The TWIN'S Daughter

The TWIN'S Daughter

LAUREN BARATZ-LOGSTED

BLOOMSBURY

NEW YORK BERLIN LONDON

First published in the United States of America in September 2010
by Bloomsbury Books for Young Readers
www.bloomsburyteens.com

For information about permission to reproduce selections from this book, write to
Permissions, Bloomsbury BFYR, 175 Fifth Avenue, New York, New York 10010

Library of Congress Cataloging-in-Publication Data
Baratz-Logsted, Lauren.
Twin's daughter / by Lauren Baratz-Logsted. — 1st U.S. ed.
        p.   cm.
Summary: In Victorian London, thirteen-year-old Lucy's comfortable world with her
loving parents begins slowly to unravel the day that a bedraggled woman who looks
exactly like her mother appears at their door.
ISBN 978-1-59990-513-6
[1. Twins—Fiction.   2. Aunts—Fiction.   3. Murder—Fiction.   4. London (England)—
History—1800–1950—Fiction.   5. Great Britain—History—Victoria, 1837–1901—
Fiction.   6. Mystery and detective stories.]   I. Title.
PZ7.B22966Tw 2011   [Fic]—dc22   2010008234

Book design by Danielle Delaney
Typeset by Westchester Book Composition
Printed in the U.S.A. by Worldcolor Fairfield, Pennsylvania
2 4 6 8 10 9 7 5 3 1

All papers used by Bloomsbury Publishing, Inc., are natural, recyclable products
made from wood grown in well-managed forests. The manufacturing processes
conform to the environmental regulations of the country of origin.

For Melanie

The TWIN'S Daughter

Part 1

· One ·

I was thirteen the year everything changed with a single knock at the door.

It was a strong door, sturdy oak, the kind designed to keep the worst of the world's elements outside while keeping safe the occupants on the inside. My mother was making the rounds of the neighborhood, as she often did on weekdays, preferring the use of her own feet to the carriage, while my father was no doubt at his club, regaling his friends with stories concerning the progress of the latest novel he was writing; born into great wealth, my father could afford to treat his career with leisure.

I don't know where the servants were when that knock came. For surely it should have been one of *their* jobs to answer it. But as I sat on the floor of the back parlor, in front of the fire, my long skirts all about me on the carpet with the drawings I was working on spread out along the perimeters of those skirts, the knock came again, more insistent this time. I thought to ignore it—the self-portrait I was working on, showing my long dark hair off to best advantage, was really coming along too nicely to be disturbed! It was probably just one of my mother's friends. Or perhaps it was one of the beggars who occasionally found their way to our front steps, quickly made short shrift of by Cook providing food we no longer wanted at the back. But then the thought occurred to me: what if it was something—however improbable—important?

With reluctance, I set down my charcoal pencil. Brushing off my skirts to straighten them as I rose, I made my way to the source of the knocking, opening the door just in time to see the caller turning away.

The caller's back to me, from behind I made out the tall figure of a woman, so painfully thin as to make me want to feed her, her long gray dress bearing the stains of the elements we usually tried to keep out. Her hair, also glimpsed only from behind, was a naggingly familiar thick hank of gold that no amount of living hard could tarnish, nor could it be kept completely under control by the pins that sought to bind it up in a twist; the tendrils would escape, wisping their way onto the air. Both hands were gloveless despite the frigid day, and in one she carried a threadbare carpetbag.

· "Can I help you?" I asked, catching her attention before she started away.

She turned slowly. At first, her eyes were downcast, but as she moved them upward to meet mine, there came a shock of recognition as I took in the familiar bright blue of her eyes and knew where I had seen that hair before. It was the same place I had seen that porcelain skin, although, I must confess, I had never seen it quite like this: with soot smudges on it. It was as though she had been cleaning out fireplaces herself and hadn't a looking glass to consult before leaving her home.

I couldn't prevent a gasp from escaping my body. "Mother?" I said, reaching a hand out to her. "What has happened to you?"

. . . . .

Of course, as it turned out, it wasn't my mother who had come knocking on the door. Does not a child recognize her own mother?

"Is Aliese Sexton at home?" she asked, speaking in an accent reflective of her lower class attire, naming my mother and ignoring my gasp and what I'd said.

"No, she is not," I said.

"I hope you won't mind, then," she said, slithering around me and into the entryway without so much as a by-your-leave, "if I wait inside."

Shutting the door behind her—it felt good to shut out the cold—I turned just in time to catch sight of the surprise and surprising visitor taking in our vestibule. She nodded as her eyes swept across the soaring height of the ceiling, as though approving it, nodding a second time at the pink marble floor, a third time at the ornate hat rack with its mirrored back and bench seat.

I started to offer to take her cloak, as I would that of any visitor arriving in the winter—or as my parents or the servants would—but then I stopped myself short. Of course, she hadn't a cloak.

"Would you like to leave that here?" I said, indicating the carpetbag she still clutched and pointing at the bench.

"If it's all the same to you," she said coolly, "I prefer to keep it close to my person."

"Of course," I said, trying to smile, trying to appear natural, trying to behave as I thought the adults I knew might behave in similar circumstances . . . as if there ever *could* be similar circumstances. "I don't think Mother will be much longer," I said. With a hand I gestured toward the front parlor. My drawing things, which I was missing now with that longing you have for safe objects when the world has turned confusing, were in the back parlor, but I couldn't bring her there. That cozy room was for family, while the front parlor was for more formal visitors and was surely where my parents or the servants would have shown this woman. "Perhaps you would like to wait in here?"

She followed the direction of my hand, seating herself on one of the white silk sofas, her back ramrod straight, hands tightly clasped in her lap, her carpetbag so close to her legs it touched against the ankle of one of her worn boots. She did not change her position even when I called a servant to bring tea and the tray arrived, the servant barely containing her shock at the appearance of my guest. For my part, it surprised me that the woman did not take any refreshment, since I would have thought she would have accepted a cup, if only to hold something warm in her hands, which I could see now were chapped and raw.

I sat with my own teacup and saucer balanced in my lap, my legs delicately crossed at the ankle beneath my skirts, and it occurred to me for the first time: I didn't even know her name! And yet how do you ask that of someone *after* you have invited them into your home and *after* you have offered them tea and a comfy seat in the front parlor? Do you say, "Oh, by the way, and what are you called and who might you be?" Just as odd, when I stopped to think about it, she hadn't asked my name at the appropriate juncture either, and so that time had passed.

"I don't think Mother will be much longer," I said again, striving for a bright tone, while inside I was hoping my father would arrive first. My father, even if he had been drinking with his friends, would still be better equipped than Mother to deal with whatever . . . *this* was.

"I can wait," the woman said. "I have waited for a very long time."

And so that is what we did: waited, waited, waited in silence as the ornamental clock above the fireplace ticked away the seconds and minutes, eventually striking a new hour.

We both started at the sound of the front door opening, followed by heels tapping on the pink marble floor. I knew from the quality of the tapping that I had not been granted my wish; it was not my father's step.

"Lucy?" I heard my mother's voice call out, and I could picture her removing her gloves, followed by her wrap and finally the pins from her hat, which she would toss blithely at the rack, laughing if she missed the hook. I heard that laugh. "Where are you?" I heard her call to me. "I have missed you." I could hear her step growing closer to the doorway, and I rose from my seat thinking to go to her, to warn her somehow first—although warn her of what exactly, I couldn't say—but her energetic glide was too quick for me and as she blew into the room, the woman who had been seated across from me rose as well.

I stood between them looking from one to the other: the one who was dressed and coiffed in a way that showed she had every advantage in the world—my beautiful, *gorgeous* mother—and her mirror image, but dressed and coiffed far differently. I can say with near certainty that I am the only child in the world who can claim she was there the first time her mother met her twin.

My mother fainted dead away.

· Two ·

My father was considered to be an exceedingly handsome man, having grown more so as he aged. I shared his coal black hair, although his curls were short while my mass stretched down to nearly my bottom when I let it, and I shared his dark eyes. Twelve years my mother's senior, he had met her when she was in her seventeenth year. I had not, of course, been there to witness their first memorable meeting. But I had heard stories.

Both of my mother's parents had died during my early years: my grandfather to a disease when I was an infant, my grandmother to a different disease when I was just three. I had no memory of the former, rendering him no more to me than a stern face in a portrait, but I had a few memories of the latter: long afternoons when Mother had me accompany her as she visited her own mother in her illness; my grandmother, even though sentenced to her bed, finding entertainments or trinkets with which to occupy me while she and Mother chatted away.

As for my father's parents, they lived out in the country and only came into the city when there was absolutely no other choice. In truth, I found them to be rather stultifying people and far preferred to have them there than here. Besides, when they were with us, they had little to say of interest about the past, a subject that interested me greatly, save to say that my father had been an intelligent boy.

As if anyone had ever doubted *that*.

Since Mother was an only child, this state of affairs left only my father's older sister, my aunt Martha, as a source of family lore. Aunt Martha, seven years my father's senior, had never married and was as tall as her brother, which meant very. The graying black hair she wore coiled around her head like a nimbus made her appear just a smidgen taller; I suspect my father found this annoying. She had the lean look of someone born of far less affluent parents, and I often wondered how she could stand to live with those parents in the country, but then would remember that perhaps this was why she so often visited with us.

"The day we chanced upon your mother strolling with her mother in the park," Aunt Martha would say, recalling my parents' first meeting, "was a truly great day in my life. I had despaired of Frederick ever finding a woman to marry. Lest you think that no one would have him, on the contrary. From the moment he was out of britches, one female after another set her cap at him. And yet he was quite the choosy fellow. Any woman who became *his* wife had to be perfect. She had to be one of a kind."

"And when he met Mother," I would say eagerly, "she was that woman!"

"Yes," Aunt Martha would agree. "Aliese was that woman. She was like a diamond pulled from one of those mines in southern

Africa: the golden color of her hair, the cut of her figure, the clarity of everything she said."

"And my father fell in love with her that very first day and told Grandmother he would make Mother his wife!"

"A month later they were married. It was astounding how quickly they planned it."

"And my father put a ring on Mother's finger."

"Yes, the symbol of unity, in this case made of cobalt blue and diamond, fashioned into the shape of forget-me-nots."

"Which Mother lets me wear sometimes."

It was true. Mother gave me freedoms I couldn't imagine any of the other mothers I'd ever met giving their own children. But then, Mother wasn't like any other mother.

Whereas every other mother I'd ever encountered was eager to pass her children off to the nearest nanny, Mother looked forward to our time alone. Indeed, on sunny days, or beastly ones—Mother hated in-between days—Mother would send Nanny, when I was still young enough to have one, to help elsewhere in the house, taking my care upon herself.

Once we were alone, Mother would help me with my drawing. Better still, she would invite me to help her spin stories of things that had never happened but might be. Mother loved stories as much as my father did, but whereas all his stories found their way into and out of his pen, hers came straight from her mind to mine, twining together before I sent the stories back to hers. Best of all, Mother would encourage me to act out the stories we created together.

Her favorite thing to act out, and mine, was something we gigglingly referred to as "The Wedding Game."

Mother would place her own wedding veil upon my head and give me her special wedding slippers to wear, although my feet swam in them. Then she would lend me her wedding ring, so that I might feel a complete bride. To finish the picture, she would run from the room, gliding downstairs to steal flowers from one of the vases. Heaven forbid that a bride should have nothing to carry. What would she do with her hands?

After humming a march as I processed across the nursery, Mother would lead me to her room, where she would stand me in front of her full-length looking glass so that our side-by-side reflections, so very different from each other, gazed back at us.

Her blue eyes meeting my dark ones, she would say, always using the exact same words, "Your hair may be a dark cloud, but no matter what the weather, on your wedding day the sun and stars will shine."

And then we would dissolve into yet more laughter as we collapsed upon the bed she shared with my father, giggling at the silliness of it all.

• Three •

My father arrived home, entering the front parlor just as Mother was swimming back up to consciousness. If Mother had fainted in any of the number of ways that women usually faint, my father would have asked me what had happened to precipitate the event. But these were not normal circumstances. There was nothing usual going on here.

He need only glance from me, bending over Mother on her right, to the caller bending over her on the left. One look at the caller's face, turning up to meet his at the sound of his tread, was all he needed to know immediately that these were very extraordinary circumstances indeed.

"Go upstairs," he ordered me.

"But I—"

"Now, Lucy!"

I rose to my feet with as much dignity as I could muster. I could not believe I was being sent away. It was as though I were a mere *child*! Had I no right to know what was going to happen next? I lived here too, after all.

Still feeling the imperative to move with dignity, I forced myself to glide from the room and to the foot of the long curving staircase. My parents had lately tried to impress upon me the importance of gliding.

"A lady always glides," Mother would say, prompted by my father to see to my deportment. "It should appear at all times as though a lady is floating across the floor. Only common women do something as vulgar as walk—or, worse still, *stride*." She would of course tell me these things while wearing a good-natured smile upon her face, as was her habit, leading me to wonder how much stock she herself invested in such rules.

I had noticed one thing about the caller, in the few brief steps I witnessed her take: She didn't glide. She walked. She *strode*.

And I had noticed something else, in the few brief moments when the caller and I had been bending over Mother's prone form on the floor, before my father's entrance: Transferring my gaze from one to the other repeatedly, I saw that I had not been mistaken in my earlier impression. The two women did indeed bear the exact same face. If the caller had more to eat, and cleaner clothes, she would be the image of Mother.

At the bottom of the stairs, I placed my booted foot on the first step, charging up them so that the adults below would be sure to hear the racket I was creating. What they could not know was that when I gained the top landing, I sat, removed my boots, and then crept back down the stairs on cat's feet, stopping on the sixth step from the bottom so that I was close enough to hear but not close enough to be seen. It was a trick I had learned over the years, something I did when there was a party going on or when I thought my parents or other adults might be discussing something interesting.

I quietly seated myself on that sixth step just in time to hear my father saying, with all his authority, "Could you please tell me what your name is and what business brings you here?"

"My name's Helen Smythe," I heard the caller say, in a proud tone suggesting she was trying to force a dignity into her speech. "I came to meet my sister." She paused. "My twin."

It was odd. These were the most words I'd heard her speak in the space of a minute since first setting eyes on her. And it was odd too because, once removed from the visual confrontation of seeing her face side by side with Mother's, it was as though she had come from a different world. Her voice was so coarse, when compared with my memory of Mother's lovely one, using a base contraction that Mother would never use—*My name's Helen Smythe*—as though she could have been one of the servants helping Cook work in the kitchen.

I wondered if my father would question this Helen Smythe's authenticity. He had long been fascinated with the story of Edward Rulloff, a thief, lawyer, doctor, murderer, and professional impostor who earlier in the century had been executed in New York, over in America.

My father was fascinated by the very idea of impostors, by the idea of people being something very different from that which they appeared to be, although I suspect his fascination did not extend to having one try to deceive him. Would he accuse Helen Smythe of being an impostor?

But no.

My father might have been given to arguing with his learned friends over the most trivial pieces of historical fact, but even he could not deny the truth his own eyes were seeing, the truth Helen Smythe had spoken.

Her face was her proof.

Now that he knew her name, he left off wondering about the precise nature of her visit, proceeding to:

"I must say, this is a fantastical thing . . . I cannot imagine . . . how did you come . . . you must tell me . . ." It was almost painful to hear my well-spoken father lose the sure-footedness of his speaking so, to stutter as though he could not put a complete thought together.

Apparently, Helen Smythe had mercy on him at this point, perhaps on Mother too, for she began with no preamble to tell her tale.

"My parents"—here she paused and I could imagine her looking meaningfully at Mother as she corrected to—"*our* parents were not really our parents."

"That is not so!" Mother cried, speaking to Helen Smythe for the first time. "Of course they were my parents!"

"Yes," Helen Smythe said evenly, "and no. They were the people who raised you, but they were most definitely not our parents. Our real mother was a maid. Our real father?" I imagined her shrugging. "I've no idea."

"But that is impossible!" Mother interjected again.

"Of course it's possible. The people who brought you up were very wealthy, as you no doubt know. But the woman? Much as she'd have liked, she couldn't have her own children. When the maid found herself in the family way, the people you think of as your parents took her out of the country. They told everyone else that your *mother* was pregnant and that she needed peace. When the maid bore twins, those people decided they didn't want more than one baby. So they consulted a fortune-teller."

I imagined Mother raising an eyebrow at this startling news. No one we knew consulted *fortune-tellers*!

"Apparently," Helen Smythe went on, as though people's fates were decided thusly every day, "whatever *she* told them caused them to make a decision. When they returned to England, they brought you home with them. They placed *me* in an orphanage."

"But how did you know all this?" Mother asked, and I could hear the wonder in her voice. "How came you by this knowledge when I have none of it?"

"At the orphanage," Helen Smythe said, "the mistress there used to taunt me with it whenever she thought I'd done something bad. She would say that I was so bad, even the people who should have kept me didn't want me. The other children soon took up her cause. I became known as the 'rich little poor girl.'"

It occurred to me as I listened to this, in shocked surprise, to wonder what it must be like for Mother to learn that what she had believed all her life of her own parents—of the people who raised her, as Helen Smythe put it—was a house of lies from the foundation up.

It was my father who spoke next. "Why have you come here," he asked, "after so much time? You must have been released from the orphanage many years ago."

"Yes." I could almost picture her face smiling wryly here. "But sometimes life conspires to get in the way. I'm here now, though. I've waited thirty-one years to lay eyes on my sister, my *twin*, and now I've done so."

"But how did you find—"

Later, it would occur to me that my father was about to ask "But how did you find your way here?" or "How did you find where we live?" But he never had the opportunity to finish, at least not then, for it was at that moment that I, having leaned far forward to clearly hear every word, overbalanced, toppling down the stairs.

Rushing feet, and then my father was at my side. "Are you all right?" he asked anxiously. Once I assured him that I was, hastily scrambling to my feet to demonstrate just how all right I was, I saw anger enter his eyes. I would no doubt later be berated for my foray as an eavesdropper. But not now. Now, almost as soon as the anger entered, it was replaced by a softness. I could not tell if it was a happy softness or a sad softness. Perhaps it was both.

Gently, he took my hand in his. "Come, Lucy. There is someone you must meet." He led me into the parlor, where now I could see my mother and her twin again. I realized this was the first time I was seeing them together where each knew who the other was.

"Lucy," my father said, "I should like you to meet your aunt Helen Smythe."

"We have met already," I said, stating the obvious, at the same time realizing we had never met like this. I dipped a curtsy, as was only proper when faced with an older relative. "How do you do?"

With a smile I could not read upon her face—was it joy I

saw there? mockery? sarcasm?—Helen Smythe dipped a crude curtsy in return. "The pleasure's mine," she said. "I'm quite well now, thank you."

I moved to take a seat on the sofa where my father indicated I should, but my aunt remained standing. Then she reached down, grasping the handle on her carpetbag with one of those raw, chapped hands before rising again. "Thank you for seeing me," she said. "And now it's time for me to go."

"But—" This time it was Mother speaking, her one word sounding a different kind of protest than what she'd voiced earlier.

"It's getting dark," my aunt said. "I should like to find a place to stay before nightfall."

"But—"

"I only just wanted to see you," my aunt said directly to Mother, "just once. All my life, I've wondered what you looked like. I wondered: Did you look like me? Did you look completely different? Would I know you if I saw you in the streets? Now I've my answers." She shrugged. "And now it's time for me to go."

"You said you need to find a place to stay," my father said. "Don't you live somewhere?"

"I did," my aunt admitted, "but I could no longer pay the rent, so I was put out. Now I shall have to find somewhere cheaper." She looked at all three of us at once, as though taking in a whole picture. "Thank you again for today."

She started for the door.

My father looked at Mother, raised his eyebrows until she nodded back. Her nod at first was like a stutter, unsure, then it became a vehement thing, as though she'd grown eager.

"Stay." My father's voice stopped my aunt's step. "Please stay, if only for the night. It is dark already, you see." He turned to the window, as though illustrating the coming of the night. "And it is cold. Please stay tonight."

"If you wish it." My aunt smiled at us all. "Then I shall."

• Four •

"Lucy, why don't you go up to your room?" my father said. "It has been a long and unusual day for you, not to mention the tumble you took down the stairs earlier. You must be tired."

It was our family's custom, when both my parents were at home, for me to dine with them, however late that might be. But when my father made his statement—more of a command than a suggestion, really—adding that he would have Cook send a tray up so I shouldn't starve, I obeyed. I recognized that the advent of our visitor, and her staying on, meant that I had escaped my father's wrath at catching me eavesdropping.

And so I went.

I did not try to stop and listen on the staircase again. I had already attempted that trick once, with mixed results. I would not get away with it a second time, not on that night. Whatever else may have been said by the adults after I left the room, I was to hear none of it.

When I gained the landing, entering my room on the right

side of the corridor, I looked at my familiar surroundings. Already it seemed smaller than when I'd last been in it, just hours previous.

Shortly, the maid brought up my dinner: mutton, potatoes, and something green that looked as if ideally it should have been greener. But I ate nothing. Whatever appetite I might normally have had at this time of day was stalled by the thoughts ranging through my head. Even the pudding did not tempt me.

I had a new relative! An aunt! And she was spending the night!

Where would she sleep? I wondered.

The servants' quarters were on the fourth floor, my parents' on the third. For as long as I could remember, I had been alone on the second. But, perhaps I would no longer be so?

Through my closed door, I heard movements in the room across the corridor. It was the sounds of a servant or two bustling, getting a room ready.

The room across the corridor had originally been intended as a nursery. Twice, that I could remember, Mother had grown big with child. Both times had caused great excitement in me, as I longed for a brother or sister. As wonderful as Mother always was, as good as my father could be when he was so inclined, it was not the same as having another child with whom to share things, particularly since whatever child I envisaged would naturally be younger than me and hence at my beck and call. But the two times Mother had grown big with child resulted in . . . no child.

"That is all right," Mother had said to me one time, still weak, still recovering from the loss of that second child that was not to be. "I do not think I could love more than one of you"—here she had smiled a smile that looked as though she was trying to be stronger than her body would allow—"and I mean that in only the nicest way."

Since that last loss, the room across the hall from me had remained as a nursery, either as testament to what never was or false promise of what might yet be.

Was the visitor to be placed so close to me then?

I realized with a massive yawn that my father was right: I had exhausted myself.

But after changing from my day clothes into my night ones, and crawling between the cool sheets, I discovered that sleep would not come. I could not stop my mind from wondering what my parents might be discussing with our visitor—my aunt!— downstairs.

What do you say to a relative, a sister, you never suspected you had? It was a question, the answer for which I could not fathom.

So then my mind turned to wondering what *her* life had been like in the thirty-one years before she came to knock on our door. An orphanage, she had said. Mother and I, when playing our pretend games, sometimes joked about orphanages.

"If you are not good, child," I had been known to command her when she was of a fancy to let me be the parent, "I will send you to the orphanage!"

"Oh, no!" she would cry in mock horror. "Not the orphanage!"

It was a bad joke, our laughter a giddy and uncomfortable thing, like laughing nervously at the undertaker when he passes by because you know whoever is in the box is not you . . . and yet, it could be.

No, I thought as I lay there, gazing at the early moon shining its way into the room through the curtains, an orphanage would be an awful place to grow up. It was a place my curiosity had no desire to lead me into. But what about the years since then? What had—I hesitated over the name—*Aunt Helen's* life been composed of between those years and this day? Thinking on her clothes and the general bedraggled nature of her appearance, I could not imagine that life had been anything good.

It was as I was still trying to conjure that life in between that sleep finally came and awake thoughts ceased.

. . . . .

I dreamed I was in a room with Mother and Aunt Helen. I could not see their faces—both were turned away from me—and yet in that peculiar way that dreams have, I knew without doubt it was them. The chairs they sat in had high backs, but I could see their golden blond heads peeping over the tops from behind. They sat very still, as though each was trying to perch a teacup on her knee.

"Mother!" I called. "Aunt Helen!"

Their faces turned to look at me, as though each head was attached to the same unseen wire. Behind them, the fireplace blazed—I had not noticed that before.

Nor did I have time to note it long now, although later, in memory, I would see it as a wall of flame blazing around their faces.

But now I was too busy to register it for long. I was too busy screaming.

The two faces that looked at me—I could not tell Mother from my aunt—they were exactly the same.

. . . . .

I did not scream myself wholly awake—just enough to register hurrying footsteps, the sound of a door pushed open, a face leaning over me before I drifted back to a more peaceful sleep. Was the face Mother's? Was it Aunt Helen's? I could not say.

When I woke again, it was a new day.

• Five •

The sun shone through the curtains, waking me as it warmed my eyelids. Immediately, my eyes opened, my mind so much more excited at the prospect of facing this morning than the one that had gone before. Yesterday I had awoken to a day I thought would be like every other day. But now? There was so much to look forward to, so much that was different, new.

I sprang from the bed, not waiting for a servant to come for me. Glancing at the door on the other side of the hallway, shy now, I was surprised to see it wide open. Tiptoeing across the corridor, I hesitantly poked my head around the corner, only to be faced with ... nothing.

Used to beds that had been made to perfection by capable, work-roughened hands, I saw that the bed my aunt had slept in had been put to rights crudely, as though the hands doing so had no experience with tidy corners or were in great haste. On the counterpane was a note. I hurried to pick it up.

Deer Neece Lucy,

   Im afraid I must take my leeve. I
wantd to meet your mother. Now I hav.
It wood be rong for me to stay her.
   It wood hav bin nise to get to know
my neece, but Fortune I think has
always had other plans for us all.

                    Wishing you well,

                    Aunt Helen

I tucked the note into a pocket in my nightdress, not stopping to think long about why my aunt had addressed her good-
bye to me and not my parents. Racing down the stairs, though,
my mind started to work over that, at last settling on: *Why shouldn't
she address me instead of them? Perhaps she felt a deeper kinship with
me, a kinship like what I had started to feel toward her.*

Sliding into the dining room on bare feet, I saw that my parents were already at breakfast: my father with his nose in some
book, Mother poised with the jam knife over her toast.

"Aunt Helen—," I started, breathless.

"'Aunt Helen' is it already?" My father looked up, amused.

"—has gone away," I finished, ignoring his amusement at me.

"Gone away?" Mother asked. "How do you know that?"

"The door to her room was open," I said. "I looked in—I
swear I wasn't snooping; the door was wide open!—but she was

gone." I confess, I did not tell them about the note. It had been addressed to me alone.

"Perhaps she went for a walk," my father suggested. He glanced out the long window behind him. "I am sure it is still cold, but it looks as though it is going to be a lovely day."

"No, I am positive she is gone," I said. "Her carpetbag was gone too. She would not have taken that if she were going for a mere stroll. She must have sneaked out while you were still sleeping, which is why you did not hear her go. I am positive she has gone"—I paused meaningfully—"for good."

My father looked at Mother, and she returned the look. It shocked me, for it was a complicit look, as though this turn of affairs was perfectly all right with them.

"She was supposed to leave today anyway," my father said with a shrug.

"Perhaps this is for the best," Mother said.

"*For the best?*" I practically shouted. I was not accustomed to shouting at my parents and yet I found that I could not keep the dual sounds of outrage and derision from entering my voice. "How can it be *for the best*? Aunt Helen is *your sister*. She is your *only* living relative now. How can you not be curious? How can you not want to know where she has gone? It is probably to some awful place—"

"Enough." My father's one word halted all mine, and yet when I turned to him, though his palm was facing me as if to physically stop my speech, his expression had softened. He turned to Mother.

"She is right, Aliese. We may have raised an unnaturally outspoken termagant," he added with an appreciative smile, "and yet she is right. Now that we know of Helen's existence, we cannot turn our backs on her. What would people say of us if they knew? And, of course, it would simply be wrong; even if no one ever knew, we would know. It would be wrong." He repeated that, as was his habit, as though repeating words could convince other people of the need to yield to his way. "And you must recognize, however confusing and wretched this whole business may be for you, it is not your sister's fault. It is your parents', curse their wretched souls."

"Yes," Mother said, "I suppose you are right." She shuddered, though it wasn't cold in the room, not like it no doubt was outside, wherever Aunt Helen might be. "For the first time it occurs to me: It could have been *me*. *I* could have been the child my parents gave away."

I did not say, but the same thought had occurred to me as well when my father cursed her parents.

No sooner had I won my battle—convincing my parents of the need to get Aunt Helen back—than I realized that there was yet a bigger battle ahead. How could we ever find her? London was a big place!

I said as much.

"Do not worry about that," my father said, throwing down his linen napkin and rising from his chair with more energy than he was used to showing in the morning. It was as though he felt what I did: that life suddenly had more to offer us. There was excitement in the air.

"After you went up to bed last night," Mother informed me, "Helen told your father and me where she had been living before coming here. Perhaps your father thinks he will start looking for her there."

"I want to come with you." I spoke to my father without thinking first.

He studied me closely.

Of course he would say no.

Then:

"Yes," he said. I thought I sensed a new respect for me in his eyes as he smiled. "But you must hurry and dress," he said, "for I will not have the carriage wait for you if you are not ready before I am."

Then he raced to the stairs to change his own clothes—my father racing?—and I raced after him.

. . . . .

The descent from where we lived in London to where we were going to look for Aunt Helen did not take long in time measured, and yet it might have, given how very different one place was from the other: from the relatively scentless place where we lived to the manure and decomposing cabbage around Covent Garden— barely mitigated by the girls selling flowers on the street corners— past St. Paul's Cathedral and the City with its banks and money, the invasive odor of wet rags and hot metal as we progressed, and the final turn into a dark lane in an area my father referred to as Cheapside. And, too, everything was suddenly so loud! We were in the same city, and yet we were not. I had never entered such an area before. There were two worlds, it seemed, within one world. How had I not known this?

I did not go out often with my father in the carriage, unless it was to church, and I might have been more excited at the novel event were my mind not occupied with our mission. My mind also wondered why Mother had not asked to come with us. But then it occurred to me that she might not wish to see how her sister had been living.

The horses reined up in front of a shabby dwelling that I assumed was the address my aunt had given my parents. My father told me to wait in the carriage as he leaped down, making his way to the weather-beaten door. I watched as he knocked firmly, could hear the sharp sound his knuckles made. In a long moment, the door was answered. Peering out of the carriage, I could see an elderly woman in the crack. It was difficult from the distance to make her features out clearly, but I thought I saw a snaggletooth glint against the sun.

"I am looking for Helen Smythe," my father said, his voice a peculiar combination of friendliness and command.

"She ain't here," the woman said. "I put her out early yesterday."

"Yes, I am aware of that," my father said. "But I was wondering if you could tell me where she might have gone to."

"I'd imagine that sorta information should be worth somefin," she said craftily.

I saw my father extract a shilling from the billfold in his pocket, handing it over to the woman.

"Try down the pub." She jerked her head toward the end of the street.

My father tilted his head up at the sky, the rare blue expanse and few passing clouds, as though he might find a giant clock up there. He looked back at the woman. "Is it not still early in the day for the pub?"

The woman barked another one of her coughing laughs.

"Maybe for some," she said, then she shut the door in my father's face.

Early in the day as it was, the noise coming out the door of the public house as my father opened it could have been coming from the middle of a busy night. I resented being told to wait in the carriage again and, once the public house door had shut behind my father, I slipped down from the seat, checking to make sure the driver was paying no attention. I saw that he was indeed nodding off in his high perch as I crept up to one of the grimy windowpanes. Peeking over the sill, I was there to see it when my father first spotted my aunt among the noisy crowd, saw her turn when he must have called her name, saw her smile flash before her expression turned grim. His back was to me and, unlike at the snaggletooth woman's house, I could hear nothing of what was said. Aunt Helen continued to look grim, angry almost, shaking her head several times. I had no idea what my father said, but suddenly all those grim head shakes turned into a single radiant smile. A moment later, they were heading toward the door. My father had one hand on Aunt Helen's elbow, steering her, while in the other he carried her carpetbag.

I scurried back to the carriage so as not to get caught looking.

· · · · ·

The ride back to our home was silent, but I was content, squeezed in the back of the carriage between my father and my aunt. Occasionally, I would steal a glance at her. She always caught me looking. She always smiled back.

· · · · ·

Mother flung open the door just as my father reached for the doorknob. And so I was there, a witness, as she embraced her sister for the first time.

"I am glad," I heard Mother whisper into my aunt's ear, their two blond heads pressed together at the cheek, "that you came back." Then louder, brighter, to the rest of us: "Come. It is time for lunch."

As we sat down at the long table, my parents at the head and foot with Aunt Helen and me facing each other in the middle, Mother regarded Aunt Helen's clothes with a studied eye.

"Tomorrow," Mother said to her sister, "I will send for my dressmaker. You shall have some new things." She turned to my father. "Is that acceptable to you, Frederick?"

"Oh, quite," my father said, placing his napkin in his lap.

I saw my aunt watch what we did, carefully placing her own napkin in her lap.

The repast before us was a generous one, far more so than would have been our usual custom at lunch. It was a veritable feast, a meal as though in honor of the homecoming of a queen.

One of the servants brought in the soup course, placing a bowl before each of us. Not waiting this time to study us first— I suspected she was very hungry—I saw my aunt reach for the smallest spoon among the many at her place setting.

"That is a pudding spoon," I corrected my aunt, "not a soup-spoon. The soupspoon is the largest one."

Even before my words were finished, I blushed at my own impertinence. Who was I, to tell any adult how to behave, how-ever incorrect their behavior might be?

An awkward silence followed.

It was my aunt who broke it, turning to face me head on with a bright smile that was wide, generous even.

"It's all right to correct me," she said. "How am I to learn to become a member of this family if someone doesn't teach me the proper way to behave?" Then she placed the pudding spoon back down, taking up the correct one.

And so the education of Aunt Helen began.

• Six •

Yesterday having been Sunday, there had been no time to call for the dressmaker. But it was a new week, a new day was upon us, and Mrs. Wiggins had been sent for first thing.

And now she stood before the three of us in Mother's bedroom, her jaw dropped in shock.

Mrs. Wiggins was an older woman, her ample bosom nearly exceeding her wide girth, her hair the color of steel mixed with some dirt. There was always something a bit sloppy-looking about Mrs. Wiggins, as though she had spent too much time laboring over everyone else's attire to have any energy left to labor over her own. She was a poor advertisement for her own trade and yet she had been making Mother's dresses for years. On this morning she had arrived with her usual basket containing the tricks of her profession—measuring tape, pins, and such—as well as several bolts of what I assumed to be the latest rage in expensive fabrics to show off to Mother. It was immediately obvious that she had assumed, wrongly, that Mother was to be the dressmaker's dummy.

I had to repress a near hysterical impulse to giggle. Someday, I thought, the sight of Mother and her sister thrust upon someone who was yet unaware of the new development in our lives would cause a heart attack or cause the viewing party to question their own sanity.

This, clearly, was a reaction we were going to have to get used to. Just as each of us—my father, Mother, myself—had been stunned by the appearance of Aunt Helen, so would the world, or at least each person in *our* world, one at a time. I wondered how the servants were taking it. My father, I decided, would have seen to that.

As for there being three of us facing Mrs. Wiggins in that room on that day, I was fast learning that if I kept my own counsel, if I merely quietly followed along as others moved to and fro, it was amazing how much I would be allowed to witness. Indeed, at times now it felt as though my parents did not notice me when I was there and yet, at the same time, I felt that Aunt Helen always noticed.

"Look at this lovely satin." Mrs. Wiggins practically coughed the words out, having only just barely recovered her composure.

"It is lovely," Mother said, wistfully fingering the smooth emerald green fabric. Indeed, such a color would be stunning with her hair. "But it is not for me."

Mother stood aside, indicating that Helen should step forward.

"I see," Mrs. Wiggins said, and yet it was obvious that she did not as she regarded Helen: Helen, in what seemed to be the only dress she owned, the gray one we had first seen her in; Helen, whose drab garment hung so closely to her painfully thin frame it was obvious to anyone looking that she wore no petticoats underneath.

It must, I thought, *be awful to be so poor.*

"This is Helen Smythe," Mother said, forcing a regal tone into her voice as she added, "my sister."

"Yes," Mrs. Wiggins said, "I do see that much. And what would you like?" She removed the measuring tape from her basket. "For me to make a gown for her?"

"A *gown*?" Mother laughed. It was a genuine laugh of glee, the first of its kind I had heard from Mother since she'd arrived home Saturday only to find history waiting for her in the front parlor. "*A* gown?" Another delighted laugh. "Surely you must see, Mrs. Wiggins, my sister needs *everything*!"

Mrs. Wiggins replaced the emerald green bolt of satin in her stack, reaching instead for what I guessed to be a cheap muslin.

"Oh, no," Mother said with great energy. "No, no, no. It must be the best of everything and plenty of it. Imagine it was *me* you had come here to dress, that I had lost everything in a great fire and now you have to outfit me fully from the inside out."

"Very well," Mrs. Wiggins said, putting aside the muslin with a heavy sigh. *What a waste of fine fabric,* I imagined Mrs. Wiggins thinking as she regarded Aunt Helen. *Such things are not meant for the likes of one such as you.*

I listened to them debate the relative merits of two different silks.

"Now take this black grosgrain," Mrs. Wiggins said, addressing Mother more than Helen. "We can make a narrow-yoke petticoat with this, then smooth-fitting gores on either side and the front, a full back-breadth gathered at the top. And if you like, we can do a small ruffle of the same silk with a pink edge, perhaps in lace, to decorate the bottom."

"What do you think?" Mother turned to Aunt Helen.

Aunt Helen shrugged. It was difficult to tell if she was indifferent to the garment or if she merely did not know what to make of it.

"Very well." Mrs. Wiggins reached for the taffeta silk, which was a pure white color. "There's a lot you can do with this. Of course it too would be gored, but the ruffle at the bottom would be much wider, in keeping with the bias Spanish flounce for the lower part. And as for the decorations? Well, we can do wide ribbon-run beading with the ribbon formed in rosette bows at intervals or we can do a triple box-plaited silk ruche to trim the flounce near the top."

Mrs. Wiggins paused, which was perfectly fine with me since I was not as fascinated with rosettes and ruches as the others were. Again, the dressmaker looked at Mother expectantly. Again, Mother turned to Helen.

"I don't know which is better," Aunt Helen said. "The first one seems nice enough. The second is much more fancy." She turned back to Mother. "Which would you choose?"

"I would choose both and in several colors." Mother smiled warmly. "As should you."

Aunt Helen hesitated. Then at last she turned to the dressmaker. "Yes. All right then. I'll have both."

From petticoats the talk turned to dresses proper as Mrs. Wiggins pulled sheets of illustrations, fashion plates, from her basket.

The first sketch was of a tailored dress with moiré vest and revers, large pointed lapels. It looked more to me like something staid that Aunt Helen might wear were she to apply for a position as governess, but she seemed to like it well enough.

There were two sketches of gowns that were obviously for fancy evening dress. One had jeweled embroidery, while the other had an embroidered waist. Mrs. Wiggins suggested this one would be best in green velvet, the low neck draped with white chiffon and lace, clustered flowers holding the drapery on the front and shoulders.

"But of course"—Mrs. Wiggins hesitated over the words she spoke to Aunt Helen—"you might not need anything this elaborate." She turned to Mother. "I only showed these to you because I thought you might want to see the latest things from Paris."

"Please do make one of each for my sister," Mother stated with a firmness that brooked no arguments.

Of the dresses proper, the only one that truly appealed to me was a costume with bolero and velvet vest. In the sketch, which was black illustration on white paper, the vertical bars of cords looked like keys on a piano. But then Mrs. Wiggins suggested it be made in gray blue cloth with the vest and revers in dark blue velvet fabric, and then I did not like it half so much.

As they at last moved on to overdresses, my mind moved away. What care had I for the intricacies of cloaks, mantles, and capes?

I looked around at Mother's lushly appointed bedroom, thought of the wonder on Aunt Helen's face when she'd first set eyes on it. How different it must appear to her when taken in comparison with what must have been her lean lodgings at the snaggletooth woman's boardinghouse, a still starker comparison to whatever the orphanage must have been like for her. Even her room here was nothing like this. Her room here was a nursery. Painted walls, white woodwork, chintz curtains, floor of hardwood with a removable rug that was replaced by a square of matting in the summer, a gay Japanese screen that matched with nothing. Blue and white Dutch tiles surrounding the fireplace depicting pictures of the finding of Moses.

"And how long will it take you to make all these clothes?" Mother asked as Mrs. Wiggins at last set to taking Aunt Helen's measurements.

"Well, it is a tall order," Mrs. Wiggins said, looking exhausted at the size of the prospect. Then she could not prevent a certain glee from entering her eyes as she added, "And it will be expensive." I imagined her thinking that while she did not mind making so much money from one order, she still regarded it as a waste that the money should be spent on Aunt Helen.

"I would not want you to rush," Mother said, then she regarded Aunt Helen in her drab gray dress, "and I do want you to leave enough room in the seams of each garment. It is my hope that my sister will soon put on some weight."

. . . . .

The visit from the dressmaker had eaten up all the morning, bleeding into the early afternoon. Hats, boots, gloves—all would be ordered separately based on the extensive measurements Mrs. Wiggins had taken. By the time we sat down to our late lunch, I was famished, not caring about how unladylike my manners might seem as I tucked into the repast with relish. But I needn't worry about my father criticizing as I slathered more butter on my toast, for my father wasn't there. Squirreled away in his study as he often was when in the midst of a project, he'd sent word to have his meal delivered there.

No sooner had I laid down my linen napkin after I had been sufficiently stuffed than Mother suggested a walk. Despite the cold weather, a daily constitutional in the park after lunch was our practice whenever she was at home.

I don't know why it should fill me with such excitement, Mother suggesting something that was almost as regular as eating, and yet it did. I suppose I was already anticipating the novelty of having Aunt Helen accompany us. I did not mind being alone with Mother—indeed, previously I had treasured our time together—but that did not mean I was averse to change.

As Mother rose from her seat, I rose from mine, thinking to hurry and fetch my cloak. I saw Aunt Helen start to rise too, the same eagerness in her eyes as there no doubt was in mine, as though we three were a set. But then I saw Mother's eyes shoot to Aunt Helen's and, just as rapidly, Aunt Helen sat back down again.

"Your aunt has had," Mother said, "what must be for her a very exhausting day so far. I am sure she would prefer to rest."

"Yes," Aunt Helen said. It was impossible to read what she was thinking. "I'm tired now."

I was puzzled. Why wouldn't Aunt Helen want to go outside for a bit? Who *wouldn't* want, even on the coldest day, the freedom at least for part of it from feeling cooped up?

Then it struck me: Mother did not want her sister to be seen, not yet, not by any members of our acquaintance we might chance to run into in the park. She was ashamed of her.

And Aunt Helen knew it.

. . . . .

That afternoon's stroll with Mother was a staid one for me. I didn't like to talk to her just then, not thinking what I was thinking about her now.

Since I was disinclined to chat, or even answer simple queries, and since the air truly was frigid, Mother cut short our walk.

"I have not had a chance to ask," she said as we neared our front door, "how do *you* feel about Helen coming to live with us?"

I regarded her with a coolness I do not remember ever feeling toward her before.

"It is wonderful," I said. "It is a fine thing."

. . . . .

That night, my parents went out as was their frequent habit whenever my father was not off by himself somewhere. They may have gone to visit friends or to the theater—I paid no attention, although I usually would have.

I felt Aunt Helen watching me as I knelt, elbows propped atop the back of the sofa, peeking out the window as the carriage disappeared from view.

Turning around, I saw mirth on her face and when I giggled, her giggle matched my own. There may have been plenty of servants afoot, but it was as though we were two children left with no one to tend to us.

Which was perfectly well.

"We're alone at last, niece," Aunt Helen spoke, a devilish gleam in her eyes as her words echoed my thoughts. For the first time, it occurred to me that there might be something dangerous about Aunt Helen. "What," she asked, that gleam still there, "would you like to do?"

I suggested playing charades.

She did not know that game and, when I explained it to her, said she did not think it was a game she could be good at. She did not think she would make a very good actress.

I suggested we take turns drawing pictures. Mother would sometimes compete with me to see who could draw the better version of any of the number of vases of flowers that filled our home.

But no. Aunt Helen did not think drawing imitations of life would be her talent either.

I was nearly out of ideas. "I suppose," I said with a shrug, "we could just talk . . ."

"Talk." The gleam in Aunt Helen's eye came back with new strength. "Now there's something I think I could be good at."

We settled down with great purpose upon the sofa, side by side. Then:

Silence.

Long, protracted silence, finally breached when Aunt Helen mercifully leaned in a hair closer to me, whispering, "What would you like to talk about?"

Like a cork removed, I burst out with it: "Why did you come here now? It seems, from everything you have said, that you have known of your sister's existence for a long time, nearly your whole life. And yet you waited until now, after all these years, to come here. Why now?"

It was rude of me to ask her that. I knew it even as the words were flying out of my mouth. And yet I could not stop myself. It was a niggling thing that had been gnawing at my brain. She must have been released from the orphanage long ago. *Why wait? Why now?*

Rather than looking affronted by my outburst, however, Aunt Helen answered very coolly.

"Remember when I referred to the place I was put in while still a baby as an 'orphanage'?"

I nodded, feeling the beating of my heart, which had been speeding to keep pace with my own outburst, subside just a little. "Yes."

"Well," she said wryly, "the more proper word is 'workhouse.' It's a wretched place where they work human beings like draft horses."

Not having ever been inside such a place, hoping I should never come to know firsthand what she had seen, I shuddered.

"Yes, it was awful," she said with a smile that was almost friendly.

There was a long moment, during which I suspect we both thought of where she had come from.

"You're not a stupid girl, Lucy," she said, surprising me with her choice of words. "Think, for a moment, what it must've been like, what *I* must've been like when I first came out of the work-house. It took me that many years to refine myself into something fit to show myself on your doorstep. It took me years—improving my speech, my manners, earning enough to buy better clothes."

This was a huge thing to digest: the idea that it had taken her years to rise merely to what I saw before me now, someone who would have been sent to the back door without question, had it not been for her relation to Mother.

Up until this point in my life, I do not think I had known what it was to feel real sympathy for a human being not myself. But I felt it now.

"I am sorry, Aunt Helen," I said, embracing her.

"It's not you who should be sorry," she whispered into my ear.

It did not seem like another serious word could be spoken after that.

A moment later, Aunt Helen asked me if I could teach her how to play charades.

Our joint laughter heralded our motion as we raced through the house.

• Seven •

"Now that we know that Sister Helen's body is to be properly attired," my father announced the next morning over breakfast, "we must see to the development of her mind. I have engaged the services of a special schoolmaster who will come here, to the house. He can educate Lucy at the same time."

There was a jocularity in my father's voice. Not for the first time, it struck me that my father regarded the advent of Aunt Helen in our lives as some sort of great joke or, at the very least, a game.

"I had a devil of a time securing a suitable schoolmaster on such short notice," my father went on, "but when I offered to pay him double his wages, he was made to see reason. I am told he is the very best."

Previously, my education had been seen to by one Miss Walker, a private tutor, but apparently my father did not feel her talents sufficient to teach Aunt Helen as well.

The schoolroom was attached to my bedroom, and it was in

this room that Aunt Helen and I waited for the new schoolmaster to arrive, Aunt Helen once again wearing her drab gray dress. Was Aunt Helen as nervous as I was? As excited?

Mr. Samuel Brockburn, when Mother led him in, appeared to be a serious man with a sense of humor, for he carried himself so erect it was as though he was attempting to prove, single-handedly, that we were not descended from apes. And yet, when he looked down at Mother from his great height, there was a twinkle of merriment in his eyes.

Mr. Brockburn was also an astonishingly handsome man.

He had the same dark hair and eyes that my father did, only in Mr. Brockburn's case those eyes contained an even greater depth. I guessed him at being just a few years older than Mother, and his hair had a wildness to it. I quickly saw it was his habit to use his long fingers to rake through his locks as though he might yet rein in the untamable.

"Mr. Brockburn," Mother announced, "I should like to present your two new pupils: Miss Smythe and Miss Lucy."

Immediately, I rose and dropped a perfect curtsy, as I had been taught. Aunt Helen, trying to follow my lead, was a beat behind me and less successful in her execution. The curtsy she dropped in haste was not so deep as to mimic mine and it threw her off balance enough so that she bumped against the table. Moreover, her curtsy, I saw from her sardonic grin as she rose from her stumble, had somehow lacked sincerity.

I suppose we should have warned her, prior to the schoolmaster's arrival, that while I as a child would be expected to curtsy properly, she as an adult in the household would not, certainly not to someone my father was paying to be there.

As Mr. Brockburn, who it appeared had fine manners, reached out a steadying hand to Aunt Helen, he took in her face for the first time, his attention having been riveted upon Mother when they had first entered.

I saw the shock register there, recording the echo in her to another close by. Then a startling thing happened. It was as though, unlike with the others, he wasn't in the slightest bit disconcerted by seeing my mother's highborn face attached in a very different way to another body. He smiled at Aunt Helen with great sympathy, turning what I can only describe as a harsh eye on Mother. He looked as though he was seeing something quite clearly right then, but what that something might be, only he could say.

"Thank you, Mrs. Sexton." He addressed Mother in a peremptory and dismissive fashion. It was unlike any way I had ever heard her addressed before, unless the addresser was my father. "I believe I have everything I need right here."

"Very well," Mother said, clearly confused by the change in his manner, but departing the room and shutting the door behind her nonetheless.

Once she was gone, Aunt Helen and I returned to our seats, eyeing Mr. Brockburn warily as he stood before us. What could we expect from a schoolmaster who had turned away my gentle mother so? And what, pray tell, did he expect from us?

"Let us begin," Mr. Brockburn announced. "First, we must ascertain where you are in your learning. What have you been reading?"

I went to the glass doors of the bookcase and removed a copy of the latest book my father had told me to read. It was John Bunyan's *Pilgrim's Progress*.

"How far along in it are you?" Mr. Brockburn asked.

"Not very, sir," I replied, retaking my seat. "I am just at the part where Evangelist comes by to direct Christian for deliverance to the Wicket Gate."

"Very good," Mr. Brockburn said. "It is an edifying tale." He turned his head slightly. "And you, Miss Smythe?"

For the first time ever, I saw what looked to be a blush color Aunt Helen's pale cheeks. "Oh," she said softly, "I'm not much of one for reading . . . *sir.*"

"I see," Mr. Brockburn said. Again, it was as though he was seeing something beyond what was in the room. Indeed, there was a soft sadness in his look. "Very well. Perhaps we would do better to begin with some of the rudiments instead. Mathematics?" He shook his head at his own suggestion. "No, I do not think that would be the best place to start. It is of course a worthwhile thing to know a little something about, but perhaps another time. Geography? What do my new pupils know about geography?"

"Geography?" Aunt Helen echoed as though the term might be unfamiliar to her.

"Yes, geography," Mr. Brockburn reiterated. "You know: the science that deals with the description, distribution, and interaction of the diverse physical, biological, and cultural features of the Earth's surface."

Aunt Helen puzzled over this overdefinition for a bit.

I had only been in Mr. Brockburn's presence for a short time and yet already I suspected he might be even more intelligent than my father.

As Aunt Helen continued to puzzle, perhaps to save her embarrassment, Mr. Brockburn turned away and began arranging on the table some sheets of paper, writing implements, and school-books he had brought with him. I took this opportunity to lean close to Aunt Helen, mouthing the word "places." When she remained perplexed I took the chance and whispered, "He's talking about *places*."

Aunt Helen coughed, clearing her throat.

"Do you mean places?" she asked Mr. Brockburn. Had she not believed me?

Mr. Brockburn looked up, nodded.

"Well, I know we're in London," Aunt Helen said. "I know that London is in England." She paused, thinking. "And England is in the world."

Mr. Brockburn let show a smile of delight that was, well, a delight to behold.

"Someone once said the very same thing but in a much more verbose fashion," he addressed Aunt Helen directly. "But I do think I like your succinct version much better. It hits the main points while leaving out the boring bits."

Aunt Helen looked startled to be receiving a compliment and then pleased at the fact even while I suspected she had no clue as to what Mr. Brockburn was referring. It made me sad to think she had lived a life that should be so lacking in compliments that even one she did not understand should serve to please her so.

"Perhaps, though," Mr. Brockburn said as he handed sheets of paper to us, "now that we have reduced the universe to the one pinpoint on it that truly matters, we should turn our attention to the basics of writing."

It occurred to me that even though Mr. Brockburn chose to use the word "our," he was focusing far more of his attention on Aunt Helen than on me. I suppose it exposes me as somewhat small-minded to confess it, but such a thing would normally bother me—the relegation of myself to the periphery in a situation where I expected to be central. And yet, somehow it did not. It was as though I saw that Aunt Helen needed what Mr. Brockburn might have to offer far more than I did.

"I will dictate a series of words," Mr. Brockburn announced, "and you will write them down as best you can."

The words he began with were simple enough: "Mother." "Father." "Aunt." "Niece." I suppose that, knowing we were a household here, and further guessing my relationship to Aunt Helen, he assumed these would be easy words for us to spell.

I set them down on the paper with ease and then glanced over at Aunt Helen's paper to see how she was progressing. The first three she had accomplished well enough, but the fourth was again misspelled as it had been in the note she left me on the morning she left: "Neece." It occurred to me then that the things I took for granted—being able to read a book if I so chose, being able to spell correctly as though it were second nature—were freedoms that were not available to everybody.

Mr. Brockburn looked at what we had written. He took up the pen and, rather gently I thought, corrected Aunt Helen's misspelling.

"It is an easy error to make," he said. "You would be surprised at how common it is."

I do not think Aunt Helen liked being put in a class with what was "common."

I saw Aunt Helen look over at my paper, my paper on which Mr. Brockburn had had to correct nothing. What must it be like for her, I wondered, to realize that her thirteen-year-old niece—not *neece*—could read better than she could, could write better too? It must be awful, I thought, to sit in a schoolroom with a child when you were not one and be treated like one yourself.

And yet, there was something special in the way Mr. Brockburn treated her. Another man might have had trouble concealing his contempt for her in such a situation, as though he were her better despite that she lived in this grand house while he was merely employed there. Mr. Brockburn, on the contrary, showed no such contempt. Rather, he appeared to treat Aunt Helen as though some great mistake had been made by the universe and he was now here to help rectify that.

Aunt Helen studied the way Mr. Brockburn had written the offending word. "Huh," she said at last. "An *i* instead of an *e*. Who would have guessed?" Then, with great care, she copied out the word correctly several times. "I'll remember it now," she said, satisfied.

"Do you have a good memory, then?" Mr. Brockburn asked.

"I've an excellent memory"—Aunt Helen gazed at him steadily—"when I'm shown things."

"I have an idea." Mr. Brockburn tapped the pen against his lips. "Since you say you have an excellent memory when you are *shown* things, rather than waste your time with dictation, I will just write out words for you to copy. The English language is a notoriously fickle thing and for the first time I am thinking this would be the best approach to learning."

Aunt Helen's eyes practically gleamed at that.

I recognized that my presence had been forgotten. "And what am I to do while you are both doing that?" I did not like to appear complaining, and yet the prospect of a whole hour during which I would be expected to write out words like "cat" and "ball" repeatedly did not appeal.

Mr. Brockburn handed me a volume, the book I had pulled out earlier. "You can continue," he said, "with *Pilgrim's Progress.*"

And so I sat in solitary silence, reading, as Mr. Brockburn and Aunt Helen sat in communal silence, writing.

An hour later, I heard Mr. Brockburn ask Aunt Helen, somewhat solicitously I thought, "Isn't your hand getting cramped yet?" In the short time he had been with us, he had already been changed much by her presence.

"No." She laughed. "I could do this all day. I *want* to learn."

Mr. Brockburn appeared charmed by her response.

"Be that as it may," he said, "this is a good place for us to stop for the time being. You have learned much already. If you try to do it all at once, it will become overwhelming, and you will start to hate it."

"That could never happen," she said with strength.

Again, Mr. Brockburn appeared charmed.

Then Aunt Helen looked down at the words she had copied so carefully, filling sheet after sheet. She looked from her pages to Mr. Brockburn's and then to my lone page with the four short words I had written earlier. Her face fell.

"The way I make my letters . . . ," she started.

"You mean your penmanship." Mr. Brockburn supplied the correct word.

"Yes. That. My"—Aunt Helen paused, her face a picture of struggle as though determined to get it right this time—"*penmanship.* It's not very good, is it?"

Kind as Mr. Brockburn might wish to be, even he couldn't lie about what was obvious, so he settled for one word: "No."

I glanced over. The letters were uneven, spiking and going off every which way. Then, too, it was obvious from the darkness of the letters that the hand holding the pen had been bearing down mightily.

Mr. Brockburn brightened. "But," he said, raising an instructive forefinger, "just because you have always done a thing poorly does not mean you need go on doing so. Since you are excellent at learning when you are *shown* things, instead of merely writing the letters as you see me write them, why not copy my hand, or even Miss Lucy's?"

"Please don't be offended," she said, "but copying your hand, however fine—it's still a man's hand. As for Lucy . . ."

She trailed off, but I knew what she was going to say. No matter that I could spell circles around her, it was not an adult hand forming the letters.

"I know!" I exclaimed, wanting to be a part of things. "Aunt Helen could borrow a piece of Mother's writing and learn from that."

"What a perfect idea," Aunt Helen said with enthusiasm. "Perhaps then I could learn to copy how a real lady makes her letters."

"You really are determined to be a good student and to learn," Mr. Brockburn said, appreciation in his eyes.

"Oh, yes," Aunt Helen said. "I aim to be the best."

. . . . .

Mr. Brockburn had departed the schoolroom for the day.

I turned to Aunt Helen.

"He is a handsome man," I said, "is he not?"

"Is he? Is he really?" Aunt Helen looked surprised. "I hadn't noticed."

. . . . .

We laughed our way down to the lower floor of the house, where Mother was enjoying tea in the back parlor.

She looked up, startled at our loud entry.

"How did it go?" she asked.

It felt odd, to stand there before her as though aligned with Aunt Helen against her somehow. Previously, I had been on my own before my parents. And, in terms of the greater world, it had always felt as though I was alone, unless I had Mother beside me. But now it felt different—yet another change.

"It went very well, thank you," Aunt Helen said formally. Then a grin began to fight with the corners of her mouth, ultimately winning the war. "The only problem is," Aunt Helen sputtered, "Lucy . . . Lucy . . . Lucy thinks the schoolmaster is . . . *handsome!*"

I do not think Mother caught the joke. In truth, I do not think I caught it entirely myself. But Aunt Helen's hilarity, such a rare thing, was so infectious, I could not help but join in. Before I knew it, I was doubled over with the overwhelming humor of it all.

We were laughing so hard I didn't hear the door and only realized our home had a visitor when one of the servants came in, delivering a card to Mother on a silver tray.

Mother glanced at it. "Mrs. Carson is here," she said.

Mrs. Carson was a neighbor of ours, living in the next street over, and a nosy one at that.

"Tell her I will meet her in the front parlor," Mother informed the waiting servant.

I controlled my laughter and straightened my skirts, preparatory to following Mother out of the room. Mrs. Carson may have been nosy, but it was fun to listen in on the gossip she so often delivered.

As though I were a duck and she were my duckling, Aunt Helen made to follow me.

Then Mother turned, stopping our progress.

"Perhaps," she said, "it would be best if I saw Mrs. Carson alone today."

It was as though I had been struck. Immediately, as I watched Mother leave the room, I caught the implications: not only was Aunt Helen not to be encouraged, *allowed* to go out, but neither was she to be part of our normal family life when visitors were seen in. Had Aunt Helen caught the implications too?

I looked at her face:

She had.

"It doesn't matter," she said to me. "I suppose Mrs. Carson is a silly woman."

"She is," I said, forcing a smile in the hopes of taking the sting out of what had just transpired.

Now we were presented with a dilemma, however. We could not leave the room by the normal exit, because nosy Mrs. Carson might see us as we passed by the front parlor on our way to that staircase. And to remain in that room? It would have felt too much as though we had been consigned to a nicely appointed prison.

Aunt Helen and I used the back stairs, the *servants'* stairs, to pass upward to our rooms.

• Eight •

The next morning during lessons, Mr. Brockburn presented Aunt Helen with a gift.

"No one's ever given me a present," she said, studying the plain brown wrapper, tied with string, as though unsure as to how to proceed. "I don't know what to do."

"I think you're supposed to open it," Mr. Brockburn suggested, his cheeks coloring.

Aunt Helen did so. Inside the wrapper was a book. It was a fine dictionary.

"It's a dictionary," Mr. Brockburn informed her, perhaps suspecting she might not know what one was. "It is a reference book containing words alphabetically arranged, along with information about their forms, pronunciations, functions, etymologies, meanings, and syntactical and idiomatic usages."

"It's beautiful," Aunt Helen said, using a delicacy I never would have guessed was in her to gently page through the book.

Then she added with a mischievous smile, "Even if I don't know the meaning of nearly half of what you just said."

"Yes. Well. That is what the dictionary is for." Mr. Brockburn's blush deepened. "Now you can copy out words to your heart's content as practice work."

With the correspondence I had provided her from Mother's desk, this would make a perfect pairing for Aunt Helen's education in letters.

"Use it in good health," Mr. Brockburn said.

"Oh, I shall," Aunt Helen said. "I shall."

. . . . .

My father joined us for luncheon that day.

Just that morning, I had requested that my customary position at meals be changed so that I might sit beside Aunt Helen. My request had been granted.

Aunt Helen made a face when she first tried the turtle soup. I cannot say I really blamed her, but I did notice she used the right spoon for it now, and by the time she took the second mouthful, you could not tell from her expression if she still hated it. Already, she was getting quite good at using the proper utensils. And eating—she was getting good at that too. Mother had told Mrs. Wiggins that she planned to fatten Aunt Helen up. As I watched Aunt Helen reach for a third roll, it occurred to me that she was doing a fine job of fattening herself up.

"Now that Mrs. Wiggins is taking care of your body, at least in the matter of clothing," my father began, "and now that Mr. Brockburn is tending to the expansion of your mind—indeed, he informs me that you are quite a sponge—perhaps it is time to turn our attention to your spirit."

"You don't mean church, do you?" Aunt Helen asked sharply.

My father threw back his head and roared. "Do you hate it that much?" he asked her.

"I've never been," she said proudly.

I was mildly horrified at this, a little thrilled too. Everyone I knew went to church, and I had wondered what was to be done about it now that Aunt Helen was here. We normally went every Sunday, had not gone the last Sunday because that was the day that we had set out early looking for Aunt Helen.

"And you shall not go now either," my father said, surprising us all, perhaps even himself, but still smiling just the same. "Although the time will come, I suppose, when you shall have to. But no, I don't believe our church is ready for you just yet."

"Then what did you mean before," she asked, "about turning my attention to my spirit?" Her eyes narrowed. "You don't mean a fortune-teller, do you? Like the one who—"

She cut herself short, but we all knew what she was thinking, had been about to say: like the one who advised her and Mother's parents to take Mother home while consigning her to the work-house.

"No." My father sobered. "I was not thinking of anything like that." Then his smile returned, just as quickly as it had fled. "I was thinking more along the lines of etiquette lessons, deport-ment, that sort of thing. Perhaps 'spirit' was not the right word to use when I meant something else, when I meant something more like 'style.'"

"I've a new dictionary I could lend you," I heard Aunt Helen murmur under her breath. It was all I could do not to laugh. Then, louder, she said: "And who's to be my teacher in this . . . etiquette? This . . . deportment?"

My father raised his glass, tilted it toward Mother. "Why, your sister, of course," he said. "Who better?"

Then he turned to me. "You're looking a bit shabby these days, Lucy," he said.

I *was*?

I looked down at myself. The apron of my dress was slightly askew. I had been so caught up these past few days in all things Aunt Helen, I rushed through my own toilet far too quickly in order to see her.

"Perhaps," he said, "you could use a few lessons in etiquette and deportment yourself."

. . . . .

With no Mrs. Carson to visit us that afternoon, Mother began her lessons with Aunt Helen immediately after lunch.

They were to be held in the music room.

"I think," Mother said, looking pleased to be regarded as the expert on something, "that we should start with the simple task of walking gracefully."

Mother walked the length of the room, appearing not to take anything so human as a step.

"Huh," Aunt Helen said, as though she were making a discovery. "I don't think I ever noticed that some people walked like that. It's like you're an angel or something."

Aunt Helen and I tried to mimic Mother's artistry at floating, with mixed results. I, of course, had had this lesson before, more than once, but it did not mean I had perfected it. At least, I was better at first than Aunt Helen.

"Not bad," Mother pronounced after Aunt Helen and I had practiced floating for half an hour. "Do that for half an hour each day. I think now you should practice your curtsies. You bend the knees outward, rather than straight ahead, stepping one foot behind you. You should use your hands to hold your skirt out from your body."

Mother executed a perfect curtsy, bowing down low, although it was impossible to tell beneath her voluminous skirts just what she was doing with the positioning of her knees. Really, she could have been hiding almost anything down there.

"Now you try it," she directed.

I dipped a curtsy, not thinking it very difficult. I was accustomed to performing them whenever my parents' friends or older relatives came to call.

"Very good," Mother said. "Now you, Helen. It is important to know how to curtsy for when one encounters those of a senior social rank. And you need to know how to curtsy properly before beginning a dance."

Aunt Helen's face was practically the portrait of a sneer. "But I never leave the house," she said. "I never see anyone of a 'senior social rank.'" Another sneer. "And I certainly don't never *dance*."

"Don't say 'don't never,'" Mother corrected snappishly. Then she had the grace to color at this, at everything. "No, perhaps you do not have those opportunities now. But one day you shall."

That was enough persuasion for Aunt Helen. With great seriousness of expression she dipped curtsy after curtsy until Mother
finally said she had dipped enough.

"You are doing quite well," Mother said with a generous smile.
"The schoolmaster is right: you *are* like a sponge."

All this taking classes together—it was like having a big sister as well as an aunt, only sometimes it felt as though she were
my younger sister, since she knew less about what we were being
taught than I did.

"Next," Mother said, "I think we should work on how well you
carry yourselves in even more formal circumstances."

Our house contained many staircases. The one leading from
off the front parlor to the family bedrooms upstairs. The back
stairs that the servants used and that Aunt Helen and I had used
to escape on the occasion when Mrs. Carson had come to call.
And a third one that led up to the grand ballroom. It was to the
last that Mother led us now, having us ascend the stairs first so
that we might descend them.

"I know it may not seem to matter, but the way you carry
yourself—your bearing, as it were—is so important in terms of
the opinions others will form about you. It is paramount then at
all times, and in particular when descending a grand staircase
such as this, to be perceived as though you are floating on air."

She demonstrated, performing her angel trick again.

I followed, looking straight ahead, pretending that I had the
dictionary that Mr. Brockburn had given Aunt Helen perched
on my head all the while. If I do say so myself, my floating would
have done the queen proud.

Then it was Aunt Helen's turn.

She was so serious as she descended the first few steps, her head erect, as though there were a strong cord attaching it to the ceiling. You could not say she floated, not like Mother did, because her steps were too halting, but her carriage was regal as she walked down the dead center of the stairs, far from any railing, eyes straight ahead as though looking for a ship's arrival.

But then, something must have been on one of the marble steps or perhaps she grew dizzy from trying to walk without looking where she was going, for I saw her stumble. Immediately, she lunged and grabbed on to the railing as though to keep herself from tumbling all the way down. It would have been a disastrous fall. It was a long flight.

Having secured her anchor, Aunt Helen sat with little grace upon the step where she had been standing. Then an unthinkable thing happened: she covered her face with her hands and burst into tears.

"Are you hurt?" Mother asked in an anxious voice, starting up the stairs.

Aunt Helen lifted one hand as though to ward Mother away. "I'm fine," she gasped out between sobs. "I'm not hurt at all."

"Then what is the matter?" Mother asked, stopping where she stood.

"I'm so *bad*," Aunt Helen said, angry heat in her voice. "I'm so bad at all"—and here she waved one hand in a wild circle as though indicating a universe greater than our house—"*this*."

Mother stared at Aunt Helen as she continued to speak.

"What kind of woman am I? I must be taught how to read, how to write, how to eat—even how to walk down the stairs!" She barked a bitter laugh. "And I'm so *bad* at all of it."

And then a second extraordinary thing happened: Mother laughed.

"Are you *laughing* at me?" Aunt Helen demanded, her face as shocked as I felt.

"No, I am not laughing at *you*," Mother said, trying to control her laughter as much as Aunt Helen had tried to control her tears moments earlier. "Or at least," she added, "not directly. But I guess that I am laughing at you in that . . . you are . . . you are . . . you are taking this all far too seriously!"

"Excuse me?" Aunt Helen said.

"This." Mother waved her own hand in the air, describing a circle more ethereal than the wild one of Aunt Helen's harsh gesture. "All this. It is what Frederick wants. Frederick wants the lessons. Frederick wants me to teach you about poise and deportment. But do you honestly think it matters a whit to me? It is not that important. You should not let it upset you so. You should not let taking it all too seriously make you so unhappy."

And then a third astonishing thing happened: Aunt Helen burst into laughter too.

"You are right!" she said. "I *do* take everything so seriously!" She stood and, as though demonstrating how wrongly serious she could be, began descending the steps much as she had done before, stiff, eyes centered on nothing, as though going to meet her executioner. She stopped and laughed again, as if at herself, and then she did something she had not yet done: she held out her arms for Mother's embrace and Mother entered them.

When Mother and I had gone for a walk in the park the afternoon after the dressmaker's visit, just prior to returning home Mother had asked me how I felt about having Aunt Helen here.

At the time, I had told her, rather defiantly, that it pleased me. But, in this moment, I felt something I had never felt before, watching them embrace in their laughing sisterly fashion:

Jealousy.

Then Mother gaily called for us to follow her back to the music room—she was going to play the piano while Aunt Helen and I learned how to dance—and the bad feeling disappeared.

· · · · ·

Back in the music room, Mother seated herself on the bench in front of the baby grand piano. She began to play a tune, instructing us to waltz. Instead, Aunt Helen stood still for a time, her head to one side, listening to Mother play.

"Aren't you going to dance?" Mother asked, stopping. "Lucy knows how to dance a bit."

"You play so nicely," Aunt Helen said wistfully. "I wish I knew how to play."

"It is not very hard," Mother said, "but I am not sure I am the one to teach you. I shall arrange for someone to give you lessons."

"You would do that?" Aunt Helen asked.

"Of course," Mother said simply.

"I would like that very much," Aunt Helen said. "Do you think I could ever learn to play as well as you?"

"Of course," Mother said again. "In time." Then she put her long, graceful hands to the keys again.

This time when she played, Aunt Helen and I tried to dance as we'd been told to, with me attempting to lead her around as I'd seen my father do with Mother, but we kept stepping on each other's feet. She was too tall for me to lead her.

"I'm sorry," Aunt Helen said. "I'm not much good at this kind of dancing, and I don't think today is the time for me to learn."

I sensed that perhaps she was tired after her bout of crying on the stairs. I knew from my own experiences with crying from frustration, it took a lot of energy out of a person.

But then Aunt Helen laughed, perhaps remembering Mother's admonition not to take everything so seriously, laughing as she had earlier, as though suddenly light of heart.

Taking one of my hands crudely in one of hers, while placing her other hand firmly on my waist, she said, "Now, here's a dance I can teach you," and began leading me on a merry romp around the room.

Before I knew it, Mother was banging on the piano in a way my father would no doubt have thought unseemly had he been there to witness it. But I did not mind her banging—I had no idea she could play such a tune!—nor did I mind the romp. As we twirled faster and faster, I no longer cared if my toes were stepped on a bit, nor did I worry that I might step on any toes in turn. It felt like someone had allowed a strong seaside breeze to blow through the house. It felt clean. It felt good. It was too much of a good thing to stop.

"What is the meaning of this?" came a stern voice from the doorway.

The owner of the voice was tall for a woman, the graying black hair she wore coiled around her head like a nimbus making her appear just a smidgen taller, and she was very lean.

Aunt Martha had come to call.

• Nine •

Aunt Martha moved her gaze from Mother to Aunt Helen. If her expression had been severe before, that expression solidified in her features now as she took in the startling similarities and remaining differences between Mother and Aunt Helen.

Whatever Aunt Martha saw, whatever she thought, it was obvious she did not like it.

"What is—," she began to demand a second time, but Mother cut her off.

"I should like to present," she said, "Helen Smythe." She turned to Aunt Helen. "Helen, this is Frederick's sister, Martha Sexton."

Aunt Helen executed what could only be termed a saucy curtsy.

Before Aunt Martha could respond, Mother rose from the piano bench and stepped away from the instrument.

"Let us adjourn to the front parlor," she suggested to Aunt Martha. "Perhaps the sunshine in that room will improve your mood."

Aunt Helen and I moved to follow them, but Mother's words stopped us.

"Perhaps," she suggested, "it would be best if you two went upstairs and left us alone to talk in private."

"But—," I began to object.

"Now, Lucy." Mother's tone was firm.

As Mother and Aunt Martha turned left into the front parlor, Aunt Helen and I turned right, beginning our ascent. But when we reached the sixth step, I tugged on Aunt Helen's sleeve.

She looked down at me, a surprised expression on her face as I took a seat on the stair, gesturing for her to do the same.

She raised her eyebrows at me as she sat, opening her mouth to speak, but I put a finger to my lips.

Then we sat in silence, together, listening.

The conversation was heated, and we could hear every word with crystal clarity as though we were in the same room as the speakers.

"Helen Smythe is my twin sister," Mother said with simplicity.

"That is obvious," Aunt Martha returned. "What is not obvious is why I have never been informed of her existence before. What is not obvious is what she is doing here now."

"I did not know of her existence myself," Mother said, "until recently. Has it been a week now? More?" I could picture her shaking her head over the elusive nature of time. "It is hard to say. The days are all so strange now, so different from what they once were. It is no matter. Whatever the day, when Helen first arrived I was as shocked as you are today. More so—I fainted. But when I came to, Helen told me a story that I had not previously guessed at, nor would I have believed it even then, had I not the bodily proof of it staring me in the face. My parents, you see, *our parents* were not who I thought they were. Our real mother was unable to keep us . . ."

I noticed that Mother did not mention that her own real mother had been a maid. For the first time the thought occurred to me: perhaps she found such a notion disturbing? The very idea that she, brought up among wealth and privilege, was in fact the descendent of a servant and that a mere accident of fortune had elevated her in the world. What would Aunt Martha think if she knew? What did my father think? He had known Mother to be one person and now, in a sense, she was another. Did he see her differently, now that she was a maid's daughter? Come to that, did I?

"Had you given me ten minutes on my own after seeing this . . . *Helen Smythe*," I heard Aunt Martha say, "I might have deduced the circumstances. Not the exact circumstances, perhaps, and I do have the feeling you are not telling me everything you know, but the physical connection is obvious."

Mother said nothing to this. Perhaps she worried that if she did, Aunt Martha might specifically ask just whose daughters she and Aunt Helen were.

"Tell me," Aunt Martha asked, "have any of your friends met this Helen Smythe yet?"

"No." Mother's tone was surprised. Obviously, this was not the question she had expected to be asked next.

"That is all to the good." Aunt Martha sounded satisfied. "You are ashamed of your new sister, then, are you?"

"Of course not." Now Mother sounded horrified at the notion. "I simply do not think she wishes to be seen yet."

This struck me as being in direct contradiction to all I had observed, confirmed when I studied Aunt Helen's suddenly grim profile now, but I was in no position to make my objections heard.

"Whatever the reason," Aunt Martha said, "it is all to the good."

"That is the second time you have said that," Mother said. "What is 'all to the good'?"

"It is simply this," Aunt Martha said. "If no one else has seen her, except for the servants, who can easily be paid off, then no one will be the wiser when you tell her it is time for her to leave."

The idea of no one else having seen Aunt Helen was not strictly accurate, of course. There had been the dressmaker, Mrs. Wiggins. There had been the schoolmaster, Mr. Brockburn. If Aunt Martha was made aware of their having seen Aunt Helen, would she suggest they be paid off as well?

Mother's voice had sounded horrified just a moment ago, but it was nothing as compared with the raw emotion with which she spoke now.

"I'm not going to *send her away*!" Her words could have filled the whole large house. "She is my *sister*! I will *not* send her away!"

"Tell me," Aunt Martha said, "what does Frederick make of all this?"

"How do you mean?" Mother asked.

"He cannot be happy about the situation," Aunt Martha said. "I cannot imagine that my brother would want that woman, who is not at all like us, under his roof."

The wall separating us might just as well have been made out of thin glass, because I could have sworn I saw the straightening of Mother's spine as she bit out the words:

"Then you do not know your brother." And then it was as though she was trying to temper her anger, softening as though straining to achieve conciliation. "Your brother says it is just like *Comedy of Errors*, save that it is a tragedy and no one is laughing. It was, in fact, mostly Frederick's idea that Helen stay on with us. He would not, you see, have it any other way."

"Then you are both insane," Aunt Martha declared.

"I beg your pardon? The woman is my sister. Can you not see—"

"Can *you* not see, Aliese, what that woman is? Look at that woman with your own eyes, see her for what she is. You could spend a fortune trying to transform her into something else. It will do you no good. She is not one of us, never will be. Do you know anything, really, of what her life has been? Have you any idea of what things she might be capable? I would swear on my life, that woman is dangerous. And if you allow her to remain here, you will no doubt come to regret it greatly in time."

"I think it is time for you to go, Martha."

"Are you ordering me out?"

"Ordering? No. I just think that if you come back on another day, you will see things differently. At least, that would be my hope."

I liked that Mother, having previously hidden Aunt Helen away here, stood up to Aunt Martha now on her behalf at last.

As we heard Aunt Martha prepare to depart, Aunt Helen and I hurriedly crept up the stairs. When we attained the safety of the landing, Aunt Helen turned to me.

"Aunt Martha has never been married?" she asked.

I shook my head.

"They are always the worst," she said.

I did not know what to make of this, but Aunt Helen spoke again almost immediately, obviating any need for a response on my part.

"That one," she said, "will always be trouble."

· · · · ·

More people entered our lives: a woman to teach Aunt Helen how to dress her own hair, so that it looked just like Mother's; a piano teacher, one Mr. Chambers, whose job it was to instruct Aunt Helen how to play. When he finished with her, if there was time, he spent a few moments instructing me.

Perfumes, ribbons, lotions—all were sent for and arrived to adorn Aunt Helen. At last, the day came when the dresses and other items Mrs. Wiggins had been hired to make began to arrive.

Mother was out when the first packages were delivered, while Father was off in his study, either writing or reading or sleeping— one could never be sure. Even though Mother had been the one to order everything for Aunt Helen, I sensed that Aunt Helen was not disappointed at having Mother away from home just then. Indeed, I surmised it must be a relief for her, because now she would not feel forced to show immediate gratitude for that which should have been hers all her life.

Still, as one of the servants moved to follow Aunt Helen's instructions to bear the packages up to her room, she turned to me, genuine excitement in her eyes.

"Come with me, Lucy," she said, eyes sparkling. If she were the kind of person to impulsively touch others when overcome by great feeling, I imagine she would have grabbed on to my hand

then and there. "I want to try everything on, but I'll need someone to help."

"That's what the maid—"

"I don't care about the maid. I'd be shy around the maid. I
want you." Then she grabbed on to her skirts, racing up the stairs.
"Come on!" she called over her shoulder and I raced after.

In her room, door closed and locked, she spread out the
packages on her narrow bed.

She gave that bed a moment's consideration. "I wonder how
long I'll be kept in a nursery." Her words were barely audible, yet
they filled me with a chill.

Of course it was only natural she should feel resentment at
being kept in a room created for a child. Of course it was only
natural that she should want to move to a more suitable room
and that, eventually, my parents would see that. But I did not like
the idea of being left alone again on the second story, with
nobody else.

This was not a day for melancholy, however. It was a day for
joy. And, no sooner did the clouds enter Aunt Helen's counte-
nance than they rolled right back out again, leaving only the sun
behind.

"Look at all this, Lucy!" There was awe in her eyes as she
unwrapped package after package, revealing garment after garment. "I've never had such things before!"

Before I knew it, Aunt Helen was rapidly removing her drab
gray dress. In a moment, she was naked before me.

I was not accustomed to seeing naked bodies, but I thought
that Aunt Helen's, while still too thin, must be considered beautiful. No sooner had I registered that willowy beauty, however—the

swell of breasts and hips, not so very different from my own changing body, separated by a smooth, flat stomach—than Aunt Helen was reaching for one of her new things to try on.

If I had been asked to select what she would choose first, I would have sworn it would have been one of the dresses, but I would have been wrong. Aunt Helen reached for one of the petti-coats, stepping her bare feet into it and covering the lower por-tion of her nakedness. It was the black grosgrain petticoat with its narrow yoke and smooth-fitting gores on both sides and the front, a full back-breadth gathered at the top. The bottom was decorated with a small ruffle of the same silk with a pink edge, in lace.

"I've never had one of these before." Aunt Helen's voice was small as she smoothed the fabric, the touch of her fingers light and then more forceful, as if the very hands themselves could not believe what they were touching.

Then Aunt Helen did what I could not imagine her doing a short time ago. Grabbing on to my hands with hers, still naked from the waist up, she danced me around the room, much as she had danced me when Mother played the piano for us on the day Aunt Martha came to call.

Every now and then, Aunt Helen would pause long enough to pick up one of the new dresses, throwing it up in the air until it rained down on the narrow bed. At last, when we were too exhausted to dance any longer, we collapsed onto the bed, com-ing to rest side by side, faces turned up to the ceiling, our backs cushioned by a sea of silk and velvet and lace.

• Ten •

The next day, for our lessons with Mr. Brockburn, Aunt Helen put on one of her new dresses. She spent much time with me, debating over which would be best. I did not want to exercise any undue influence—it was, I felt, her choice to make—but I was pleased to be consulted.

When Mr. Brockburn entered the schoolroom, Aunt Helen and I were already seated at our table, side by side. So I was there to witness it when Mr. Brockburn was brought up short by the vision of Aunt Helen for the second time. The first had been on the day when he originally met all of us, recognizing that Aunt Helen, in her drab gray dress, was Mother's sister. Now he was brought up short by this new vision of Aunt Helen, that of a woman transformed.

Aunt Helen sat there properly in her gray blue costume, with its vest and revers in dark blue velvet fabric. She even wore the hat that went with the costume. This was an odd thing to do indoors, particularly in a schoolroom, but I cannot say that I blamed her for this fashion misstep. I could well imagine how, having lived in drab gray for what must have felt like an eternity, it must now feel to her as though she had been set free.

"Miss Smythe." Was that a blush I saw in the schoolmaster's cheeks? "You look most becoming today, if I may be so bold as to comment."

"You may." Aunt Helen bowed her head demurely, but then it dipped up just enough and . . . was that a coquettish look directed at Mr. Brockburn from that one eye visible under the brim? "Thank you, sir, for noticing."

Mr. Brockburn cleared his throat as though discomfited.

"Good day, Mr. Brockburn," I said, wishing to remind them of my presence.

"Oh?" Mr. Brockburn tore his gaze from Aunt Helen, looked at me, blushed again. "Yes, Lucy. Yes, it is." Another clearing of the throat. "Shall we get down to our lessons?" He did not wait for an answer. "Now, where did we leave off yesterday?"

"I was working on my penmanship," Aunt Helen supplied. Then she produced the sheets she had been working with previously, along with the letters of Mother's I had purloined after suggesting she copy Mother's penmanship in perfecting a graceful hand.

"Ah, yes. Of course." Mr. Brockburn leaned over Aunt Helen's shoulder, the better to closely observe her as she worked.

While they did that, I went to get my copy of *Tom Brown at Oxford* from the glass cabinet. I'd finished with *Pilgrim's Progress*, and my father had suggested this next.

And so we passed the next few hours, Mr. Brockburn's dark head nearly side by side with Aunt Helen's blond hatted one,

while my own head was in a book. Their occasional murmured
voices created a soothing sea sound in the background, but I did
not try to pick out the words. I was happy enough to have Aunt
Helen learn to make her letters better, but I did not need to
know all about it.

It was half twelve before anyone addressed another word that
might concern me.

"Of course, it is still cold out," Mr. Brockburn said, a hopeful
expression on his face, "but it is such a sunny day. Would it not
be better, this once, to continue our lessons in the park? Surely
we can discuss geography there just as easily as here."

My inclination was to decline for both of us.

"I don't think that is a very good—," I started, but then
stopped.

I saw the look in Aunt Helen's eyes. It was a pleading look. It
occurred to me then how awful it must be to be kept in all the
time, how desperate she must be to get out, if only for an hour.

"Mother is out on visits all day," I reviewed the facts aloud,
repeating what Mother had told us at breakfast, "and my father is
in his study, writing. I don't suppose anyone would notice if we
slipped out just this once. Provided we're not gone for very long,
no one will even miss us."

We did not tell Mr. Brockburn why it mattered so much that
no one see us go out, but a look of knowledge came into his eyes
as I spoke. He did not comment on whatever he was thinking, but
he did go along with us as we moved down the staircase, proceeding with slow creeps from step to step as though we might be
three burglars.

At the bottom, I peeked around the corners on both sides,

making sure there were no stray servants beating draperies or stoking fires. Seeing no one about, I made a mad dash across the vestibule, gesturing for the other two to follow me. Reaching the door, I all but yanked it open, immediately feeling the fresh air on my face. In another instant, I was outside; another, and Mr. Brockburn and Aunt Helen were on the step beside me; one more, and we had shut the door behind us.

. . . . .

Aunt Helen's breath made tiny puffs of clouds against the air as she spoke, but I did not note the words. I was too happy to be outside, walking with Aunt Helen between Mr. Brockburn and me as though we were her protection.

I could feel the excitement coiled up in the woman beside me until she was near to bursting with it, causing me to share—as close as I could—that excitement. What must it be like, I thought, to be outside at long last? And what must it be like, to be seen by the world for the first time in raiment that one has never been permitted to wear before?

Aunt Helen still strode more than glided, but her head stood so proud. Did she feel different? She looked different.

The sun was as high as it could get for that time of year, and strong, as Mr. Brockburn had promised, the air as crisp as a snapped sheet. Little patches of snow still covered much of an earth that would fill again with grass and flowers in a few months' time. Where the snow had melted, the ground was mucky and it occurred to me that I would need to remind Aunt Helen to scrape the earth off the bottoms of her boots when we returned home so that no one would suspect where we had been.

Even though the sun was bright, the air was still too cold for more than a few hardy souls to take advantage of the chance to stroll out of doors. The park was therefore sparsely populated, which suited me perfectly.

"Aliese!" a strident voice called out, halting us.

I knew that voice. It belonged to Mrs. Carson.

Our nosy neighbor's body was as unattractive as her voice. She was stocky, and had an ill-fitting wardrobe. Mother often wondered, outside of Mrs. Carson's hearing, why she should choose her clothes so poorly when it was widely thought that the Carsons had more money than anybody. On top of Mrs. Carson's wattled neck was a head slightly out of proportion to its body, erring on the large side. Her hair was a flat brown, not always as clean as it might be, and her brown eyes were shrewd, always watching one too closely.

She knew who we were, however, or at least she *thought* she knew who two of us were, and we could not ignore her.

We stopped, turned, faced her.

"Why have you changed your dress?" Mrs. Carson demanded of Aunt Helen. "When I saw you at Mary Williams's this morning, you had on a different one. I think it suited you more."

"Mother spilled something on it," I said, speaking for Aunt Helen, before she had the chance to speak and give herself away. Aunt Helen had never met Mrs. Carson before. She could not know what sort of dangers such a woman presented.

But then I decided that I did not like what I had said. It cast Mother as a clumsy sort when she was anything but. I did not like to think that by day's end Mrs. Carson would have returned to Mary Williams, telling her that Aliese Sexton could no longer balance her own teacup, so I amended to, "That is to say, a servant, overeager, placed a tea tray down too abruptly, causing it to spill on Mother's sleeve."

"But I thought," Mrs. Carson addressed her words to Aunt Helen again, "that when I saw you, you distinctly said you would be spending the entire day paying calls."

Aunt Helen gazed at Mrs. Carson steadily, finally parting her lips as though to speak.

I could see why she did this—she probably guessed that by now Mrs. Carson was wondering why her good friend Aliese Sexton was not speaking—but I could not let her.

"Mother grew tired," I said. Then I lowered my voice, as though we were conspirators. "You know how tiring Mary Williams can be—all that gossip she engages in."

I was rather proud of myself for thinking to say this. It has been my experience that when people are guilty of a thing, they always mark the flaw in others, never themselves.

"Mother just needed a rest," I went on in a more normal volume. "She just needed a spot of tea. But look at her: she is fine now."

I regretted saying that last. It wouldn't do to invite Mrs. Carson to look at Aunt Helen too closely.

But then *I* looked at Aunt Helen, and the thought struck me:

There were still marked differences between Aunt Helen and Mother. Chiefly, the former was still a bit thinner than the latter. But I could see now that in her new peacock finery, and if she didn't speak, thereby revealing the speech differences that still lingered, one could mistake one sister for the other.

"Lucy," Mrs. Carson said, "you must endeavor to learn not to speak for your mother. It is quite impertinent that you should do so. I do not remember you being thus before."

"I shall try, Mrs. Carson," I said.

Mrs. Carson turned her attention to Mr. Brockburn. "And who is this—," she demanded, leaving an audible silent slot in which she would normally have slipped the word "gentleman." Mr. Brockburn dressed respectably enough, for a schoolmaster, but he was not in attire that any in the neighborhood would term "one of us" in the way that, say, my father was, or even Mr. Carson.

"This is Mr. Brockburn," I said proudly, running the risk of a second admonishment for impertinently speaking out of turn. "He is my schoolmaster."

Mr. Brockburn tipped his hat, executing a surprisingly elegant bow in Mrs. Carson's direction.

She all but took a step back, away from him.

It was easy to read what Mrs. Carson was thinking: *The* schoolmaster? *The Sextons are now taking strolls with their* schoolmaster?

As she took hasty leave of our company, I prayed that something more momentous than us should fall into Mrs. Carson's path as she continued her journey, so that when she made her gossipy rounds through the neighborhood she might have something else to wax on about.

I had had enough heart-stopping adventure for one day.

"It is time to go back," I announced.

No one argued with me.

Our walk back to the house was far more sober than had been the one when we set out.

"Thank you," Mr. Brockburn addressed Aunt Helen, prior to taking his leave at our doorstep, "for a lovely afternoon."

. . . . .

My father had not been seen since breakfast time, but as he joined us for dinner, he looked at his recently acquired sister-in-law.

"There is something different about you tonight, Helen," he said, his brow moving into an exaggerated arch of puzzlement, as though it were a question mark lying down.

"I—," she said.

"She—," I said at the same time.

"No." My father waved his hand. "Do not tell me. I wish to guess." He puzzled some more. Then his eyes lit with knowledge. "You have learned where New York is!"

That's when I knew he was teasing us.

I couldn't help it: I giggled.

Aunt Helen giggled too.

"No," she said, mirth in her eyes. "That was last week."

"Hmm," my father said. He drummed his fingers against his chin. "What else could it be?" The light of knowledge again. "I know!" He snapped his fingers. "You have acquired a new kitten!"

"No." She giggled.

"But she would like one," I added, giggling some more.

"This is terrible," my father said. "And here I have always thought myself to be an intelligent man." He frowned. "Well, apparently, I am not nearly as intelligent as I thought." But a moment later he collapsed against his chair back, as though relieved of something. "I have finally worked it out," he said, smiling. "You have a new dress."

"Yes, I do," Aunt Helen said, more soberly now, "thanks to you and my sister." She nodded at Mother.

"And it is very becoming on you," my father said warmly, ignoring the words of gratitude. He turned to Mother. "Isn't it, Aliese?"

"Indeed. But I do think, Helen," Mother said, "that you might take the hat off when at table. It is not customary to wear one's hat while at home."

. . . . .

I had caught a chill in the park that day, although my parents did not know how or where I caught it. But the next morning, when I had not improved, Mother ordered me to spend the day in bed. Mother was always concerned that any cold I acquired might lead to my death.

"If you ever died," she would say, "I would cry forever."

My father, hearing her say this, would tell her that she must not speak to me so, that I would feel responsible that her happiness was too bound up in me and that this would turn me into the sort of namby-pamby person he despised.

But I never minded when she spoke those words. It was somehow nice to think that at least one person in this life loved me so much, if I should die the world would stop for them. And I understood how she felt. For, as much as Aunt Helen being there had disturbed things in our household, as much as the constantly changing swirl of it all had served to alter the balance between

Mother and myself, Mother was still the one person who, were she taken from this world, her absence would cause me to cry forever.

And so I bore my bed sentence with as much stoic grace as I could. And so I was not there in the schoolroom when Mr. Brockburn came to give the day's lesson and Aunt Helen took that lesson for the first time alone together. I should like to have known what they talked about with no one there to hear their words. Did he ask her about her past? Did he inquire as to how she had come to be the way she was when he first saw her and how she came to be here now?

It is impossible to know.

• Eleven •

One month passed, then two.

My father once told me that he had dreamed briefly, when he was younger, of a life in the navy, but that being the only male child, he had been compelled when grown to manage the family fortune.

Perhaps from time to time the idea of a life missed preyed on my father's mind, bleeding out into his reading choices for me. At those times I would be forced to read a seafaring novel such as the one he'd recently given me, Frederick Marryat's *Mr. Midshipman Easy*. Apparently, my father was longing for his unrealized life at sea again.

Which was why I was in the back parlor, alone, plugging away at the book. I cannot say I was overly impressed with Mr. Marryat's writing. But at least I could be comfortable while reading the wretched book. I could recline on one of the sofas in the back parlor, book in one hand, crunchy apple in the other, even resting my booted feet on the soft fabric because there was no one there to see me.

But then the book really became too much, making me want to hurl the thing across the room.

Book unfinished, I put my finger between the pages where I had stopped reading, tossed the apple core on a plate, and went off in search of my father. I suspected this was not a book he had in fact read himself, that he had only selected it for me based on the title and, if I had to suffer at the hands of Mr. Marryat's philosophizing, well, my father would too.

But as I approached the door of his study, my purposeful stride slowed as a timidity crept into my resolve. My father did not normally like to be disturbed when he was working. His study was his sanctuary. He often said as much, causing me to wonder if Mother and I were so distracting that a man should need a refuge from us.

I raised my fist to boldly knock, drew my fist back to my side. What if my father became angry at being interrupted? What if he was at a critical juncture in his novel writing and I, tearing his attention away at just the wrong moment, became the cause of his never creating a sentence that would have been sheer brilliance?

It was as I was about to turn away from the door that I heard the sound of laughter coming through it.

This was odd.

I was not in the habit of walking past my father's study often while he was working, but the few times I had, I had never heard laughter.

The happy sound of that laughter gave me courage now, and

this time, when I raised my fist, I followed through with a bold knock.

"Yes?" I heard my father's voice call out, as though it was a slight effort to turn his attention away from whatever amused him.

Timid once more, I turned the knob, pushed open the door.

My father's study, in an octagon shape at the back corner of our home, had books soaring all around from the baseboards to the heights of the ceiling. The walls, what you could see of them, were painted dark cobalt with a blinding white trim. In one corner of the room roared a fire; in another was a trapdoor, which he said led to the cellar, although I had never been. The room contained a sofa and chairs surrounding a centrally located table for when he wanted to read or think, instead of write. As for the writing; that was done at a large walnut desk, its back to the long French doors that let in abundant light and from which my father could enter his own private garden.

It was that desk at which he was seated now, the light behind him causing me to blink as I adjusted my eyes to it.

It was only after I made that adjustment that I realized he was not alone. To the right of him was Mother, her skirts not far from the strong hand he used to hold his pen. Her back was to me, the dress she wore white shot with gold. Whenever she wore it, which was not often, for it showed dust and dirt so easily, it always made me think that it was what it would be like if you could take the palace at Versailles and spin it into a dress.

Mother twisted her waist to look back over her shoulder, an anxious expression on her face that disappeared the instant she saw me. What was she doing sitting on my father's desk? It was not like her. I had never seen her do such a thing before. But before she could speak, my father spoke again.

"Yes, Lucy?" my father said. "You wanted me for something?"

I raised the book in my hand halfheartedly, no longer caring about the issues I had wanted to raise. "This"—I waved *Mr. Midshipman Easy*—"it isn't very good."

"No? It's a good thing you told me, then. Now I won't have to bother reading it." He cleared his throat. "Your aunt Helen was just helping me with my book," he said.

I nearly dropped *Mr. Midshipman Easy* on the ground at this.

"Yes," the woman who I had thought just a moment ago to be Mother spoke. And in that one syllable, although the differences between them had closed so much, I could still hear that this was Aunt Helen. The voice was almost Mother's, but not quite. Or, perhaps I only knew it was Aunt Helen because my father had just said so. Even now, it is still so hard to say.

"What are you doing in Mother's dress?" I blurted, without stopping to temper what Mrs. Carson would no doubt call my impertinence or the outrage in my tone at this offense.

"I have grown bored with my few dresses," Aunt Helen said, "but there has not been time for the new ones I ordered to arrive. That Mrs. Wiggins can be so slow. Aliese said she wouldn't mind if I borrowed any of hers in the meantime, anytime I liked. She has so many and, after all, we are now nearly the same size."

"I am sure she does not mind," my father said. "In fact, I hardly ever remember seeing her wear that dress." My father gazed at me sternly. "Not that it is your place to question your aunt as to what she does or does not do."

I suppose I should have bowed my head in submission, but I was not used to bowing my head to anyone, not even my father.

"You said that Aunt Helen has been helping you with your writing," I said, still puzzled by the very notion.

"She has a wonderful ear," my father said. "When I came to the part that was giving me so much trouble, she administered the perfect prescription for helping me over the hurdle. We were laughing at that when you knocked."

"We were," she confirmed.

I did not know what to say to any of this: the idea that my father would share his work with anyone but his editor before publication; the idea that Aunt Helen should turn out to be the sort of woman who was capable of giving profound editorial advice concerning a plot hurdle.

"I suppose I should leave you to your work, then," I said.

Back out in the hallway, having closed the door gently behind me, I shook my head as though trying to wake myself from a confusing dream.

Then I thought about how I had believed the woman sitting on my father's desk to be Mother, how disconcerting it was to learn I had been wrong. And it *was* disconcerting—daily, more so—the idea that the face I loved more than that of any other could be so easily confused with that of another. It was as though they were the same person, but different.

I shook my head again, hefted my copy of *Mr. Midshipman Easy*, and moved on, away from the closed door.

. . . . .

Another month passed, and another.

Aunt Helen and I were once again in the schoolroom with Mr. Brockburn.

The weather had changed much since our first schoolroom lesson, much more since that one day we three had gone to the park together. While the windows looked out upon other houses across the street, I felt as though I could see through those buildings to the flowering buds on the trees in the park beyond, see the grass sprouting up green and strong, see younger children playing games I no longer played. I yearned to be there, seeing all that in person, feeling the sun on my face. Later on, I would regret longing for this, regret having wished time away.

Aunt Helen spent a large portion of our hours in the school-room that day also looking out the window. No longer the "sponge" that made her teacher's pride, she was restless now, as I was, look-ing out the window as though anxious to be gone, like a prize pony who has had a whiff of the air beyond the stable yard. Or perhaps . . . I don't know. There was a gleam in her eye, as though she was waiting for something only she expected to happen, wait-ing for something only she could see speeding toward us.

As for Mr. Brockburn, there was a certain desperate sadness about him. He kept trying to pull our divided attentions back to himself, that center upon which we had been content to devote so much energy before. But whatever he attempted—discussing books that would normally pique my interest, complimenting Aunt Helen on her lightning progress through everything he could teach her—it was all to no avail. We remained with our minds and souls outside of that room, me at the park while Aunt Helen was wherever she had gone to.

At last, a quarter hour before our lessons normally ended, Mr. Brockburn informed us that he had an announcement to make. Reluctantly, we turned our twin gazes upon the schoolmaster.

"Mr. Sexton paid me a visit early this morning just before I left to set out here," he began.

My ears pricked up at that. It seemed unusual enough to me, that my father should take the time to pay Mr. Brockburn an early-morning visit, when early mornings were rarely my father's finest hours, rather than waiting to talk to the schoolmaster when he came here.

"Mr. Sexton wanted to tell me," Mr. Brockburn went on, "that my services here would no longer be required. I was—" His breath caught. If he were a child, I would have imagined him choking on a tear. "I *am* surprised at this. I had thought that our lessons together would continue until some time in the distant future. But, apparently, I was wrong."

Aunt Helen's look betrayed nothing, nor did she speak.

So it fell to me to ask, "But why? Why end it? Why now?"

Mr. Brockburn shrugged here, as though defeated. "Mr. Sexton says my work here is done. He says my . . . *job* was to give Miss Smythe intellectual confidence and that now that task is complete. Her education is complete."

I stole a glance at Aunt Helen.

She looked pleased. I cannot say that I blamed her. Apparently, there had been some sort of test going on and, even though no one had informed her of that fact, she had still managed to pass. No, I could not blame her for being proud of all she had accomplished.

But then the thought occurred to me: Of course Aunt Helen's education was complete, or whatever education my parents had wished her to have, but what of me? What of *my* education?

As though reading my mind, Mr. Brockburn looked at me with a sad smile. "Your father tells me that he will be once again employing your former tutor, Miss Walker, to see to your education."

So there it was.

Aunt Helen, according to my father, no longer needed Mr. Brockburn; so for me, it was back to studying with the innocuous Miss Walker.

Then Mr. Brockburn did a surprising thing, given who he was, who I was. He came to my side, bent down, and laid a gentle kiss upon my cheek. "You are an intelligent girl, Lucy," he reassured me. "You will do fine."

Then, slowly, Mr. Brockburn gathered up his things for the last time. I watched Aunt Helen watching him, and I noted a coolness in her look. But as he paused beside her seat, I saw that look warm.

Mr. Brockburn bowed stiffly. "It has been my pleasure, Miss Smythe. I hope that this is not the last time we shall meet."

"I don't see why it should be," Aunt Helen said. "Indeed, I am sure that it is not."

Perhaps emboldened by her words, a look of hope now in his eyes, he turned to me.

"Lucy," Mr. Brockburn said, "could you please tell your father that I wish to speak with him before I go?"

. . . . .

"What did Mr. Brockburn wish to discuss with you?" Aunt Helen asked my father at dinner.

"There will be time enough to discuss all that later," my father replied. "In the meantime, we have something more pressing to discuss. Aliese and I have decided that it is time for you to be presented to the people of our world."

Part II

• Twelve •

Winter, as has been noted, had turned into spring. Now spring had turned into summer and it had been decided that Aunt Helen's first formal presentation into society was to happen upon the occasion of the celebration of Mother's birthday, *their* birthday, July 6.

The invitations had gone out. The Carsons. The Williams family. Andrew and Penelope Sexton—my father's parents. Aunt Martha. The Tyler family.

The Tylers were a family who had recently purchased the house next door. I had not met them yet, nor even seen them, but my parents said they supposed if they were inviting everyone else in the neighborhood, they would feel as though they were not being properly hospitable, were they not to include these new people.

Invitations went out to about forty other people as well, some business associates of my father's, mostly friends of the family.

Mr. Brockburn's name was not on the list.

The invitations all said the same thing:

Mr. and Mrs. Frederick Sexton

cordially request the honor of your presence

. . . .

to celebrate
Mrs. Sexton's Birthday.

. . . .

At that time, they should also like to
introduce into society her sister,
Miss Helen Smythe.

. . . .

R.S.V.P.

I cannot imagine what people made of that invitation. As far as I knew, the only person on the list who knew of the existence of Mother's sister, had met her, was Aunt Martha. Of course, Mrs. Carson had met her too, that day in the park, but she hadn't known it at the time.

There had been much debate as to how the name was to appear on the invitation. It was the name Helen that was in question, and it was Aunt Helen who was bothered by it most.

"Never mind Smythe," Aunt Helen said. "Helen, when taken side by side with Aliese, is too common-sounding by half."

Aunt Helen thought perhaps she should become known as Helena, that it had more of a regal sound to it, but she was not sure if she could learn to answer to a name that wasn't hers.

"What if someone speaks to me and I don't reply because I

don't remember what I am now to be called?" she would say. "They would think me very rude. I am not sure I could ever get used to a new name."

But still she wavered. Even after the invitations went out, she maintained that she could still change her mind up to the last minute, that guests could always be told that the name on the invitations was a misprint.

She vacillated right up to just a few minutes prior to the grand event. And what finally swung her one way over the other? It was the vicar, Mr. Thomason.

Aunt Helen had yet to attend church, but my parents had thought it would bring good luck to the proceedings to have Mr. Thomason arrive early to give a blessing. Mr. Thomason, an unmarried man of advancing years, had been warned in advance of the startling resemblance between Mother and Aunt Helen; Mr. Thomason was widely known to have a weak heart, and no one wished to be the cause of that heart finally giving out.

Upon introduction, Mr. Thomason took one of Aunt Helen's now beautiful and pampered hands in both of his gnarled ones.

"Helen," he said warmly, a smile on his face as though he only wished himself young enough to pay suit to the woman whose hand he was holding. "That has always been one of my favorite names. It always puts me in mind of Helen of Troy."

"Helen of Troy?" Aunt Helen's expression was puzzled. Helen of Troy had not been covered in Mr. Brockburn's lessons.

"Oh, yes," said the vicar. "Helen of Troy. Her abduction by Paris caused the Trojan War. You know," he added confidentially, "they say her face launched a thousand ships."

Aunt Helen smiled back warmly in return, radiantly even.

I rather think she liked the idea of causing a war, of launching a thousand ships.

· · · · ·

It was as though our house had been holding a breath for half a year, waiting to see if our world would approve of Aunt Helen.

I stood beside Mother, with Aunt Helen between her and my father, as the guests arrived.

My father looked handsome in his dark suit. Mother, beautiful as always, had surprised us all by wearing a salmon dress that, while pretty enough on her, was one she had worn on a few social occasions previously. At first I thought she'd done it so that those who had already seen her in the dress could readily tell the two women apart. A little further thought on this matter, however, and I deduced a generosity behind her decision: Mother was doing her best not to outshine Aunt Helen on this day. Myself, I had been ordered a new party dress in the blue that was Mother's favorite shade. I rather fancied that I looked smashingly sophisticated in that dress.

And what did Aunt Helen wear?

White. A white so blindingly pure, it might have just as easily been her wedding gown.

We stood at the top of the stairs, greeting guests at the entryway to the ballroom.

My father's parents were the first to arrive. They always were the first at any event, as though anxious to get to a thing so they could get it over with and go home, a theory borne out by the fact that they were always the first to leave.

One would think they would be as startled as everyone else always was upon first seeing Aunt Helen, but one who would think that had never met my grandparents.

"How nice for you," Grandmother said tepidly to Mother, "to finally have a family member of your own."

"Refreshments inside, are they?" Grandfather asked my father, clapping him on the shoulder and then turning toward the ballroom without waiting for an answer.

Aunt Martha came up the stairs next. The brown dress she had on made me think she might have made more of an effort.

"I see you have acquired finer clothes since last I saw you." Aunt Martha addressed Aunt Helen directly, not even bothering to greet Mother and my father first. "But I seem to recall that you can rub the outside of an apple until it shines without ever eradicating the worm within."

Mother slipped one hand firmly around Aunt Helen's waist. In that moment, as I looked at the twin cameo heads of Mother and aunt side by side, I saw that Mother's was all defiance. She would defy everyone, including my father's own sister, to say that *her* sister did not have a proper place in our home.

"You have always been welcome here, Martha," Mother said, "*before*. But if you cannot bring yourself to—"

"Yes, Martha," my father said evenly, effectively supporting Mother while preventing her from making a breach that could never be mended, all at the same time. "Father and Mother are all alone in the ballroom. Perhaps you should go keep them company until the other guests arrive."

Aunt Martha turned away without another word.

The new neighbors came next, the Tylers.

Mr. Tyler was a tall man with blond hair and a genial smile. His wife, nearly as tall, was elegant with auburn hair that was like a fireball. Between the two stood a boy. I guessed him to be about sixteen to my fourteen; I'd had a birthday since Aunt Helen came to stay. The boy was nearly as tall as the man beside him. He had blond hair, like the man, but in his case that blond was not dulled by time. Rather, it was vibrant, like flowers tipped with gold. His eyes were green and, at present, they looked bored.

"John Tyler," the man introduced himself. "My wife, Victoria. Our son, Christopher."

"We call him Kit," Mrs. Tyler provided cheerfully.

"How do you do?" Aunt Helen said, when it was her turn to acknowledge these new people. Aunt Helen said the same thing to each new person she met, and each time she said it, she sounded exactly like Mother. All remnant differences in their speech were now gone.

Unlike the rest of the guests, the Tylers had no cause to react with shock upon seeing Aunt Helen, or at least no more than anyone normally would upon meeting identical twins. As far as the Tylers were concerned, they had merely been generously invited to a party. To them, and them alone, nothing was amiss.

"Pleased to meet you," I said to the Tylers when my turn came. "And you," I added shyly to Kit.

Briefly, his bored expression lifted, causing me to wonder if he was seeing the possibilities in me that I was seeing in him. There had never been any people my age right next door before. Not even having cousins, it seemed my whole life had been centered on adults. Seeing Kit now was a revelation, an unexplored country. It was like meeting something I'd been missing all my life without knowing it. What was he like? Would he be like boys I had read about in books? Too soon, he was gone.

After the Tylers, there came many more family friends, some with children, followed by a long string of my father's business associates. These last were a mixed group. Many of them brought their wives, but several had never married and came alone. Of this latter group, more than one developed a gleam in his eye upon meeting Aunt Helen.

Last to come, after all these people, were the Carsons.

An unpleasant light of awakening knowledge appeared in Mrs. Carson's eye at the sight of Aunt Helen. Was she remembering that day in the park, putting one and one together and coming up with Aunt Helen and me?

And then Mrs. Carson narrowed her eyes and asked the one thing no one else yet had dared to ask: "Where have you been hiding all these years?"

It was not a kind question, not like if, say, you were to use the same words in application to someone whose sudden presence in the world gave you immeasurable delight.

"I grew up in an orphanage," Aunt Helen said evenly, holding her body with an amazing show of dignity. "How about you?"

Mrs. Carson looked affronted at this boldness, as Aunt Helen no doubt meant her to be.

"Circumstances separated us at birth." Mother, exercising all her considerable charms, stepped in to save the moment. "Sad circumstances. But now Fortune has decided to be more benevolent and has happily reunited us, as you can see."

Even a woman like Mrs. Carson was forced to knock over the king on her own side of the chessboard, at least for the time being, in the face of Mother's dazzling assurance.

I did wonder how long it would take Mrs. Carson to spread her newfound knowledge of Aunt Helen's beginnings like wildfire.

But there was no more time for wondering now as the Carsons passed into the ballroom.

It was as though the house at last let out that long-held breath as we four entered the ballroom ourselves.

So far, things were going all right.

· · · · ·

Overhead, the many chandeliers, having been polished especially for this occasion, gave off sparkle and light.

The entire center of the ballroom had been left empty for the dancing that would occur later. Lining three walls were chairs for people to sit upon. The fourth wall was taken up with a long buffet, upon which was every food imaginable—roast beef, a ham, game birds, fish, fresh breads, fruits, vegetables, and a myriad of puddings that should be enough to keep everyone satisfied. There was also plenty of wine and spirits; more than enough, if the increasing noise level was anything to go by.

I was too excited to feel any hunger, and so I made the rounds of the room, picking up snatches of other people's conversations as I went.

"That woman is a stunner," Herbert Dean, one of my father's unmarried acquaintances, observed to another.

"Would you like to wager a bet," Alistair Roman returned, "as to which of us she will consent to dance with first?"

I moved on.

"Have you noticed," Victoria Tyler observed to her husband, "how everyone else keeps staring at Miss Smythe?"

"I suspect," her husband said, "that it is rare enough to see a great beauty reach her age and not be married." He turned a brilliant smile upon his wife. "I suspect it would be much the same for you if you had never married me."

I moved on.

"I think I saw her once before," Mrs. Carson said, "but I cannot be certain."

"I know I saw her once before," Aunt Martha said. "I cannot say I like her any better on this meeting."

"Did you know she grew up in an orphanage?" Mrs. Carson asked.

"Oh, yes," Aunt Martha said. "It has occurred to me: What would have happened if the two had been assigned their fates differently? Would Fortune have delivered Helen to Frederick instead? And what would Aliese have been like?"

I did not like the implied aspersions to Mother—as if she could ever be a different person than the wonderful person she was—but I did know one thing: everywhere I turned, all people were talking about was Aunt Helen.

She did not appear to mind being the center of attention in the slightest.

. . . . .

I had finally managed to eat something, which was a good thing. What with the excitement and the heat, for it was high summer, I had begun to feel light-headed.

"I can think of a hundred things I should like to do better right now," a voice at my elbow said as I raised a heavy linen napkin to dab at the corners of my lips.

The voice belonged to Kit Tyler.

Up close, the need to be demure removed since our parents were no longer with us, I had the opportunity to study him more thoroughly.

I cannot say that blond hair on males had ever appealed to me much before. I loved it on Mother and Aunt Helen, but I suppose that perhaps due to my father's influence, I had previously favored coloring that more closely matched his, like Mr. Brockburn's. It seemed to me that darker characteristics made a male somehow more, well, male. But I didn't think that when I looked at Kit.

And his eyes?

Earlier, I had thought them a simple green. But, up close, I saw they were more complex than that. One time, my father had taken us to see the ocean, and I thought Kit's eyes had something changeable like the sea in them as I looked upon him now.

"And what," I asked him, "are some of these hundred other things you'd rather be doing?"

"Walking in the park." He shrugged; obviously his desire for the park was not affected by the fact that it was nighttime. "Playing chess." He shrugged again, having no way of knowing he had named my father's favorite game, a game he had taught me to play fairly well, although I did not always like to play. "Reading."

"I like reading," I said, wanting to say something.

"I would rather be reading anything instead of doing this," he said.

I stood up straighter. "Then you have never read *Mr. Midship-man Easy.*"

"*Mr. Midship*—?" He looked perplexed. "What?"

"You are clearly not as well-read as you think yourself to be," I said.

His jaw dropped.

"I'm sure my parents would be pleased to learn how boring you find it here after they were kind enough to invite you," I added, turning on my heel.

There, I thought. Over in one corner, several much younger children played. *Let him find his entertainment with them,* I told myself now. *Let him see if he can do better.*

· · · · ·

The music played on, the crowd became louder, fighting to be heard against it so that conversations that might normally have been held to a whisper were being carried on at nearly full shout.

"I have stayed away since the first day I met that woman," Aunt Martha said. "I only came today because I received an engraved invitation, but I doubt I shall be repeating that mistake anytime soon."

"Really?" Mrs. Carson said. "It seems to me the situation *exactly* calls for a wise woman, such as yourself, keeping a close eye on it."

I looked to the very center of the room, where "that woman" they were discussing danced. *That woman* had been dancing for hours, it seemed, with one partner after another.

In that dress, swirling faster and faster, *that woman* looked untouchable.

She was like an angel, dancing on top of the world.

· Thirteen ·

The next day presented a very different picture.

All the adults, perhaps having had too much pleasure the night before, remained in bed until well past the summer sun had crossed the center of the sky.

And so I was left, for many hours, to occupy myself.

Instinctively, I moved through my own home on tiptoes as though sensing that any undue noise on my part would bring down the wrath of one or more people upon my head. As I moved, I couldn't stop myself thinking about Kit, even though he'd perturbed me when we talked. I couldn't stop myself wondering when—if—we might meet again.

I had already eaten two meals alone—breakfast and lunch—and was thinking of calling the maid to bring an early tea, when Aunt Helen made her yawning way into the back parlor. I suspected that if propriety did not mitigate against it, she would still be wearing her dressing gown. On the first day she had come to us, her attire had been shabby, and yet I'd come to realize in retrospect that she had in fact taken pains to look as dignified as possible on that day. But I had never seen her looking so disheveled as she did now, not like this.

"I feel," Aunt Helen said, flopping down unceremoniously at the opposite end of the sofa, "as though tiny carpenters have taken their tiny little hammers and are hammering on my brain."

"Shall I send for tea?" I offered.

"Please," she said.

"Does it feel so very awful?" I asked, curious, after I'd dispensed a servant on the tea mission.

Aunt Helen's head was tilted back, eyes closed. I saw a smile lift the corners of her mouth. "Not entirely," she said. "In fact, I feel rather alive at the moment, if also a little dead." She paused. "If that makes any sense."

Another pair of groans from the doorway and there were Mother and my father, also looking the worse for wear, also looking as though they too would have liked to have been still attired in their dressing gowns. They too took seats on sofas without the usual grace they normally would have shown. Of the three adults in the room, my father looked the freshest. I supposed it was because he was more accustomed to overindulging than the others were.

"I've sent for tea," I offered helpfully.

"I always said you were a clever girl," my father said.

"I bless the day you were born," Mother added.

The servant came in with the tea tray. She asked if they'd be wanting any more to eat.

"A late breakfast," Mother said, head back, eyes closed as Aunt Helen's had been, "but please serve it in here." She opened one eye, looked over at my father. "The dining room table seems very far away right now, does it not?"

My father allowed that it did.

It was strange. Seeing the way Mother and my father were suffering, to their varying degrees, it was as though Aunt Helen gained in strength.

"It was a success," Aunt Helen said with a wide smile, "was it not?"

"If you mean the party," my father said, "I should say so. I shall practically have to write another book to pay for what all those people ate and drank, so I would say it must have been a huge success."

Of course my father was making a joke. He had his family fortune to fall back on, as had his father before him, and his father's father before that. My father often commented on how interesting it was, how money kept begetting more money. If he never wrote another word as long as he lived, he would want for nothing. None of us would. Although his joke did make me wonder something I'd never thought to wonder about before: *did* his novels make him any money?

Now Mother had both eyes open, and they were both looking at Aunt Helen.

"It went exceedingly well, I thought," she said. "I was very proud of you."

I felt that now familiar frisson of jealousy I sometimes experienced when Mother bestowed a great compliment on Aunt Helen, but it disappeared as quickly as it had come when I realized how happy I was for Aunt Helen and even more when I considered the alternatives: What would the aftermath to the party have been if things had not gone well? Would Aunt Helen have been forced to remain in hiding in the house forever or even possibly been forced to go?

"Elizabeth Carson did have a sour expression on her face all evening," my father said, making one of his own. "I have never been overly fond of that woman."

"Your sister was not much better," Mother said wryly.

"No, she was not," my father said. "I wonder why that was?"

"Perhaps she ate something that disagreed with her," Mother suggested.

I knew then that Mother had never shared with him the details of that visit Aunt Martha had made to the house several months back, the one during which she had suggested that Aunt Helen might be dangerous, that Aunt Helen should be told to leave.

True, Aunt Martha had left herself that day on bad terms. But it seemed an odd thing to me for a wife to hold back from her husband.

And my father's own attitude made it obvious that Aunt Martha had never shared her concerns about Aunt Helen with him. Perhaps Mother's own disapproval had somehow tempered her usual instinct toward outspokenness?

The servant returned with the requested breakfast—eggs, bacon, toast with butter and jam, orange juice—and set it out on the low table. If the servant wondered how they intended to eat this meal without the benefit of the usual dining room table, her expression did not betray as much.

Aunt Helen sat forward on the sofa, picked up one of the plates, balanced it on her knees.

"So we are agreed," she said, "that with the exception of a pair of disgruntled guests, everything else went according to plan?"

"Outside of those two exceptions," my father said, "it could not have gone better, I shouldn't think."

"I am glad you think so, Frederick," Aunt Helen said. "And now that we have the success of the party behind us, perhaps you could answer a question for me."

My father merely raised his eyebrows at her.

"A few weeks prior to the party, you dispatched Mr. Brockburn," Aunt Helen said. "On his last day, he asked Lucy if he might have a word with you. At dinner that evening, I asked you what that word was about but you would not say. Instead, you said we needed to talk about the party you proposed. Now that party is behind us and I am returning to the subject of Mr. Brockburn. What was that word?"

"Oh. That."

"Yes. That."

"Do you know, Helen, if you ever grow tired of your life of leisure here, I do think you would make a fine solicitor." He considered this. "Of course, your gender might get in the way."

"I assume there is a compliment buried in there somewhere," Aunt Helen said, "but I don't care to dig for it at this time. You are evading the question."

Could one party change a person so much? I hardly remembered ever hearing anybody hold their ground in such a way against my father. Certainly Mother never had. And yet, judging from my father's expression, he was rather enjoying what for him must have been a novel experience.

"It is simply this," my father said. "Mr. Brockburn wished my permission to ask for your hand in marriage."

A marriage proposal from the schoolmaster!

I shot a look at Mother. Her expression revealed shock as great as I felt. So, just as she had been keeping secrets from my father, he had been keeping secrets from her.

Aunt Helen's expression was not shocked. It was severe.

"Don't you think you should have told me of this offer before now," she asked with ice in her tone, "instead of waiting weeks?"

My father took a bite of his toast, shrugged. "We had the party to plan." Another shrug. "I thought it best to wait."

"Would you even have said anything *now* if I had not brought it up first?"

My father's shrug was his answer. He'd just as soon let it go.

"But I am an adult woman! This was an offer for *me*!"

"You live under my roof, my protection. All such offers must come through me." He considered this. "I do hope this won't become a regular thing, suitors knocking at my door to ask for your hand."

My father's words might have appeared pompous on the surface, but what he spoke was accurate: He was the man. This was his house. We all lived at his whim. And we all knew it. Or at least, most of us did.

"And did you also answer the proposal for me?" Aunt Helen said through gritted teeth.

My father appeared surprised at this. "Oh, no. That would hardly be my place to decide for you, would it? Although I do have my opinions on the matter."

Aunt Helen glared at him some more. I think now the heat of that glare must have proved too much for him, for he picked up his plate, rising.

"I have some work to do," my father said. "Perhaps, anyway, this is something you would do best to discuss with Aliese."

No sooner had my father's shadow passed from the room than Aunt Helen turned on Mother.

"I suppose you've known about it all this time too?" she demanded.

"I swear to you, I would never keep such a thing from you!"

"No," Aunt Helen practically muttered, "I suppose that you would not."

Then her expression suddenly lightened, and she let out a loud laugh.

"You know," she said, "this is the first invitation of marriage I have ever received!" And, just as quickly, her expression soured again. "Well, *I* did not receive it," she added. "Frederick did."

"Never mind all that now," Mother said in a soothing voice. "What do you think of it?"

The silence that stretched out after this question was a lengthy one. It was long enough for me to consider what *I* thought about it.

So Mr. Brockburn, the schoolmaster, had asked for Aunt Helen's hand!

I had never thought much before on the idea of people falling in love. I read books, so I knew that it happened. But the only real-life story of such a thing that I knew about was the story Aunt Martha used to tell me about Mother and my father's first meeting.

What was it like, I wondered now, being in love? Would I ever experience it?

I could see, of course, why Mr. Brockburn loved Aunt Helen. She was beautiful, like Mother. More than that, in her own way, she was full of life.

"What do you think of it?" Aunt Helen asked now, turning the question back on Mother.

Mother blew out a breath, surprised to be consulted. "I am not sure I know. I suppose you could do far worse. Mr. Brockburn is a nice man."

"He is *the schoolmaster.*"

"Which also means he is more intelligent than most men. At the very least, he knows more about a variety of subjects."

"He *is* the schoolmaster."

"He cuts a handsome figure. Not to mention, it must have taken a great deal of bravery on his part to approach Frederick in this fashion. He must love you a great deal."

"And he will always be *the schoolmaster.*"

"Then he is not good enough for you?"

"I did not necessarily say that. But he would not be good enough for you, would he?" Aunt Helen said. "Then why should he be good enough for me?"

"Then you do not like him?"

"Did I say that? Of course I *like* him. But he is—"

"I know." Mother cut her off. "He is the schoolmaster."

"Yes," Aunt Helen said.

"Then you should tell Frederick to tell him no," Mother said.

"Yes," Aunt Helen said again. And then she smiled. "But it is nice, to be asked."

Poor Mr. Brockburn.

I wondered about something my father had said earlier: would there be other men, more suitable suitors who would call on Aunt Helen?

I thought about what Aunt Helen had said the day Aunt Martha visited, something about women who never married being the worst kind.

Aunt Helen was now thirty-two and yet she had never married. Was she prepared to become one of "the worst kind"?

• Fourteen •

A few days later, Victoria Tyler, the new neighbor from next door, came to pay a courtesy call. She wanted to thank Mother for including her family in our family's celebration. In Mrs. Tyler's company was the boy she had brought to the party, her son, the bored yet oddly intriguing boy known as Kit.

Our home had seen several callers since the night of the party. Apparently the neighborhood, in the persons of Mrs. Carson and Mary Williams and others, wanted to see Aunt Helen up close, learn more of her history away from the pull of the crowd. So far Aunt Martha, despite having told Mrs. Carson she would keep a closer eye on things, had kept away.

"What a lovely home you have, Mrs. Sexton," Mrs. Tyler said, having been led into the front parlor.

"Thank you," Mother said, "but I am Mrs. Sexton."

Mrs. Tyler had mistakenly addressed her remark to Aunt Helen. Really, the only thing to tell the women apart now were their dresses, and a person needed a knowledge of both ladies' wardrobes to be able to pull off that trick. Not to mention, ever since the day I had seen Aunt Helen in my father's study, wearing one of Mother's gowns, they did occasionally share things for variety.

"I am sorry," Mrs. Tyler said, blushing so furiously her cheeks nearly matched the color of her hair. "It's just that you are both—"

"It is an easy mistake to make," Aunt Helen said with a pleased smile. "Sometimes, when I look in my mirror, *I* don't even know which of us I am seeing."

"Is it ever disconcerting for Mr. Sexton?" Mrs. Tyler asked. If anyone else had asked such a question, it would no doubt have come across as nosy. But coming from Mrs. Tyler, who in every way seemed one of the most sincere women I had ever met, it smacked of pure intellectual curiosity, not intrusion. It was a shame, I thought, that her son did not share her winning disposition.

"Not at all," Aunt Helen spoke for both of them. "My brother-in-law can easily tell us apart. He knows *me* to be the outspoken one."

I did not like this very much. It cast Mother as some sort of mouse by comparison.

"And he knows me," Mother said evenly, "as any man knows his own wife."

Good show, Mother! I could not help but think to myself.

All this time, the boy, that annoyingly bored *Kit boy*, had said nothing.

"Lucy," Mother instructed, "why don't you entertain Kit while we ladies talk?"

I did not know why I must be called upon to be an ambassador of . . . *entertainment*, but Mother did not look as though she were in any mood to hear an argument on this. And, indeed, I suppose it would have been rude of me to make one just then.

I realized I did not know how to talk to someone close to my own age, particularly a boy. And something about this boy made me *want* to be rude.

"Did you enjoy playing with the other children the night of the party?" I taunted Kit now.

"Not particularly," he said. "They all seemed very immature to me."

"That is funny," I said. "I would have thought that would have suited you perfectly well."

"I suppose you need to work on your needlepoint while the ladies talk?" Kit all but sneered at me. "Isn't that what girls are supposed to do?"

"*Needlepoint?*" I sneered right back. It took everything in me not to stamp my foot. *Needlepoint?!* "I do not do *needlepoint*," I said, grudgingly adding, "or at least, not unless someone makes me." I folded my arms across my chest. As my arms brushed against my breasts I felt instantly self-conscious for the first time in my life of having a body that was distinctly different from that of half the world's population. I pushed the feeling aside. "How about a game of chess?"

"*Chess?*"

"Yes. Chess. Is there something wrong with your hearing? That night at the party, you said it was a game you liked to play. We have a set." I indicated with an airy wave of my hand the table in the corner, upon which was still the game caught in mid-play that my father and I had been battling over the night before. "Why don't we play?"

"Very well." He took white's seat without asking my preference, leaving me to black.

He studied the board from last night's game.

He let out a low whistle. "White really has black's back against the wall here."

"White was the color I played last," I said imperiously, sweeping the men from the board.

In truth, I had not been playing white the night before.

Why had I lied? Why did I want Kit to think better of my... *chess prowess*? What did I care what he thought?

"I'm sorry." He looked embarrassed as he started to rise from his chair. "I should have asked first which you preferred before sitting down."

"Sit. Sit!" I waved my hand at him impatiently. "What do I care if I play black or I play white? I am good at either. I excel at *both*. Why, only just recently I played black." *"Just recently," as in "last night,"* a voice in my head taunted. I sought for something appropriately scathing to say, at last settling on something I'd heard my father say before: "What does such triviality matter to me?"

Without waiting for another word out of him, I commenced setting up the board as he retook his seat.

To say that he beat me would be to state the case mildly.

. . . . .

I was tempted to overturn the table.

Indeed, if I did not know that Mother would censure me greatly for this, I would have done so in an instant.

"You played that very well," Kit said.

"What are you talking about?" I bit off the words. "*I lost.*"

"Yes, well, perhaps that part wasn't so very impressive. But up until that point"—he shined a smile at me, the first I had ever received from him; it was a radiant thing—"you really played impressively!"

I folded my arms across my chest again. If Mother were paying attention, she would have accused me of slouching in my seat. If my father were in the room, he would tell Mother that I needed to be taught deportment and all that other nonsense all over again.

"I did not play as well as you." I sulked.

"Not today." He shrugged. "But you might, in time. I don't see why you shouldn't. After all, I am older than you. I have had more years to practice."

"That's a nice about-face," I said, "given your previous snide comments about 'needlepoint.'"

In truth, I did think it was a nice about-face. But there was no reason why he should know I thought that.

"I'm sorry." He shrugged. "We hadn't played chess yet when I made those comments. I take them back now. I think having you next door will be as good as having another boy."

Five minutes ago, I would have taken offense at this . . . loudly. Now I chose to take it in the spirit in which it was intended.

"Thank you." I bowed my head slightly. "Did you know that chess is the oldest skill game of record?"

"Oh, yes," he said eagerly. "Backgammon is older, but it is a game based on luck."

"Well, then, speaking of backgammon, did you also know that

backgammon was first mentioned in print in *The Codex Exoniensis* of 1025? Or that it was originally called 'nard' or 'tables'? *Or* that it was banned for a time as being gaming—which, of course, it is in a sense, being a game—until Elizabeth the First brought it back?"

"No, no, and no!" he said enthusiastically. "I knew none of those things!"

"It is one of the chief advantages of being a novelist's daughter," I said with feigned hauteur. Then I could not stop myself from adding with a smile, "I am forced to listen to all manner of boring trivia whenever my father is doing research."

"I've never met another girl like you." He shrugged. "Actually, I don't think I've ever met *anyone* like you."

"How do you mean?" I was wary, as though an insult might be hiding in his remark, ready to jump at me at any moment.

"I'm not entirely sure," he said. "It's little things, like how interestingly *different* you are, so much so that even when you insult me, I don't mind." He shrugged get again. "If I could explain it to myself, I'd explain it to you."

Then he looked over both shoulders, as though checking to see if anyone was listening in on our conversation.

They weren't. As far as I could tell, the three ladies were talking about flowers or fashion, perhaps both.

"Do you know," Kit whispered, leaning across the table, "our houses are connected?"

"What," I said witheringly, "are you talking about now?"

"All right," he said, blushing. "I'm not entirely certain, but I think it's possible that both houses once belonged to one family and that there is a connecting tunnel underground."

If it weren't for the fact that I hesitated to touch him, I would have leaned across the table in turn, placing my palm against his forehead to check for fever. As it were, I settled for:

"Of course there isn't! I've lived here my whole entire life!"

"Shh!" he cautioned me, which I must say, I found annoying. Still, I continued in a whisper:

"Don't you think I'd know if such a thing existed? And you—what—live here for about five minutes, and now you are educating me as to the architecture of my own home?"

"Is there a trapdoor anywhere in this house?" he asked, as though I hadn't been rude to him in the slightest.

"Why do you want to know?" I asked, narrowing my eyes at him.

"Because there's one in ours. I discovered it in the kitchen one night when I couldn't sleep and was hungry. I was looking around, and I noticed an uneven patch in the floor. When I pried it up, there were stairs leading down."

"And you investigated?" I didn't want to admit it, but I was impressed by his bravery.

"Not that night. It was getting close to dawn, and I didn't want to scare the cook by popping up again through the floor."

"That was thoughtful of you," I grudgingly allowed.

"But the next night," he went on, "just after everyone else was asleep, I went back. This time, I was prepared. I had a candle with me, and a compass as well. It was dark down there, and the path was long." I pictured him late at night, beneath the earth in his nightclothes. "When I arrived at the end there was a door. It wasn't easy getting it to open. I formed the impression it had been a very long time since anyone had tried to. Then, when

I did get it open, I saw what looked like a large room. You'll probably laugh at me, but I grew scared then and closed the door back up." I wasn't laughing. "I realized that room was under someone else's house. That's when I looked at my compass and realized it was *your* house."

"But I don't understand."

"A compass is a device for determining directions by means of a magnetic needle or group of needles turning freely on a pivot and pointing to the magnetic north."

"I'm not talking about that!" I practically shouted, causing Mother to shoot a sharp glance in my direction. "I know what a compass is," I hissed out the words in a lower voice. "But I don't understand how a trapdoor in your house could somehow lead to a similar place in my house . . . and I not know about it."

"You never answered before: *is* there a trapdoor in your house?"

"Yes." This time I answered immediately. "In my father's study, but it doesn't lead to any tunnel. It only leads to a cellar."

"Have you ever been down there?" he shot back immediately.

"Of course not. It's *a cellar*!"

"Yes." He nodded. "I think that part is right. But I think there's a door in that cellar, that cellar you've never seen, and that door leads to a tunnel that stretches between our houses."

I finally had to admit: there was no reason for him to make up such a story.

"Fine," I allowed. "So there are trapdoors and secret tunnels."

"Tunnel. Singular."

"Fine. *Tunnel.*" I shrugged, as he had done so many times earlier. "What does it matter?"

"I don't know, do I?" He looked enigmatic now. "But it is interesting, isn't it? It's *different*."

I hesitated, nodded.

"Do you think you might ever investigate the tunnel yourself?" he wondered.

"You mean go down into that cellar?"

He nodded.

"I suppose I might, someday. I don't know. I already said the trapdoor is in my father's office and he spends a lot of time there. I think he'd be a little put out if I ever tapped on his door and said, 'Oops! Don't mind me! Just here to check out your trapdoor because the nosy boy next door wants me to!' But I might. Someday. When he's not around."

"That's good." Kit nodded. "You never know when such a thing might come in handy."

"Kit!" Mrs. Tyler called. "We're leaving now!"

Five minutes later, they were gone.

"Well, that was pleasant," Aunt Helen said. "That Mrs. Tyler seems such a nice woman."

With half a mind, I wondered if she meant that as a compliment or not—something about her tone of voice suggested that *nice* might not be such a very good thing at all. The other half of my mind was still occupied with trapdoors and secret tunnels. Sorry. *Tunnel*.

"And I thought it was very nice," Mother said, "how you and Kit got on so well. At first I was worried about you two, but then it looked like things grew much better. Such a nice boy, isn't he?"

I pulled a face.

· Fifteen ·

I had just cracked open the spine on a new book when the knock came.

Knock.

My father lately had been distracted from his usual mission to guide all my reading and so I had selected a volume that I thought would interest me.

Knock.

It was George MacDonald's *The Princess and the Goblin,* and I was very comfortable in my curled-up position in the corner of the sofa.

Knock, knock, KNOCK!

I tossed the book aside in disgust. Sometimes I wondered why my father bothered paying all these servants. Didn't anyone else ever answer the door around here anymore? Next thing I knew, I'd be doing the cooking and cleaning as well.

When I opened the door, I saw Aunt Martha standing on the stoop. On the ground beside her feet was a large bag. In her hand, she held a wooden cane with a sterling silver lion's head for a handle. Immediately, I wondered if she really needed it—she had never needed one before and it made her look so much older—and I also wondered if that was what she had been using to hammer on the door.

"Lucy, why are you answering the door?" she demanded.

"Because no one else does anymore," I countered.

"Please call a servant to carry my bag in," she directed, brushing by me as she began to remove her gloves. "Aren't your parents at home?" she asked after a servant had carried in her bag.

"Mother is out with Aunt Helen, paying courtesy calls," I told her. "My father is in his study. I believe he is writing."

"Well, don't dawdle." She banged her new cane against the floor for emphasis. "Tell Frederick I am here."

When I knocked on my father's door and he at last responded, I poked my head into his room.

"Yes, Lucy." He barely looked up before returning to the pages he was studying. "What is it?"

"Aunt Martha is here. I think she means to stay."

"Oh!" He buttoned his coat as he rose.

· · · · ·

"Sister," my father said when he saw Aunt Martha's new cane, "have you been injured?"

"Of course not," she snapped with some asperity.

It was strange. All my memories of Aunt Martha from my early years, the talks we used to have—I used to remember her as a kind presence. But now that perception had changed. *She* had changed.

"But we are none of us getting any younger," she went on. "I thought it time to acquire an aid before I needed one. Better to prevent a fall than to try to repair the damage afterward."

"I see," he said, although he still looked bemused by the notion of a wholly healthy person using a cane she didn't need, as was I. Still, he continued brightly, "Well, I am very relieved there is nothing wrong with your health. But what brings you here today?"

"What? Am I no longer welcome to visit my own brother's family without a written invitation?"

"Of course not. We are always happy to see you. All I meant was—"

"Our parents have become insufferable. Insufferable, I tell you!"

"Oh?" He looked only mildly surprised at this outburst. "What have they been doing now?"

"It's what they don't do. They don't do anything. Do you have any idea what it's like, what it's *been* like for me all these years, living out in the country with those insufferably boring people? While you have had all the advantages here? I wish to have some excitement before I die. Or, at the very least, some stimulation over and above which fairy cake to eat at tea."

"So you have come to stay for . . . a while?" Surreptitiously, he consulted his pocket watch as though trying to ascertain just how long that "while" might take.

"I have come to stay for good."

. . . . .

By the time Mother and Aunt Helen arrived home, Aunt Martha had already been installed in her new bedroom. When they were informed of the new addition to our household, Mother, perhaps seeing no choice in the matter, hurried upstairs to ensure that Aunt Martha had been made to feel comfortable.

It was like when Aunt Helen had come to stay with us, and yet it felt far different.

"What room has she been given?" Aunt Helen asked.

I told her. Aunt Martha now lived on the same floor as Mother and my father, the third floor, in a large room all the way at the end that overlooked my father's private garden in the back behind his study.

"Hmm," was all Aunt Helen had to say in response.

I never did make it back to *The Princess and the Goblin* that day.

· · · · ·

It took Aunt Martha a few days to settle into the household, and then a few more days after that to get truly comfortable. She thought the curtains in her room were too thin, letting in too much sun, so new ones had to be ordered, and she said the bed was too large but she was willing to wait on that. She thought the food Cook prepared was too rich and that our mealtimes were all askew. Breakfast, lunch, dinner—they all needed to be moved up one hour. Aunt Martha liked her bath before everyone else's, if there were baths to be had, and whenever she sat anywhere she required a footstool upon which she rested the leg that was supported by her new cane; not because there was anything wrong with the leg, but just in case. It did strike me as a trifle mad, and yet it obviously made her happy.

"She's as bad as Lear," my father said to me one evening after what he considered to be a too-early dinner, only this time he didn't look as though he found it funny anymore, "except for the fact that she didn't arrive accompanied by one hundred soldiers for us to shelter and feed. I suppose we have at least *that* to be grateful for."

After she'd been with us a week and the house, while not necessarily breathing a sigh of relief, had at least settled down to the adjustments she'd insisted we all make, she asked me to join her one morning while she enjoyed her tea and cake.

It didn't take long for me to realize that she'd requested this tête-à-tête because she knew Mother and Aunt Helen were out together, paying calls, and that my father was in his study. Aunt Martha, we had all learned, no longer felt she was of an age where she should be expected to pay calls. People, according to Aunt Martha, should come to her.

Aunt Martha sat on the sofa, her body arranged at such an angle that there was not sufficient room for me, and I had to make do with a chair.

"Where have they gone to this time?" she asked me, forking off a last large bite of cake.

"I believe they planned to start at Mrs. Carson's," I said.

"A fine woman." She held her plate, the cake now reduced to a few crumbs, out to me to place on the table for her. I had to get up from where I was sitting to do so. "Please get me my needlepoint," she said before I had the chance to sit down again. "It should be in that basket under the window."

I did as I was told.

"Shouldn't you be working on your own needlepoint?" she stated more than asked after I brought hers to her.

I returned to the basket, returned to the chair with my own wretched needlepoint.

Aunt Martha was very enthusiastic about her needlepoint.

"Must you make those stitches so wide?" she said to me now. "You could do worse than to pursue this with greater vigor. Men like a woman with accomplishments."

Accomplishments? *Do you have any idea how much I hate needlepoint?* came the unbidden thought, following which I could not prevent a wry smile at the remembrance of Kit taunting me about this feminine activity I so despised.

"I do not see that I have said anything funny, Lucy. I haven't, have I?"

I bowed my head to my work. "No, Aunt."

"I didn't think so." *Stitch. Stitch.* "Your . . . *other* aunt doesn't do needlepoint, does she?"

I did so wish she would not call her that.

"I have never seen her occupied so," I said simply.

"Then what does she do with all her time?"

What do any of us do with our time? I wondered.

Out loud I said, "She eats, she sleeps, she visits friends with Mother, she visits with those same friends when they come to us."

I had no idea what Aunt Martha wanted from me, but now I was sure she wanted something.

"And do you . . . *like* your . . . *other* aunt?"

I set down my needle, looked her in the eye, but she was studying her own work so closely she did not catch my look. "Yes. I do."

"It is kind of you to pretend," she said, her placid stitches of a moment ago turning to pricks and stabs as she went on, "but there is no need for that with me. Anyone would understand if you were jealous of her. As a matter of fact, I do believe that if you went to your parents, and explained to them how unhappy you are with her here, how much you dislike her, I am quite certain they would—"

"I don't dislike her." I cut her off. I couldn't remember then if I'd ever interrupted an adult like that before. If I had, it was beyond my powers of recollection. I put my hand over her needle-point so that she could no longer work, so that she would have to look up and face me as I spoke with great deliberation. "And I don't just *like* Aunt Helen. I *love* Aunt Helen."

I think I stunned myself as much as her.

I had been thinking a lot about love lately, wondering what it was, what it meant. I had come to realize that there were not many in this world I had that depth of feeling for: Mother, always; my father, about half of the time. And no one else, until Aunt Helen. I knew there should be more, maybe one day there *could* be more. But for now, that was all there was.

Into the silence that followed my impertinent pronouncement, I heard the creak of a footstep on the stairs.

It was only later on that it would occur to me that whoever had made that creak did not mind if they were heard.

· · · · ·

A day went by, then two.

I could feel a silent storm gathering, could almost smell it on the air.

But whatever conversations transpired, whatever was said or not said, done or not done, I was privy to none of it.

The only thing that was made known to me was the outcome.

In a rare show of sensitivity, it was my father who told me of the changes to come, late one night after I had already climbed between the sheets. He sat on the very edge of the counterpane, no parts of our bodies touching.

"I am sorry to be the one to tell you this," he said gently, "but your aunt will be leaving us on the morrow, probably before you have even risen."

"*What?*" I rose up sharply. "Where is Aunt Helen going?"

"I am sorry again. I should have clarified right away: it is *my* sister who is leaving us. Your mother's will be staying on."

That was a relief.

"Your mother would have told you herself, but she has been very distressed about all this. In truth, I feel the guilt is mine. I should have anticipated this. I should never have let Martha stay on here."

So, Aunt Martha was out, and Aunt Helen was in.

I looked at my father's troubled face and in that moment saw him as a man who *did* strive, sometimes against worse instinct, to do what was right. If he took things too lightly at times, at others he took things too hard.

I remembered what I'd been thinking of love a few days earlier, that I loved my father about half of the time.

This was one of those halves.

When he placed a gentle kiss upon my forehead before departing the room, I smiled up at him, hoping he knew how I felt.

. . . . .

As it turned out, Aunt Helen took over the bedroom at the end of the hall from my parents after Aunt Martha took her leave.

How, I wondered, would my father and his sister ever heal the rift between them? And what in the world had caused it?

Of course, Aunt Helen did not take over *right* after Aunt Martha's departure. First, she prevailed upon my parents sweetly, the room needed to be redone. She wanted Aunt Martha's heavy curtains removed and lighter ones moved in to replace them. She wanted the floral wallpaper ripped down and, in its place, something brighter put up: perhaps something with cleaner lines, like vertical thick cream stripes alternating with a thinner cranberry, maybe some draped accents across the top border in a contrasting pattern. The candelabra fixtures in the wall looked tarnished; something in a shiny brass would do nicely instead. The mirror should be bigger. Just one carpet extending not far beyond the edges of the bed would be fine; she liked the hard-wood floors once they were exposed. And that bed. It really did have to go. Too many people had slept in it before. And so, a large bed, the head- and footboards hand-carved out of rosewood, was commissioned.

And then it was finished.

She said I could visit her, even invited me for tea on her first afternoon there, and I went.

"That really was a useful trick you taught me," she said, surrounded by the splendor that was her new room.

"'Trick'?" I echoed.

"Yes," she said, "the one about listening from the stairs."

I still did not understand.

"That day you were talking with Martha," she said, seeming impatient now with my slowness. "I came back early from making the rounds with your mother. I had a headache, I think, told Aliese to go on without me. As I was heading upstairs, I heard Martha mention my name. Well, of course I had to stop and listen..."

Now I saw it all clearly: Aunt Helen had heard Aunt Martha infer that if I told my parents I no longer wanted Aunt Helen here she would be banished ... and then Aunt Helen had told Mother ... who had told my father ...

"More tea, dear?" Aunt Helen offered.

Aunt Helen said a short time later, as I was leaving, that I could come to visit her there as often as I wished, and I did, at first, but it wasn't the same, not like when she had been just right across the hall.

It was as though she had become one of *them* now, and I was left, back to being on my own.

• Sixteen •

Time marched on, as it has a tendency to do, and I continued my studies with Miss Walker.

Time, which had not stopped for me, had marched on for everyone else as well. My father, at forty-four, had not changed at all, save for a new wrinkle or two around the eyes, which he attributed to much laughter. He said he had no interest in trading these lines for a smoother appearance, since such a trade would mean relinquishing the considerable joy he had in life. As for Mother and Aunt Helen, they were both thirty-two now. Guests often commented how much like a young woman Mother still looked—a girl even! And the same was certainly true of Aunt Helen.

But there was a difference.

For while Mother had already been married for fifteen years at this point, Aunt Helen had never been married for even a minute.

"She is like Penelope, entertaining and rejecting suitor after suitor," my father observed with a wry grin, "but with one difference: there is no Odysseus in sight, no earthly reason for her to turn all these men away."

"Perhaps there is no earthly reason," Mother said, "so perhaps there is a divine one?"

"How do you mean?" my father asked. "Surely you are not suggesting that Helen is preparing to pledge her life to some church."

"Of course not. I only meant that perhaps Helen does not want to marry for anything less than love."

"*Love!*" my father scoffed. Then, catching the expression on Mother's face, he amended that scoffing. "I am not saying, my dear, that love does not matter. Indeed, where would you and I be without it? But we met when the bloom was still on your rose."

"But if you are saying that the bloom is *off* Helen's rose, then you are saying it is off mine as well since we share the same face. Are you saying that I am some sort of old hag now?"

"Hardly. If anything, you are more beautiful than ever. And, of course, by natural extension"—and here he coughed nervously— "Helen is as well. But she is a little old to still be seeking a first husband, and to be doing so at such a leisurely pace! I must confess, I have long suspected that we would one day be compelled to house a spinster aunt, but I had always assumed that spinster would come from my side of the family, not yours."

My father had never stated, explicitly, how he felt about Aunt Martha leaving. This was not something I could question him on, but hearing his words now—the sardonic sentiment warring with an unmistakably wistful undercurrent—I suspected he felt both relief and loss.

As did I.

. . . . .

The stream of men had started appearing not long after the party celebrating Mother and Aunt Helen's birthday.

One man after another presented himself at our home.

They would come to call, invite Aunt Helen out for a stroll in the park, always inviting Mother too for propriety's sake. If the stroll went well, and the strolls always did, further invitations would follow: from my parents asking the men to dine with us, from the men inviting my parents and Aunt Helen to some entertainment.

"Do you like any of them particularly?" I asked Aunt Helen one day when we were alone together.

"I do not know that it is a matter of 'like,'" she answered. "But at least they pass the time."

Given his comment at the twin birthday celebration that "I always thought Frederick had stolen the jewel in the crown when he married Aliese, but now I see there are other gems in the world," it took Herbert Dean a surprisingly long time to find his way to our door.

Herbert Dean had been a friend of my father's for as long as I could remember. Another writer who rested on a pile of family wealth, like my father he could write what he wanted without being overly concerned what the wider world made of that writing. He was neither particularly tall nor short, neither particularly thick-haired nor bald, neither particularly fat nor thin.

Despite what Mother had always termed his "indolent life of unwed leisure," he was a chiefly pleasant human being with regular brown hair and regular brown eyes to match. In appearance, he was average down to the bone. In personality, he was inoffensive, although he did present one slight advantage over the previous men: he was unstintingly generous with his purse, lavishing upon Aunt Helen all manner of fine gifts and always insisting on paying for everybody—it was Mother who told me this—whenever a group went out.

One night, when Herbert Dean had purchased six tickets to the opening of an operatic play called *Patience* at a new theater called the Savoy—Mr. Dean said he was thrilled at the prospect of the new theater, lit entirely with electricity; Mr. Dean said that it would be nice for once to see a show in the autumn where not only would he be able to *see* the show, but he would also not have to worry about freezing while doing so!—it turned out at the last minute that the Tylers could not go. Kit was sick, Mrs. Tyler would not leave him, and Mr. Tyler would not leave her.

I was very worried on Kit's account when I heard of this, but I must confess to being overjoyed when it turned into a boon for me after no other couple could be located to take up the other two tickets.

"Why don't we bring Lucy with us?" I heard Mr. Dean suggest to my father. "I think she is old enough now to enjoy Gilbert and Sullivan, and Helen loves her niece so. You know, I do not mind spending money and getting something in return, but I detest the notion of spending and receiving nothing. At least this way, one of the two remaining tickets will not go to waste."

My father having consented, I rushed to get ready.

Once the opera started, however, it could not hold my interest.

A languid love for lilies does not *blight me!*

Lank limbs and haggard cheeks do not *delight me!*

And what in the world did *This costume chaste/Is but good taste/Misplaced* mean? Or *I do* not *long for all one sees/That's Japanese* for that matter?

Perhaps, I thought, I was not as cultured as I'd deemed myself to be.

But that was not it, or not entirely.

In our rush to take our seats, we had sat in haphazard fashion, with me somehow winding up dead in the middle, the two men flanking me, the women flanking them. And whatever Gilbert and Sullivan might have to offer—and, judging from the roars of the crowd, they must have offered *something*—it could not compete for my attention with the drama playing itself out on my left.

That was where Mr. Dean sat.

I studied his profile as he, in turn, studied Aunt Helen's. I wondered what that was I saw on his face. Was that love? Was it some other feeling that I had no familiarity with? Whatever it was, it captivated him the whole time we were there. He was getting nothing out of this opera itself, despite his words to my father earlier that when he paid for something he liked to get something in return.

I could not stop thinking about this "love" thing, questioning it, turning it over in my mind to look at all sides. I understood, had been given to understand, that love was what my parents felt for each other at first sight. And I had taken this fact for granted. But how did it happen between people, really? And how, having happened, did it then grow?

If it grew between Aunt Helen and Mr. Dean, I supposed that eventually he would become my uncle. Was I to be a witness, on this very night, to such an outgrowth of feeling between these two adults to my left? Was I to see new adult love firsthand?

But as I craned my neck forward, not so much as to be obvious and yet just enough to take in Aunt Helen, I saw that perhaps this was not to be. For it did not matter how long Mr. Dean gazed at her, she only had eyes for the stage. When the audience laughed, she laughed, and so quickly that it was impossible to tell if she was laughing of her own accord or merely following their lead.

At one point, only one, I saw her turn her head to him, bestowing upon him a smile of tolerance and gratitude. It did not look very encouraging to me, but he seemed to take it so. In an almost shocking public display, I saw him take his hand and cover one of hers with it. But she allowed it to rest there for only the briefest of seconds before snatching hers away again so that she might clap in glee at something being enacted upon the stage.

And so it always ended the same, even for Herbert Dean. A man would ask my father's permission to ask for Aunt Helen's hand in marriage, that request would be passed on, but without the delay my father had imposed upon Mr. Brockburn's request, and Aunt Helen would answer no.

Always, the answer was no.

· · · · ·

"What is she waiting for?" Aunt Martha demanded outside of Aunt Helen's and Mother's hearing.

Aunt Martha, now age fifty-one, had managed to age more

than anybody, her graying dark nimbus of hair growing a little lighter, a little thinner.

Aunt Martha had been exiled for a time after her rift with my parents over Aunt Helen, but my father had no inclination to allow that rift to remain permanent, nor was Mother inclined to make him.

"I only have one living relative in the world," I heard him tell her one night, when Aunt Helen was out with one of her suitors.

"What about us," Mother said, "your wife and daughter? What about your parents?"

"I didn't mean you," my father said, "and you can hardly call my parents 'living.'"

"That is true enough," Mother conceded.

"I merely meant that Martha is the only person I have known going all the way back to earliest memory, who is still worth knowing, and I do not wish her banished from my home permanently. She has so little joy in her life, I cannot see why we should not share some of ours with her."

"So long as you can prevail upon her not to try to get us to toss my sister out again," Mother said finally, "I see no reason why she should not return."

And so, every Sunday, Aunt Martha came to dine with us after church. But she was always careful now, always careful to not spend time alone with Aunt Helen or to be heard to be critical of her, at least not in either Aunt Helen's or Mother's presence.

Indeed, Aunt Martha had developed a new tactic. Presenting herself as the soul of generosity, she said that she could think of any number of available and suitable men off the top of her head that might wish a union with such a woman as Aunt Helen.

I wondered what these "number of available and suitable men" would be like. Probably one foot in the grave and the other foot on another continent, far, far away.

"Perhaps I could arrange . . . ?" Aunt Martha left the question open-ended one afternoon when Mother and Aunt Helen were out and my father had taken a rare break from his work, joining us for tea.

"I am sure your heart is in the right place, Martha," he said, showing an assurance I did not share, "but I do not think that is the solution. I am sure that Helen already knows, through Aliese, that I am perfectly prepared to lavish a generous dowry upon her and pay for any marriage that might come her way. Were we to present her with a parade of men now, it would look as though we were trying to force her out. You tried that once. Aliese will not tolerate it again. And, I must confess, I have grown accustomed to having her sister here. It may not always be easy, but at least it is never dull."

"But I don't understand," Aunt Martha said. Then she again added, "What is that woman waiting for?"

It was a question we all should have liked an answer to, although for some of us, we wanted the question answered solely for the purpose of satisfying curiosity and not because we had any desire to see that matter resolved in a direction that would mean marriage.

I must confess, it would not necessarily have suited me for Aunt Helen to marry. Oh, it is not that I minded the notion of marriage so very much. In fact, the idea of a big celebration did hold some measure of appeal, particularly since I considered I was of an age now where I might play some sort of pivotal role at such an event. And it is not that I did not want Aunt Helen to be happy; I did, very much so.

But were Aunt Helen to marry, she would no doubt move out from under our roof. It was inconceivable that she would remain on here after taking her vows. If she were to marry, she would be expected to go live under her husband's roof or under some other roof they both picked out, unless of course that husband could not afford a worthy enough roof, like Mr. Brockburn so long ago had not been able to, but in that case such a suitor would not even be entertained in the first place. And I did not want her to go away. I loved Mother more than I loved anyone else, but I did not want to live in this house again without Aunt Helen.

Still, the fact that Aunt Helen remained unmarried?

It was a mystery.

• Seventeen •

The morning after we went to the Savoy to see *Patience*, I walked over to the Tylers' next door to see how Kit was feeling.

I had by now been to the Tylers' home many times since they had moved in. On the outside, it was not very dissimilar to ours—large and made chiefly of stone—but the inside was different, far different than it had been under the previous owners. While the furniture was all well chosen, there was an undeniable comfort to even the smallest picture, as though Victoria Tyler's personality had permeated all that surrounded her.

It took so long for someone to answer my knock, I was beginning to think no one was at home, but that didn't make sense, so I persisted. At last a servant answered. In one hand she held a cloth that she was using to cover her nose and mouth.

"Is young Master Ty—," I began, but she wouldn't let me finish.

"You must go, miss," she spoke hurriedly. "No one is allowed in, save for the doctor. Master Tyler is very sick. It's the typhoid."

I tried to ask further questions but was prevented doing so when she, in an act no servant had ever performed upon me before, shut the door in my face.

"*Typhoid*," I said to myself, my pace slowed on the walk back home after what I'd heard. It was confusing. I knew that typhoid had killed off Queen Victoria's consort Prince Albert, but that was before I was even born, and I didn't know much else about the disease. Prince Albert had died of it nearly twenty years before, though. Surely it could not still be so deadly.

Feeling the urgency of life all of a sudden, I hurried on.

Arriving home, I did not even spare a moment to remove my cloak before heading straight to my father's study and pounding on the door, hard.

"Yes?" I heard him call, in a voice that sounded put out at having been interrupted, but I did not care at that point.

I opened the door. When my father looked up and saw that it was me, saw the expression on my face, his own expression softened.

"What is wrong, Lucy?"

"What is typhoid?" I asked without preamble.

One thing about my father: no matter what else might be happening, he never could resist the opportunity to show off his knowledge of a thing.

"Typhoid fever," he said, "is an acute infectious disease acquired by drinking infected water. Symptoms include high lingering fever and intestinal discomfort, chills, prostration, and, I am sorry to be indelicate here, diarrhea. At the end of the first week rosy spots appear on the victim's chest and abdomen. The disease takes approximately three to four weeks to see its way through to its conclusion." Suddenly he laid down his pen, looked at me closely. "Why do you ask? What makes you want to know about typhoid?"

"Because," I said, "I went next door to see how Kit was feeling and was told that he has it."

"Oh." His eyes turned serious. "Oh, that is very bad."

"But is it? Is it really? Prince Albert died of it so long ago. It cannot still be so very deadly, can it? The servant said I could not even see Kit, that no one could except the doctor."

"Oh, it is still very deadly," my father said. "The servant did right to turn you away."

"You mean Kit could really die from this?"

"It is a possibility." His expression was solemn only for a moment. "But let us hope for the best. You must not visit your friend again until the danger has passed, but in the meantime I will ask around to see if I can learn more."

"Do you think it would be all right," I asked, "for me to write letters to Kit? It must be frightfully boring, being in bed for so very long with nothing to do. At least I might take his mind off it for a bit."

My father studied me. "You are a kind girl, Lucy, aren't you?" Then he took up his own pen again, effectively dismissing me. "By all means, write your letters to Kit. But you should be warned: It is entirely possible that he will be too sick to read them. And, above all, you mustn't expect any reply." He paused, did not meet my eyes. "There may never be any reply."

October 11

Dear Kit,

It feels strange to be writing you a letter when I have never done so before. How are you feeling?

Oh, I could hit myself in the head for writing that! "How are you feeling?" Of course you are feeling wretched, and that is why I have to write to you!

Hmm...what can I write here that will take your mind off your own troubles? We went to see the new Gilbert and Sullivan opera at the opening of the Savoy last night. But no, I suppose that won't interest you. For one thing, it was you being sick that prevented your parents from going, which in turn enabled me to go. Then, too, I cannot imagine it is much fun reading about an opera when opera involves singing and you cannot hear that in a letter.

If you will only get better soon, if you will get well enough that I can come see

you, I would gladly try to sing for you
whatever I can remember from <u>Patience</u>.
It will probably only be a line or two,
and those lines incomprehensible, but they
should be enough for you to know that you
have missed nothing if you have never seen
Gilbert and Sullivan.

> Your friend,
>
> Lucy Sexton

. . . . .

October 18

Dear Kit,

My father says he has learned that you
caught the typhoid from a maid—or at least
that is what I <u>think</u> he implied, as she has
since died of the same disease now afflicting
you. If I understand what he told me
correctly, apparently she was already ill
when she brought you a glass of water, and
she must have somehow infected that water.
Not being a physician, I am afraid it is
something of a muddle to me, so perhaps
I have my facts wrong. I am not sure

which I am sorrier about, the death of the
maid—for it is always sad when anyone dies,
unless of course that person is perfectly
villainous—or that she somehow infected you
before her own passing. My father does say
that so far no one else in your household
appears to have been infected, and I suppose
for that we must all be grateful, but my
father also says your fever is very high now
and that it is said you have periods of
delirium.

You know, when I first met you, I cannot
say that I liked you very much. First, you
had the nerve to be bored at my family's
party. Then you accused me of being the
sort of girl who would do needlepoint
and—worst sin of all!—you beat me at chess.
But things between us have changed since
those early days.

Do you know, I don't think I ever had a
friend before I met you? I should be very
sad if you were to die.

But let us not talk now of death. I
refuse to allow myself to think that such
will be the outcome here! So, instead, let
me tell you something of my aunt. No one
outside of my parents and me know her
whole story, but since you are indeed my
friend, I cannot see the harm in sharing

it with you now. When Aunt Helen and
Mother were born...

Your friend,

Lucy

. . . . .

October 25

Kit,

A peculiar thing happened today.
Everyone else was out of the house, Aunt
Helen and Mother having departed before
I even arose, and I grew bored. The book I
was reading did not interest me, we know
how I feel about needlepoint, and after
spending some time at the chessboard by
myself devising a strategy for beating you
when next we play, I decided to take
myself for a little stroll. Usually, I do
not go anywhere by myself, but I decided
that just this once there would be no harm
in going to the park in the middle of the
day unattended. I can hear you admonishing
me for my lack of caution—no doubt, if
anyone here knew what I was planning, I
would have been tied to the bedpost!—but I

sneaked out all the same, wearing an old dress and with my bonnet shrouding my face in such a way that I might not be recognized.

The park was lovely. You really must get better soon so that you can see it in all the riot of color it is now. I strolled around the perimeters, watching the children play, watching nannies with babies, people walking in twos: mostly women together, but there were a few pairings that were man and woman. It was one of these latter pairings that finally caught my eye.

Seated on a bench was one of the women from my household. She was wearing a dark cloak, befitting the weather, and beside her was seated a man. At first I thought it was Mother, and I was wondering what she was doing talking to a man in the park that was not my father, but then I realized it could not possibly be her; she would never do such a thing. I was standing off to the side of the bench and the man was between us, his back facing me. From the way they were seated together, almost intimately, I felt certain that this was not their first time meeting each other. For some reason, I decided I did not want

Aunt Helen to see me there—or perhaps it
occurred to me that she might not want
me to see her there—so I stepped back out of
her view.

The two appeared to be engaged in a
rather heated discussion, judging from the
expressions I could glimpse on Aunt Helen's
face, but I could not hear any of the
words, for they were whispering. It was
all very frustrating. I could see nothing
of the man, save for his back: a coat, of poor
quality both in fabric and cut; unruly
brown hair peeking out from beneath the
back of his hat, which was also of poor
quality—the hat, not the hair. Unable to
hear anything, and now fearful of being
seen, I quickly left the park and
returned home.

Now here is the odd thing—two odd
things, really. One, why did Aunt Helen
not meet with this man at home? It is not
as though she is not allowed to have visitors
here. Two, who was he? For he was so shabbily
dressed, that of one thing I am certain: he
is no one from our acquaintance. I suppose,
reading this paragraph over, that number
two answers number one. She did not have
him here because she did not think someone
dressed as he was would be welcome here.

When Aunt Helen returned a short time later, I was back at the chessboard again, laying plans on how I might beat you. "How was your walk?" I asked her. "It was fine," she said. "Did you meet anyone interesting?" I asked her. "I saw no one," she said. As I say, it is all very peculiar.

My father says that they thought you were starting to get better but that complications have set in, that your high fever is a constant thing now. I do not wish to think about what that might mean. Do you know, I never did get to see that tunnel you claim runs beneath the earth, connecting your home with mine? My father is almost always in his study when he is at home. And, even when he is not, I fear that if I were to enter his study by myself to access that tunnel, I would surely get caught. But if you will only get better, I will steel my bravery and give it a try.

Please get better, Kit. Please.

Lucy

. . . . .

November 1

Dear Lucy,

I am feeling much better now. I am fairly
certain it was your letters that kept me alive.

Thank you.

Kit

· Eighteen ·

With each day that passed, Kit got a little better, a little stronger.

But his mother was still concerned, lest the excitement of visitors cause him to turn for the worse again, and so I was not permitted to see him, nor was he permitted to leave the house. And so we had to content ourselves with letters back and forth.

At last, two weeks to the day after receiving my first letter of reply from him, I received the following:

Dear Lucy,

I have lived. Now it is time for you to fulfill your end of the bargain. Meet me tonight in the middle of the tunnel after our households are asleep. Say at two a.m.? Don't forget to bring a candle to light your way. It is dark down there.

Kit

. . . . .

The remainder of the day passed in a sea of anticipation and anxiety: anticipation over finally seeing Kit again, particularly after the intimacy of our letters, anxiety over going down into the tunnel.

It was difficult to assess which emotion ran stronger.

It was not as though I'd ever considered myself to be a fearful person, but the idea of being beneath the earth did put fear in me. What would it be like down there? Would it be cold? Damp? Would there be rats? What if Kit slept through the appointed time or fell sick again, grew delirious, and I became trapped somehow with no one knowing where I was? I could die down there!

The idea of getting caught was not pleasant either.

For it seemed easy for Kit to propose what was to him a simple thing—*Meet me tonight in the middle of the tunnel after our households are asleep. Say at two a.m.?*—but it was far more difficult for me to achieve in practical terms. Sometimes, our household was awake well into the early hours of the morning, what with guests and such. And even if there were no guests, what if my father, unbeknownst to me, was at one of those critical junctures he seemed to have more and more often in his writing? What if I thought he went to bed with the others, but he stayed up late instead to work, enabling him to catch me red-handed—or, red-footed might be more accurate—as I tiptoed into his sacred study with the intent of doing something he would no doubt disapprove of? What if he was asleep, what if they were *all* asleep, but what if I barked my shins against some inconveniently placed piece of furniture, involuntarily let out a cry of pain, roused the house around me, and, and, and . . .

I was working myself into a state.

This had to stop.

So I went about my business, pretended it was just like any other day, even did needlepoint to innocently pass the time.

When I thought, with excitement, about seeing Kit again, the clock moved at the pace of a *tick* waiting a long time for its companion *tock*. But when I thought, with trepidation, of what I was going to have to do in order to see Kit, the twin hands sped around the clock face as though trying to see who would win the race.

"You are in an odd mood today," Mother observed at tea-time. "I have never known you to take up your needlepoint before without someone insisting you do so first."

"Are you all right?" Aunt Helen asked at dinner. "You do not seem yourself."

"Perhaps you should go to bed early," my father suggested. "I know you have had no contact with Kit in weeks, but there has been typhoid in the neighborhood. It would do you well to get more rest."

"An excellent suggestion," I agreed, grateful for the excuse to escape those six prying if loving eyes. Two more, and they could have been a spider.

Alone in my room, I paced, paced, paced. Then, realizing that someone might come to check on me, I put on my nightdress and climbed into bed.

And there I waited, waited, waited.

Thankfully, there were no guests that night, and before too many hours had passed, I heard the household preparing to put itself to sleep.

"I thought you would be asleep by now," my father said. "Good night."

"I'm sure you will feel better in the morning," Mother said. "Good night."

"Are you sure you aren't up to something?" Aunt Helen said.

"Good night," I said.

I lay in the half dark of the moon-filled room, drumming my fingers against the top sheet.

You would not think that a person could be filled with so much anticipation and dread and have sleep threaten to take over all the same, yet I wound up having to pinch myself repeatedly over the next few hours, sometimes quite hard, to keep myself awake. In the end, by the time the clock called me to get out of bed at half one in order to begin my preparations, I had pinched my cheek so many times on one side, I probably looked as though I had been attacked by spiders there.

I removed my nightdress, located a day dress that was in such deplorable condition—it seemed that I always spilled whatever I was eating on it whenever I wore it—that, should it get dirty in my foray into the underworld, no one would notice it missing if I burned it in the fireplace afterward. Then I took a large dark-haired doll that I hadn't played with in many years and tucked it into bed with its back to the door, using pillows artfully placed beneath the sheets to create the impression of a body so that on the off chance one of the adults rose in the night to check on me, they would be fooled when they peeked in at the door.

It seemed too risky to put on my boots just then—I feared making a clumping racket in them as I negotiated the stairs— and so I tiptoed my way gingerly down, boots in one hand. Nor did I dare to put them on, I warned myself, until I had attained the safety of my father's study, only stopping briefly along the way to light the tallest candle I could find from one of the wall sconces, taking it with me.

Just as I was slowly opening the door to my father's study, I expe- rienced a moment of heart-stopping fear when I imagined I heard a noise coming from within. For the first time, it occurred to me that I might not be the only one in the household capable of traversing the floors on cat's feet, capable of hiding on stairs unseen and unheard. Perhaps my father had risen in the night and, unable to sleep, had gone back down to do some work, tiptoeing as I had done so as not to rouse those who yet slumbered in Orpheus's arms?

And was that a light under the door?

But, having already partially turned the knob—if someone was inside would they have seen or heard that?—I saw no choice but to turn it the rest of the way, pressing the door open.

My heartbeat returned to something approximating normal when I saw that, thankfully, the room was empty.

The clock on the wall said I still had ten minutes remaining and I took the time to look around the room, thinking how differ- ent, how odd it looked without my father in it. Finding a holder in which I could rest my candle, I sought to choose a seat where I might rest while lacing up my boots.

Stealing rare opportunity, I chose my father's big chair behind his desk.

How unusual it felt to sit there, I thought, settling cautiously into the leather cushion of the seat as though it might reject me somehow. How extraordinary—how magical! This was what my father saw when he looked out at the world; this is where he sat when he created worlds, ordering them as he pleased.

I wondered what it must be like to be him.

But there was no time for such meditations, no time for any more thoughts, for my boots were laced, my candle had been taken up again, and I had pulled open the trapdoor—drat! that creak was loud!—and was lowering myself down the stairs.

The stairs were narrower and steeper than expected, but at the bottom was a small cellar, just as my father had always said there was.

I did not tarry in this room for long, however. It was small, dank, and had dark corners that were the stuff of nightmares. If rats lurked down here, no doubt they collected themselves in those corners.

I was not here to see rats. I was not here to see this room. That door, right across on the other side: that is what I had come here for.

The door looked so old, it might have been there even before the house built over it, and its hinges creaked with the sound of an animal surprised at being attacked when I forced it open. Apparently, with the exception of Kit's use of it when he had first discovered this place, no one else had used it for a very long time.

It's hard to say what I expected to find on the other side—no doubt a room similar, if longer and narrower, than the cellar had been. But such was not the case.

I held the candle up, moving it in every direction. The floor, the generously spaced walls, the ceiling soaring overhead when I had expected to be cramped into a humpbacked position—all was fashioned out of wide, flat stones, and good quality stones at that, placed with great care. Yes, the stones were cool beneath my fingers, but not cold, not damp. A lot of time, effort, and expense had gone into building this place, but who had done so? And why?

I held the candle straight ahead of me and walked on toward my destination, now hearing a matching echo to my tread coming from the exact opposite direction, echoing louder and closer with each step.

. . . . .

We met in the middle.

No, I had not brought a measuring device with me, nor did I know how far behind him his end of the tunnel stretched; and yes, he was far taller than I was, so his stride being far longer than mine, if each of his steps had echoed mine, then he had covered more ground to get to me than I had to get to him.

Still, that is the way I thought of it: we met in the middle.

In the glow of our candles, I saw how much thinner he'd become since I'd last seen him, how much paler his face—the typhoid had robbed him of so much. Still, when he smiled, he was every inch Kit.

"You made it," he said, his grin shining behind his own candle.

I had not realized until that moment how much I had missed him, how happy and relieved I was to have him still in this world. All my life, I had been unaccustomed to having a friend close to my age in the neighborhood. Mostly, I moved in a universe where everyone was an adult, leaving me to feel like the lone visitor from another planet. I had not realized until that moment how much less alone he made me feel.

I wanted to reach out to him, touch him to make sure he was really there, embrace his thin shoulders.

But I couldn't do that.

We may have been friends, but it was not as though he was another girl whom I might touch either casually or even with warmth.

So instead I contented myself with a saucy, "What? Did you think I would prove too much of a coward in the end?"

"Never," he said with a twinkle, "but I did think you might sleep through it."

It was a good thing, I thought, that the candles probably did not give off enough light for him to see my pinched cheek.

"What are those marks on your cheek?" he asked.

Blast.

"It is nothing," I said. "Tell me"—I swept my candle, indicating the space around us—"do you have any theories as to how this place came to be?"

"Indeed, I do."

"And are you going to share them with me? Or do I have to stand here and guess?"

"I think that, once upon a time, someone in my house and someone in your house loved each other very much. But, for whatever reason, they could not permit themselves to meet aboveground. And so this place was built, with great love and determination."

"Kit Tyler!" I laughed. "Who would have ever thought it? You are *a romantic*."

He did not blush as I thought he might at my teasing. Instead he asked, "Would it be so awful if I were?"

I had no comfortable answer to that.

"Why did you want so very much for me to see this place?" I asked.

"Because you have known about it ever since I first told you about it—how long ago was that?—and yet this is the first time I have persuaded you down here. I think it's healthy to have curiosity, don't you? You should have more of it."

"I only came this time," I said, "because I made that stupid bargain with you when I thought you might be dying. Now I regret my haste."

"Do you? I don't. I'm glad I lived so that I might hold you to it."

I couldn't help myself. "I'm glad you lived too," I said.

"I also wanted you to meet me here tonight so that I could thank you properly in person."

"For?"

"My life."

This was a different Kit now than the Kit I had known before he fell ill. I did not know what to make of this Kit, what to say to this Kit.

He solved the problem for me.

"You may go now," he said.

"Excuse me?"

"I have achieved my goal for the night, and I do not want to keep you so long that you walk into a household already risen to greet the day. I don't want you to get in trouble. You may go now."

• Nineteen •

I was so tired the next morning at breakfast, I kept drooping over my eggs.

"And here I thought," my father said, "the extra hours of sleep last night would have left you refreshed this morning, but I see now you are even worse. Are you sure you are not unwell?"

I was saved from answering, which would no doubt have involved me uttering a lie, by the sight of a servant entering with a letter on a tray.

"What's this?" my father asked, slitting the envelope open with the knife he'd been about to use to butter his toast.

His eyes rapidly scanned down the page.

"Oh, no!" he said. "Martha has injured her leg!"

"How bad is it?" Mother asked, concern furrowing her pretty brow.

I roused myself enough to steal a glance at Aunt Helen. I cannot say she looked distressed over Aunt Martha's misfortune.

"Well," my father said, "she assures us most explicitly that she is not going to *die*, but she does add that being cooped up with our parents even more than usual is nearly driving her mad."

"Oh, how awful," Mother said, hastily adding, "not being with your parents, of course—but I do think that someone who likes to get out and about as much as Martha does must be very vexed by this turn of affairs. Perhaps she can come stay with us for a while?"

I stole another glance at Aunt Helen. Now she did look distressed over Aunt Martha's misfortune.

"That is very kind of you, dear," my father said, "but Martha already suggests and then immediately rejects such a solution in her letter. Apparently, she feels that such a long carriage drive might do further damage to the leg."

"Then we must go to her!" Mother said.

Mother may have been upset at one point about Aunt Martha's machinations concerning Aunt Helen, but her natural instinct was one of forgiveness, and she hated to see anyone hurt.

But my father had his work to do and everyone agreed that I looked too tired to undertake the journey. As for Aunt Helen, well, she did not offer, nor did anybody ask.

And so it was agreed that Mother would go alone. Within the hour she was packed up, everyone had been kissed, and she was gone.

No sooner did the door close on her back than it occurred to me how impossibly empty the house felt without her. True, she was often gone in the day visiting with friends and was just as frequently out in the evening, fulfilling some sort of social obligation. But it had never been like this. It had never been her going away for an entire night, or more.

The minute she was gone, I longed for her return, shivered at the sudden unwelcome thought of what the house would be like if we were one day to find ourselves permanently without her.

"You are cold," Aunt Helen observed, seeing me shiver. "Why don't you come into the parlor with me and warm yourself by the fire?"

"No," I said, "I am not cold. I am merely still so very tired." I yawned. "I think I will go lie down. Perhaps a nap will refresh me."

. . . . .

Still in my clothes, I slept through lunch and no one woke me, slept through tea and no one woke me, slept through dinner and no one woke me.

When I at last opened my eyes it was to a dark and silent house. Somehow, I had managed to get my natural clock confused, exchanging what should have by all rights been day for evening.

I shivered in the dark, recalling the last dream I had had. In it, I was buried alive. No one knew where I was and the ceiling of earth above me kept inching down, ever closer to my face, the walls tightening as well. On some level I must have known that the dream stemmed from my secret meeting with Kit the night before—perhaps guilt was playing a trick with my brain?—but it is hard to rein in terror and hold tight to reason when you wake in your stale clothes in the dark, confused about the time or even what day it is.

Despite my age, I wanted my mother.

Halfway up the stairs to the third story, however, I remembered that she was not at home. And yet I continued on to her door, thinking that for once my father would have done just as well. There had been times, although rare, during my younger childhood when he had soothed me over some wound, physical or emotional. If he had done so before, he could do so again.

But when I tapped softly at his door, it swung open because it had been left ajar. Peering inside, whispering his name, there was no answer. I stepped into the room. There was no one there.

He must not be able to sleep without Mother here, just as my sleep has now been disturbed, I thought. *He must have gone downstairs for a drink or to work, perhaps both.*

I would not disturb him in either case, knowing that disturbance from me now would be unwelcome. But I did still feel the need for comforting, did feel the need to have human arms around me.

Shutting my parents' door, I tiptoed down the hall to Aunt Helen's room. This door was shut. But before I could tap softly, I heard her from within. She was making moans, groans unlike anything I had heard a human being make before. I didn't know what I was hearing.

Was she in pain?

And yet somehow, it did not sound like pain.

I thought to call out to her, see if she was all right, but some instinct held me back.

I hoped Mother would be home in the morning.

· Twenty ·

My body had been changing.

I had known this would happen to me one day, hadn't I? Surely I had known, if nothing came to kill me first, that I would inevitably complete the transformation from girl into woman?

And yet, it had always seemed such a long way off.

And yet, now it was here.

Over the past year or so, hair had begun to sprout, slowly, under my arms, on my legs, even between my legs in that place I had no name for. I tried to regard these changes scientifically, but I could not help but think that were I a blonde like Aunt Helen and Mother, these changes would not seem so shocking. As it was, with my black hair, each new strand that erupted, however short, created a stark distinction against my pale skin. Then, too, the flesh in my breast area had grown yet larger as well. The whole—the hair and the flesh—made me feel as though I were a tree in the garden that had looked the same all its life, barren, and yet was now through some alchemy transforming itself into an entirely different and exotic tree.

I had even grown a little taller.

No one in my home hardly ever remarked on these changes, and that made me feel odder still. My father said nothing at all, as though it were not happening, while Mother merely commented that soon we would need to have Mrs. Wiggins come to remeasure me for new clothes.

My parents and Aunt Helen were entertaining the Carsons and the Williamses. Herbert Dean, while having been given no further encouragement by Aunt Helen, was in attendance. The Tylers, sadly, were not. Christmas was fast approaching and Mrs. Tyler had insisted on the family going to visit her parents before spending some time by the sea. It might have been cold out, but she thought the air would do Kit's body good after his bout with typhoid.

Normally, I would have enjoyed staying up late and listening in on the adults, but on this occasion, with Kit gone, no sooner had we finished with the pudding than I began to grow bored with all the talk of books and plays and, on Mr. Carson's part, money. I did not care what he thought was a good investment, and I certainly had no wish to hear his wife gossip about Mrs. Tyler, which she had begun to do roundly in her usual insidious fashion.

In addition, all through the meal, I had not felt completely well.

"I'm going up to bed now," I informed Mother, gently and deliberately laying my napkin beside my plate.

. . . . .

I awoke in the middle of the night to a strange cramping sensation in my lower abdomen.

Pushing the sheets down away from my body, half rising, I saw bloodstains on my white gown.

Oh, no! I thought as a strange guilt flooded through me. *Have I somehow broken something in myself?*

Having already panicked that I'd done myself some harm, I forced sanity to flow back in. I had no idea what I was looking at, but I deduced that it was somehow part and parcel with my changing body: the new hair, the larger breasts. Or at least that is what I tried to tell myself.

It's a good thing, I told myself as I climbed out of the bed, *that I am such a sensible girl. Elsewise, I might think I was bleeding to death.*

I suppose I might have stayed in bed until morning, waiting for someone to find me, hoping that whoever found me first could tell me what I was to do about this latest development. But I did not want to wait. I did not think I could get back to sleep just then, not with everything that was happening. Then, too, I worried that if something wasn't done about it immediately, I really might bleed to death.

Taking up the candle I had lit before falling asleep, I tamped the panic back down again as I ascended the stairs to the third floor in search of help.

My first instinct was to go straight to Mother, but as I raised my hand to knock, I hesitated. If I woke her, surely my father would wake too. I looked down at the bloodstains on my white gown. I did not want my father to see me like this. So instead I proceeded down the hall to Aunt Helen's room at the very end.

It occurred to me that if I knocked, others might hear me;

but that if I didn't knock and merely walked up to the side of her bed to wake her, I might scare her half to death. So I settled on turning the knob gently and poking my head into the room just enough to whisper, "Aunt Helen?"

"Lucy?" She sat up in bed, looking as beautiful as Mother in the light of the fire she had burning in the grate. "What is the matter?"

I entered the room, closed the door behind me, showed her.

"Oh!" She sounded surprised. "I was sixteen when it first happened to me," Aunt Helen whispered. "I would have thought that you would have still had another year or two before you for this."

"I would have thought so too," I said wryly, having no clue as to what she might be referring. Was she really suggesting that it was the normal course of events for a female to one day find herself bleeding between the legs? In fact, I would have even thought "never." Then I added, the fear creeping its way back, "Could something that I have, er, *done* caused this to happen to me?"

"I hardly think so!" She laughed. "Unless by 'done' you mean the mere act of growing older."

At least, I thought, one of us had found something to laugh about in all this.

She must have seen my dismay, for her expression grew concerned.

"Are you frightened?" she asked, rising and sashing a gown around her waist.

"Not frightened," I said, realizing I wasn't, certainly not now that I was with her. "But I would like to know what to do."

Aunt Helen strode swiftly to her wardrobe, removing some

items from the drawer. Then, going over to the washbasin, she took a cloth and moistened it with water.

"Remove your gown," she directed me. "I don't think you'll want this one anymore," she said, taking it from me, tossing it on the fire. "When we're done here, I'll go to your room and get you a fresh one."

Then she got down on her knees and cleaned off the place between my legs. The wet cloth felt soothing against my skin.

"Here," she said, holding up one of the items she'd removed from her wardrobe. It was a fairly large piece of cotton fabric, about two feet by one foot in measure. The central foot or so, lengthwise, was comprised of a thicker material, terry cloth, and I watched as Aunt Helen folded the whole into thirds. Then she showed me how I was to wear it on my body so that it would catch the flow of blood that would come at regular intervals now at the space of once a month and lasting each time approximately a week.

"That often?" I wondered. "And for that long?" I did not like to complain, but it was a bit much.

"Oh, yes," she said. "Now you are a woman."

Did she have to point that out to me? Not that I was believing it for a second. Yes, my body was changing. Yes, I was changed. But a woman? Not now. Not yet.

"Wait here," she said.

Several minutes later, longer than I would have thought it would take her to run down to my room and back up again, she returned with a fresh gown for me, helped me as I slipped it over my head.

"There," she said.

Then she told me she'd taken it upon herself to wake one of the servants, directing that my bed should be remade with fresh sheets so that I would not have to sleep in soiled ones.

"It should be ready in a few minutes," she said. Then she put her arms around me, a nice touch. "Or you could stay here with me tonight."

"I am not scared," I protested.

"I know," she said, "I know. Only, sometimes, there are things that happen in life that can make a person feel lonely."

Suddenly, I knew exactly what she meant. Suddenly, I felt that if I returned to my bed alone right now, after all that had happened on this night, I should feel very lonely indeed.

"Well, if you do not mind . . . ," I said.

In answer, she pulled back the sheets on her big bed, held them open for me.

I climbed in and she climbed in after me, banishing the feelings of aloneness that just a moment ago had threatened to creep in.

Aunt Helen put her arm around my shoulders, let me rest my head against her shoulder.

I was tired now.

"This changes everything," Aunt Helen said to the top of my head.

"It does?" I stifled a yawn.

"Oh, yes. Now you can make babies."

"How do you mean?" I asked.

Then Aunt Helen explained to me the making of babies. She explained it all.

I was not entirely sure I believed her at the time. The very idea of it seemed almost fantastical, filling me with the sense I had sometimes when, presented with certain unusual foods, the thought occurred to me, *Now, what ever possessed a human being to think there might be tasteful nourishment in* that? But it was certainly a good story.

• Twenty-one •

Christmas had passed, the Tylers were back in their home, and New Year's Day was fast approaching.

Decorations still adorned our home, although we would be sure to remove them before Twelfth Night was upon us. Wreaths and holly were everywhere, every staircase railing adorned with garland that was in turn decorated with French horns, ribbons, and candles.

The large tree, centerpiece of our downstairs this past week, had been moved up to the ballroom. It still wore its candles, its paper cornucopias filled with treats, its Dresden ornaments that looked like metal but were in fact cardboard painted in silver, gold, and copper, fashioned into the shapes of animals and toy trains. Then there were the wax ornaments in the form of angels, children, animals, and fruit; I suspected the wax children were meant to be charming, but they always unsettled me. Last, there were the few blown-glass balls, my favorites.

The tree had been moved in preparation for the New Year's Eve party my family was hosting.

It was to be a grand affair. Everyone was invited.

I had on what I thought of as my first truly adult dress: apple green satin with crepe over it, the trimming minimal. My hair was even done differently. Normally, I wore it down with pins holding it back at the sides so that it wouldn't fall in my face, but now it had been swept up and there were pins all over my head, making me feel elegant, if something like one of the cushions in Aunt Martha's sewing basket.

I was already in the ballroom, having left my parents and Aunt Helen behind in the receiving line, when the Tylers walked in.

Kit was more dressed up than I had ever seen him: black super-fine dress coat with matching trousers, well cut; patent leather boots; white vest and cravat; he even had a white cambric hand-kerchief poking out of his pocket, and on his hands were white kid gloves. Kit had always been handsome, I thought now, but nothing like this. Now he was splendor itself.

I wondered, if we played chess right then, if he'd let me beat him.

Mother, at my father's insistence, had tutored me in the finer points of ball etiquette. Where, normally, if Kit were here on a regular visit I would go to greet him, I now knew that a lady was not supposed to cross a ballroom unattended. So I waited for him to come to me.

Kit gave a slight bow.

Then he looked at the table behind me, picked up a dance card.

"Let me see, Miss Sexton," he said with a twinkle in his eye, "what will be your pleasure this evening? I see there are four sets here—sixteen dances! Will you dance with me the schottische, a polka, the Lancer's Quad? I know!" He snapped his fingers. "The Last Waltz!"

"Are you *insane*?" I laughed.

"Possibly." He set the card back down again. "But it might be fun, you know, to dance."

"I know how to dance," I said. "I've been taught them all, but it doesn't mean I think it would be any fun."

"Ah, well. Are you hungry?"

"No."

"Thirsty?"

"No."

"Then I suppose we shall just sit down here, like so, and watch the others."

And that's what we did, for hours, it seemed. We didn't talk, as we usually might have done. Too stiff in our new clothes, we barely said a word.

"Is it loud in here?" he asked.

"Yes."

"Is it too crowded?"

"Yes. And," I added, "all these pins are making my scalp itch."

"Yes," he said, "I can see where they would. I'm afraid I can't do anything about the pins—I'm sure your mother would notice— but I think I have the solution to everything else. Come on."

"Where are—," I started as he rose.

"Come on," he said over his shoulder, adding in a whisper, despite the noise all around us, "no one will notice we're gone."

Outside the ballroom, the noise receding behind us, he grabbed my hand and pulled me down the stairs.

. . . . .

"The trapdoor in my father's study?" I was incredulous. "Have we not done this already?"

Through the ceiling, I could hear the muffled footsteps of the party overhead, the sounds of dancers, the music vibrating the walls.

"Come on," he said, grabbing a candle to light the way. "I've never entered it from this side. I always wondered what it would be like, if it would feel different than entering it from my kitchen, if I'd gain a greater sense of what it was originally used for."

"I thought you already had a theory on that."

He shrugged. "I might change my mind." Another shrug. "Or confirm it."

Cautiously, I climbed down after him.

"As you can see," I said when we were about halfway through the tunnel, somewhat ruffled at having allowed myself to be drawn into this, "it is not any different at all. It is the same as it was before, the same as it has no doubt always been: lots of stone, the sense of earth around it, the only light that which we bring with us."

Kit extracted a gold watch from his pocket, held it up to the flickering flame.

"Look," he said. "It is just turned midnight."

Then, before I could think what he was about, he lowered his face toward mine until he blocked out the sun of the candle, and laid a feather kiss on my lips.

We both pulled back almost instantly, as though we'd burned each other.

"Happy New Year, Lucy," he whispered.

I couldn't help it. Involuntarily, my fingers moved to my lips as though I might feel a searing brand there.

My lips felt the same—plump, soft—yet changed forever.

"They will miss us if we don't return soon," I said.

"I hardly think so," he said. "There is so much revelry going on in your household right now, I doubt they should miss us before morning."

It was a tempting thought: the idea of remaining in that tunnel with Kit. Perhaps, if we stayed, he might kiss me again. And when we at last emerged from here, it would be a sunny new day and new year, even though I knew we would of course not be stepping from here into the outdoors; we would be stepping into my father's study or Kit's family's kitchen.

"Don't worry," he said, when I failed to respond, the first minutes of the new year ticking out silently ahead of us. "I won't try to keep you here. Of course you must go back."

Then he took my hand, warming mine in his.

"I'd ask you to race me back," he teased, "but I know how competitive you are, and you look so pretty tonight in that gown, I would not like to see you strive to beat me, in which case you might trip, thereby ripping your dress."

"Do you have any other solution?" I countered.

"We could run together," he said, holding my hand yet tighter, pulling me along at his side as we raced back together through the passageway.

. . . . .

We were still giggling as we approached the underside of the trapdoor leading into my father's study above.

"Shh," I shushed Kit, barely able to contain my own mirth.

I held the candle as, exercising excruciating slowness, Kit pushed upward against the trapdoor.

On the one hand, I could understand his hesitance, but on the other I could not help but wonder: What did the speed he used matter? If my father had decided to take a respite from the party and go in there, or some other guest had gone there for whatever reason, speed would make no difference in terms of saving us. After all, it was not as though, were he to push the trapdoor up at a creeping pace and were he to spy feet in the room above as he peeked over the edge, he could then close the door back over us without us being seen. Speed, stealth—if someone were in the room neither would save us. A bell had been rung. As my father liked to say of bells, it could not now be *unrung*.

Gripping the candle tighter in my hand, I brushed past Kit, pushing up against the door so hard that it flew up with the sheer force of it, snapping back against the wooden floor above.

"Are you *insane*?" Kit looked as though he was unsure about whether he wanted to laugh hysterically or possibly see if he could find someone to accompany me to an asylum.

But I did not answer him as I went ahead, pulling myself up into the room, quickly glancing around me.

"We are safe," I announced, looking down upon him.

Then, realizing our exertions had taken a toll on him, given the relatively short time ago that he had been deathly ill, I reached out my hand to help him up.

Not wanting to tarry any longer, lest we get caught, after returning the trapdoor to its proper position, we extinguished the candle and hastily made for the door.

This time, it was I who exercised silly overcaution, poking my head around the corner.

No one was in sight.

"Hurry," I urged Kit, indicating he should follow me.

Still breathless from our recent run, we had closed the door gently behind us, had made it nearly out of the corridor when Mother rounded the corner, nearly crashing into us.

"You startled me out of my life," she said, raising a hand to her chest.

"We're sorry," I apologized. "Why aren't you at the party?"

My assumption in asking this question was that if you don't want to be asked a thing yourself, it struck me as best to ask the other person the very same thing first, thereby putting them on the defensive side of the chessboard.

It seemed like an eminently sound strategy to me.

"I could not find your father anywhere," she said, "so I came looking for him. I thought he might be hiding out in his study. I could not find your aunt either."

"He is not there, neither of them are," I said quickly.

Too quickly, apparently, for she raised her eyebrows, for the first time taking in Kit, who had come to stand beside me.

"And what are the two of you doing here?" she asked, eyebrows still raised as though the wonder of it all might cause them to remain thus poised permanently. "Were you seeking your father as well?"

"No." I could feel the blush in my cheeks.

"It became so noisy," Kit said, saving me, "and you know I am still not completely well. Lucy was kind enough, when I complained of a headache, to suggest I escape for a moment's quiet and further kind enough to accompany me down here so that I would not have to suffer alone."

It did not impress me as being a solid story. Why, Mother could just as easily ask, if he was feeling unwell, did he not ask his parents to accompany him home? Or even go himself if he did not want to disturb their good time? Why, in a house so large, did he need to go into our most rarely used hallway rather than one of the more public parlors?

One thing that did impress me: the unblinking, unflinching way he gazed into Mother's eyes: not as though he were defying her—no, not that—but rather as though he was defending my honor, as though he was insisting through posture and look that I would never be party to anything that could be anything less than good.

"Thank you for explaining that to me," Mother said to him evenly. "Now if you wouldn't mind, and if you are feeling well enough to rejoin the party, I wish that you would do so, that I might have a word alone with my daughter."

He may have been proud and valiant, but he could not deny Mother that.

"Of course," he said. He even gave her a courtly half bow. But as he passed away from us, I could not help but strain up a bit on my toes to see over Mother's shoulder, going up just high enough so that I caught a glimpse of him looking back over his shoulder as though to ensure I was all right.

Was that a *wink* he gave me?

I felt another blush rise.

But when I at last turned back to Mother, her expression was one of amusement, not anger.

I could not help myself. "What is so funny?" I practically snapped, embarrassed.

"I don't know if it is so much that anything is funny," she said. "But you must admit, it is . . . *something*—the way when you first met Kit you disliked him so and yet now that is clearly no longer the case."

"He almost *died*," I pointed out. "Not that I have any other experience of it, but I would *guess* that when people almost *die*, their worth automatically goes up, at least to some *small* degree."

"Of course," she said. "I don't know why that theory never occurred to me before, the idea that death should increase value even of those who have previously annoyed us, but of course I see now that you are right. And it must be even more so when the person in question is someone we *do* care about."

The amusement in her eyes no longer looked as though it was at my expense. Rather, it was expressive of a happy warmth like I hadn't seen in those twin pools of blue in I could not say how long.

"I have no idea what you are talking about," I insisted.

She reached out a hand, touched my lips where Kit had kissed me, where I had touched myself in the startled wake of that kiss.

Again the blush came. That wretched, damning blush.

There was no way she could have missed that coloring of my

cheeks, although there was also no way she could be sure of its significance. But still, mercifully, she failed to comment on it. Instead, with the same hand, she brushed a stray hair back from my forehead, smoothing it away with a mother's benediction.

"Your hair may be a dark cloud," she said, "but no matter what the weather, on your wedding day the sun and stars will shine."

I was shocked. "I am *fourteen!*" I said, at last thoroughly annoyed by everyone and everything. "Why are you talking to me now about my wedding day?"

"Because you won't always be fourteen. Because one day things will change."

• Twenty-two •

I should have known something was wrong right away.

The house was too quiet as I stepped over the threshold.

In the corner of the entryway, the grandfather clock ticked loudly. Later on, remembering, I would think that steady *tick-tock* had a mocking quality to it.

It was nearly a year to the day since Aunt Helen had first come to us.

When I had arisen that morning, early, it had been different from the morning that followed the party for Aunt Helen back in the summer. Rather than a quiet house to myself, Mother, my father, and Aunt Helen were already up and at breakfast, discussing the festivities of the night before. They were pleased that a good time had been had by all. But they were also tired, Mother in particular.

"I'm not feeling myself this morning," she'd said, taking up a cup of tea as she rose. "I think I'll go back to bed for a bit." Before leaving the room she'd stopped long enough to lay a kiss at the top of my head. "You looked beautiful last night, Lucy." Then she leaned down, whispered in my ear, "I love you."

It wasn't so much that it was odd for her to voice her affection, but it was odd for her to do it where others might overhear her.

For answer, I smiled my affection back at her in return.

As Aunt Helen and my father had discussed their immediate plans, I was only half listening. Already, my mind had flown ahead to the park.

Last night, as the Tylers were leaving, Kit had taken advantage of the relative privacy of the adults talking all around us to suggest a New Year's Day rendezvous. Why not meet, he'd said, take a walk in the park, so that we could greet the opening of the new year together?

At the time, when I'd said yes, I'd assumed everyone else would be sleeping when I set out, but such was not the case.

"Be sure to wrap yourself up warm," my father had said when I informed him of my intentions to go for a walk, although I neglected to add whom with.

"Oh, yes," Aunt Helen had added. "We would not want anything to happen to you."

Outside, meeting Kit between our houses, he'd seemed jovial, as though nothing strange had happened between us the night before. I certainly was not going to bring it up. And so we had gone to the park, as we might have done on any other day. Of course, normally we would have been accompanied by others for propriety's sake.

It was almost too cold to be out.

After midnight at some point, a snow had started to fall, was still falling. But it was a slow, soft snow, the kind that covered the grass but melted on the streets. Still, the paths we walked had some ice on them, and Kit put his hand beneath my elbow, steadying me. This was something new.

"What are you doing?" I asked, trying to make a joke of it.

"I just want to keep you from falling," he said, trying to inject a note of jocularity into his own tone.

But it did not feel that way to me.

Everything was the same. Everything was different, changed.

The park was nearly deserted. It was too dangerously cold for nannies to bring babies out. Couples, whom we would normally see promenading, were kept away. The benches were too icy to sit on. And so we strolled the perimeters once, twice, making stabs at jokes or casual conversation, eventually falling into silence.

Everything was the same. Everything was changed, different.

"I suppose," Kit said at last, one deathly quiet hour having succeeded another, "I should get you back home. I do not think your father will thank me if you freeze to death while in my care."

And now I was back home.

Tick-tock. Tick-tock.

I liked to joke that I was the only one in the house who ever answered the door anymore, but this wasn't, strictly speaking, the truth. In fact, whenever I returned home from being out, someone almost always came at the sound of the door opening, at the sound of my booted foot on the marble floor. One servant or another was bound to appear shortly, helping me off with my cloak, hanging that cloak up for me if I had already taken it off myself.

But none came that day.

Tick. Tock. Tick. Tock.

I removed my own cloak, tossed it on the hall bench, removed my gloves, tossed them on top.

I remembered that Mother had said she was going back to bed, but she should have been up by now. And if she wasn't, then I would wake her up.

"Mother! Aunt Helen!" I called cheerfully, wanting some company, wanting something to take my mind off this new strangeness between Kit and me. "Mother! Aunt Helen!" I called again.

But no one answered.

To this day, I don't know why I didn't check the parlors first. Was it some sort of prescience on my part? It is impossible to say.

Whatever the case, whatever my thinking might have been, I did not go to those likely rooms. Instead, I made my way to my father's study, that room I went to least, knocked. Receiving no answer, I turned the knob, pushed the door open, and entered . . .

. . . an empty room.

It was only then that I remembered dimly registering over that morning's breakfast, that for some strange reason seemed an era ago now, my father saying that he would be going out as well; that he saw no reason why he alone should spend the dawn of the new year a slave to a desk. And so he would go out, after he'd breakfasted and dressed, would meet up with some of his friends at their favorite drinking club.

I gently pulled the door closed behind me.

Tick. Tock. Tick. Tock.

Now that I was in the corridor again, I had a sudden urge to run for the front door, to escape . . . I knew not what.

That is silly, I told myself. *Perhaps Mother is still sleeping. Perhaps my father is still out.*

What had Aunt Helen said she would do with the day?

I could not remember.

Tick. Tock. Tick. Tock.

I lifted my skirts, hurried up the stairs—one flight, two—thinking to burst into Mother's bedroom. "Wake up, sleepyhead!" I would say. "If you sleep any longer, you will sleep the whole year away!"

But when I threw open the door, shouted my greeting, she wasn't there.

Nor was Aunt Helen in her own bedroom.

Back down two flights, moving at a slower pace now, thinking, thinking . . .

Near the bottom, near the step I usually sat to listen in on, I picked up speed again. I am not sure now if I was more worried or angry, angry like a child who has been tricked by far bigger and faster children into playing hide-and-go-seek.

Tick-tock, tick-tock.

The front parlor? No.

Tick—

I found them in the back parlor.

At first, I didn't know what I was looking at: all that red, so much red, splattered behind them like a wall of flames.

For the longest moment, I could not take in the size of what I was seeing, had to force myself to narrow my focus on what was right in front of me.

It was Mother and Aunt Helen, lashed side by side to straight-backed chairs, separated by no more than a foot of space.

At first, I thought they must both be dead. All that red, all that red—how could anyone survive it?

The one on the left's head was flung back at an impossible angle, as though it were only hanging on to the body by a thread, a bath of blood drenching the front of her dress.

The one on the right was covered in blood too, but I saw now that this one was merely splattered with it, as though she had been painted in it, not drenched. The one on the right's eyes were open—I saw that now—but they were staring straight ahead as though blind, taking in nothing.

The one on the left was dead—there was no way she could not be—but this one was yet alive.

But which one is it? my mind suddenly, silently screamed. *WHICH ONE?*

Frantically, I looked at their clothes more closely, even the dead one, although I was reluctant to draw nearer. But that was no help, I soon realized. How long had it been, I wondered, since the last time I could definitively say which garment belonged to which twin?

Which one? WHICH ONE?

They looked the same, the same.

It couldn't be Mother, I told myself. It could not be Mother.

Before that moment, I would have said I loved Aunt Helen, greatly, and I would have meant it. But Aunt Helen was not my mother. There was only one woman whom I had ever loved with all my heart and she could not be dead now.

There and then, I begged God in my heart. *Please, God, if one of them has to be dead, please, please let it be Aunt Helen!*

The eyes of the live one had turned, were looking at me now with a puzzled expression in them.

I ran to her, dropped behind her chair, tore at the bonds that still held her wrists crossed so tight it was as though twin streams of rope had been embedded in the delicate skin, scrabbled at the rope with my nails until her hands were at last free. Then I moved around to the front again, looked down at her. *Who was she?*

"Lucy?"

She held out a trembling hand, a hand with much blood on it.

I went to that hand, not knowing whom I was going to, fell at her feet, took that blood-covered hand in both of mine and laid my cheek against it.

It was then, with the back of that sticky hand against my cheek, its copper scent in my nostrils, that I became aware that it was her left hand against my cheek and that there was something else I should have been feeling against my skin and yet didn't.

Gently, I removed that hand from my cheek, studied the back of it as though I expected to find the answer to the mystery of the universe there.

And I did find the answer to the mystery, although it was not the answer I'd wanted. This hand was naked. There was no wedding ring on it.

"Aunt Helen." I spoke the words flatly, having now realized which twin had survived.

She pulled back, startled, withdrew her hand from mine, studied the back of it as I had done.

"What? Where is my ring?" she asked, puzzled.

"Where is *your*—?"

"That's right," she said. "I remember now. *He* took it from me."

I had no idea what she was talking about, but as her eyes searched the room frantically, my eyes followed wherever hers looked.

And then, there it was, halfway across the room: a tiny flash of metal, only a tiny flash because most of the ring was covered with blood.

I raced to it, brought it back to her. Somehow, it seemed important to both of us that she have it back as quickly as possible.

Immediately, she slipped it on her finger, blood and all, looked at it.

"There," she said, looking oddly pleased.

And I was oddly pleased too, seeing that familiar ring there: the symbol of unity made of cobalt blue and diamond, fashioned into the shape of forget-me-nots.

So Mother was alive after all!

But now that she had her ring back, confusion settled over her face again. It was awful to see.

"Lucy?" She placed her other hand against my cheek. "What has happened?"

I followed her eyes as they took in the room around us, the river of blood.

Then I started to scream.

Part III

· Twenty-three ·

No one came.

ticktickticktick

"Where *is* he?" I asked Mother, the urgency in my voice threatening to spill over into hysteria. "Is he still in the house?"

He. Mother had already indicated a man had done this when, referring to her absent ring, she'd said, "*He* took it from me."

"Who?" Mother still looked puzzled.

"The person who did this!"

"No." Still that vacant, perplexed look. "He left." Her eyes were the picture of someone trying to piece together the order of impossible events. A moment ago she had asked me what had happened. Now it was as though she were struggling to return from a faraway place. "That must have been when he dropped the ring. He ran away when first we heard you call out."

This made little sense to me in my own confusion. Would a man who was capable of doing all . . . *this* suddenly run away at the calling out of a mere girl?

And where had he run to? I had not passed him coming in. Had he escaped through the door leading out to the private garden behind my father's study? Had he gone to the kitchen, disturbing Cook and the servants as he escaped through the door back there?

The kitchen . . . the servants . . .

Where were the servants???

Why had they not stopped *this*?

And then my father was there, covered in soot.

I didn't understand anything—nothing made sense anymore. Had the whole world gone mad? Aunt Helen dead, my father's skin darkened as though he had been cleaning out chimneys, the servants nowhere to be found. Had the servants all been slaughtered as well?

Was I dreaming all this? *Please, God,* I prayed, slamming my eyes shut, praying to a deity I did not often think much on, *let these images go away.*

But they would not.

"Lucy, what has happened?" my father demanded of me. Everyone was demanding it of me, it seemed, as though I were the one witness.

As I saw my father's eyes frantically move back and forth between the faces before us—my aunt's dead one, Mother's still living but so changed—I could not help but find it an eerie echo of the first time he saw the two women together, that night so long ago now when my aunt first came to us.

I knew what he was doing. It was what I had done. He was trying to figure out who had died, who had lived.

With a chin nod in the direction of the blood-drenched body, the one with its head thrown back, a mere thin stalk still attaching that head to its lifeless body, I put him out of his misery.

"That one," I said, barely able to look at her, "that is my aunt." I held tight to Mother's frozen fingers. "This is Mother."

I saw his shoulders sag with unmistakable relief.

What an odd feeling for someone to have at such a moment, in the midst of all this carnage: relief. And yet, I knew what he was feeling. I had felt it too, a feeling of such shameful relief that already I knew in a part of my mind that guilt must surely follow—if not today, it would be here tomorrow.

Even Mother looked relieved, if also still confused.

We were all glad—is that even the right word?—that if one had to die, it was Helen.

. . . . .

"Who did this?" my father demanded, striving to keep a gentleness in his tone, but not quite achieving it.

"He was a monster . . ." Mother shuddered.

And then the house began filling up with people.

First the servants straggled in. They, too, were covered with soot. It was all so confusing. Why was the world suddenly covered with soot? One servant screamed, fainting upon seeing the grotesque tableau created by my aunt and Mother. The others were equally shaken, although no one else fainted, and my father prevailed upon the strongest-looking one to go for help. The servant did not want to leave—we had to reassure her repeatedly that her mistress had survived—but did when my father at last shouted at her, "*I* cannot leave my wife like this! *GO!*"

When the servant returned, she had Victoria Tyler and Kit

with her. A few minutes later, John Tyler followed, a constable in tow. And shortly after that, a superintendent, one Chief Inspector Daniels.

Chief Inspector Daniels was a short man, looking like nothing so much as a basketful worth of dinner rolls held together by the occasional bone and some sinew. He seemed as confused by the horror of it all as any of us as he bumbled his way through his instructions to people: telling the servants to stay, then telling them to go to their own quarters of the house accompanied by the constable until he should call for them; asking Mother, after her wrists had been bandaged, if she would like to change out of her blood-spattered garments, then gently requesting she wait; asking my father what part of the house the fire had taken place in and then, not waiting for an answer, sniffing the air and announcing firmly that there had been no fire here.

I was outraged that no one more competent had been sent. Still, I followed as Chief Inspector Daniels led the main family away from the scene of the slaughter.

"Where can we go to talk privately?" he asked my father as we exited the room. "I need to question you and your wife."

"My study?" my father immediately suggested. It struck me as odd that my father, always so definite about everything, should phrase it as an interrogatory and not a clear statement.

"Very well," Chief Inspector Daniels said. He turned to Mr. Tyler. "Go find another constable. Tell him to send for the coroner." Then to Mrs. Tyler and Kit: "Please stay available in the house. I'm sure Mrs. Sexton and the girl will need friends close by afterward."

The last thing I saw before Chief Inspector Daniels shut the door to my father's study was the look of concern on Kit's face. How far we had come since our innocent walk that morning.

No sooner had the door shut, however, than my father issued a gentle command to me.

"Leave us, Lucy," he said. "You must wait outside with Kit and Victoria. I do not want you exposed to any more unpleasantness."

"No." I stood my ground with that one firm word: "No."

I was not going to be banished along with the tearful servants, only to be later served a sanitized version of whatever had transpired. This was my home. This was my world that this had happened in.

My father opened his mouth, no doubt to press his suit, but Chief Inspector Daniels cut him off.

"Your daughter is right, of course, Mr. Sexton," he said. "She was the first to happen upon the scene of the crime. She must stay."

My father, not accustomed to taking orders from others, shut his mouth all the same.

Chief Inspector Daniels took hold of Mother's hand gently, tucking it inside the crook of his arm as he slowly led her to a sofa.

Mother having been seated, Chief Inspector Daniels settled his soft bulk upon the seat right beside her.

"Mrs. Sexton," he said, still holding her hand, "you have had a bad day here today."

I thought, ruefully, that Chief Inspector Daniels was a master of understatement.

As though reading my mind, he amended, "No doubt, this has been the worst day of your life. Be that as it may, I will need all your help in bringing the guilty party or parties to justice. So I must ask you, although it is soon and however painful it may be for you to discuss, what happened here today?"

"There was a man . . ." Mother's voice drifted off.

The silence stretched out long before she continued.

"I was looking out the window in the front parlor, watching the street." There were still falters, but as she spoke, her voice gained a degree of strength. "I was trying to decide whether to go out or stay in when I saw a man come running down the street."

"Did you know him?" Chief Inspector Daniels interrupted.

"No." Mother shook her head vehemently. "I never saw him before today." She paused, visibly seeking to gather more strength. "He ran straight toward our door. A moment later, I heard a knock."

"And you answered the knock?" Chief Inspector Daniels asked. "You didn't wait for a servant?"

"No." Again the head shake. "I was standing right near the door, and there was something about him. His every movement spoke of a great emergency. I thought perhaps an accident had befallen Frederick." Here she looked at my father. "I thought he was bringing bad news."

"So you answered the door," Chief Inspector Daniels said.

"Yes," Mother answered, "and the man said there had been an emergency, only nothing like what I had imagined."

"Oh?"

"He said there had been a bad fire at the Carsons'. He said that it was still raging and he begged the loan of all the servants to help with the bucket brigade."

The Carsons lived in the next street over. Why had Kit and I not noticed the smell of smoke when we returned from our walk in the park? I supposed we were so caught up in thinking of what had transpired between us the night before, caught up in thinking about the changed way things were between us now, all London could have burned and we might not have noticed the conflagration.

"It is true," my father spoke, breaking into my thoughts, breaking the flow of Chief Inspector Daniels's interrogation of Mother. "I saw a shot of flame in the sky as I was returning from my club. When I went to see what was causing it, I came across the fire at the Carsons'. All our servants were already there." He looked down at his soot-stained suit. "I stayed to help them." A horrified look crossed his face. "Perhaps if I had not stopped—"

Chief Inspector Daniels held up his hand to stop my father's words. I suspected he had no patience for self-recriminations, not at this moment.

"So you did send the servants," Chief Inspector Daniels addressed his words to Mother, "as the man requested."

"Yes," Mother said. She looked up at my father, adding dully, "What of the Carsons? Did Elizabeth survive?"

"The house was completely destroyed, but they are both fine," my father reassured her.

"And the man departed with the servants?" Chief Inspector Daniels asked Mother.

"No," Mother said, the puzzled expression returning to her face. "I left him on the doorstep, went back inside the house to give the servants instructions, and they of course left through the back door. When I returned, I saw the servants parading in military fashion up the street below. The man had seemed so urgent, I thought surely he would go back with them. At the very least, I thought he would go knocking on other doors in the street—you know, to raise more help."

"But he didn't."

"No."

"You said you were watching the street when you saw him come running. He never stopped at any of the other houses?"

"No. I suppose I should have thought it strange at the time. He ran right past the Tylers'. I saw him run straight to our door! But I was so immediately worried about the Carsons, it wasn't until the servants departed and he remained behind himself that the first feeling of unease set in."

I suspect the same thought occurred to us all at once: the fire had been deliberately set so that the man could come to our house, drawing the servants away.

"Then what happened?" Chief Inspector Daniels asked.

"The man asked if he could have a drink of water. His skin was covered in soot"—she turned briefly to my father—"as Frederick is now. And I had no servants left to send for the water. He had obviously been helping to put out the fire. How could I deny him?"

Her question was a plea for which no one had an answer.

"I told him I would bring him a glass and to wait there, but as I turned away, I felt an arm grab me tight around the waist, the hand on the other arm drawing a blade close to my throat as I heard the door being kicked shut behind us. 'Where is Helen?' he hissed in my ear."

Mother stopped as though she would not, could not go on.

My father moved behind Mother, placed a protective hand on her shoulder. She flinched at the touch. I supposed it was not surprising, given that the last time a man had approached her from behind a knife had wound up at her throat.

"And where was your sister?" Chief Inspector Daniels asked in a voice so soothing, he might have been a mesmerist.

"H-h-h-helen was in the back parlor," Mother said at last. "But I refused to answer his question!" she added with some degree of pride. "I could tell that if I did, it would not end well."

Mother, I thought with an awful ruefulness, could give Chief Inspector Daniels a run for his money in the field of under-statement.

"He told me he would kill me right where I stood if I did not tell him where she was," Mother said, "and still I did not answer. But then Helen was there. She came out from the back parlor. I could see from the look on her face, she knew him right away. 'Let Aliese go,' she commanded."

"Did she call him by name?" Chief Inspector Daniels asked.

"No, but I wish she had." She looked closely at Chief Inspec-tor Daniels. "That would be valuable information to have, would it not?"

Almost imperceptibly, he nodded.

"It is too bad, then," Mother said, "that I never heard it—not then, not . . . later."

"But the man did not let you go?"

"Oh!" Mother looked surprised that he did not know this, as if we all should have guessed. "He did. Well, that is not exactly how it happened. Helen—you should have seen how brave she was!—told him to let me go, that it was her he really wanted. That's when he told her that if she did everything he asked, I would not die. He told her to lead us to a room that could not be seen from the street, which was how we ended up in the back parlor. Then he directed me to sit in a chair, took a length of rope from his cloak, commanded her to bind my hands behind my back. He told her the instant she ceased to obey him, he would kill me. Helen obeyed. Then he pushed her into the chair beside me, tied her hands behind her back, and then . . . and then . . . and then he slit her throat."

I couldn't help it: I gasped at the suddenness. It was as though, so long as Mother kept telling her story—if she could somehow go on telling it forever—it would not end the way it had ended.

"And then," Mother said, followed by a soft sigh, as though the telling of the tale had been somehow even more awful than the living of it and now she was tired out, "Lucy came home."

"It had to have been someone Helen knew from before," my father said darkly.

"Before what?" Chief Inspector Daniels, still an innocent in the ways of our family, asked.

So my father explained, beginning with the birth of Mother and my aunt, hitting all the high points between then and now, concluding with, "We never met any of the people from her past. We have no way of knowing what lurid things might have existed in that past! The man could have been anybody."

Yes, someone from Aunt Helen's dark and mysterious past— that made sense. But why would anyone want to murder her? And why now?

"What did he look like?" Chief Inspector Daniels asked Mother, a question I wondered at his not asking before this.

"He was the biggest man I'd ever seen," Mother said with a

shudder. "He was incredibly tall, he had red hair, he was hideous. Oh, God." Fear entered her eyes. "What if he comes back?"

Chief Inspector Daniels hastily assured her that this was unlikely, as the house was now full of people, many of whom were officers of the law.

Mother abruptly turned her gaze on my father, anger filling her eyes. "Where were you today?" she demanded. *"Why weren't you here?"* Then her gaze shifted to me, her eyes only slightly less angry. "Where were you?"

That accusatory gaze, that question: it would echo in me for the rest of my life.

A madman could subdue two women easily enough with the threat of a knife. But a madman, even a monster, could not have succeeded had there been four of us there.

Of course the police did search the neighborhood for the man, but he wasn't found. And they asked the servants, the servants who had paraded by our door as Mother stood talking to the strange man, but none of them had noticed him—they had been too busy thinking on the seriousness of their purpose. Nor did any of the others at the fire, including my father, remember such a man—again, they had been too busy trying to put the flames out.

And the only other witness—Aunt Helen—wasn't talking.

• Twenty-four •

It was difficult to believe that our home had been the site of a great party less than twenty-four hours before. People had laughed, eaten, danced, drank—some of us had even kissed. Those had been other people. It had been another world.

My father had said that Mr. Carson would need to spend some of his tightly held fortune to repair their ruined home. Well, it would take a lot more than money to repair the one room that had been damaged in ours. Once the police had completed their investigations there, once my aunt's lifeless body had been taken away for further investigation—a process none of us could bear to watch—my father ordered the back parlor boarded up. Scrub away the stains on the chairs, floor, and walls? Spend money on new furnishings? I doubted enough scrubbing could be done, nor enough money spent to persuade me to ever set foot in that room again. If the room could have been cut neatly away from the rest of the house, like a gangrenous limb sawed off a wounded soldier, it would have suited me perfectly well.

The remainder of that dark day passed in a fog, prelude to a more proper mourning. Mother at last was permitted to change out of her blood-spattered dress, giving it to the police as yet more evidence. A servant from the Carson household, unaware as to what had passed in our household, came with a message of thanks from the Carsons for all the help my father and our servants had provided, further informing my father that the Carsons would be moving to their other home in the country until the one here could be rebuilt—as if any of us cared about that right now. As for the Tylers, they stayed on until late in the afternoon, seeking to distract us from the reminding sounds of policemen scurrying hither and yon, providing comfort when necessary, providing silence when that became even more necessary, urging us all to eat at least a little something. But none of us could eat. Food? Sustenance? What was that now?

Knowing that Kit was in the house did help. From reading books, I knew that some people run from tragedy, fearing that proximity could invite it to spread into contagion, while others race toward it, not from any noble feeling but rather with the joy-tinged excitement of one watching a play enacted upon the stage—it is not real if it is not happening to you.

But there is also a third kind of person who sticks to tragedy in order to see if they can genuinely help, the impulse coming from a generosity of spirit combined with an empathic nature that immediately recognizes that if *they* were to ever find themselves in such straits, this is how they would like the world around them to respond.

Kit belonged to this last group; I think that all the Tylers did, and for this I was grateful.

And yet, I could not keep Kit in my thoughts for very long. I had always been the kind of girl who could think of two things simultaneously: I could hold down my end of a spirited conversation with my father about literature, while planning how best to beat Kit at chess the next time we should meet; I could read a book, taking in the words on the page, while at the same time working through another problem in my mind entirely. But now there were too many things crowding that mind—my shock and sadness about my aunt, my concern for Mother and my relief at her survival, followed hard by my guilt at having wished my aunt the dead one so that Mother might live, not to mention my crushing guilt at having been away from home when the madman came to call. There simply was not any room left for one more thing.

Eventually, as day turned into evening and then night, like spectral figures fading one by one from a house they had mistakenly been haunting, everyone disappeared. The last to go out the door was Kit.

And then we three were alone.

. . . . .

My father cleared his throat.

"Aliese?"

She did not look up at the sound of her own name. So deep was her shock, there had been moments scattered throughout the day where it seemed she did not even know where she was, who she was. She would alternate between offering the Tylers a drink—as if this were an ordinary social occasion!—with these moments of distant staring.

"Mother." I touched her sleeve. "Father is talking to you."

At last she looked up at him, but she did not speak.

"Perhaps we should all go up to bed?" he suggested, adding with a bluff assurance, "Sleep, time—that is what we all need right now."

But even then I sensed that for once my father was wrong about something.

Time could not heal all wounds.

Time, which had already played such a dreadful trick on us— what if we had all stayed home that day? Could what had happened still have happened?—would never heal this.

. . . . .

Alone in my room at last, I was finally able to let grief overwhelm me. Lying on my bed, still fully clothed, I cried as I had never cried before or since.

No one in my world had ever died before. True, Mother's mother had died, but I was small then, and she was not someone in my daily orbit. But this? It was as though one of the stars had been ripped from Orion's belt. The sky would never look the same again.

I now knew that I could lose things—*people*—in a way that I had not known that fact the day before. When Kit caught the typhoid, I had worried, daily, that he might die. But I had never really believed in that possibility, not really, nor had I understood what such a fact would mean.

And now I did.

Sobs racked my body, sobs like giant waves assaulting a beach with so much force they would reset the shoreline, sobs so big it reached the point where I thought they would rend my body in two. And still I could not stop. I did not *want* to stop, for if I stopped, it would be as though I were saying that already the loss meant a little less this minute than it had meant the moment before.

The thing that finally did put an end to my loud show of grief?

The thought entering my brain that I might be so loud I would further disturb Mother. For this, I felt, I had no right.

Biting on to my own hand to keep the sounds from coming out of my body, in the sudden stillness of my room, against that backdrop of silence I could now discern the noises of someone abruptly moving about on the floor above me.

Impatiently brushing away the tears from my face, I rose, went up to investigate.

My parents' bedroom door was shut, but at the end of the hall—in what had formerly been my aunt's room—the door was open, a lamp was lit, the light mockingly blazing good cheer after the gloom of my bedroom.

I blinked against its glare, trying to make sense of what I was seeing.

The woman, dressing gown sashed tightly at the waist, was moving briskly from bed to wardrobe, tossing dresses into boxes that were scattered haphazardly there. The frenzy of activity created the impression of a woman packing for a trip she'd only just been notified she would be taking. Looking at that golden swirl of hair, the hair having been let down for the night, for one moment— for one brief, glorious moment—I believed that I had been granted my earlier wish, that the events of the day had been erased, rendered a bad dream; I believed that I was looking at Aunt Helen again.

Of course I was not.

"I don't understand why your mother feels the need to do this right now."

I turned at the sound of the voice, almost a whisper, saw my father seated in a chair in the corner of the room, legs crossed. He, too, wore his dressing gown.

Mother continued with her movements to and fro, seemingly oblivious of being talked about.

"What is she doing?" I whispered back.

I don't know why I whispered, save that he had done so and it seemed like the proper thing to do, as though we were witnesses to some solemn church service or a one-character scene from a play upon the stage.

"She is packing her sister's things away," he said.

"I am not *packing* them away!" Mother paused long enough to spit out the words with heat. "I am boxing them up. Then I want them all *burned*."

"But surely, Aliese, this can wait until morning? Or even another day?"

She did not respond. Instead, she returned to yanking dresses from the wardrobe, tossing them at the boxes on the bed.

"Your mother is not herself." Wearily, my father rose, placed a hand on my shoulder. "Perhaps you will have better luck at talking some sense into her. I fear that if she goes on like this, she will make herself sick."

And then he was gone.

This was the first time Mother and I had been alone together since I had come upon her and my aunt in the back parlor.

I sat on the edge of the bed, unsure of what to do. Sadness?

Tears? I would have known what to do with those things. I would have held Mother in my arms as though she were the child and I the parent, stroking her hair until there were no tears left to cry. But this? This barely coiled anger of hers? I had no prescription for it. I had never seen Mother like this before.

And then it struck me: As devastated as I was by what had happened, how much worse it must be for Mother. I had lost an aunt. But she had lost a sister, and not just any sister—an identical twin! Surely it must be a loss beyond what anyone who was not a twin could understand. The surviving twin, she must feel incomplete. No. More—it was almost as if Mother had died herself.

Now I felt I *could* fathom her anger. A grief as enormous as hers must be, were she to cry, she really would never stop. And yet the depth of emotion must come out somehow, and so it came out as this. If she could stay angry forever, she would never have to be sad again. There would be no need to accept what had happened.

Still, I could see that my father was right. If Mother kept on at this rate, she would wear herself out. And she would need her strength for what was yet to come: the funeral, seeing her twin put in the ground.

"Will you sit with me, Mother?" I asked softly. "Just for a moment?"

I did not think she would stop for me, her movements had been that hurried, but it was as though my words had let the wind out of her sails as she settled into port, on the edge of the bed beside me.

Reaching out a hand, she tucked a stray hair behind my ear; with a finger, traced the trail of an earlier tear down my cheek.

Then she looked into my eyes as though really seeing me there for the first time.

"You really did love your aunt, didn't you, Lucy?" she said with wonder in her voice.

"Of course I did! Did you ever doubt that?"

"Maybe once." She smiled an odd smile, neither happy nor sad. "When your aunt Martha tried to convince us all that you were secretly jealous of her, I thought perhaps she was right. I thought perhaps you wished she had never come."

"No!" I said. "I was *glad* when she came! And I am . . . I am"—I closed my eyes against the threat of more tears—"I am sorry that she is gone now."

I opened my eyes at the feel of Mother's fingers beneath my chin, tilting my head upward to face her.

"I suppose," she said, "that is as it should be."

Then she rose, returned briskly to her earlier task.

"Father is right," I said, hoping to stop her. Something about the way she was immediately dismantling Aunt Helen's presence from the room—it was unsettling. "This can wait until morning or another day. I will even help you when the time comes."

"No, Lucy." This time, she took the briefest of moments to fold the dress in her arms before dropping it into a box. "I feel I must finish this tonight."

"But don't you want to keep any of it? You and Aunt Helen used to trade clothes so often. Wouldn't you like to keep a few things to remember her by?"

"Only this," she said, removing an item from the very back of the wardrobe and showing it to me.

It was the drab gray dress, the one that Aunt Helen had been wearing when first she came to us. I was surprised Aunt Helen had kept it all this time.

"This is the only reminder I need," Mother said, folding the tattered garment with great gentleness over her arm before regarding the boxes on the bed, a hardness settling over her expression as she added, "The rest will burn."

. . . . .

Much later—Mother having since returned to her room and I to mine—I crept back up the stairs to the third story, crept past my parents' closed door to Aunt Helen's open one at the end of the hallway. I was not sure exactly what I sought: some sort of answer, perhaps? Some clue as to why this awful thing had happened? Maybe I just wanted a few moments alone in the room, surrounded by the scent of her that yet lingered faintly on the air before it disappeared forever.

As I tiptoed into the room, candle in hand, I saw that the doors of the wardrobe were still flung open, and that's when I saw that Mother had left something behind: Aunt Helen's old carpetbag.

I placed my candle in a wall sconce and lifted the carpetbag with great care as though it were some precious and irreplaceable relic destined for the museum. As I set it down on the bed, I felt something shift within it. Opening the carpetbag, I reached inside and extracted a slim volume. It was crude: tattered boards for covers, the pages protruding beyond the borders of the covers as though they'd come loose from the binding, the whole held together with a piece of graying string.

What manner of book was this?

I undid the knot, peeled away the front cover, and saw that I was holding a diary.

Aunt Helen's diary.

My heart began to beat faster with excitement. Aunt Helen had kept a diary! Perhaps there were answers here. Perhaps I would discover the identity of the monster, maybe even uncover a motive.

The scrawled handwriting on the first several pages was as childish as I remembered it from when Aunt Helen first came to us. She had obviously started keeping the diary not many days before she knocked on our door, for the first pages were all filled with her fears and hopes over the prospect of finally meeting her twin. It made my heart ache to see that childish scrawl, those poorly formed letters and poorly spelled words, made my heart ache further still when I came across her impressions upon first meeting me: she had liked me right away, considered me her one true ally here.

Oh, Aunt Helen!

I brushed tears from my eyes and read on, saw the penmanship transform itself, improving as the pages flew past until I reached the entry that had been written on the morning after the joint birthday celebration she'd had with Mother, and I saw that Aunt Helen's handwriting was now indistinguishable from that of her twin. I turned the page, saw nothing. Flipped through the remainder of the diary with increasing speed: more nothing. It was as though, having achieved some sort of imperceptible goal, Aunt Helen had lost the need to record her story.

Immediately, all the excitement I'd felt earlier left me. There had been no mention of people from her past, no mention of monsters. There would be no answers tonight.

Still, after placing the carpetbag back on the floor of the wardrobe, I clutched the diary to my chest. I would take it back to my room, hide it away in my own wardrobe. It had been important to Aunt Helen to keep this diary, despite that it revealed little of import, and so from now on I would keep it for her.

Taking my candle again, I exited the room.

It was as I was creeping past my parents' door that I heard Mother cry out: the sound of someone waking from a nightmare only to discover that the nightmare yet went on.

"The blood!" I heard her cry. "All that blood!"

"There, there, Aliese," I heard my father's more muffled voice soothing her. "It will be all right."

"But what if he comes back?"

"It will be all right."

"The blood! Did you see it all?"

Unwilling to eavesdrop any longer on Mother's pain and my father's inadequate efforts to comfort her—how could there ever be enough comfort in the world after such a thing?—I tiptoed on.

There were, I was certain now, more nightmares in our future.

. . . . .

At breakfast the next morning we were no more hungry than we had been the night before.

Everything—toast, eggs, even tea—sat untouched.

Another thing had not changed: Mother's barely contained anger.

"I wish," she informed my father, "that when Helen's body is returned to us, she should lie in state in the ballroom for two days before the funeral."

"Well"—my father stumbled over his words—"that is not the usual . . . that is to say . . ."

I knew what he meant. Aunt Helen having been neither the master nor the mistress of the household, it would be peculiar to accord her such an honor now.

"I do not *care* what is the usual!" Mother shouted at him. "Do you think I care for that now? My sister—let me repeat, *my sister*—was never given what she should have been in life. Let her at least have it now, *in death*."

Mother looked so guilty as she spoke her angry words. It occurred to me then that just as I felt guilty for being relieved it was Aunt Helen who had died instead, Mother felt guilty for having been the one who had survived. No doubt, in her mind, life had always dealt more kindly with her than it had with her twin, was doing it still in death. And so, if she could not erase the unfair past, she would at least grant her sister parity now.

It was my father's turn to feel guilty; over what, I could not say. Perhaps he also felt bad about his relief that it was Aunt Helen who had died.

"Of course, dear," my father said, his cheeks coloring. "I only meant—"

A servant entered.

"Chief Inspector Daniels is here to see you," she said.

"Please," my father said, "send him in."

And then that man, with all his rolls of soft fat, was among us again.

After the briefest of preambles, stating that he hoped we had been able to sleep the night before, he announced:

"I'm afraid the medical examiner turned up some shocking evidence when he was examining Miss Smythe's body."

Shocking evidence? What could possible be more shocking than what had gone on already?

"Were any of you aware," he asked, studying each of us in turn until his gaze finally rested upon Mother, "that Miss Smythe was pregnant?"

· Twenty-five ·

"Herbert *Dean*?" my father said in shocked, scathing response to Mother's suggestion after Chief Inspector Daniels had departed, after we had all recovered as best we could from this latest shocking revelation.

"Who else could it be?" Mother countered, eyeing my father coolly. "Who else could the father possibly be? He was the man she spent time with most frequently, was he not?"

My father considered this, yet another blush coloring his cheeks. It was so strange. I did not recall my father ever blushing over anything before Aunt Helen's death. Now he did it all the time. "Who else, indeed?" he said at last. Then he shrugged. "I suppose it does not matter now, does it, who the father was? The child will never be born."

I wondered at the coldness in his response.

"And you knew nothing of this?" my father asked Mother.

She looked surprised at his question, offended almost. "Of course I knew."

"You . . . ?" He was stunned.

"We are, *were* sisters, after all."

"And when were you planning on telling *me*?"

To this, Mother said nothing.

It occurred to me then: if Herbert Dean had been aware of Aunt Helen's condition, perhaps he had arranged for her murder in order to avoid the scandal that would no doubt attach itself to an unmarried woman being with child?

But then, just as swiftly, I rejected that notion. Herbert Dean had loved Aunt Helen. Had he known, he would have married her.

· · · · ·

That night I awoke to sounds coming from upstairs. I had heard similar sounds when I was younger, but much softer than this. I had not known what they were back then, and it had been a long time since they had disturbed the night, but I had since come to realize that they were caused by the act between a man and a woman that Aunt Helen had once described to me. These sounds, though—they were so loud, almost violent, like two people at war with each other, so different from anything I'd ever heard before.

My house was changing.

· · · · ·

My grandparents, my father's parents, were the first to arrive.

Mother and I were dressed in black merino wool, my father in a black suit, as we greeted them outside the ballroom. In a perverse re-creation of the night we had introduced Aunt Helen to the people of our world, we were all gathering again, only this time it was to begin the process of saying good-bye to her.

"I am sorry for your loss," my grandmother said to Mother, but I saw no evidence that she understood the weight of the occasion.

"I suppose," my grandfather said, "this would be more difficult if you had known her your whole life."

"Please go inside," my father said with an abrupt gesture of the hand, barely able to contain his outrage at their lack of sensitivity.

Aunt Martha came next.

"Aliese," she said, stumbling up the stairs with her cane. I had no idea now if she really needed it, nor did I care. "I wanted to come as soon as I heard."

Aunt Martha held her arms out to Mother.

"You never liked her," Mother said, taking a step back.

"Oh, Aliese." Were those tears I saw in Aunt Martha's eyes? Whatever she was feeling, whatever she felt she had a *right* to feel, she swallowed it. Perhaps she recognized that now, of all times, she had no rights at all here. With a heavy sigh, she continued. "You are correct, of course," she admitted. "I was worried about you. I was worried about *my family*." The tears were back now. "But you cannot possibly believe that I ever wanted *this*!"

She held out her arms again.

This time Mother consented to the embrace, but as Aunt Martha's arms closed around her I saw her recoil.

Mary Williams, Mrs. Carson.

The former's brightness of spirit could not lighten that day for me. As for the latter, having returned without her husband for this sad occasion, well, as far as I was concerned, she might just as well have saved her condolences.

The Tylers.

John Tyler shook my father's hand with great feeling, while Victoria Tyler embraced Mother as if they might be as close as sisters.

Kit stood before me, hands carefully clasped in front of him, as did I. I should have liked to grasp on to one of those hands for strength, but we among all those in our families could not touch, not here, not with everyone looking.

"I was sorry the other day," Kit said simply, "and I am still sorry. I shall be sorry about all this for the rest of my life."

In a universe turned vastly imperfect, it was the perfect thing to say.

"Thank you," was all I could say in reply. As he passed into the ballroom with his parents, I saw for the first time that he was now taller than his tall father. When had that happened? I wondered dimly. Really, my Kit was practically a man.

· · · · ·

The casket, black-painted oak with silver handles, was set up on its shallow platform in the center of the room, on a spot I imagined as being the very spot upon which I had seen Aunt Helen dancing, merrily spinning away the hot July night—how long ago was it now? Could it only have been a half a year?

Aunt Helen had been washed and dressed by hands that did not know her. The undertaker had measured her body, crafting the coffin by hand, returning to our home with it under cover of darkness. I wondered at the delicacy. If we did not see him arrive, would she be any less dead?

I approached the casket.

The upper portion was open, but a blanket had been placed over Aunt Helen's body up to her chin—I supposed however great the undertaker's artistry, he could do nothing about that grave wound.

I stole a glance at Aunt Helen's face.

There was a book I had read once where a mother lost her child. Viewing his body, she'd exclaimed, "Ooh, look! He looks so peaceful! It is as though he is merely sleeping!" What a simpleton. A dead body, I now learned, did not look like it was sleeping. There was no mistaking Aunt Helen's deadness now. Nor did she look peaceful.

Standing there, I could not shake the feeling that I was looking at Mother, that this is what *she* would look like dead. But I forced that grim imagining from my mind. Mother would *not* look like this dead. Mother would not die, pray God, for a very long time.

That night, when I retired to my bedroom early, sleep refused to come. All I could think through that long night and the next was of that coffin with Aunt Helen in it, lying dead in the ballroom.

· · · · ·

The day of the funeral dawned brittle as broken glass, the coldest day so far that year. It was as though the frozen fingers of Milton's hell, where Satan had been encased in a block of ice so he could not move, were reaching up through the earth, seeking to drag us all downward.

Breakfast, as can be imagined, was a somber affair. None of us, I don't think, had managed more than a few morsels since the unspeakable events of a few days before.

Mother looked at my father across the table, then she pushed the plate of toast toward him, the jam too.

"Eat, Frederick," she said. "Just because I have completely lost my appetite, it does not mean you should not indulge yours."

He was hesitant at first, but he was, in the end, a man. We women were used to subsisting on not very much, so that our stays might close around our waists, but my father could not continue on so little.

At last, he took a nibble of toast, and then another. Then some bacon. Then some eggs.

My father did not usually have seconds of anything—drink was more his habit. But when he had cleaned the first plate, Mother urged seconds upon him.

He ate them.

. . . . .

The bell tolled.

"I cannot believe my sister is dead," Mother said as she entered the church, supported on either side by my father and myself.

Mother looked around the interior of the church, stunned, as though seeing it for the very first time.

I cannot say that her reaction surprised me. Given all that had changed in the world, it was continually surprising how much of it remained the same. Stone buildings? The post coming through the mail slot? Strangers making noise in the street? None of it stopped for death, no matter how much one might feel that it should.

We had followed on foot, walking between the tracks created

by the hearse carriage, the vehicle itself drawn creakingly on by black-plumed horses. Our friends, walking behind us, carried flowers—not for their beauty but rather, as was the custom, to mask the odor of any unpleasant smells that might arise.

The vicar, Mr. Thomason, was still ancient, still gnarled. As he took his place at the altar, I could not help but think, *Why should one so old get to go on living when my aunt—so young!—was dead?*

"We are gathered here today," Mr. Thomason intoned, "to bid farewell to a woman we knew all too briefly . . ."

You did not know her at all—I could not prevent the thought from forming. That day, I was so bitter, it was as though my mouth had been stuffed full of dandelion greens, my ears stopped up with almonds; despite the flowers all around me, horseradish dripped from my nose. *You only met her that one time you came to the house, when you told her she should keep her name because it reminded you of Helen of Troy.*

It was true.

Aunt Helen had never set foot in the church. After her introduction to our society, it seemed natural that she would then accompany us every Sunday. But she never had, despite Mother's entreaties.

"God and I have always known exactly where we stand with each other," she would say. I could never tell if her words truly scandalized Mother or if they filled her with the same giddy feeling at hearing the utterance of such blasphemy as they filled me. "I do not see that stepping inside *a church* will do anything to further clarify that relationship."

The church was filled with our family, our friends. With the exception of us and the kindly Tylers, I thought bitterly, they were not Aunt Helen's family, not her friends.

Directly behind me sat Kit. I did not turn to look at him. It was enough to know that he was there.

"I cannot believe my sister is dead," Mother said again, this time in a hushed whisper.

And I cannot believe she is here! I thought. How ironic she would find all this, I thought: Aunt Helen was at last attending church. How uncomfortable it all would make her. The dirgelike quality of the hymns, the pretentiousness of the liturgy—she would have hated it all.

At the very least, she would have laughed at it.

As for those stained-glass windows, depicting scenes of biblical agony with little redemption, they were the stuff of nightmares.

· · · · ·

The earth was so cold, the gravedigger's spade broke against its impenetrable hardness, and we had to wait for a replacement to be fetched. As we waited, I could not escape the feeling that the woman in that box did not want to be buried.

Don't bury me, I imagined her whispering in my ear, using the crude accent that had characterized her speech when first she came to us.

I do not want to, I whispered back inside my mind.

Don't forget me.

I never will.

We kept up our silent dialogue—her entreaties, my

reassurances of faithfulness—until the hole in the ground was completed and the first clod of earth struck the top of the casket.

. . . . .

That night, deep in the night, again unable to sleep, I thought I heard a noise coming from downstairs. Making my way through the quiet house, I found Mother on the sofa before the front window. She was in the same position I had been once, very long ago, as Aunt Helen and I had kneeled on the cushions side by side, elbows propped up against the back of the sofa, watching my parents depart for an evening out.

On that night, I had asked her about her previous life in the workhouse. She had given the briefest of answers, referencing the obvious awfulness of the place. At the time I had not pressed for further answers—like how she had ever found us—and now I would never have them.

"What are you looking at, Mother?" I asked her, startling her into turning half around.

"The street," she answered, looking back out at it. She had the look of a caged bird trying to peek out at the greater world. I supposed that made sense: the extended period of mourning we were about to embark on would curtail our normal life; not that, under the circumstances, we would mind.

Still, it was odd, I thought. What was there to see out there in the cold blackness?

"Come," she said, turning fully around, patting the cushion beside her. "Sit with me. If neither of us can sleep, we might as well do it together."

After all that had happened, I could no longer count myself a child, not in the sense I used to be. And yet, sitting close to her like that, I felt all the anger and bitterness leave my body as I sagged against her, as though I were a child half my age who had exhausted herself, playing too long at the park.

"Here," she said, putting her arm around me, so that now my head rested between her neck and breast.

There was something I suddenly wanted desperately to know.

"Do you think she found any happiness here?" I asked Mother.

She brushed my hair with her fingers and soothed my brow. Then she waited until I looked up, until our eyes met.

"If I am certain of nothing else in this life, I am certain of this," she said. "*You* made her happy."

· Twenty-six ·

Time had one more trick to play on us: it marched on.

We all began to eat again, to sleep.

The black crepe bunting was removed from the ballroom; the black sheets covering all the mirrors were taken down. People talked, sometimes not even trying to keep to whispered tones, although no one laughed, not yet. Some days, the sun even shone through from behind the gray white clouds of the late winter sky. The back parlor had not been reopened, but I now realized that, in time, it would be; we could not live in a house with one room eternally boarded up—it would be too big of a reminder, somehow worse than it already was. Unless we were to move to a new home, and no one was suggesting that, then we would need to remodel the room. One day, it would need to be opened again.

There was one thing that had changed, drastically: the relationship between Mother and me. Before, when Aunt Helen had first arrived, we had needed to expand to accommodate another;

and now we needed to contract again to fill in the vacancy she had left.

It was awkward.

One morning over breakfast, hoping to bridge that space between us, I suggested we go for a walk together in the park.

"I am not sure that it is yet—," my father began.

"Is yet *what*, Frederick?" Mother demanded, pushing the serving plate toward him.

Mother still ate little, and yet I had noticed that she went on urging more food on my father at every mealtime and that he, after all she had been through and thus perhaps hoping to please her in at least this one small thing, accepted it. My father had been the same size for as long as I had known him, but already he had needed to call in the tailor to be measured for new trousers. At night now, he drank more too. It was as though something was troubling him—more than just the obvious—but what that something was, I could not say.

"I only *meant*—," my father began.

"I think it is a fine idea." Mother turned to me as if he had not spoken. "If I stay in this house another minute, I shall go mad."

. . . . .

This was the first time either of us had been out of the house since the funeral, save to go to church, and it felt good. True, late winter's icy fingers still sought to freeze us within her grasp, but it was bracing in a curiously pleasant way, as though so long as we could keep alive in the cold, the freedom was good.

This was also the first opportunity since the funeral that I had had to properly observe people outside of our own circle of acquaintance, and I jumped at the chance. All the way to the park, I swiveled my head to and fro, searching, searching.

And once we were at the park? I continued my searches.

That man slouched in the corner of that bench? Even with him sitting down, I could see he was too short.

That man over by the tree? Too skinny.

Those three men entering together just now? Blond, blond, and blond, and therefore wrong, wrong, and wrong—I was not looking for blonds.

"Lucy, what *are* you doing?" Mother asked me. "Ever since we left the house, your head keeps bouncing all over like a ball!"

Despite the cold, my cheeks flushed hot.

"I am searching," I admitted haltingly, "for the man who murdered Aunt Helen."

I would not have imagined that Mother could laugh at anything having to do with that tragic event, but laugh she did.

"And you think you will find him in *the park*? You think that, a citywide manhunt involving every policeman in London having failed to turn him up, *you* will now stumble upon him here?"

I knew it was foolish. Even before her scathing utterances, I had known it. But, still, I had to try.

Apart from the funeral, this was the first time I had really been out of the house since . . . *that day*, and the man could be anywhere!

"He has no doubt fled the country by now," Mother said, as though responding to my unspoken words. "Only a madman would remain behind after what he did."

Her words were bluff and blunt, but it sounded as though she was trying to convince herself of our safety as much as she was trying to convince me. I knew she still had nightmares that the monster would come back, still heard her scream out about the blood at times in the night.

"Lucy?"

The speaker was not Mother.

It was a tall man.

I had been looking for a tall man, had I not? But I had been looking for a monster with red hair. This tall man did not have red hair. Rather, he had thick black hair peeking out beneath his hat, dark eyes too.

"Mr. Brockburn!" I could not prevent the joy at the sight of him from entering my voice. It had been a long time since I had seen him last and in a world gone dark, the sight of him was an unexpected bright light.

"Lucy!" he exclaimed again, taking my gloved hands in his, spreading our joined hands wide. "Let me look at you! You have changed so much!"

I blushed at the attention. "I hope you have been well, sir, since . . . since you left us," I hastily added, not wanting to say "since you were dismissed."

"Oh?" he said vaguely. "Oh, yes."

I had noticed that not once while we were talking did he glance at Mother beside me, nor did she try to speak to him. It was as though, for some reason, he was avoiding her.

At last he turned to her, tipping his hat with a grand nervousness.

"Miss Smythe," he said with a bow, "I cannot tell you how happy it makes me to see you again."

I felt her stiffen beside me. Mother had been inside the house for so long, her face was practically the color of paper, but at the sound of Mr. Brockburn's words, I saw her blanch further still.

Well, who could blame her? If it had been shocking to be mistaken for a twin before, it would be doubly shocking after the murder.

"Miss Smythe," he repeated again warmly when she did not immediately respond, holding out a hand as though he wished to clasp on to hers.

"Mrs. Sexton," Mother corrected, drawing back from him.

"What?"

"I am not Miss Smythe," she declared with hauteur.

"But of course you are," he said, confused. "At least . . . when I first saw you . . ."

"Aunt Helen is dead." I delivered the news as gently as I could, placing my hand softly on his sleeve. "She was murdered this past January."

"But that is not possible!" he cried. "How could such a thing happen?"

"Did you not read about it?" I said. "It was in all the papers."

He shook his head in confusion, shock. "I was in Italy," he said. "After your father dismissed me, I took a position with a family who was traveling there and have only returned to London this past week."

"I am sorry, then," I said, "to be the one who had to tell you."

"No," he said, regaining his manners, despite his own obvious devastation at the news. "It is I who am sorry. This must all have been so dreadful for you." He stood back, for the first time taking in our black mourning garments, recognizing them for what they were.

"I am so very sorry," he said again. "Lucy." He tipped his hat at Mother. "Mrs. Sexton. I shall leave you to your walk."

I watched him stride away, slowly at first, then more briskly, as though leaving something behind him.

Somehow I was sure that I would never see him again.

"Well, Lucy," Mother intruded upon my thoughts, "what shall we do now? Are you going to continue trying to locate the murderer?"

I could not remember Mother ever having been so... sardonic before, but I supposed I was going to have to get used to it. What had happened to our family had changed each one of us, Mother most of all.

. . . . .

In truth, I *did* plan to continue trying to locate the murderer.

If all London gave up looking for the guilty party, I never would.

Not only that, but exercising my mind was the greatest antidote I knew to crushing sadness.

"Father!" I banged on the door to his study as soon as we arrived home, turning the knob without even waiting for a response.

"Yes?" my father said, seeing me.

He was seated at his desk, working, a large glass filled with whiskey off to one side. It seemed to me that it was early in the day for that, but it was not for me to say.

"Do you have any books of detective fiction?" I asked with a breathless eagerness. "I do not have any among my books in the schoolroom and I wish to read one. Really, I should like to read as many as possible."

"An odd request," he said. Still, he rose from his desk, scanned the titles in his bookshelves.

"Here," he said at last, holding out a volume to me.

The title read *The Experiences of a Lady Detective*. The author? Andrew Forrester.

"Oh, yes," I said, with the first real excitement I had felt in a long time as I grabbed on to the book with both hands. "This is *exactly* what I wanted!"

"There are seven cases collected in there," he said, "each one solved by a character named Mrs. Gladden. Mrs. Gladden has a most unusual sense of evidence." He chuckled. "An expert at interpreting boot marks, she says that more men have been hanged because of boot marks than because of any other evidence in the world. Indeed, she advises the criminal who would succeed to bring an extra pair of boots along for just such a purpose."

I liked that the detective was a woman. It was wonderful to think of a woman being able to do such a thing when the women I knew were mostly adept at needlepoint, gossip, and singing in church.

"Do you think that is true?" I asked.

Perhaps if I searched London for the biggest boot marks I could find, I would find her killer.

"I do not know," my father said. "I suppose it would be nice if it were." He looked at me more closely. "Why the sudden interest in detective novels?" he asked.

I thought to lie, not wishing to be laughed at again as Mother had laughed at me. Still, I took the chance.

"I want to learn the art of detection," I said, straightening my spine to show that I would not be mocked. "The professional detectives have failed to solve the mystery of Aunt Helen's death. Perhaps if I gain greater knowledge concerning how a person goes about the process of solving crimes, I can figure it out for myself." I could not stop myself from adding, "I will not rest until he is caught!"

But my father did not mock me, as I had feared. Rather, he reached out a hand, stroked his finger against my cheek. He was so close, I could smell the strong whiskey on his breath.

"You are a good girl, Lucy," he said with a wondering sadness. "Aren't you?"

. . . . .

As it turned out, Mrs. Gladden was quite a talented amateur detective, solving all seven of her cases when the police could not. Indeed, Mrs. Gladden clearly regarded the constabulary as being less competent at solving crimes than her dog.

From where I was sitting, I could not say that I blamed her.

. . . . .

MURDERER
APPREHENDED!!!

The headlines blared a week later.

The article went on to say that the monstrous red-haired giant had been seen coming out of a pub in one of the seedier

parts of the city. He was so drunk, so huge, it had taken six officers to subdue him sufficiently enough to take him into custody.

"Fine," the story quoted the murderer as saying, "I confess. I
did it!"

"You would think," my father said, throwing aside the paper
in disgust, "that we would have been notified first, rather than
stumbling upon the information like *this*!"

No sooner did he speak than there was a knock at the door,
followed by a servant leading in Chief Inspector Daniels.

Immediately, he took in the discarded newspaper on the
breakfast table.

"I am terribly sorry," he said, sounding sincere. "I would have
liked to be the first to tell you of these latest developments, but I
am sure that, being a man of great literary talent, you know how
these mere newspaper hacks are. One was in the pub at the time
of the arrest and apparently felt no scruples about publishing
the story before the family was notified."

My father was hardly mollified at this. "I am only glad," he
said haughtily, "that you have finally caught him, that justice will
be served at last."

"I wish to see him with my own eyes," Mother said abruptly,
rising from the table.

"Dear!" my father said. "Do you think that is wise? It would
only upset you!"

"Your wife should identify him," Chief Inspector Daniels
said, "even though the man fits the description she gave perfectly and he has already confessed."

"He killed my sister." Mother addressed my father with steel.
"What more reason do I need?"

"I will get my coat then," my father said, starting to rise.

"No." Mother stopped him with a word. "I must do this myself."

. . . . .

An hour later, Chief Inspector Daniels accompanied Mother back home again.

Immediately, my father was out of his chair. "Are you all right, dear?"

"I am going to lie down now," Mother said vaguely, heading upstairs.

"What happened?" my father demanded once Mother's footsteps had safely retreated out of hearing distance.

For once, Chief Inspector Daniels looked perplexed.

"We let the prisoner go," he said simply.

"You *what*?" my father practically shouted, forgetting the need for silence.

"We had to." Chief Inspector Daniels shrugged. "When we showed your wife the prisoner, one Paul Peter, she was outraged. Well, why wouldn't she be? He had, after all, murdered her sister. But then when we asked her, for mere formality sake, if this was the man who murdered Miss Smythe, she opened her mouth, started to say 'y—,' hesitated and then shook her head no. 'No,' she said. 'This is most definitely *not* the man who killed my sister.'"

"But the man confessed!" my father said.

"Yes," Chief Inspector Daniels said. "Yes, I know. So I sent Mrs. Sexton into the other room and asked him about that. He said he had simply been drunk and tired of getting beaten up by the constables. He said it was easier to confess than resist. We would have liked to keep him, if only on general principle, but Mrs. Sexton was so adamant and she was the only witness to the crime."

"So you let him go," my father said.

"We had no choice."

• Twenty-seven •

"I wanted so badly to have someone else to blame for what happened," Mother said the next day. "And when I first saw this Paul Peter, I half convinced myself that he *was* the one." Her expression showed real regret as she sighed. "But then I was forced to admit he was not. And I could not allow someone else to hang for a crime he did not commit, however much I might want *someone* to hang."

. . . . .

And then Aunt Martha came back.

Well, strictly speaking, she had never been away.

She had gone on accompanying us to church every Sunday, coming back to the house afterward for Sunday dinner. It was near the end of one of those dinners that Aunt Martha, with a rare nervous clearing of the throat, pled her case.

"I have been thinking," she said, addressing her words directly to my father. She paused, cleared her throat one more time before starting again. "I have been thinking that it would be best for everyone concerned if I were to move back in here again... permanently."

The startled look on Mother's face revealed that as far as she was concerned, the only person such an arrangement would be "best" for was Aunt Martha.

"Oh?" My father raised his eyebrows as he lifted the glass before him to his lips, draining the last of the wine.

Aunt Martha colored. It occurred to me that when she had planned this, she hadn't anticipated having to explain the logic behind her reasoning to her own brother, despite how things had ended the last time she'd sought to live with us permanently.

"It is just that all that has happened has put such a strain on poor Aliese. If I were here, I could help her with the managing of the household. And," Aunt Martha continued, "there is Lucy to consider. She is getting older. Do you not think it would benefit her to have the example of *two* proper women to guide her on her own road to womanhood?"

She did not add, but we all knew, that the prime motivation behind this was her desire to escape her own parents.

"I realize that you and Aliese do not go out in the evening now, while she is in mourning, but the time will come when you will return to society. At that time, again, would it not be good in the evenings to have a woman here with Lucy who is not a servant?"

Mother had said nothing through all this.

"And, Frederick, I am getting older." Here I thought Aunt Martha looked her most sincere, wistful too.

Aunt Martha's great distinctive nimbus of hair had thinned

and lightened from its graying black, so that now it was a mere wispy cirrus of white, all threat of storm removed.

"Indeed," Aunt Martha continued, "some days, I do not feel as though there are very many years remaining to me. I should like to spend what is left with my own brother, friend of my youth."

Based on my father's wistful expression, it was obvious that he too was imagining simpler times.

It is odd to try to picture one's own parents as having been children once. Mother, whenever I tried to envision her thus, I could just make out a glimpse of a golden-haired child chasing jewel-colored butterflies on an emerald lawn somewhere. But my father? I had only ever seen him in my mind as a properly suited gentleman . . . even when he was wearing his dressing gown! And Aunt Martha, well, even in my earliest memories of her, she had always seemed so much older than my parents. But now I pictured the two of them, Aunt Martha and my father, as being yet younger than I was now. It was a curiously happy picture: a dark-haired girl, even a *pretty* dark-haired girl, sternly cautioning her bare-kneed younger brother not to be so loud in church, then bending down to whisper with a mischievous smile, "If you can only sit still for five more minutes, once we are out of here I will play a great game with you. You will enjoy it." Flash of merry dark eyes. "There will be *worms* involved."

"I will not be any trouble," Aunt Martha hastily added now. "I only want to help out. If there is something I do that you do not like, you need only ask me to stop, and I will do so immediately."

"What do you think, Aliese?" my father asked Mother.

It struck me as odd that my father would ask Mother such a question publicly, but then it occurred to me that after the debacle of Aunt Martha's previous stay with us, he wanted all such matters to be carried out in the open, however embarrassing they might be for some parties. I suspected he was tired of being positioned between the two women.

It was obvious what Mother thought. She thought it to be a horrendous idea. And who could blame her? Although she had seemed to forgive Aunt Martha when she reluctantly submitted to an embrace on the day of Aunt Helen's lying in state, I had seen the recoil. I knew she had not truly forgiven her, not in her heart. Not to mention, just as I had resented ancient Mr. Thomason for going on living when Aunt Helen was dead, so must Mother resent that my father's sister went on living while hers was in the ground, being eaten by worms.

Still, Aunt Martha was being so supplicating, she was practically *begging* to be allowed in, that it would have taken the hardest heart in the world to deny her one last chance.

The hardest heart in the world? Despite what had happened to her, the changes I saw in her—the abruptness she often exhibited since Aunt Helen's murder, particularly when she addressed my father; the anger that seemed to ever lurk beneath her formerly placid surface—that was not Mother.

"And you will not ask for the bedroom to be redecorated again?" Mother said at last, turning to Aunt Martha.

When Aunt Helen was still alive, Aunt Martha had once asked me what had happened to her old bedroom here after Aunt Helen inherited it. I had described it to her in detail, only to have her respond with outrage, "It sounds as though that woman has turned my tasteful room into a bawdy house!"

Now all she said was a meek, "I am sure it will be fine."

"Very well," Mother said. Then she turned a warning look upon my father. "We can *try* it."

"Now that that is settled," my father said, patting his growing waistband, "I think I shall retire to my garden for a cigar."

My father had never been a smoker before. But Mother, having recently seen a sketch of a gentleman smoking a cigar in one of the newspapers, had decided that my father would look handsome with one in his hand and had further taken it upon herself to order him a box.

He had taken to them, you might say, like a house on fire.

· · · · ·

I was fifteen, I was sixteen.

And Kit was now eighteen.

I had long since given up searching passersby whenever I was outside of the house, hoping for a sighting of the red-haired man, finally admitting to myself that Mother was right: a man so noticeable, he had no doubt fled the country. I still believed that one day I would find him, or at the very least get to the bottom of the mystery, but that this would not be accomplished by hoping to stumble upon him in the park.

Aunt Martha had kept to her word. She never sought to redecorate Aunt Helen's old bedroom, she did not try to prevail upon us to have all our meals served one hour earlier as she had the last time she lived with us; she made no trouble at all.

Indeed, there was something that was somehow sad about seeing a woman who formerly had such strength of personality reduced to the cautious peepings of a mouse.

But no matter how much Aunt Martha tried to please Mother,

it was obvious Mother only tolerated her but did not like her, nor would she even sit and do needlepoint with her as had been their habit together once upon a time. The needle, the thread, the constant stitching—Mother now claimed that it all gave her a headache.

And so it fell to me to sit with Aunt Martha whenever she timidly asked me to, engaging in an activity that I myself found odious.

In truth, were it not for the needlepoint part of it, I would not have minded these tête-à-têtes so much. Not wanting to offend Mother, Aunt Martha was almost as obsequious with me, and it was good, as she had said, to have another grown woman in the house to ask about certain things.

In the time since Aunt Helen's murder, Kit and I had continued in our friendship. More, we had continued, albeit cautiously, in our explorings of each other. It did not happen often, but occasionally we would meet in the tunnel where we could talk and kiss, sometimes a little . . . more. And when I was alone in my room at night, I saw his face.

When I was younger, I had not felt the difference in our ages very much—perhaps because I had insisted on viewing him as "that bored boy." But now that I was sixteen and he was eighteen, with him very much focused on what he might do in the greater world, I did feel it. He really was a man now, while my family at times still infuriatingly regarded me as a girl. And, I must confess, the subject of love was on my mind.

I wanted to know how a person knew that was what they were feeling. Were a racing pulse and rapid heartbeat when in the presence of the object symptoms? I did not want to open myself up to ridicule. But I did want to know more about love, like, say, how you knew the object was the person you wanted to one day marry.

"Did you ever consider getting married, Aunt Martha?" I asked coyly as we stitched together.

When I was younger, I had taken Aunt Martha's spinsterhood for granted—after all, when you are a child you do not question those kinds of things. Rather, you simply think, if you think about it at all, *This is the way this is*, because it had always been that way. But now that I was older, I did wonder because, frankly, it was odd for a woman from a family of wealth to have never been married.

"There once was a boy," Aunt Martha said, not looking up as she stitched away.

This sounded promising. "Yes?" I encouraged, hoping that the eagerness, easily misinterpreted as nosiness, did not show in my voice.

"Oh, yes." Reflective pause. "He was a very handsome boy."

"What was his name?"

"Alfred."

"And how old was he?"

"Eighteen."

"And you were . . . ?"

She looked at me sharply. "You are not writing an *article* for the *newspaper*, are you?"

"Oh, no," I said, cursing the blush that betrayed me when what I was trying to do was convey an air of innocence. "No, no, no." I shrugged, still striving for nonchalance. "I was merely curious."

Aunt Martha surprised me by laughing. "I was just teasing you, dear." Aunt Martha teasing? This really was a new Aunt Martha! "It is only natural," she said, commencing to stitch again, "for you to become curious about such things at your age. Yes, Alfred was eighteen and I was the same. I thought we were the perfect match. He did, as well."

"Then what happened?" I asked, puzzled, no longer able to hide my great interest in this topic. I could not understand it. If they had *loved* each other, if they had been *perfect* together, why had they never married? Had he fallen ill? Had an accident? Went off to a war? Had he *died* somehow?

"My father said Alfred did not have enough money," Aunt Martha said with the slightest of shrugs, as if it no longer mattered. "His family, you see, was not as wealthy as ours. Almost, but not quite. And my father did not approve of this."

"But if you wanted to marry, how could he stop you?"

"How little you know, Lucy. My father," she said, "refused to provide me with a dowry if I persisted in my intentions to marry the man I wanted to marry."

"But I don't understand! Why did you listen? You have already said that this . . . *Alfred* had money—why could you have not married without a dowry?"

"Because Alfred's father would not permit him to. He said that, despite the fact that his family could afford me, if my own father would not endow me with a dowry, he could not possibly believe that I was worth anything."

"That is awful! What did Alfred do?"

"Oh, he obeyed his father. His father threatened to disinherit him if he did not, so what choice did he have?"

It seemed to me that there was always a choice, in everything, unless someone was holding a knife to your throat, even if that choice was not an easy one.

But Aunt Martha did not see it this way.

"Our parents disapproved," she said, "and we could not possibly disobey them."

"How . . . tragic!" I said. "Did you ever see him again?"

"Oh, yes. When I still lived at home, I used to see him in the village all the time . . . him and his wife."

So he had married while she had not.

She leaned closer, speaking in a conspiratorial voice. "But I had my revenge on my parents."

"Oh? How is that?"

"After they sent Alfred away, they did want me to marry someone, almost *anyone* so long as that person had enough money. But no matter whom they brought before me, I shook my head no. I have stayed a spinster all these years, you see, to devil them. And, if I may say so, I have done a good job."

Knowing what I knew, that they drove her equally crazy, I did not see that this was entirely true.

"Was that the only reason?" I asked. "You have refused to get married, all your life, merely to devil your parents?"

"No, that is not the only reason."

"Well, then?" I persisted.

She settled back into the sofa.

"I never again," she said, "found someone to love."

• Twenty-eight •

The Carsons' home had at last been rebuilt, but Mrs. Carson would never live in it again. On the day they were to move back, Mrs. Carson had taken the unprecedented step—for her—of suddenly dying. In the aftermath, Mr. Carson declared himself to be tired of London, placing the house on the market and returning to reside in the country permanently.

When you are very young, you imagine that no one you know will ever die, and that death, when it occurs, happens to other people in books and in far-off places. But once that first significant death occurs, as it had for me with Aunt Helen, you realize that more people will follow until everyone you know has died or you have died yourself.

I cannot say that Mrs. Carson's passing brought a tear to my eye, as it did to Aunt Martha's, but I marked it off in my mind as a further shrinking of my already small world, one less person to know.

It was good, then, that Mrs. Carson's passing also heralded

an increase: a family with the last name of Clarence purchased the Carsons' rebuilt house in the next street. It was a large family, consisting of the usual mother and father, in addition to which were four daughters—Dora, Flora, Ivy, and Julia, all younger than me—and a fifth sister, Minerva, seventeen, her age placing her directly between Kit and me.

Minerva Clarence was a tall colt of a girl with flaxen hair streaming down her shapely back, her eyes the color of violets in shade. Indeed, we were so dissimilar in appearance that the first time I stood next to her I felt myself dwarfed, like a common building forced to coexist side by side with a toweringly beautiful church spire.

I had never really felt compelled to compare myself to any other girl before, did not like the experience, wondered if what I felt was something akin to what Aunt Helen had when first standing beside Mother.

Mother and I had called on the Clarences in order to welcome them to the neighborhood. Mother later said we should have written, notifying them of our intentions first, for when we arrived the house was in chaos.

"I do not *wish* to have a bath today!" Dora, the youngest at four, was shrieking.

"But you have to," Flora, two years older, said, "elsewise you will stink up our bedroom."

"It is Wednesday," Ivy, the eight-year-old, said. "You always take your bath on Wednesdays."

"It is not Wednesday yet!" Dora said. "It is still Tuesday!"

"It is not Tuesday or Wednesday," ten-year-old Julia said. "It is already Thursday, which is why you stink so much."

It was in fact Wednesday, something the others could not persuade tiny Dora of as they chased her around the parlor. I could see where the child did need a bath, should have had one the day before, because her honey-colored hair was so straggly it looked like there might be twigs settling in to form a nest, her grimy hands leaving prints on the furniture she grabbed on to as she raced to avoid capture, her rosy cheeks stippled with various bits of dried food.

"I really should have had five boys instead of five girls," Mrs. Clarence said as though she'd had some choice in the matter, causing me to wonder if she truly understood how procreation worked. "Boys are so much more civilized." But she laughed when she said it, as though oblivious that her household was any different from anyone else's.

"What profession does your husband pursue?" Mother asked politely.

"Oh? Do you mean Gerald?" Mrs. Clarence asked, as though there might be someone else to whom Mother was referring. "He is a judge."

As I sought to keep the teacup that was balanced in my lap from spilling when Dora leaped over the back of the sofa from behind me, Minerva made her first entrance.

She was like an angel.

"Dora, you little urchin," she said, her syllables tinkling like good-natured Christmas bells, "what are you playing at now?" She stopped at the sight of her mother's visitors. "Oh, hello," she said to me, blushing when she realized she had failed to greet Mother first. With an embarrassed curtsy, she did so, before turning back to me.

This was the part where I made the mistake of standing, sitting right back down again when I saw how she towered over me. Already I sensed that she was not someone I wanted to find myself compared to by others, not ever.

"It will be so nice to have you close by," Minerva said in a sunny voice, once it was explained who we were and where we lived. "The place we used to live, there weren't any girls even close to my age." She smiled ruefully at her four young sisters. "Only these lot."

"What day is it, Minerva?" Dora asked. In the few minutes since Minerva had entered, Flora, Ivy, and Julia had succeeded in wrestling Dora to the ground, where they now sat on various parts of her body. "Julia says that it is Thursday, but I am fairly certain we have not finished with Tuesday yet."

"It is Wednesday," Minerva authoritatively announced, as though she'd been personally responsible for ordering the days of the week. Then she laughingly unearthed Dora's body from beneath the others, tickling the younger girl's stomach until she laughed before throwing her over her shoulder like a sack of wheat. "If you do not take your bath this very second, I shall declare it Wednesday every day from now on, and I don't think you will like that."

"Oh, no! Not that!" Dora shrieked as Flora, Ivy, and Julia crowded after them as though wanting to make certain that the grimy little thing wound up in the tub. "Not that! Never that!"

But I could tell Dora didn't mind. I could tell that, once Minerva came into the picture, she was happy to do anything her oldest sister wanted her to do, so long as they could be together.

For myself, I was not sure how I felt at the prospect of this Minerva living so close by.

"I do not know what I would do without Minerva to help out with the children," Mrs. Clarence despaired to Mother, and even I could see that she'd be lost without her, as she clearly had no idea how to rule her own family. "Nor do I know how we will ever find five husbands for our daughters," Mrs. Clarence further despaired. "At least in your case, you only have to find a husband for one."

· · · · ·

When the Clarences returned the courtesy, calling on us the following Wednesday, we already had other visitors: Victoria and Kit Tyler. And, of course, Aunt Martha. Aunt Martha's cane could always be heard thumping its way into the parlor whenever anyone came to call.

Unlike the other day, the younger Clarences were now all neat as pins, even Dora, with every hair in place, and with solemn faces as though they were about to be baptized.

"Now remember what I said, girls," I heard Minerva whisper as everyone took seats, "no speaking unless spoken to and do not take anything unless it is offered to you."

This last proved a problem for Dora when, having enjoyed the first fairy cake she was offered, she reached for a second.

"Dora!" Minerva admonished. "Put that back right this second!"

"Oh, it is quite all right," Aunt Martha said, nudging the plate toward Dora in an uncharacteristic move; usually, Aunt Martha liked to keep the fairy cakes close to herself. "It is good to see a girl with appetite. Why, around here, no one ever seems to eat very much except for my brother."

And yourself, I thought uncharitably.

"But it is good of you to mind the manners of your little sisters," Aunt Martha went on. "So many young people these days—all they do is think about themselves."

"Oh, Minerva is always thinking of the well-being of others," Mrs. Clarence said. "One day, she will no doubt make some lucky man a wonderful wife."

Minerva did not look embarrassed, as I would have done at such obvious pushing on a mother's part. Rather, she continued with her ministrations to her four sisters as though she did not mind being talked about in the slightest.

"Lucy, fetch me my needlepoint," Aunt Martha said. "My fingers feel so stiff today and that always seems to help them."

"Oh, what a pretty piece that is!" Minerva observed when I had brought the required object.

"Do you do needlepoint?" Aunt Martha asked.

"My stitches are not as fine as yours." Minerva blushed. "But I do love it."

It was all I could do not to roll my eyes. From the look on Mother's face, she was tempted as well.

"Here," Aunt Martha offered, holding out the canvas and needle. "Why don't you try a few stitches?"

"Oh, I couldn't, Miss Sexton," Minerva said, only accepting the items when it became apparent that resistance was futile.

And so the next five minutes passed, the room in a complete state of hushed silence as the others watched Minerva stitch away.

"You stitch beautifully," Aunt Martha observed at last. "Your mother is right: a girl with your accomplishments, you *will* make some lucky man a fine wife."

Minerva blushed again, prettily.

I glanced at Kit to see what he was making of all this nonsense, but I could not catch his eye.

"I say," he said, "I don't think I've ever quite understood the charms of needlepoint before, but this is beautiful. It makes me wish I could ply a needle."

I was disgusted. It was one thing for Kit to be polite to the new neighbors, but this was really taking things too far.

"Come on, Kit," I said. "Why don't we play a game of chess while the others continue doing . . . *this*?"

"But that would be rude," he said. "And besides, I am enjoying watching Miss Clarence stitch."

Miss Clarence.

"Fine." It was hard not to grit my teeth when I said it. "Then I shall get my sketchbook."

And so, as the others sat in a circle around Minerva, watching her work as though it were the most fascinating thing that had ever happened in the history of the world, I sat in my corner drawing the object of their attention.

. . . . .

"She seems like such a fine girl, does she not?" Kit said, at last joining me. "She is so sweet. And the way she looks out for her younger sisters, it makes me wish *I* came from a bigger family."

I did not say anything.

"Is something troubling you?" he asked, as though suddenly seeing me for the first time. "You are not yourself today."

"I am not the only one," I muttered under my breath.

"Come again?"

So many people did not seem themselves to me all of a sudden, and that included Kit and myself. I was not used to seeing him pay attentions to another girl, and so raptly, was not used to feeling such strong stirrings of jealousy within my heart.

But I could not tell him any of that, so instead I settled for:

"Does it ever strike you that Mother is not as Mother used to be, before Aunt Helen died?"

Kit shrugged. "I suppose that is to be expected, is it not? She has suffered an enormous loss, been witness to the most violent of crimes. I cannot see how that could *not* change a person."

"I suppose," I reluctantly conceded. "But sometimes, it is as though she is not even herself."

"How do you mean?" he asked, then he laughed. "Who else could she be?"

I merely shook my head. To this, I had no answer.

Kit waited patiently, as though he knew I was not finished with this subject yet. Of all the people in the world, Kit knew me so well.

"And then there is the way she is with others," I went on, "the way she is with my father now—not to mention the way he looks at her sometimes, as though he does not know her anymore or is made uncomfortable by her somehow. Even the way she is with me! Sometimes, when she looks at me, I do not know how to describe it, but it is not the way I've ever seen her look at me before."

"Her world has changed, Lucy," he said calmly, "and the eyes with which she sees that world have naturally had to change accordingly."

God! Sometimes his reasonableness was maddening!

But I would not give up, not even in the face of evidence, of reason.

"And then there is *both* she and my father! You would think they would be more interested in finding Aunt Helen's killer, you would think that at the very least they would be encouraging the police to continue searching! Why don't they?" I held up a hand, stopping him before the words could come out of his already open mouth. "I know what you will say. You will say that a man of such a noticeable appearance, a monster, he would have been found by now if he was still in London. You will say that it has been a year and a half, and he must be long gone. That is what they all say. That is what I tell myself. But the fact of the matter is, *he is still out there*! He murdered my aunt. He is still a threat, so long as he is still alive and free, he could still come back someday . . . and yet no one else seems to care!"

Kit's eyes narrowed. "What are you trying to say, Lucy?"

I shook my head, as though waking myself from a fever dream.

"I don't even know myself," I said at last. "I only know that something is not right."

He looked at me then as though he would save me if he could, if only he knew how.

But not knowing how, and with me giving him no help in that regard, he did what others often do when tense conversation meets with a dead end: he changed the subject.

"What are you drawing?" he asked, coming to stand behind my shoulder, taking in the picture I had drawn: the body was equine, with four long legs and a swishing tail, while I had placed, where the horse's head should be, the profile of our most honored guest.

"That is uncharacteristically uncharitable of you, Lucy." The disappointment was clear in his eyes. "You have married Miss Clarence's head to the body of an animal! *I* happen to think it will be jolly to have her as a neighbor."

"Then if you think *that*," I seethed, "why don't you go back there with all the rest? I am sure that any minute now she will stitch the greatest stitch that anyone has ever seen."

I did not have to ask him twice.

With Kit gone, and disgusted with myself over what I recognized to be my own jealousy, I flipped the page and began a fresh one. This time, I sought to render Mother's image as she sat across the room.

But however much I worked at it, somehow, the resulting picture reminded me more of Aunt Helen.

· Twenty-nine ·

Whatever designs Mrs. Clarence might have had on her eldest daughter's behalf where Kit was concerned—and I was certain she did have them—they were not to be. At least not yet.

Kit had elected to join the military.

To be specific, he was to be an officer in the Second Life Guards.

"What are you talking about?" I said when he first told me. "No one can buy a commission anymore—my father told me this—and you have not even been to military academy yet."

"In truth, I have," Kit said proudly.

"What are you talking about now?" I said, growing unease and alarm coming out as impatient anger in my tone.

"I have been at Sandhurst."

"No, you have not," I insisted. "You have been here!"

"Have I?"

"Of course. I have seen you!"

"But have you seen me as much?" Before I could object further, he went on. "A year ago, I sat for the entrance examination and passed. In the twelve months since, I have been training at the Royal Military College in Sandhurst as a cadet in order to earn my commission. You should be proud of me, Lucy: I have earned it."

"How is this possible? I would have noticed if you were away for a whole year!"

"Of course you would have. Or, at least I like to think so." He laughed. "But I have been home sometimes for weekends, for the whole of the summer holiday, for breaks at Christmas and Easter. Really, I have not been away all that much more than I was when I was at school."

I could not believe this. Important things had been going on in the world around me and I had remained unaware.

"How could you have kept such a secret from me?" I demanded. "Why did you not tell me sooner?"

"Because I did not want to see the disappointment in your eyes if I failed in my goal."

"Disappointment?" I was stunned at this more than any-thing else. "I could never—"

"As an officer with the Second Life Guards," he went on with excitement, "I shall be part of the heavy camel regiment known as the Camel Corps."

"You are going to ride a *camel*?" I said, disturbed at a situation that was fast spinning out of my power to control it. If I could raise enough objections, if only I could shout loud enough, he would never go away. "I don't recall ever having even seen you ride a *horse*!"

"I used to ride very well," he said, adding with an infuriating show of equanimity, "Not camels, of course, but certainly horses."

"If you like horses so much, why did you ever stop? You know, you could stay here and ride horses again. You do not need to go away to ride camels."

"I stopped riding horses," he said, flushing with shame, "because even after I recovered from the typhoid, Mother would not allow it and Father agreed with her."

"So start riding again!" I said. "You are eighteen now! What can they do to stop you?"

But he merely shook his head.

Of course I now saw the source of all this sudden . . . military fervor. Having been treated like a child by his parents during the years since his illness, he now wanted to acquit himself as a man. He wanted to prove, once and for all, that he was not the frail and sickly thing his parents, his mother in particular, took him to be.

"Where will you go with your . . . camels?" I said.

I don't know why, but for some reason, the camels in particular nettled me.

"To Egypt," he said simply.

"You are going to ride *camels* in—"

And so we went on, with me expressing outrage at what I saw as his whimsical decision, while he parried my outraged utterances with a reasonable calm that made me want to slap him.

"Your mother must be devastated," I said.

"She is," Kit allowed, "and for that I am sorry. But she has had a year to grow accustomed to the idea, and I will not change my mind."

"And what does your father say?"

"That he had thought I would attend university and then follow him into the law."

"I must say, your father's plans for you sound more sensible to me than your plans for yourself."

"He thought so too. But when he saw that I would not be moved, he accepted it. He even came along when I went to have my uniform fitted." His eyes lit up. "You should see it, Lucy! The tan tunic and breeches—I suppose that is so we blend in with the desert; the boots; the hat. The hat actually looks like a hat for playing polo."

"No doubt it is too big for you. It probably comes down half over your eyes. Oh, no!" I put a palm against my cheek in mock horror. "With that big hat, how will you ever find your camel?"

But Kit ignored my sarcasm.

"And we are given this band of bullets to wear across our chest," he said excitedly, illustrating how it would drape his body from shoulder to waist.

"Be careful that you do not shoot yourself," I said dryly, but again my words had no impact, not even when I added, "And for God's sakes, don't shoot your own camel!"

We carried on that way right up until the night before his departure.

In the dead of night, as Kit had bade me do so, I met him in the tunnel.

"I cannot say good-bye to you properly in the daylight," he'd said, "not with everyone else looking on."

"Have you come to your senses yet?" I asked now, neatly side-stepping his grasp as he sought to embrace me. "You know, it is not too late. You could still resign your commission."

"Of course it is too late!" For the first time, he showed

exasperation with me. "There would be great dishonor in backing down now."

"*Dishonor*," I echoed the word disdainfully. "A word no doubt invented by some *man*."

"Do not pretend you do not care about honor, Lucy." His words were soft again now, dangerously soft, so much so that I feared that if he went on in this vein I might shed tears in front of him. "I know you better than that," he continued. "You would fight to the death over a matter of honor."

"Ohhh . . . you think you know me." I folded my arms tight against my chest.

"Better than anybody." He put his hands on my forearms, gently tried to tug the armor of them away from my chest, but I would not let him. "And you me."

"You are just saying that," I said, refusing to relent. It was a trick I had learned from Mother after the death of Aunt Helen: so long as I stayed angry, I would never have to be sad. "No doubt, as soon as you leave me here, you will go to meet Minerva Clarence in some . . . clandestine tunnel too. You will whisper pretty words to her about honor and . . . and . . . and . . ." I could not find a word I felt as contemptuous about, having already overused "camels," and so at last I settled lamely on, "*Helmets*."

"Silly Lucy." He traced a fingertip like a feather from my temple to my chin. "We have so little time remaining. Why do you insist on spending it all on nonsense, fighting over trivial things? I *like* Minerva Clarence—"

There! He had confessed!

"—but I *like* her in the way you like any nice person. You must admit, in a world filled with complicated people, it is a relief to occasionally meet someone who is exactly as they seem: nice, sweet."

"If you think she is so nice, then . . . if you think she is so sweet—"

"Oh, shut up, Lucy," he said, pulling me to him, crushing his lips to mine.

Kit had kissed me before, more times than I could now count, but even our first magnetic kiss in the tunnel had not been like this. The room spun away from me, my knees threatened to give way beneath me and would have done so had his arms not been so strong around my waist, his tight grip telling me he did not want to let me go, not then, not ever. I think now I felt so dizzy, so weakened, because I feared losing him so much. A world without Kit? Might as well tear down the sun as well. The world would not need it again.

He broke away first. Had it been up to me, that kiss would never have ended.

"You will look in on Mother for me from time to time, won't you?" he said. "I hate to think of her being lonely."

I promised that I would.

"And you will write me? For I will write you every day, or at least as often as I can, and it would be crushing if you did not write me back."

I promised that too.

"Be *proud* of me, Lucy. Your high regard matters more to me than I think you know."

"If you want me to be proud," I said, tears at last filling my eyes, so that the image of him swam before me like an image of something already fading away, "then you must promise me not to *die*, for if you *die*, it will be very hard for you to know that I am proud."

"I shall try, Lucy," he promised. "I will do my best."

. . . . .

The next morning, I rose early to see him off with his family.

We stood beside the carriage that was to take him away from us, the horses stamping their impatience.

Do not hurry time, I silently begged as the dawn mist circled all around us, so thick it was impossible to see the end of the road. *Only speed up again once he is away, and then hurry him back to me.*

"This is a fine adventure you are embarking upon." John Tyler's voice was cheerful as he clapped Kit on the shoulder, but he did not fool me. "And when you return, there will be time enough for us to see to your finishing your studies and entering into the law."

"I look forward to that day, Father." Kit returned the manly shoulder clap.

Men, I thought. Why did they not simply embrace? It was so obvious they wanted to.

"Now, you must remember to eat regular meals," Victoria Tyler cautioned.

"Of course," Kit said with a patient geniality as she threw herself at him.

I would not manfully clap him on the shoulder, nor would I hurl myself at him. I would maintain my calm, I would hoe the middle row, I would—

"Books!" I shouted at him, incipient panic sneaking up my spine. "Books! I had set aside some wonderful ones for you to take with you! If you just wait I will go back and—"

He grabbed on to my hand, then raised our joined fists to my lips, the back of his knuckle gently stopping my words—the fact that his parents were standing in full view of us be damned.

"It is all right, Lucy," he said. Then he laughed gently, patted his bag. "I have already packed a few of my own. So you see, when I am not busy shooting myself or my *camel*, my time will be gainfully filled."

On another day, I would have had my revenge on him for mocking me. But instead, I tilted my chin upward proudly, as he would want me to, and witnessed him toss his bag into the carriage, pulling himself up afterward.

And then he was gone, disappearing into the mist.

· · · · ·

"You saw Kit off?"

My father's words startled me as I entered the house, sagging back against the door I'd just closed. It had taken all that was in me not to collapse in the road.

"You are awake early," I said.

Either that or he had not gone to bed yet, I thought. Sometimes now, my father drank so much and so late into the night, it must be difficult for him, I thought, to know where one day ended and the next began.

But no, I saw now. He did not think it was still night. He had on his dressing gown, so he must know that it was morning.

"I was worried about you," my father said. "I know how close you and Kit are. He is your friend. I did not want you to be alone when you came back."

"Kit is not *just* my friend, Father," I said. "He is my *only* friend."

"Oh, Lucy."

I fell into his open arms, allowing him to hold me while I cried.

· Thirty ·

"I am not sure of this, Aliese," I heard my father say.

"Oh, really?"

"Yes, really. I do not think it is a good idea."

"Then that is too bad, because *I* think it is an *excellent* idea. What's more, your sister happens to agree with me."

Since when I entered the room they ceased talking—my father departing for his study, while Mother said she had many letters to write and that she'd best get started—I returned to my reading.

I had persuaded my father to purchase for me a subscription to the *Boy's Own Paper*. I had not told him why I wanted the weekly publication, but it was so that I could learn more about a life I would never have the opportunity to live: the life Kit had lived, being away at school.

I cannot say that I was very impressed with what I read. Still, it was rather thrilling, all the same: boys lived in such a different world than I did, a world where boarding schools and wars were almost regarded as one and the same. When Kit had been here, I could fancy we lived in the same world, but now I had to face the fact that that was not the case, now that he had gone away.

"And are you feeling more *Christian* yet?" my father inquired, interrupting my reading.

"Pardon me?"

"*Boy's Own Paper*. Did you not notice? It is published by the Religious Tract Society. No doubt, it is not only meant to encourage you to read, but it is also intended to instill Christian morals in you." That last time he said "Christian," he rolled the word pompously, wiggling his eyebrows at the same time and causing me to laugh.

"I do not know if it is making me more moral." I giggled. "But now at least I know that when five hundred boys are gathered in one place, it is likely that mayhem will ensue."

"I would like to see just what it is that you have persuaded me to purchase for your reading matter," he said with a mock seriousness.

He held out his hand for the paper, and I handed it to him, looked on as he perused it with amusement.

"Father, what were you and Mother discussing earlier?"

"What are you talking about?"

"I heard you say that you thought something was a bad idea and then she said it was a good idea. What was all that about?"

"Oh. That." He had sobered instantly. "That you shall have to take up with her."

. . . . .

But when I asked Mother, she would not tell me. All that she would say was that we were to have a party for which Mrs. Wiggins had been commissioned to make me a new gown.

"What party?" I asked. "What is the occasion?"

But Mother would not say.

When the gown was delivered, I saw that it was a rich satin, royal purple in color.

"Try it on!" Mother urged me.

I did so, standing in front of the long looking glass in her room to take in the effect. But as I studied my profile, first the left and then the right, fists boldly placed on hips, I did not see a young woman in formal dress.

"What do you think I would look like in tan?" I asked absently.

I was envisioning myself in a tan tunic and breeches, high boots polished to a shine, a long braid of bullets cascading across my chest. The picture in my mind made me think that I would make a fine officer, although I could not see myself ever killing anyone.

"*Tan?*" Mother's tone was exasperated. "What are you talking about, Lucy? No girl wears *tan* to a ball!"

· · · · ·

I was late to the party.

Having grown tired of *Boy's Own Life*, I had taken up *Treasure Island*, finding Mr. Stevenson's tale of buccaneers and buried gold to be more to my present taste. I at least had my gown on already, but I was lying on my stomach crosswise upon my bed and had just passed the part where Jim's father dies, when a servant came to remind me that my presence was required.

Hurriedly straightening the creases I had created in the skirts of the gown, I hastened to the ballroom only to find the space already filled up with people.

The only person close to my own age that I recognized there was Minerva Clarence. But there were at least a dozen young men, scattered amongst the adults, I didn't recognize at all.

"Who *are* all these boys?" I asked Mother, having located her.

"Don't you recognize any of them?" She looked surprised. "They are family to our friends, friends to our friends."

"No," I said. "I have never seen any of them in my life."

"Surely you must know him." With a slight jut of the chin, so as not to rudely point, she indicated a blond boy standing in the corner. He looked amiable enough, but he was a sloucher. "That is Mary Williams's nephew, James."

"If I had met any nephews of Mary Williams, I am certain I would remember it."

"Oh? Then how about him?" Another chin jut. "Alistair Roman's much younger cousin, Arthur."

Arthur Roman had dark sideburns so thick, they looked like they might be part of a theatrical costume, and a chin that looked like he used it for a chisel.

"I do not know him either."

Nor did I know Bertram, Cecil, Cyril, Edward, Ernest, Garnett, Harry, Ransom, Thomas, or Victor, although Mother took great pains to detail for me their connections to various adults there.

"It is wonderful to know the lineage of everyone present," I said, unable to mask my sarcasm, "but what I don't understand is why they are all here in the first—"

But I did not get to finish asking my question, because someone had tapped tentatively on my shoulder.

I turned to find that the tentative tapper had been James Williams, who was now bowing down low.

"Miss Sexton? I wonder if I might have the pleasure of this dance?"

James Williams was not half so good a dancer as Kit, and I could feel the sweat of his palm bleed through the fabric of my dress, but it did feel nice to be whirled around the ballroom. At the very least, it was good exercise. And when he stepped on my toes, I tried not to let the grimace show on my face.

"I say," he said, "this is a rather lively tune. I always think that if there must be music, let it at least be lively."

"Yes," I could not help but agree, if only to have something to say. "That does sound like a good policy."

No sooner did I finish dancing with James than Arthur Roman came to tap on my shoulder.

"Have you read any good books lately?" I asked, hoping to have a more fruitful conversation than my last one as he slowly waltzed me around as though the only shape one could dance in was a very small box.

"Books? Hmm." Arthur Roman cleared his throat, eyes on his own feet, the tip of his tongue protruding between his lips whenever he was not speaking. "I try never to read books unless I absolutely have to."

When Thomas—or was it Victor?—came to tap on my shoulder next, I did not even try to engage him in fulfilling conversation, only answering his feeble queries with monosyllables as I bided my time, waiting for the music to end.

Despite more young men asking me to dance, I pleaded the need to eat. Alongside the buffet that had been set up, I found Minerva Clarence, tapping her dainty little foot in time to the music.

"Do your parents always throw parties like this," she asked, "with so many young men?"

"Not in memory," I said wryly, helping myself to a plate of food I did not want before one of the young men I'd just refused could ask me to dance again.

"I had the devil of a time getting away," Minerva said, her cheery tone belying the frustration in her words. "Dora would not go to sleep until I finally promised to bring her back a treat. Do you think your parents will object if I take her one of the little cakes?"

I pictured her in her pretty aquamarine gown, borrowing a linen napkin in which she'd wrapped a tiny sliver of cake to take home to her youngest sister; or better yet, concealing it in the satin folds of her skirts, not minding if the icing ruined her gown. I was forced to admit, grudgingly, that Kit was right: she was indeed a nice girl.

"No." I shook my head. "I am certain they will not mind."

"So many young men here," she said again, delightedly, as though we were surveying the treats upon the table.

But none of them are the right young man, I thought.

"That one with the bristly dark mustache," she said. "He is handsome, is he not?"

I could not recall if the one she was indicating was called Cecil or Cyril, nor did I much care.

"If you think *that*," I said, moving on, "then you are welcome to him."

"I do think that it is going well, Martha, don't you?" I heard Mother ask as I came up behind her.

"Oh, yes," Aunt Martha said. "It is exactly as—" Then she caught sight of me over Mother's shoulder and reddened, scurrying away as best a person could scurry away with a cane.

"Mother, what is going on? And why are not the Tylers here tonight? At least if Mrs. Tyler were here, I might ask her if she has received any letters yet from Kit."

"Kit," she said. "You always talk of Kit." She looked sour, but then her eyes suddenly glittered with satisfaction. "You cannot tell me you are not having a good time. I am sure I saw you dancing every dance. It certainly looked to me as though you were enjoying yourself."

"It does not matter if I was enjoying the *dancing*!" I said. And then it hit me. "The Tylers not being here—there was a deliberate decision *not* to invite them, wasn't there?"

"Well, I don't know about *deliberate*." She looked flustered now. "But I did think it would be more enjoyable for you to meet some new young men if they were not present."

"You *thought*?"

"Why, yes. Aunt Martha and I both agreed, what with Kit gone now, it would be a welcome diversion, that it would be good for you to enlarge your social circle."

"But I don't want *a diversion*! I don't want to *enlarge my social circle*!"

"Lucy." Her whisper might have been a shouted command. "Lower your voice, this instant." Her expression softened, taking on an almost begging quality. "You must be reasonable, Lucy. Kit is gone now, and it may be years before he comes back. I do not want to be the one to say so, but it is entirely possible that he may *never* come back."

I did not understand it, did not recognize this Mother.

Why had she changed so? Why had her relationship to *me* changed so? She never would have dismissed Kit's importance in my life so cavalierly before, as if one person could just as easily be replaced with another, as if *he* could ever be replaced. She had met and married my father almost immediately when she was not much older than I was now. Could anything have dissuaded her from that path, that love? I liked to think not. And yet, apparently, she thought that as soon as Kit was removed from the picture, out of the country, I should be content to move on. It was almost as though she did not want him to come back, I thought wildly. It was almost, my mind raced yet more wildly still, as though she wanted me to meet someone else quickly, so that *I* might sooner be gone.

I had never been so angry with her in my life.

"He will come back," I said, willing tears of anger and fear not to spring to my eyes, not in front of her, not now, not here. "He *will* come back."

· Thirty-one ·

At last—at long last!—letters from Kit began to arrive.

It was too bad, then, that the first one opened:

Dear Minerva . . .

"What is he doing writing to you?" I demanded when she came by the house to show me the letter that had come to her.

She looked perplexed at my question, perplexed at my anger too, causing her to respond with the counterinterrogatory, "Because, before he went away, he said he would?"

"Yes," I pressed, "but why is he writing to you *first*? I don't believe even his mother has received a letter yet!"

She looked puzzled by this as well. "Perhaps because *C* comes before *S* and *T* in the alphabet? You know, Clarence does come before Sexton and Tyler."

"What kind of schooling did you receive?" I raised my eyebrow witheringly at her, a gesture I had learned from Mother.

Of late, I had noticed Mother using that gesture increasingly on my father whenever she found something he said to be in some way lacking.

"I am quite certain, Minerva, that however mail delivery is determined, it is *not* alphabetically."

"Then I don't know—"

"Oh, will you please be quiet so that I can read this letter!"

> It is very hot here, although the camels do not seem to mind it. With twenty-some-odd officers and over four hundred men in our regiment, making for nearly five hundred of us, it almost feels like being at school again!
>
> How is your fine mother? And how are your sisters? On particularly hot days here, I picture you trying to herd Dora, Flora, Ivy, and Julia in from a sudden downfall with Dora always refusing to come in out of the rain so that everyone else becomes drenched as they chase her about. Odd, but the vision of other people as cool and wet has become my own personal oasis here.
>
> Wishing this finds you well,
>
> Kit

"He does not say much, does he?" I thrust the letter back at her. "The heat? Well, anyone with a sense of geography could have guessed at that. And he appears to have become obsessed with water. But other than that? It does not really tell us anything."

"It tells us that he is alive," Minerva observed stoutly. "At least each letter one of us receives does tell us that."

· · · · ·

Dear Lucy,

Let me say first: Egypt is NOT England! (And here I hear your voice in my head, "But Kit, why did you have to go all the way to Africa to learn that? I could have told you—I read about it in a book!" I will endeavor to ignore that voice, at least when it hectors and lectures me, although I do hear your voice, often; in fact, I hear it all the time.) Back home, there were sodden months when I longed for just a peek at the sun. Well, let me tell you, I have now acquired what I wished for. Do you think I might exchange it yet again? To say that it is hot here is an understatement. And that sun? When you are out in it, there is nowhere to hide. I see now why the ancients worshipped it as a deity. That celestial orb is a relentless god, burning all who would get too close.

What is the weather like in England now? Many is the moment when I wish I had listened to you, when I wish I had gone to Oxford

instead, where I might get soaked by the rain
while reading Homer in the yard.

Missing your hectoring
and lecturing,

Kit

. . . . .

Dear Lucy,

   Imagine my surprise. I send you a heartfelt
letter, and what do I get in return? A brief
missive saying that if you wanted a report on the
weather, I could save myself the trouble of writing
because you would get that information from my
letters to Minerva.
   Dearest Lucy, why must you always be so . . .
INSANE? You do not feel that I tell you
enough? If more than I would ever tell anyone
else, could tell anyone else, is the only thing for
it, then you shall have everything.
   I hate it here. Our ultimate objective, I have
learned, still a long way off, is to cross the
Bayuda Desert from Korti to Metemma. (Do not
expect me to draw a map for you here. If you
wish to know where I am talking about, you may
consult your globe.) Once there, we are to position
a force close to Khartoum. Its purpose? To

reinforce it while we wait for the remainder of the British army to make its way up the Nile. We have guns, we have ammunition, we have native drivers to help with the camels.

The camels!

Now here is something I suspect you do not know, despite all your opinions about camels: the camel is quite adept at desert travel, but he is no horse. Rather, he is as slow as a donkey, nor can he be mounted or dismounted from with ease. This means that once we come to the battle part of our operation, we will be forced to do so on foot. And what will we use for cover? (Oh, already I hear you laughing as I come to this part!) Since the camels are so precious to our mission—they do, after all, carry everything—we are told that we must not use them to shield ourselves from harm. Rather, they will be lashed together in the center of square formations and given cover by us! We, who will only be permitted to use saddles and boxes for cover.

The oppressive heat, the stupidly slow camels, the fear of our mission perhaps being a futile exercise in loss of home and life—some days, it is a bit much. It is a lot to hate. I think now that war is something men do, not necessarily with rhyme or reason.

And do you know what I hate most of all, Lucy? I hate being away from you. Do you know that when I kiss you, your hair smells to me like the rain? That is why I "miss water" so much, as you put it in your letter: because it reminds me of you. The heat, I find that I can live with the heat—and I will; much as I hate it here, I will stay on because I know our cause is just. At least, I do tell myself that. But I find that I cannot live without the rain, Lucy; I cannot live without you.

So do not talk to me any more of Minerva. "What's Hecuba to him or he to Hecuba . . . ?" Hamlet asks. Well, what is Minerva to me? Silly Lucy. I have already told you: she is a nice girl, no more, no less. But it is you I think about out here in the desert. It is you whose face I see, whose voice I hear, whose lips I taste, whose rain-scented hair I still can smell when I close my eyes.

I know that I should not speak so to you, but being here—knowing I may never be back there— makes me bolder than I would be if you were standing right before me. Here is what I want you to know: my body thinks often of your body. Do you know what I mean?

I hope you will forgive the forwardness of my words, but I would not want to die without you knowing that I love you, with all my heart and all my mind and, yes, with my entire body. You will no doubt laugh again here. You will tell me

you do not know what I am talking about or you
will tell me that I do not know what I am
talking about. But hopefully, when you are finished
laughing, you will see the truth in what I write.
What's more, I pray you will return it.

                Yours, with my camel in
                the desert, always yours,

                Kit

. . . . .

Kit,

    I cannot imagine a letter less conducive
to inciting laughter. Did you purposely
design it thus? You promised me laughter.
Well, I did not laugh once—not once!—and
now I am feeling very hard done by.
    As for the rest, I know exactly what you
mean. In fact, since you are so concerned
about dying—which I do think you might
have thought about before you left!—I will
confess something too. My body has thought
of your body in the way that you indicate
for more than two years now.
    So now I am the indelicate one, but
what do I care? At least now when you are
out under the stars—for I do know that that

is one advantage of being where you are as opposed to being where I am, a star-crammed sky where all I have is fog and lonely Orion—you will have that picture to keep you company.

But you will not die, Kit. In an ever more confusing world where everything has gone mad on me—an aunt murdered, a father ruining himself with drink for no good reason, a mother sometimes changed beyond recognition—you are the one solid thing in that world. You are my family. So no, you will not die. I think now that I could get used to anything, so long as I never have to get used to that. And so, I simply will not allow it.

Love,

Lucy

Thirty-two

Kit loved me!

   ... I love you, with all my heart and all my mind and, yes, with my entire body ...

Were any written words ever more wonderful?

But he was a world away, while I yet had to live in this world.

     . . . . .

"I am worried about your father," Mother said.

"How do you mean?"

"Surely you have marked the changes in him over the past few years."

Indeed, it was impossible to miss them. The eating, the drinking, the smoking—if I happened by his study, I could smell the smoke from his cigars. Even though he only engaged in this activity in his own private garden, the scent managed to snake its way into the study itself, further snaking its way out under the door and into the house proper. As for the first two items—the eating and the drinking—he had always indulged in the latter, but now overindulgence in both had resulted in a body that would not have been recognizable to those who had not seen him in two years. And the drinking, which had never appeared to affect him before, did confuse him at certain moments, even muddling his speech so that now there were times when talking to him was like talking to a watercolor painting of a person you once knew.

"Yes," I said. "The changes started right after Aunt Helen died."

"We all miss Helen," she said, "but that is no reason for any of us to let ourselves go in such a grotesque fashion." Her words were severe, only mitigated when she added, "I fear that if he does not make some changes for the better soon, he will not be long for this world."

It seemed like a peculiar way for Mother to talk to me—she had never talked in such a way before—but then the thought occurred to me: perhaps it was because she had never viewed me as an adult before. Perhaps now she saw us as equals.

Trying to respond as an adult might respond, I impulsively covered her hand with mine.

"You are worried about him, aren't you?" I said.

"Of course I am worried about him." She yanked her hand away, seemed offended at the very question. "He is my husband, is he not?" Before I could respond, she added, "And have I not already said as much?"

And yet when she spoke of him, there was so much disdain in her voice.

That same night, as I again heard those disturbing man-woman noises coming from the floor above, I wondered that she could expend so much of that kind of energy on a man she so obviously now held, for whatever reason, in contempt.

. . . . .

There were eleven at dinner: the four of us—Mother, my father, Aunt Martha, and myself—as well as the Williamses, the Tylers, and the Clarences, accompanied by Minerva.

I thought it odd, given Mother's ostensible concerns over my father's well-being, but she had decided that a dinner party was in order.

Twin candelabra displaying blue tapers adorned the ends of the linen-draped table, while for a centerpiece there sat a shallow bowl of irises that had had their stems neatly chopped off.

"I hear that Joseph Carson is planning to remarry," Mary Williams announced cheerily as I picked up the tiny fork at my right and removed an oyster from its shell.

"That is sudden," my father said. "How long has Elizabeth been dead now?"

"Less than a year," Mother answered. "Still, I suppose that it is harder for some to be alone than it is for others. Perhaps he missed the companionship."

"Then he will not return to London?" my father asked, indicating that the servant should pour him more wine.

. . . . .

Soup replaced the oysters.

"Have you received any new letters from Kit?" Minerva asked Mrs. Tyler as I raised my soupspoon.

It was a question I had wanted to ask, but did not want to ask too early in the evening, and now I was frustrated that she had done so before me.

Kit had originally said he would write me every day, but it had been two weeks since I had had a letter from him. Not that I minded, not very much, for I worried that if he did write me daily, he would ignore the more important business of staying alive. It was a recurring nightmare of mine: Kit, out in the desert somewhere, writing to me and never seeing the bullet that would take his life.

Mrs. Tyler's brow furrowed with worry, but she also looked pleased to have the opportunity to speak of Kit.

"I had a letter just today," she said. "Kit writes that his camel is still alive." She forced a bright smile, adding, "I suppose we must count that a fine thing."

"Thank heavens the camel is still alive," Mother said. "I think this calls for a toast. Frederick?"

My father called for more wine and, when the glasses had been filled, raised his. "To the camel!"

Then he drained it dry.

·　·　·　·　·

Fish course, meat course.

"How have you been occupying your time since Kit's departure?" I asked Mrs. Tyler.

I felt guilty. I had promised Kit that I would look in on his mother regularly but had failed to do so as regularly as I might have. It was not that I did not like her—I liked Mrs. Tyler, very much so—but seeing her was a sword with two edges. On the one hand, when I saw her I saw him, for they were so alike; while on the other, it filled me with an aching pain, for however much they might be alike, she was not the genuine article. No one was him.

Now when she smiled, it was genuine. "I have taken up croquet!"

"And I must say," Mr. Tyler added, "she is quite good at it."

The Tylers taking up croquet, with Mrs. Tyler winning nearly every time, apparently called for more wine.

. . . . .

Salads came, along with cheese, bread, and butter.

"And tennis!" Mrs. Tyler erupted.

"Tennis?" Mrs. Clarence was puzzled.

"Oh, yes!" Mrs. Tyler said enthusiastically. "When we are not in the mood for croquet—meaning when John gets tired of losing—we now play lawn tennis!"

"Lawn tennis," Mother mused, looking down the length of the table at my father. "You should take up lawn tennis, Frederick. Or croquet. Really, any form of exercise would be good." Then she expanded her gaze to encompass the table at large. "More wine, anyone?"

. . . . .

Pudding, fruit, bonbons.

We never did make it into the parlor for coffee, for my father's head had begun to droop, and the others thought it best to call it a night.

"But I haven't said anything about the book I'm working on yet!" my father said, rousing himself. "I have new stories to tell you!"

"Never fear," Mr. Tyler said, clapping him on the shoulder. "You can always come by tomorrow and tell me all about it."

And then our guests were gone.

"I think I may have had too much to drink," Aunt Martha said, trying to mask a hiccup behind her hand and failing miserably. "I think I had better go to bed."

"Frederick?" Mother said, blowing out a candle.

"In a while, dear, in a while." He waved her off. "I just want to finish off some work first."

"Very well," she said. "See you in the morning. Lucy?"

"I will be up shortly," I said.

"Very well," she said again, and was gone.

"Father," I said once we were alone, "don't you think you had best go up to bed now? The work will be there in the morning."

"The morning?" He looked confused by the very concept, as though variations in time meant nothing to him. "No, I do not think it can wait. So!" He clapped his hands against his thighs. "A cigar, and then work."

He was nearly out of the doorway when he turned back.

"I am sorry, Lucy," he said.

"For what?"

"For everything." He shrugged. "For things you will never know. I am just sorry."

• Thirty-three •

Thump. Thump.

I had fallen asleep on the sofa in the front parlor.

For some reason, even though I was accustomed to my father working late when "the Muse," as he put it, was upon him, I had been worried about him when he'd gone off to do so following the dinner party. Then, too, I was hoping to learn what he had meant by saying, "I am sorry." So, rather than going up to bed myself, I'd lain down with my copy of Lewis Carroll's *Through the Looking-Glass*, intending to stay awake until my father emerged, and yet sleep had overtaken me.

But I awoke now at the sound of:

Thump. Thump.

My father had put on so much weight over the past two years that now whenever he ate or drank too much, which was pretty much daily and nightly, he ran the risk of suffering an attack of gout in the left leg. Whenever this affliction was upon him, the sound of his footsteps became heavily biased to one side, making me think that he should really borrow Aunt Martha's cane. It also made it possible to hear him coming from a mile away, as it were.

Thump. Thump.

"Lucy, what are you doing still up?"

As I dragged myself to a sitting position, the open book rolled away from my chest, thudding to the floor. I rubbed the dream from my eyes, saw that the fire in the grate had nearly burned itself away to nonexistence.

"I guess I fell asleep while reading."

He regarded the book where it lay on the floor.

"Ah, Carroll," he said. "His use of mirror themes is excellent." Then he sighed. "Some days, I wish *I* could make time run backward."

"If you could do that," I asked, trying to appear blithe in my questioning, "where would you make time run to?"

It was as though he sobered instantly. "To that New Year's Day," he said, "when we found your mother and Helen."

I saw it all clearly then: he still felt guilty, as I felt guilty, for having been away from home that awful day. Had we both been here . . .

"I feel so responsible," he said weakly, then he jerked his head toward the ceiling. "I am sure *she* blames me as well. Although I sometimes wonder if . . . actually, I often wonder . . ."

"Wonder what, Father?"

"It never should have happened," he said with sudden strength. "And since that day? It has all been such a muddle, such a waking nightmare for me. That baby . . . There are times when I don't even know who . . . ?"

"Who," what? What was he talking about?

He shook his head.

Then he collapsed on the seat beside me, his bulk making the sofa shake like a small boat tossed by strong seas, the cloud of alcohol rolling off him in waves.

He put his hands to his face, fat sausage fingers covering his eyes.

His peculiar behavior solved no mysteries, only raised more questions.

But I could not press him further, not in his condition. There would be time enough when morning came, or perhaps the next day, or the day after that, when he was feeling better, stronger. So instead I asked the question I knew would make him most happy:

"How did your writing go?"

He pulled his hands away from his face, a gleam entering his wine-filled eyes now.

"It went most excellently! I cannot wait to get back to it, so that I may return to all my characters and their fanciful world!"

But it was as if those two enthusiastic sentences had exhausted him and his hands went to his face again.

"I am so very tired, Lucy. So very tired."

"Then you must sleep, Father," I said. "The work will still be there in the morning."

"Morning ... yes ... sleep ... bed ..."

With a great effort, like a soldier trying to catapult an enormous stone over the fortified walls of a castle, he heaved his bulk off the sofa. Almost immediately, he faltered, stumbling back down again.

"Stay here tonight, Father! I can get a blanket for you. You can sleep on the sofa." I did wonder how he would ever fit on it, but still I insisted, "I can make you quite comfortable right here."

"Lucy?" Confusion had entered his eyes. It was almost as though he had forgotten where he was, whom he was with. He placed his hand against my face, tentatively felt my cheek like a blind man trying to trace the features of one who might be a stranger.

I covered his hand with mine. "Yes, Father. It is Lucy."

"Lucy." His face melted into a fond, wondering smile as he patted my cheek. "Such a good girl." And one last pat, more serious now. "I do love you."

It is not an exaggeration to say that I can count, using less than one hand, the number of times I had ever heard my father say "I love you" to me, and yet he was saying it now. For my part, I—who had spoken those words uncountable times to Mother—could tally no more than that in return. It had never been our habit.

But the situation appeared to require it now and, anyway, it was no hardship for me to say, "I love you too, Father," however unfamiliar might be the constellation of words.

"Very good," he said in a dismissively vacant tone as though already he was drifting away from me again, his hand falling away from my cheek. "Very good."

"I will get that blanket now, Father," I said, rising.

"No!" He nearly shouted the word. It was a wonder that the volume did not raise Mother, but then I remembered that both she and Aunt Martha had enjoyed a fair quantity of wine with supper themselves; not to mention that we had all grown used to my father occasionally being a little . . . *loud* at night. "No," he said more softly, his voice almost a whisper as with one final great heave he extricated himself from the comfort of the sofa. "I must go to your mother," he said urgently. "I must be with Aliese!"

"Then lean on me and I will help you," I said, insinuating myself into the space between his torso and arm, pulling on that arm until it came around my shoulders and I could hold his hand with mine, putting my other arm firmly as far as I could reach around his waist.

"Such a good girl," he murmured. Then he exploded again, "I must go to your mother!"

"Then I will take you."

It was a snail's journey from the front parlor to the foot of the stairs. And—oh—those stairs! Twice we had to stop when his breathing became too labored and once—on that favorite sixth step of mine—he teetered, nearly pulling us both back down again. But at last, finally, our pilgrims' progress attained the safety of the landing.

"We are halfway there, Father," I encouraged him. "Just one more flight—"

"Wait!" he cried. "I have to add something to my story!"

With a force and speed I would not have imagined was in him anymore, he spun away from me.

"Father! No!"

I turned just in time to see him falter on the top step, his hands going to his chest and then he was flying—I reached out, but my hand only grasped air!—and then he was tumbling down that flight of stairs.

It was a long flight.

I raced after his body, but when I reached the bottom, I saw there was no point in calling for help.

. . . . .

When I had seen Aunt Helen dead in her coffin, I had thought of a book I'd read once and a mother saying her child did not look dead, only sleeping. At the time, I could only find falseness in such an assertion: there had been no mistaking that Aunt Helen was dead. But now I saw that, even though my father's eyes stared open, a dead person *could* appear to be sleeping. It was as though he had not died, but rather, had merely left his body for a while.

I fell in a heap beside his head.

My father had always been a cipher to me; in death, even more so. Who was this man whose books were his life? Whose blood was part of my blood?

Beneath the fleshy folds of his face, I could still see the handsome man he had once been.

"Father." I whispered the word as the tears came.

If he could still speak, he would say we were like Lear and Cordelia, only it was me cradling his body in my arms, entreating, begging him to stay a little.

He was just forty-seven years old. His parents still lived. How could he die?

It was a long time before anyone found us.

I was grateful for that time alone.

Later on, the doctor would tell me that his heart had simply given out: he was dead before he hit the marble floor.

Part IV

• Thirty-four •

If I never went to another party again, it would be too soon.

I had begun to associate parties with death. I had begun to fear them, for it seemed that, nearly every time we had one, someone died in the aftermath.

Throw a party on New Year's Eve? Aunt Helen is murdered the next day. Have a dinner party? Father's heart fails to keep beating the very same night. I was done with celebrations. If I never celebrated anything else for the rest of my life, with people and food and drink, it would suit me right down to the ground.

I resolved that if there were ever again something in my life to make merry over, I would do it in the privacy of my own heart, leaving more public displays for those foolish enough to tempt cruel fate.

. . . . .

Dearest Lucy,

Never have I felt more the pain of you being there while I am yet here. I cannot escape the notion—insane, I know!—that if I had been with my parents when they came to your home that evening, your father would somehow not have died. But such is the hubris we men are made of, that we think our mere presence in a place can forestall disaster. This last is truly ironic since in my time in the desert I have seen that men are more often responsible in causing disasters than preventing them. If these were better times, you would no doubt object to my last statement. I can almost hear you laughing, saying to me in that modern way of yours, "But what about the women? Surely we are just as capable of causing great disaster! You do us an unfair injustice, sir."

But I know that you are not laughing. I know that these are not better times. I know that these are the worst of times, made so because we are not together. To think, by the time I received the letter informing me of your father's passing, the event had long since transpired, the church bells had tolled their sad song, the black cloth had been taken down from the mirrors.

If the world were fair, I would be with you right now. I would have been with you on that dreadful night your father died, even though I do know I could have done nothing to prevent it. I would have been with you in the churchyard, by your side and holding your hand on the day you saw him laid to rest.

No, my body was not beside yours through any of those awful moments. But know this, Lucy: should I survive this desert..."sojourn" of mine—and it is my every intention to do so, camel willing—I shall never leave your side again. And know this too: even when I am not with you in body, I am always, _always_ with you in your mind and in your heart. Indeed, I think that is where I live.

Love,

Your Kit

. . . . .

I fell into a well of sadness.

When Aunt Helen died, I had been devastated. But at that time I had had my anger to hold on to. Then, too, there had been the mystery of trying to figure out the truth behind what had happened to keep my mind occupied.

But this death was different. It was the death of a man who, all my life, I had known only incompletely.

And now I never would know him.

Life was a puzzle to me. Even when you thought you knew what you were looking at, there was always another world beneath the visible world.

· Thirty-five ·

Mother had taken to going out in the evenings.

At first, it was a sudden engagement once a month, then once a week, then every day. Walks to the park, never inviting anyone else to accompany her. By the time I did notice, I had also noticed that when she returned from these forays, the color in her cheeks was high, a look in her eye forbidding any questions.

So I asked Aunt Martha.

"Where do you think she is going?"

"Your mother has long since given up sharing any confidences with me," she said with asperity, as though the fault lay solely with Mother. Aunt Martha in the past two years had grown more crotchety, seeing offense at every turn but too timid to voice such offense when Mother was within hearing. But then her next words belied this tendency toward crotchetiness. "Your mother is still a relatively young woman, Lucy. I suspect it is impossible for us to expect her to remain indoors, in mourning for the rest of her life."

I digested this information.

"One thing you can be sure of," Aunt Martha said.

"Yes?"

"I am fairly certain that whatever your mother is doing, she is not out robbing banks."

Aunt Martha looked pleased at her own rare joke.

· · · · ·

I took to being watchful again.

With no other happy distraction to entertain me—Kit still being gone, what happy distractions could there be?—I determined to seek out the cause of Mother's increasingly frequent absences. Minerva, always chasing after her sisters, was hardly what I would call diverting company. Doing needlepoint with Aunt Martha had never held any charm. As for the books I used to turn to, even they had let me down of late. What use were made-up stories when every day I woke to the fresh reality that *this* might be the day a stray bullet would find Kit, take him from me? And so I resolved, for the time being at least, to transform myself back into Lucy Sexton, Girl Detective.

Of course, I was limited in the tools of my trade. Yes, I could follow Mother along in the daytime, far enough to see her go into the park, but I could not follow her into that park, lest *she* might see *me*. Yes, I could follow with my eyes the carriage as it took her out of an evening, ascertaining the direction in which it was heading, but there was no second carriage for me to follow her in, to discover her destination. And so I had to content myself with watching and listening, waiting for the opportunity to arise when I might learn more.

That opportunity came late one evening.

After Aunt Martha had gone up to bed, I had remained in the parlor. But the fire had died out with me neglecting to notice the diminishing flames, and the lull of the ensuing cold gloom had overtaken me.

I awoke at the sound of the front door opening, followed by the sound of footsteps on the marble floor:

Two sets of footsteps.

I shrank into the corner of the sofa, hoping that in the dark Mother and whoever was accompanying her would not see me when they came in. But the twin sets of footsteps did not advance in my direction. Rather, they receded off toward the long hallway leading to Father's study. In the dead stillness of the house, I clearly heard the door to that sacred room click open and then shut again.

With no Kit around to entice me to meet him in the tunnel that could only be accessed from the trapdoor in Father's study, I had not gone in there since Father's death—that room was now a relic of the family's past, only observed by the servants who went in there to dust. Indeed, I barely even used that hallway anymore.

But now I did so, removing my boots and treading down it swiftly on padded feet. I did not intend to enter, nothing so brazen as that. But I did want to listen at the door, hoping to hear the voice of whatever person it was that Mother had invited into our home.

No sooner did I skid to a halt in front of the door, however, than I heard a second door opening from within. That could only mean one thing: the door to Father's private garden had been opened. Why would Mother and her secret visitor be going out there?

I raced back down the hallway, running up two flights of stairs until I achieved the landing on the third story. There, I made straight for the end of the corridor: Aunt Helen's old bedroom, now Aunt Martha's.

Turning the knob slowly, I entered as silently as possible, crept past Aunt Martha's sleeping form as I crossed the room to the window on the other side: the only window that overlooked the garden. But I needn't have exercised such caution. Aunt Martha had always been a sound sleeper. And now that she was older, she snored, as she was doing now, the sounds coming from her prone body so loud they would camouflage anything else.

I pressed my face to the glass, relying on the strong moon to afford me a clear view of the garden so far below.

They were seated side by side on the curved stone bench.

Mother wore a pretty gown, shimmering scarlet, while the man beside her had on a dark suit. I could not see Mother's face, nor the man's. All I could see of him was that he was tall, his thick brown hair longer than the norm, causing it to curl up a bit at the ends. As I say, I could not see their faces, for the man's back was to me as he kissed her. There was something disturbingly familiar about the back of that head.

I don't think I could have been more shocked if Aunt Martha had begun speaking in tongues between her loud snores. In all my life, I had never seen Mother kissed so. It was as though this man would bury his entire body within Mother's, if such a thing were possible.

I don't know how long I stood there, witnessing, unable to

tear myself away. But then the man was pulling away from Mother, her head tilted upward until her eyes caught mine. She tapped him on the shoulder, gesturing with her chin, and then he was looking up at me too and for the first time I saw his features.

In addition to the shock of brown hair, unspectacular in its color, he had a strong jaw, and as his full lips parted I saw a set of teeth that sent a chill up my spine. I would not say they were wolf's teeth, and yet they made me think of one as the moon glinted against their brightness. His eye color was not visible at such a distance—later on, I would judge them to be hazel—but I could just make out the faint trace of a scar running from temple to the corner of his mouth.

He was not a handsome man, not by any means, and yet there was something compelling about him, something danger-ous about the defiant, self-confident gaze that met mine.

I did not want to be caught in the trap of those eyes any lon-ger, but when I looked back at Mother, I saw her mouthing my name, *Lucy*.

Struggling to open the double-hung window, I at last jerked the lower frame upward.

"Lucy." Now I could hear her. "Why don't you come down and meet the man I am going to marry?"

Aunt Martha snored on.

As I exited the room, I could not help but remember the first sight of them together in the garden, the back of that man's head.

As I walked down the staircase, I remembered once, a long

time ago, witnessing a startlingly similar tableau, a woman I knew well seated across from a man just like that. When Kit had the typhoid, I had stolen out by myself to the park one day, where I'd come across Aunt Helen seated on a bench with a man, the back of whose head looked exactly like this man's head.

And then it finally struck me: the twin who had survived had not been Mother.

It was Aunt Helen.

My knees buckled under me as I collapsed onto the step.

Mother was dead.

. . . . .

"Are you sure he is not after your money?" I heard Aunt Martha say to the woman I now knew to be Aunt Helen the next day.

The night before, I had obeyed Aunt Helen, making the long way back down to the garden to meet, as she had put it, "the man I am going to marry." But I cannot say that I registered much of the specific details of what transpired, only vague impressions. I had been too shocked: at the news, at everything, not least of which was the possessive hand the man held at Aunt Helen's spine, reminding me of a ventriloquist and his toy.

I did note that he was far younger than Father had been— more Aunt Helen's age, really—and that even though his clothes were fine, there was an impression of unkemptness about him. His words were fine enough too, but again, something about them struck me as not quite right. And there was his energy, a coiled energy coupled with an almost frightening overabundance of manliness.

I am sure I must have offered congratulations to one and best wishes to the other, as appropriate—I must have done, because good manners had been bred into me—but I have no recollection of it.

The whole time I stood before them, stunned, all I could do was try to work through things in my mind, pushing grief aside until later. For some reason, I felt that I could not, should not let show what I now knew to be true.

It all made sense now: the changes I had perceived in the woman I had thought to be Mother since the day of the murder, the new harshness in her, the way she had been with Father, even the difference in the sounds I had heard coming from their bedroom at night, so much rawer. I realized then that I must have suspected, must have known the truth all along, somewhere in the deep corners of my mind, that this woman before me was not my mother. Certainly, I knew she was nothing like the mother I had grown up with.

But why had Aunt Helen done it? Why pretend to be someone she was not?

And then I saw that clearly too. No matter how much Mother and Father had ever given Aunt Helen, *could* ever give Aunt Helen, she would always view herself as a poor relation, everything she had in this world dependent upon the benevolence of others. How it must have *galled* her all those years, to always be second best through no fault of her own. And so, when Mother was murdered, she'd seized her chance to achieve what should have been her life all along as well as Mother's: a good life, with no one to question her right to it. Perhaps she also worried, with Mother

dead, that there would no longer be any reason for Father to support her. Then, too, I liked to think: maybe she loved me so
much, she was glad of the opportunity to be my mother, with no
one else between us. Her diary had certainly indicated her
strong affection for me.

I was as shocked as a person could be to realize that it was
Mother who had been dead all along—yes, I would still need to
wait until I was alone, away from these two, to properly grieve
the loss—and yet I could not fault Aunt Helen for what she'd
done. The world had never dealt with her fairly, and so, when
opportunity came to call, she had answered.

If I exposed her now, what good could come of that? Aunt
Martha, everyone in our world, would no doubt insist upon her
expulsion from the house based on the lie she had lived. How
hard, I thought, it must have been for her to live that lie all these
years, all the things she had been compelled to do.

I did not want her gone, I suddenly saw. She was my only
remaining tie left to Mother. Not to mention, if she were exposed
as not being Mother, whom would I live with: Remain here alone
with Aunt Martha, if the circumstances of Father's will were even
such that we *could* remain on here? Go with Aunt Martha to live
with her ancient parents, my dreadful grandparents, in the country? Neither option was attractive to me.

And so, I resolved, I would live the lie too. I would help Aunt
Helen maintain her fiction, for her sake and mine.

There was only one thing I remembered clearly about meeting the man:

I had not liked him.

And then one final thing struck me. Chief Inspector Daniels had told us that the medical examiner had said the murdered woman had been with child. Now that I knew it was Mother lying dead in the churchyard, it meant it was my own brother or sister who lay in that grave with her.

When I lay down on my bed later, I had to shove the corner of the pillow into my mouth to mute the racking sobs of grief as I at last mourned the twin losses of Mother and the sibling I had always longed for and now would never have.

But now it was a new day, and it was time to pay attention. Perhaps Aunt Martha would do my dirty work for me, asking questions I had been too stunned to ask the night before.

"You have said many rude things to me over the years," Aunt Helen addressed Aunt Martha, "and I have forgiven you each time. But this really is the limit! Do you think my money is the only thing that might attract a man?"

"I am well aware that you have many attractions, Aliese," Aunt Martha said. "But my brother left you a very wealthy widow. Surely you must acknowledge the possibility that—"

"*I acknowledge nothing.*" Aunt Helen bit off the words. "The man I am going to marry has plenty of his own money."

"Oh, really? What profession does he pursue?"

"He is . . . he is . . ." In her anger, Aunt Helen stumbled over her own words. "He is a merchant," she finished at last.

"I see."

"I think it is time you went, Martha," Aunt Helen said.

"Went? Went where? Out? To bed?"

"I think it is time you leave," Aunt Helen clarified. "No doubt, now that I am to remarry, we will all be more comfortable—yourself as much as anybody—if you and I are no longer under the same roof."

"I don't understand," I said to Aunt Helen after Aunt Martha had clumped her way up the stairs to commence packing one last time.

"Surely you must see that it is not tenable to have her here any longer."

"That's not what I meant," I said, nor was it.

The idea of Aunt Martha, at her age, going home to live with her parents again—probably the last move she would make—created a sad vision. But it must have been very hard for Aunt Helen to suffer her presence for so long, given how much they had always hated each other, and while I did love Aunt Martha, I could not now blame Aunt Helen for seizing the chance to have her gone.

"What I meant," I continued, "is that I don't understand why you have to get married now. Or at all. I have only just met this man!"

It was a pitiful excuse, I knew, particularly since I was well aware that she had known him for far longer than she was saying. Had she been in love with him all these years? Had she waited patiently for Father's death, having endured being Father's wife in every way, so that now she could marry the man she truly loved?

But I could say none of that.

"I am still relatively young," Aunt Helen said, echoing the words Aunt Martha had spoken when I'd first wondered where the woman I'd previously thought to be Mother was disappearing to. "There are still opportunities to be had. There is still a lot of

life ahead of me. Don't you think I have a right to take advantage
of those opportunities, to have that life be as happy as possible?"

. . . . .

Aunt Helen was not at home when Aunt Martha took her leave.

"I hope you will be all right here without me, Lucy," Aunt
Martha said. "I fear for you alone in this house."

As so often in the past, there was an underlying harsh judg-
ment in Aunt Martha's words.

But I did not mind on that day.

She was the only tie still connecting me to Father. So rather
than questioning her about her meaning, or censuring her for
speaking the words in the first place, I merely hugged her hard,
wiping the tears from her crepe cheeks when she began to cry.

. . . . .

His name was Richard Earl.

As I say, I did not like him upon first acquaintance, nor did
I like him markedly more as that acquaintance grew. I suppose
an alienist would say that I resented the idea of seeing Father
replaced as man of the house.

Surely there was truth in this. But there was a deeper truth,
one I could not quite put my finger on. No matter how I might
try to unravel it in my mind, I still came back to the same thread:
I did not want to see another man sitting at the breakfast table
every morning, did not want to see another man occupy Father's
private study, did not want to see another man go up to the bedroom Mother and Father had shared at night.

"Someday soon," Aunt Helen said, adjusting her gown before

her looking glass just prior to leaving for the wedding ceremony, "though it may not seem so to you now, you yourself will be married. And then, were I not to marry Richard, I would be left here alone." She turned to look at me. "Is that what you want? Tell me now and I will call off the ceremony."

Would she do that? I wondered, studying the dare in her unflinching eyes without knowing the answer. But no. I would not ask that of her. She had waited patiently so long for this day. I did not want her to be left alone.

"I just want you to be happy, Mother," I said. "Are you?"

"Never happier," she said, turning back to her own reflection.

. . . . .

The ceremony was a simple one with no guests, save myself and a second witness, a maid from the vicarage, drafted into this service at the last minute. The vicar, Mr. Thomason, presided.

Studying Aunt Helen's face as she looked up at Mr. Earl, I saw that she was happy. She did love him.

And he? Suffice it to say that even standing before a man of God, there was an untamable energy that sprang between the two of them that was more animal than human.

Afterward, at home, Aunt Helen went up to change, leaving me alone with Mr. Earl.

"I suppose," he said, assuming a seat and languidly crossing one leg over the other, "you should call me 'Papa' now."

"I don't think so, sir," I replied.

"Very well, Lucy." He placed his hands behind his head and laughed, a sardonic sound. "As you wish it."

· Thirty-six ·

He had left me in the mist. He returned to me *from* the mist.

. . . . .

Aunt Helen and Richard, as I had come to think of him, had long since left for their month-long honeymoon in the Swiss lakes when the knock came. With Mother dead, Father dead, Aunt Helen away, and Aunt Martha gone, I was the only member of my family still under that roof, and it was lonely. So it was something of a relief when a knock came at the door.

A moment later, Victoria Tyler was announced, ushered in. Immediately, I saw that her eyes were rimmed red and I suspected the worst.

"This came today." She thrust the letter she clutched in her hands at me. "Here. John is still at work and I have no one with whom to share the news."

I did not want to take that letter from her, feared the words it might contain. If I never read it, then I would never learn any bad news. Father's words came back to me: *Once a bell has rung, it cannot be unrung.* So long as I remained ignorant, worse could not come to the worst. But I could not bear to see her alone in her concern and so I accepted it, unfolded the pages.

Dear Mr. and Mrs. Tyler,

I regret to inform you that your son has been wounded. I hasten to say that he is still alive! And yet, he is gravely injured. Without further preamble, let me tell you my story.

It was the 17th of January and we were marching cross-country in the Sudan to relieve General Gordon at Khartoum when we were set upon by Mahdists. We fought back mightily, and successfully turned back the attack, but not two days later we were set upon again as we approached Metemma. Once again, we were successful...and this, despite there were merely fifteen hundred of us to twelve thousand of them!

But then the tide turned against us.

It is amazing to think how much the world can change, how much can be lost in just fifteen minutes. In fifteen minutes, eleven hundred Mahdists died, an astonishing number. In fifteen minutes, nine British officers and sixty-five men of other ranks were killed. In fifteen minutes, over a hundred additional British soldiers were wounded, including my best friend in the desert, Kit Tyler, who was stabbed with a spear and shot.

It is an understatement to say that when he threw his body in front of mine, he saved my miserable life.

After that, I could no longer remember what we were all fighting for. Our column was too late to save Khartoum. Just a few days after Kit was wounded in battle, Khartoum was taken by the Mahdists. If I ever knew what we were fighting for, I know it no longer.

Normally, I do not write such long letters to people I have never met, but Kit asked me to explain everything and, as I say, he is my best friend here. Indeed, he is the finest man I have ever known. God willing and the surgeon's hand steady, your boy will be returned home to you soon, hopefully even in one piece.

With deepest regrets and fervent prayers for a bright outcome,

Lieutenant Luke Thackeray

P.S. Kit requests that you pass along a message to one Miss Lucy Sexton, a young

woman he has spoken of fondly on more
than one occasion. Indeed, every day since
we have been here. "Please tell Lucy," he
says, "the camel died."

. . . . .

"What do you make of this?" Victoria Tyler asked me.

"Well, for one thing, I think Lieutenant Thackeray is overly fond of adverbs."

My attempt at bluff humor did not fool even me.

"This was written in *January*?" I said, looking back at the top of the letter as panic overtook me. "But that is so long ago now. Anything might have happened since then!"

"'God willing and the surgeon's hand steady'?" Victoria Tyler cried. "What can Lieutenant Thackeray possibly mean by that?"

"I don't know," I said. "But at least we know one thing."

"And what is that?"

I took hold of her hands, crushing the letter between my hand and hers as I gazed steadily into her eyes as though I had the force to *make* the world as I willed it.

"When this letter was written," I said, "Kit was still alive."

. . . . .

I waited.

Daily and nightly, as though keeping watch would ensure Kit's safe arrival home, I sat at the window in the front parlor, my eyes on the street.

I don't know why I thought this vigil would help. It had taken

Lieutenant Thackeray's letter such a long time to reach us. Surely it could take Kit any length of time to return.

Or not at all, the thought arose unbidden, a thought that taunted me with alarming frequency, inciting me to tamp it back down, down, down.

I did not go out, nor did I entertain visitors in. Yes, I did leave my spot to go to the bathroom, and I even cleaned myself up occasionally. Sometimes, my eyes drifted shut in sleep, although I did not want them to. The servants became concerned, then alarmed, and finally tired of entreating me to leave off my vigil and sleep in a real bed. I would not listen. I ate in that position and when I grew sore on one side I would switch to the other. My elbows wore marks into the back of the sofa. The servants took to draping a blanket around my shoulders before closing the house for the night.

I sat like that, watching the street for two weeks.

In that time, I had discovered that there was a gap period, about an hour between when the lights from the lampposts were extinguished and the street began to stir with the activity of a new day.

It was during that gap period one day—not yet morning, no longer night—that I glimpsed a pinpoint of gold penetrate the thick mist at the end of the street.

I raced to the door in bare feet, raced outside to see what it was, the blanket falling away from my shoulders.

Whatever it was, it remained stopped at the end of the street. The golden pinpoint of light was a lantern on a carriage, I decided.

Then I heard an odd constellation of sounds—*step, tap, clack*—and then a moment later the golden light extinguished away from me as I heard the horses *clip-clopping* their way back out of the street.

But the peculiar constellation of sounds continued:

Step, tap, clack. Step, tap, clack.

It was faint at first, but as I stood in the middle of the street, hearing the sounds draw ever nearer to me, they grew in volume and speed.

Step, tap, clack. Step, tap, clack. Steptapclack.

He had left me in the mist. He returned to me *from* the mist.

He was exactly the same. He was changed.

"They killed the foot to save the man," Kit said with a rueful shrug.

These words, the first words I had heard from his mouth in over a year, stopped me dead.

Where his left foot should have been, a wooden peg rested against the street; in his left hand, a cane he leaned against now.

There was a film of fine sweat on his handsome brow, as though he had run a long race. And he looked so much older, as though he had seen the whole world.

"Gangrene," he said with another rueful shrug, as if the explanation mattered.

I had been about to launch myself at him when he told me about the foot. Now I took a step back. It was not that I was repulsed. Oh, no. Not that. Never that. But I did worry about hurting him.

"Oh, no," he said, shaking his head back and forth vehemently. "I have waited, I have dreamed"—and here his voice caught on a sob—"I cannot remember how long or how often for this moment. I will not be denied." As he held his arms wide, letting the cane drop from his hand, letting it clatter to the road, I saw the gleam in his eye, saw the tear decorate his lash like a diamond. "Fly at me, Lucy."

I flew.

The force of my flight knocked him to the earth with me coming to rest on top of him.

"Did I hurt you?" I asked anxiously, my first words.

He put his arms around me, buried his face in my neck. I heard him inhale deeply, holding the breath for a long moment before releasing it with a sigh. "I have suffered worse."

"How is Lieutenant Thackeray?" I thought to ask, not wanting to think, not yet, of what he had suffered. "It was from him that we knew you might be coming home."

"He died," Kit said.

"*Died*? Did the Dervishes get him?" I asked, as if I knew what I was talking about when, clearly, I did not.

"No. It was one of our own men. You would be surprised how often mistakes like that happen, when you have a lot of people running around with guns, but no one likes to talk about it."

"I am sorry."

"And I."

After a moment's silence:

"We are in the middle of the street," I could not help but point out. "People might see us."

"I do not care," he said. "Do you know—you still smell like the rain?"

"If you do not care about being seen, if my modesty means nothing to you, then what about a carriage? A carriage could come through here at any moment, crushing us both to death."

"I will save you, Lucy. I will never let any harm come to you."

With a great show of force, more than one would imagine possible from a man who had recently lost a foot, he rolled himself on top of me, and then rolled me over him, then him over me, over and over until he had rolled us onto the safety of the pavement.

He was changed. He was exactly the same.

He looked up at me, mischief sparking his eyes. "I say, I think you have grown *taller* since I went away!"

"Maybe just a bit," I conceded. "Why? Did you imagine that I would stay frozen as you left me?"

I did not wait for his answer.

"Shut up, Kit," I said, "and let me kiss you."

• Thirty-seven •

During the time since my revelation that the woman I had
thought to be Mother was in reality Aunt Helen, I had thought
often of that New Year's Day when I found them lashed side by
side, one murdered. The new information had caused me to
revise history as I knew it.

I thought now that there had never been any red-haired
monster, which explained why Aunt Helen had refused to identify the man Chief Inspector Daniels arrested as being the murderer: he wasn't, and she could not bear to see an innocent man
charged with the crime, knowing full well the red-haired monster was her own invention, part of the fiction she created when
she had seen her chance at a better life and seized upon it.

The only possible explanation, I saw now, was that it had
been a common robbery gone bad; the intruder having Mother
remove her ring, only to drop it in his haste to escape, bore this
out. He must have heard me at the door, panicked, and killed

her, had not had time to kill Aunt Helen too. The fire at the Carsons'? Pure coincidence.

After all, why would anybody want to deliberately murder Mother?

Aunt Helen might have had enemies from her past. But Mother?

It made no sense.

. . . . .

Of course, Kit was not exactly the same; there were things about his time in the Sudan he refused to discuss with anyone, even me.

None of us were the same, especially not Aunt Helen, who returned from her honeymoon to make the announcement that she was with child.

"So soon?" I said.

Richard had taken himself off, I knew not where.

"It only takes once," Aunt Helen said. I thought it an unseemly thing for her to say to me, the offense made graver when she added with a proud smile, "And when it is many, many times . . ."

Aunt Helen eyed me shrewdly. "You are not *jealous* of me having another child, are you? Perhaps you feel you will be displaced?"

"No." I colored at the notion, immediately damning myself for that blush. When I was younger, much younger, I might have felt such a negative emotion. But not now. "Are you sure it is healthy for you?" Since I wanted her to believe that *I* still believed her to be Mother, I added, "After the two you lost?"

"That was a long time ago." Aunt Helen waved a dismissive

hand, as if those had really been her own twin losses. "This time will be different. I just know it will."

"Yes, but you are so newly married. Would it not have been better to get used to the new husband before adding someone else?"

I confess this was my own true selfish feeling. Every time Richard came into the house or entered a room, I felt jarred by it, as though an artist had introduced a new figure that hadn't been there before to a picture I'd grown used to. It was enough to get accustomed to the idea of a new man in the house without almost instantly having to get accustomed to the idea of a new baby.

"I appreciate your concerns, Lucy, truly I do." Aunt Helen patted her flat abdomen complacently. "But this pregnancy will progress without complications. And it will not end like the others. It will end perfectly, just as I always intended."

I think it was the news of Aunt Helen's pregnant condition that killed Aunt Martha. I know that is impossible. The two could not be connected, and yet it seemed so in my mind. A week after Aunt Martha was informed of it by letter we heard from Father's parents that she was dead.

Once again, a celebration of sorts—Aunt Helen's announcement of her condition—had been followed by a death.

I mourned Aunt Martha's passing. I am fairly certain I was the only person who did.

· · · · ·

Step, tap, clack.

The first time Kit was introduced to Richard, he reacted in a way I'd never seen him react to anybody.

True, upon first acquaintance with Kit, I had thought of him as "that bored boy." But that impression had soon changed, cemented over the years by the knowledge that he was a far kinder soul than I could ever dream to be. If a person had a good quality, he would find it. If they did not, he would imagine one into existence.

And yet, as I watched him accept Richard's offered hand, watched the shake turn into a steely grip, a look of coldness entered his eyes.

"Ah," Richard said, "Lucy's soldier boy at last. Her mother has told me so much about you. How was the Sudan?"

"Have you ever been in the military?" Kit asked.

"I am afraid I never had that honor."

"Then I will tell you how it was and then you will know. People died. It was ugly. Is there anything else you'd care to ask me about it?"

"Um . . . no." Richard gave an affable shrug. "Thank you for saving me the need to enlist in order to find out for myself." He turned to Aunt Helen. "Shall we have tea now, my dear?"

. . . . .

"I do not trust your mother's new husband," Kit said to me when we were alone a few weeks later.

I had not told Kit about my revelation that the woman I had previously believed to be Mother was in reality Aunt Helen. I had debated long and hard over this—there had never been any secrets between Kit and me in the past—but I had finally concluded that I simply could not tell him. Kit was the most moral and ethical human being I had ever known, and I knew that however well he might sympathize with the reasons behind my desire not to expose Aunt Helen—my own sympathy toward her coupled with my desire to remain in the only home I had ever known, which would be doubly impossible now that Aunt Martha was dead too—he would feel compelled to do the right thing, which for Kit always meant telling the truth.

"I cannot say I care for the man very much either," I observed dryly. "But I also cannot see that there is anything to be done about it."

I had come to accept Richard as a part of life, although I was not happy about it. Many were the hours I had spent trying to figure out what exactly the history was between him and Aunt Helen, how long had they loved each other. Of course, there was no one I could ask about this, and so I had drawn my own conclusions. Based on the roughness around his edges, I thought he must have been from Aunt Helen's distant past, perhaps even as far back as her days in the workhouse. I did think that he loved her at least, and she him, but that did not improve my own feelings for him.

"There is something about him," Kit said. "He reminds me of an actor upon the stage, reading lines that someone else has written for him. And . . . what does he *do* all day?"

"Do?"

"Yes, *do*. Whenever I come to call, no matter the day of the week or the time of day, he is always here. Has he no work to go to?"

Indeed.

. . . . .

Despite that I already had some vague sense of who Richard was, a man from Aunt Helen's murky past, Kit's reaction to him, his distrust, had caused in me a desire to learn more about this man who had usurped Father's place at the table.

"Richard?" I asked the following morning as he lingered over a late breakfast and the morning papers.

Aunt Helen had not come down yet.

Often now in the mornings it would just be Richard and me at breakfast, for Aunt Helen said that her condition made her want to sleep longer hours.

"Yes, daughter?"

This was something Richard had taken to doing whenever Aunt Helen wasn't around, calling me "daughter" as though it were a taunt.

It was.

"Shouldn't you be returning to work?"

"Work?" he echoed, as though it were a new word for his vocabulary.

"Yes," I said. "You know, that thing one does to earn a living? I thought you said you were a merchant. Now here you have been on a month-long honeymoon, followed by nearly another month since you have been back. Doesn't your business need attending to?"

"My business?" He tossed the papers aside, drained the last of his coffee, threw down his napkin. "Why, yes, *daughter.* You are exactly right!"

From then on, most days, unless I was up very early, Richard was gone by the time I came down, and he stayed gone through most of the day.

This was a relief, in so many ways.

But then Kit told me a peculiar thing.

"I have been following him."

"Following who?"

"Why, Richard, of course."

"*You've* been following Richard?"

"Well, as best I can. There are two problems, you see. One, with only one good leg, I can't move as quickly as he does. And two"—here he tapped his peg with his cane—"if I follow too closely, I make a telltale sound."

"But you have seen something?"

"Oh, yes. Every day, he goes in an entirely different direction from the day before."

"Perhaps he is visiting different clients?" I suggested vaguely, not wholly certain what a merchant's day might consist of.

"Yes, but you would think there would be some main office or somewhere he would go to regularly, wouldn't you?"

I did think that.

"I tell you, Lucy, I don't think he goes to work each day at all! Who knows where the man goes?"

. . . . .

Aunt Helen was wrong.

She had said that her condition would pass without complications and yet, from where I stood, it appeared to be nothing *but* complications. I suppose it was all "normal," but daily it appeared to me there was a supernatural being that had taken over her body, causing that body to change its shape and do things it had never done: like vomit every morning, sometimes several times a day.

It was on one such unusually active day, Aunt Helen having vomited three times already, that I saw her go green around the gills. Thinking there was no time to wait for a servant, I helped her hasten to the bathroom, where she immediately emptied the contents of her stomach into the washbasin.

Afterward, weakened by the repeated offense against her body, she slid down the side of the cabinet on which the washbasin stood, settling with a thump onto the floor, her skirts spread indecorously around her. I dampened a cloth with water from a pitcher, pressed it gently against her forehead, as she remained there, eyes closed.

I felt dreadful for her. Aunt Helen had never been pregnant before, had never had a baby. I thought of how frightened she must sometimes feel at the prospect of it all, so much bigger than my own fears on the night of my first bleeding, when she had comforted me.

"It seems to me like an awful lot for a woman's body to go through," I observed.

"Yes," she said, "but it will all be worth it in the end. I shall finally have a baby."

• Thirty-eight •

Richard had employed a Dr. Channing, one of the finest obstetric physicians in London, to attend Aunt Helen in her condition.

"I want only the very best for you," I heard Richard say to her on more than one occasion.

Dr. Channing had thin brown hair plastered to his skull, as though it had been painted onto his cranium rather than naturally sprouting from that supposedly intelligent site. His bushy eyebrows were more flat than arched, and his thick mustache and beard looked all of a piece. He did smile often, which was reassuring, but his bulbous red nose gave me to believe that he enjoyed his port overmuch when he was not on duty, and the breath that floated out on his exhalations suggested that he sometimes indulged his enjoyment even when he was.

It was six months since Aunt Helen and Richard had returned from their honeymoon, and I was seated in the front parlor when I saw Aunt Helen pass by, accompanying Dr. Channing to the door. In the past few months, Aunt Helen had grown immense and I heard Dr. Channing comment on this as she saw him out.

"If I did not know better, Mrs. Earl, I would swear you were about to deliver this baby any moment now and not in the two months' time when it is due." I imagined him tipping his hat. "I shall call in again at the same time next week."

Even though I had been hearing her addressed thus for some time now, it was still a fresh shock each time I heard it: *Mrs. Earl*.

I heard the front door close, and a moment later Aunt Helen was in the room with me, her hand supporting the small of her back.

"I didn't know you were in here," she said, settling her bulk gingerly on the sofa beside me. She placed her hand over her eyes as though weary.

"Are you all right?" I asked quickly. "Is the baby all right?"

"We are both fine," she said, eyes still shut. "But could you please find Richard for me? I need to speak with him."

I found Richard in Father's private study. It was a habit of his now to spend time there upon occasion, a habit I found odious, and yet I felt I had no right to tell him *not* to go there.

After delivering Richard to Aunt Helen, I moved to go upstairs, but something stopped me and I assumed my old position as eavesdropper upon the sixth step. It had occurred to me that perhaps Aunt Helen was putting on a good front for my sake and that in fact everything was not fine with her and the baby. Why else would she need to speak with Richard right then? If such was the case, I wished to know about it.

I heard the sound of a kiss, followed by Richard's concerned voice: "What is wrong?"

It was always odd listening to Aunt Helen and Richard, so different from how listening to Mother and Father had been. The way they spoke with each other, the way they talked, the intimacy there, the words that lurked in the silences—it was like they had known each other all their lives. Like I thought of Kit and me—mates of the soul who had been born into the universe instinctively knowing of the other's existence, only waiting for the moment of meeting—so I thought of them.

I cannot say it was a happy thought. Something about Richard still troubled me so much.

"He wants to give me chloroform," I heard Aunt Helen whisper to Richard now.

"And what is wrong with that?" Richard said. "As a matter of fact, I have discussed it with him. He says that Queen Victoria herself used it when delivering Prince Leopold, and, I must say, if it is good enough for the queen—"

"Oh, *why* is everyone always throwing the queen at me?" Aunt Helen's tone was exasperated as she cut him off. "What do I care about the queen?" She barked a harsh laugh. "As though *we* have anything in common."

"But I don't understand," Richard said. "Why don't you want the chloroform? It is my understanding, though I will never have one myself, that bearing a baby is a painful business. Surely anything that can serve to alleviate—"

"Chloroform is *a drug*, Richard. A person might say anything while under its influence. What if I were to say things it would be best I did not? I might not be able to stop myself."

While no champion of pain myself, I could see why she felt this way. Childbirth, the whole notion of pushing a baby out into the world, as yet seemed to me a fantastical thing. *How did women do it?* And it would be undignified, the entire loss of physical control and having others see one thus. To add to that the outrage of being caused to babble senselessly like a madwoman—well, I could see where the thing, when taken as a whole, was more than a bit much.

Then suddenly I saw what Aunt Helen's real fear was: she worried that while under the drug, she might let slip her true identity. I wished I could tell her that I already knew, that she need not endure unimaginable pain to keep her secret from me.

But I could not tell her that.

Richard was silent for a long moment. Then: "I see what you mean." He sighed. "What is it you want me to do, though? You cannot very well have the baby without anyone there to attend you. You cannot deliver it yourself."

"I don't care who you find," Aunt Helen said, her voice steel, "so long as it is not a doctor, so long as it is not a *male* doctor who will insist on giving me chloroform." She paused before adding, "Find me someone I can trust."

· · · · ·

Mrs. Daggett did not appear to me to be the sort of person who would inspire trust in anybody. In her bedraggled clothes, she reminded me of no one so much as the snaggletooth woman I had glimpsed when Father had taken me to the seamier side of London, so very long ago, to hunt for Aunt Helen—minus the snaggletooth, of course. Other than that minor deviation, the two women were very much the same. Indeed, I had to ask her twice to wash her hands before attending to Aunt Helen.

Mrs. Daggett was the midwife Richard had found to replace Dr. Channing, causing me to think that a liking for port in a physician was not so great an offense.

The baby was arriving two months early.

Aunt Helen's water had broken at breakfast that morning, leaving behind a mark on the satin cushion of her chair. Richard had promptly sent a servant to fetch the woman he had hired, and that was Mrs. Daggett.

"Where's the room you've chosen for the birth?" Mrs. Daggett demanded with no preamble upon entering.

She was shown to Aunt Helen's old bedroom on the third story.

"I suppose this'll have to do," she allowed. "But look at this mattress," she said, throwing back the sheets. "Only one? Someone'll need to find me a second. Also, some oiled silk to put over it or an untanned skin if you have one lying about. Oh, and open the window and light that fire. Isn't anyone ready to have a baby in this house?"

"Are you sure she knows what she's doing?" I whispered to Richard, although I needn't have bothered with the caution. Mrs. Daggett spoke at such a volume I suspected she might be deaf.

He rarely let his displeasure with me show, a feeling I suspected he had often, but he did so now. "Do you honestly think I would ever do anything to jeopardize your mother's life?"

I did not. Even I could see the love in his eyes when he looked on her, concern now added to the mix.

"These are *her* wishes," he emphasized.

A moment later, Mrs. Daggett kicked him out.

I moved to follow.

"Please stay with me, Lucy," Aunt Helen said, grabbing tight to my hand. There was a look of fear in her eyes I'd never seen there before; for herself or the baby, I could not tell.

Now, twelve hours later, Aunt Helen lay drenched in sweat on her old bed.

Before having her lie down, Mrs. Daggett had instructed that Aunt Helen put on loose-fitting garments and a cap. Why a cap?

"Perhaps someone else can be located?" I suggested to Aunt Helen when Mrs. Daggett left the room without explanation, a thing she did with an alarming frequency.

"There is no time for that," Aunt Helen said through gritted teeth.

Aunt Helen's eyes had gone wild with terror like a frightened horse and then she was scrunching her eyes shut, her two rows of teeth clenched together like warring armies clashing in the middle, her knees pulled up toward her shoulders, her hand holding mine so tightly that I could feel her nails piercing my skin, the blood coming and—

There was a cry in the room that did not come from Aunt Helen, the cry of a new life.

"'Tis a girl," Mrs. Daggett said. "I do hope the mister won't be disappointed. 'Tis a pretty girl, from the looks of her, with blond hair just like her mother."

I could see that Mrs. Daggett was right as she placed the baby against Aunt Helen's breast. The baby did have a downy gold on her head.

"Your mother's a caution," Mrs. Daggett said to me. "Why, look at her. She has a baby—an early baby who happens to still be quite big!—and yet she doesn't make a sound the whole time. I've never seen one like her. Most women—*all* women—they scream their bloody heads off, as if no one else ever had a baby before."

I looked at the baby at Aunt Helen's breast: my new cousin.

Aunt Helen looked at the baby, and I looked at both of them.

I was thinking of what Mrs. Daggett had said, that she hoped "the mister" wouldn't be disappointed at not having a boy.

"Have you thought of any girls' names?" I asked.

"Yes," Aunt Helen said. She sighed a contented sigh. "I shall call her Emma."

· Thirty-nine ·

Having a baby in the house changed everything.

The sounds that filled all the rooms, the sight of baby Emma in Aunt Helen's or Richard's arms, even the smells—sweet milk and the acrid odor of nappies—were all different. And the rhythm of life was changed too.

At last, across the hall from me, in the nursery that had once been occupied by Aunt Helen when she first came to us, there was a baby.

When I was younger, I used to fantasize about this, and I freely confess: I nearly always imagined it being a girl, a miniature ally in a world almost entirely filled with adults. I pictured her being a subordinate, someone I could subjugate to my will, making her read the books I thought she should read, play the games I wanted to play. I pictured her being a tiny version of me, complete with my hair and eyes, as though she *were* me, reincarnated in doll form.

But it wasn't like that at all, not least because she did not look at all like I did, and by now I was nearly as old as Mother was when she gave birth to me.

Giving birth to Emma had changed Aunt Helen too, at least in the aftermath of that event. Having refused to employ a wet nurse for the feeding, she was constantly exhausted, as though the universe had played a grand trick on her body, with great bags under her eyes. And she worried about every little detail. Was Emma sleeping too much? Too little? Why would she not take sustenance more often? Was she growing properly?

"Nanny says that Emma is the healthiest baby she has ever seen," Richard told Aunt Helen, referring to the woman he had employed to help Aunt Helen care for Emma.

"I don't like her," Aunt Helen said. "I don't think she knows anything about babies at all. You will have to dismiss her."

"But—"

But Aunt Helen would brook no "buts," and Richard did what he was asked.

I will say this for Richard: he doted on that baby. Indeed, I had brief sparks of envy in the beginning, because I could not picture my own father ever having doted so on me, at least not until I was old enough to give him a good literary argument.

Then I would hold Emma in my arms, and all such feelings would vanish. She was so vulnerable and so extraordinarily beautiful I wanted to protect her from the world.

But that was not the job of a cousin. It was the job of a mother or a nanny. There was just one problem, two actually: Since having the baby, Aunt Helen had grown sad. And as for the nanny, having dismissed the first, that sad mother seemed no more inclined to approve the second.

"She just sits there while the baby sleeps!" Aunt Helen complained to Richard of that second nanny.

"What do you want her to do when the baby is sleeping?" Richard answered.

But his sensible approach—and his approach did seem sensible, even to me, even given how little I normally regarded Richard's opinions—did nothing to allay Aunt Helen's fears.

So Nanny Two departed, and Nanny Three arrived.

"This one does not impress me either," Aunt Helen confessed when Richard was out of the room. I think she suspected that his patience with her objections to the string of nannies was wearing thin.

"What is wrong with this one?" I asked Aunt Helen, taking care not to sound as though I was criticizing, for Aunt Helen had become very sensitive and would cry at the slightest offense, real or imagined.

"I just do not trust her," Aunt Helen said. "Do you see the way her eyes are always darting about? She is like a rodent looking for the cheese."

"I think she is just watchful," I said, "to protect Emma."

"No, I don't think that is it." Aunt Helen chewed on a finger until her cuticle became ragged, and I was tempted to bat her hand away from her mouth, beg her to stop hurting herself.

Then a light came into her eyes.

"What about you, Lucy?"

"What about me what?"

"Cannot you take care of Emma, just until I am feeling stronger?"

"Well, I don't know that—"

"Please, Lucy, I beg of you. There is no one I trust more."

It was a bit much on the face of it. What did *I* know about taking care of babies? But then, I thought, when had Aunt Helen ever asked anything of me? True, she had asked me to stay with her the day Emma was born, but I had not minded that; apart from seeing Aunt Helen in so much pain, it had been rather interesting, illuminating in a scientific sort of way. And I saw now that I did not mind this either. If I were to be called once more into the breach, as though one of Henry V's men, I would do my duty.

"All right, Mother," I said. "I would be happy to help out."

. . . . .

We took Emma to the church to be christened.

Mr. Roberts, the new vicar, had replaced Mr. Thomason, who had finally died three months earlier. It was said that Mr. Thomason had been writing a sermon one day when his pen just stopped midsentence and that was that.

Mother, Mrs. Carson, Father, Aunt Martha, now Mr. Thomason—all dead. Sometimes I felt as though we had stumbled into *Hamlet*, and I wondered who would remain living at the end of the play.

Mr. Roberts was the antithesis of Mr. Thomason: impossibly young where the other had been ancient, stern where the other had been kind.

Still, despite the creeping sense that Mr. Roberts expected us all to go to hell, as he read the liturgy I could not help but feel a proprietary satisfaction. Emma was more my daughter than my cousin now, and I could not help but delight in the belief that her soul would be saved.

. . . . .

It was not such a great burden caring for Emma.

Indeed, I received immense rewards for my efforts: a beatific smile at just a few weeks, an attempt at my name at six months. Regarding the latter, she could not get her mouth around the L, so for the longest time I was simply called by the sound of my second letter: "Oo."

I did not mind that either. Indeed, it made me feel as though I had a name that was unique in the world.

One thing I did mind—no, "mind" is not the right word; "miss" is more like it—was the company of others closer to my own age; Kit, in particular. When he would call at the door right after Emma's birth, he was turned away because Aunt Helen feared the baby having contact with outsiders was unhealthy. And since then, he had been turned away because I was too busy caring for Emma. As a result of this, I now had a new appreciation of Minerva Clarence. Previously, I had not quite grasped how helping to take care of her younger sisters should occupy so much of her time.

Despite that most babies were introduced to the outdoors at an early age, with the exception of the brief visit to church for the christening, Aunt Helen had been adamant about Emma not leaving the house.

Aunt Helen worried about everything—that the air would be too cold or hot for Emma, that someone would steal her from the perambulator, that an overzealous bird would peck out her eyes.

While I certainly did not want to see Emma harmed in any way, I did think that some of these concerns—all right, *all of them*—bordered on the insane. And I further attributed this madness to the extended condition of fatigue and gray fugue state Aunt Helen occupied following Emma's birth. But now Aunt Helen's spirits seemed at last to be lifting, her worry and madness suddenly disappearing altogether one day as though God were a portrait artist who had whipped the cloth off the easel, revealing a startling picture of the sun, and I thought it might be a good time to ask again.

"The park! Why, what a clever thought!" Aunt Helen said, as though no one had ever suggested anything more brilliant. "Let me change first."

"I don't mind confessing," Richard said, once she was out of the room, "that in the beginning, I did not think much of you."

I almost choked on my toast.

"But now that I have seen," he went on, "firsthand, the way you care for your mother and our daughter, well, I suppose I shall have to revise that assessment."

"Thank you, Richard," I said, trying to convey through a politeness of tone that his opinion mattered, when in fact it did not.

"Aren't you ready?" Aunt Helen asked, coming downstairs twenty minutes later in a beautiful dress of ice blue silk.

"Yes," I said, dabbing my mouth with the napkin. "I just need to gather up Emma."

"But aren't you going to change into something smarter?"

I looked down at what I was wearing: an old dress from a few seasons back, originally bronze in color, now faded to an unexceptional brown through repeated laundering. It had been laundered so much because I wore it so often these days, since I never minded if Emma spit up on it.

"We are only going to the park," I said. "This will be fine."

I was in a hurry to finally get Emma outdoors.

. . . . .

The day was an extraordinarily vivid one: the colors vibrant, the song of birds, the promise of flowers on the gentle breeze.

It seemed that all of London was in the park that day.

And they were all thrilled to meet Emma.

I was so proud of her. But when Aunt Helen lifted her out of her perambulator so that Mary Williams might get a closer look, I confess to a frisson of jealousy: not that Emma was the center of attention, but that it was Aunt Helen showing her off, rather than me.

"Where is Emma's nanny?" Mrs. Williams asked after having made the appropriate appreciative noises over Emma.

"Oh," Aunt Helen said, entranced with the baby in her own arms, as though meeting her for the first time all over again. "We dismissed her."

We dismissed three! I thought.

"She was not working out," Aunt Helen added vaguely.

"But this is most irregular. You must have a nanny for your baby!" Mrs. Williams insisted, as though to raise one's baby oneself were some sort of crime against the Crown.

"I suppose you are right," Aunt Helen conceded the point to Mary Williams.

"We missed you at the party last week." Mary Williams changed the subject.

"What party?" Aunt Helen asked.

LAUREN BARATZ-LOGSTED

"Why, the one we had on Saturday. Everyone was there."

We weren't, I thought.

"I must confess," Mary Williams continued, "I was surprised when you never responded to the invitation."

"I'm so sorry," Aunt Helen said with a blush, "but I never saw it. I'm afraid I have been lax about reading my correspondence of late."

This was an understatement. I knew well that on the table in the entryway at home there was a mountain of correspondence Aunt Helen had been steadfastly ignoring these past several months. Richard liked to joke that it was a good thing Aunt Helen was not responsible for paying the bills.

"Mrs. Williams?" A tinkling voice, like bells, intruded on my thoughts.

I looked up to see Minerva Clarence standing at Mrs. Williams's elbow. Minerva had on a girlish pink satin dress that was in marked contrast to my drab brown one and her hands were wrapped around the arm of a young man: Kit.

I told myself that he was merely being kind, doing the gentlemanly thing in holding her up so that she should not fall flat on her pretty face.

"I just wanted to thank you," Minerva went on, "for the delightful time we had at your party the other evening."

"Oh, yes," Kit added, looking at me. "I cannot remember the last time I laughed so much."

"I am so glad," Mary Williams said warmly. "It was wonderful seeing the two of you dance together—and so many dances! I must admit, I would not have thought it possible for a man who relies on a cane to dance so well!"

· Forty ·

I was angry with Kit for going to Mary Williams's party, even though I knew it was unreasonable to feel so, and further angry with him for dancing with Minerva in my absence.

I was used to being central in my world, central in Kit's world, as Mother had been in her own before Aunt Helen came along—only in that case, I knew, it was Aunt Helen who'd had the right to feel resentment and not the reverse.

The thought of Minerva, with her pretty hair and her pretty face and her pretty voice and her pretty body and all those... *sisters*, dancing with Kit, *my Kit*—it made me want to smash something. It made me want to smash everything.

But then I thought: just because caring for Emma kept me from the social swim, was it fair of me to expect the same from him?

And Minerva. Was it fair to judge her so harshly? I saw that it was not. It was not her fault if she was everything I was not. It was not her fault if she suited Kit far better than I could ever do.

I pictured her and Kit dancing together again. It was a painful image, but it was also a beautiful one.

And Kit. He had always been my friend, my *best* friend, the shareholder of all my most significant and greatest memories. Shouldn't I want the best for him? Shouldn't I want him to be as happy as it was possible for him to be in this world?

I wrote him a letter, asked him to meet me in the middle of the night.

For once in my life, I would be a bigger person than was my wont. I would be as big as I could possibly be.

I would let go of that which I loved most.

· · · · ·

Step . . . tap . . . clack.

Step . . . tap . . . clack.

The steps, as they drew closer to me, were halting, but I could see the candle advancing steadily all the same.

"I say, Lucy," Kit said, meeting me where I waited for him, "with all these stones—the moisture that was never here before does make them slippery!—it is not so easy negotiating this tunnel as it was before I replaced my foot with a peg. Is there some reason why we couldn't discuss whatever it is you wish to discuss *above-ground?*"

Despite the censoriousness implied by his emphasis, that feeling was not echoed in his eyes, which danced with all their usual joy.

Seeing him like that—so full of life, *so very Kit*—it made what I had come to do doubly hard.

I swallowed.

"Well," he said, when I did not speak, his eyes still dancing a tease, "what is so very important that we must meet down here?"

I wanted to reach out, touch my fingers to that familiar face one last time, but I could not allow myself that luxury. If I let myself touch him once, I would not be able to stop.

I straightened my spine into a steel rod.

"I have decided to release you," I announced, addressing my words to his nose, because I could not bear to look into his eyes.

"That is very generous of you." I had the sense of his eyebrows rising in puzzlement. "But I was not aware you had bound me prisoner. Have I missed something? Is there a chapter you have read that I have not?"

I felt the blush color my cheeks.

"You know what I am—," I started to speak, but he cut me off.

"And *will* you stop talking to my nose! If you are expecting an answer, you will only find sneezes there."

"Do not mock me," I begged him. If he no longer wanted me to talk to his nose, then I would address his ear. "I know about you dancing with Minerva."

"And . . . ?"

"And I know that you are an honorable man."

"And?"

"And I know that it has long been understood, I would imagine by just about practically everybody, that one day you and me would, that is to say you and I . . . or do I mean you and me . . . ?"

"*And?*"

There was real menace in that last *and*, causing me to feel briefly relieved that I was not a Mahdist Dervish meeting him in the desert of the Sudan and he with a bayoneted rifle in his hand.

He took a threatening step closer to me and I could hear the sound of his breathing, feel his breath on my face as I spoke the rest of what I had come to say in one great rush.

"You are released from your implied bond to me, and so now you are free to marry Minerva Clarence at your earliest convenience because I know that is what you want, so there is no need for you to wait any longer on my account and—"

He placed his hand on my body, pulled me to him.

"What are you *doing*?" I cried.

The way his fingers touched me indicated that he did indeed know what he was doing, at least on one level.

"I am trying to show you—you insane woman!—in the only way left to me, that the only woman in this world I want, for anything, is you."

I could feel my breath shortening.

"This is a peculiar way to show it," I said, striving to maintain a calm against the touch of his hand. "How did you learn how to do this?" I thought jealously of the military. Had there been women in the Sudan? I thought jealously of Minerva.

He kissed my face, my neck, my mouth.

He pulled away, pressed his cheek to mine. Despite the coldness rising up from the stones beneath our feet, there was sweat on that cheek.

"I have not done this firsthand before," he said, his own breath growing shorter, "if that is what you are thinking."

We each held fast to our candles. It is a wonder we did not set each other on fire.

"But I have always been a great reader of books," he continued, his hand caressing my body, pulling away and making me shamelessly sink into his touch. "You would be surprised what you can learn from the mere reading of books." He briefly considered this, shook his head. "Well, perhaps no, you specifically would not." He kissed my mouth again, talking between kisses. "And then, too, my father taught me my responsibilities from a young age."

His *father*?

"The Tyler men take their duties toward their women very seriously."

No wonder Victoria Tyler always looked so happy!

Still . . .

"This is no proper proposal, sir," I said, raising my hand to my mouth and indelicately wiping away the story of his kisses with the back of my hand.

"Is that what you want?" His tone was incredulous. *"Right this minute, Lucy?"*

I held firm, watched him shake his head like a wet hunting dog coming in from the rain.

"No, you are right," he said. "Or at least it is not the proposal I intended to make when I received your letter unceremoniously summoning me here. But this is."

Then Kit dropped to one knee, as best he could, taking my free hand with his free hand.

"Lucy Sexton, will you marry me?"

"Are you *insane*?"

"I may be," he admitted, "and for all sorts of reasons." He relinquished my hand long enough to reach up for my face, compelling me to look at him. "But I do know this: if I live to see every star burn out in the sky, should the ocean roll back its waves not to return, I shall never find another woman who will make me so happy, even in the moments when she most torments me. You are like no other person in this world. I love you, Lucy." Tears shone in his eyes, but they were of strength, not weakness. "Marry me."

I fell to my knees before him, set the candle to one side, took his face in my hands.

Kit. It seemed to me that everyone else I had ever known, all my life, had had some sort of duality about them, a light mixing with the dark or vice versa. Even myself. But never Kit. He had always been transparent, exactly what he was, what he said, what he did. How had I not seen this before? How had I ever doubted him?

"Do you think you could answer me tonight, Lucy?" he asked. "It is not easy maintaining this position with a bad leg." His expression clouded, concern pushing away his bluff jocularity. "And I am beginning to worry you will say no."

"Yes," I said. "Yes, Kit. I will marry you."

In the kisses that followed, his tongue traced my mouth with probing intensity. Before those kisses were through, I had occasion to remind Kit that we would need to wait until after we were married to finish what he had started earlier.

"Of course," he said, restraining himself. "Yes, we will finish then."

"How soon shall we marry?" I asked.

He pressed his forehead to mine, a groan of longing preceding his words. "Tomorrow would be good."

I began to wonder if that was the real reason he was marrying me, to gain something he could not otherwise get.

He must have seen the dismay in my expression, reading, as he was so disturbingly good at, my unvoiced thoughts.

"No, Lucy," he said firmly. "I marry you for you. Everything else is just a wonderful extra."

· Forty-one ·

My wedding day!

It was not the day following the night in the tunnel, as Kit had wanted it to be, but it was as soon as could reasonably be arranged.

"I should like to wear the wedding gown you wore on the occasion of your marriage to Father," I told Aunt Helen the same day Kit came to the house to inform her and Richard of our intent to marry.

"Do not be ridiculous, Lucy," had been her reply, equal parts sweet and sharp.

"What did you say?"

"I am sorry," she quickly mollified me. "I only meant that seeing you in it would be too much of a reminder to me and that, besides, it is your day. You should have your own gown."

At first her response puzzled me. But then it occurred to me that, perhaps, she was still jealous of Mother, perhaps was jealous of the grand wedding Mother had as opposed to the tiny one she'd had with Richard. I could understand that, at least on some level. I understood jealousy now far better than I ever had before.

With so little time before the wedding, there were not sufficient hours for Mrs. Wiggins to fashion me a whole new creation from thread and fabric to completed gown. So we bought the first white dress I found in a shop.

"Are you sure?" Aunt Helen asked. "You have not even looked at everything they have to offer."

But I did not care what I wore—they could have clothed me in sackcloth for all I cared!—so long as I was marrying Kit, so long as *he* was waiting for me at the end of the aisle. Indeed, to this day, were it not for the evidence of pictures, all I would remember about the dress I wore was that it was white.

. . . . .

We know the people in our worlds, not by what they look like, but what they say, or would not say.

Father used to claim that dialogue was character.

"A writer should be able to create dialogue such that a reader can tell who is speaking which lines without ever seeing the speaker's name attributed." That is what Father always said.

It was my wedding day.

And it was raining. *God*, was it raining!

It was as though the promise of spring weather had been canceled and a storm had come up, complete with high winds and chilling rains, battering the trees and anything that stood in its way. Apparently, winter was not finished with us yet.

But I did not care.

I was seated in front of a mirror in Aunt Helen and Richard's bedroom, still in my dressing gown, my wedding dress draped across the bed, waiting for me to wear it, as the maid fashioned my hair.

The day, happy as it was, was tinged with no small degree of sadness. I had always, when growing up, imagined Mother helping me to get ready on my wedding day, but that was not to be. Still, I contented myself that at least I had Aunt Helen with me. At least I had her.

As the maid worked, Aunt Helen fussed behind us, instructing the maid on what to do with a few stray hairs that refused to be tamed into submission, flouncing the end of the gown's skirts as if I were already wearing it and she wanted it to be perfect.

I had never seen her all aflutter like this before.

"I just want everything to be perfect for you today, Lucy," she said nervously.

"It will be," I said, not even wincing when the maid accidentally stabbed me with a pin. "I only wish Father were here."

"Yes," she said. "I am sure you would want that." She addressed the maid brusquely. "Aren't you finished yet?"

"Nearly so, madam."

"And Aunt Helen," I said, in reality thinking of Mother in my mind. "Today I find myself missing her too."

"I am sure," Aunt Helen said, placing a soft hand upon my shoulder, "your aunt would have loved to be standing by your side today."

The first maid, having finished with my hair, went to fetch another maid to help me with my dress.

Aunt Helen wrapped her arms around herself, shivered.

"If only it weren't raining so!" she said. "You will be soaked before you even reach the church!"

I met her eyes in the mirror, smiled my reassurance that all would be fine, no matter what happened.

Then she was behind me, one hand on my shoulder, and she was smiling too. In the mirror, I saw her open her mouth to speak.

"Your hair may be a dark cloud, but no matter what the weather, on your wedding day the sun and stars will shine," she said with strong assurance. "Remember how I always used to say that to you whenever we played 'The Wedding Game'?"

The Wedding Game?

It hit me instantly, like one of those bolts of lightning outside shooting down from the heavens.

Aunt Helen had never played "The Wedding Game" with me. *Aunt Helen* had never spoken those specific reassuring words to me before. Those words had been a very private thing between Mother and me. There was no way the woman standing with her beautiful hand upon my shoulder could possibly know about them, unless . . .

The first thing I experienced then was pure joy.

Mother was *alive*!

Those words: *Your hair may be a dark cloud, but no matter what the weather, on your wedding day the sun and stars will shine.* When I was younger, Mother had recited the line to me so many times it was engraved on my heart, like a talisman against bad fortune, expressive of our shared faith that good would still triumph in a world that was frequently lonely and unfair.

Mother was *alive*!

I wondered how such a thing was possible, but then I saw with a wild and giddy relief that it had only been my own self-delusion and overactive imagination that had ever told me any different. Seeing her seated down in the garden that first time with Richard, I had jumped to conclusions based on a single memory: the day I'd seen a similar picture, a similar tableau of Aunt Helen and Richard seated together in the park. It would never have occurred to me that it had been Mother I had seen, speaking so intimately with a man other than my father.

But wait a second.

Now I remembered other things. I remembered how after seeing the woman I assumed to be Aunt Helen that day at the park, when I questioned her about it later, she said she had seen no one. At the time, I had assumed her to be lying. But what if she had been telling the truth? Mother and Aunt Helen had shared clothes all the time, wore similar cloaks whenever they went out. One twin in a dark cloak looked much the same as the other. Or who knows? Maybe it *had* been Mother, and she had simply lied to me about seeing no one. It was confusing. But one thing I was not confused about any longer. The surviving twin was Mother, and it had been Mother that day in the park with Richard.

But if it had been Mother that day in the park with Richard, that day far before the murder, when, oh yes, Father had still been very much alive, what did it all mean?

I had no idea—could not fathom it, stunned as I was by this revelation—but I resolved that as soon as I swam out of this sea of confusion, I would finally uncover the truth.

I would learn everything.

My eyes yet held hers in the mirror as I forced myself to smile on as the drenching rain thundered the panes from the outside.

Tick . . . tock . . . tick . . . tock . . .

"Did I not say the words correctly?" she asked.

I forced myself to say the thing that needed to be said, so that she would not know what questions I now had about her in my mind: "Yes."

My mind reeled with shock as the woman behind me, in many ways a stranger no matter who she was, laid a tender kiss upon my cheek.

"Now you really must get dressed," she said brightly, "or you will be late for your own wedding."

It was all I could do not to wipe that Judas kiss from my cheek.

. . . . .

The day I had dreamed about forever had turned into a waking nightmare.

Does not a child recognize her own mother?

I had had this thought once before: on the day, five years ago, when Aunt Helen had first come to us, when she had stood on our doorstep with her back to me and then when she turned I saw Mother's face.

How could I have been so wrong, first in one way and then another, these last four years? How could I have not known the truth?

Does not a child recognize her own mother?

I tried to tell myself that I had been mistaken before, more than once. I had been mistaken the day I went to Father's study and seeing Aunt Helen seated on his desk familiarly, took Aunt

Helen to be Mother. I had been mistaken about Kit's feelings for Minerva. Surely I could be mistaken again?

And yet I knew that I was not.

There was something very wrong going on in my house, perhaps something had always been wrong here, and the only thing I was sure of was that it involved Richard and it involved Mother.

I wanted to shout it to the world. I wanted to renounce her there and then . . . but for what exactly?

I still did not know the answer to that.

But I would know.

Dear God.

Finally, I would know.

. . . . .

I moved through my wedding day like a ghost, seeing others as through a filmy glass as I processed down the aisle, as the assembled guests with excruciating slowness turned their heads, swinging them like pendulums backward to look at me.

One woman whose eyes I would not meet, could not meet any longer, was the beautiful blond woman standing in the front row.

So I focused instead on the back of the head of the man beside her, who had yet to turn around: Richard.

Richard had never worn his hair particularly short and now it was growing unruly again. The sight of that brown hair glimpsed from behind, I hated the sight of it—to me it was somehow symbolic of all of their lies, all of their betrayal.

I had written to Kit after that long-ago day in the park.

From the way they were seated together, almost intimately, I felt certain that this was not their first time meeting each other, I had written.

The two appeared to be engaged in a rather heated discussion, judging from the expressions I could glimpse on Aunt Helen's face, but I could not hear any of the words, for they were whispering, I had written.

I could see nothing of the man, save for his back: a coat, of poor quality both in fabric and cut; unruly brown hair peeking out from beneath the back of his hat, which was also of poor quality—the hat, not the hair, I had written.

And then later, I had told Kit, when Aunt Helen arrived home shortly after I sneaked home myself, and I asked her if she had seen anyone interesting during her walk, she had said, "I saw no one."

Of course she hadn't, if that had indeed been Aunt Helen I had spoken with upon her arrival home. Because it had never been Aunt Helen in the first place. It had been Mother. It had been Mother speaking heatedly and with such apparent intimacy to the strange man she was with, the man who was obviously no stranger to her.

And then Richard turned to me, that familiar sardonic grin stretching his lips, and I wanted to shoot him dead where he stood.

But I could not think about that any longer, not now. If I did, I would collapse or go mad.

So instead I focused on Kit, waiting patiently with his hands resting lightly on his cane, focused on those green eyes at the end of the tunnel, like the ocean calling me home.

A few moments later, I dimly heard myself being announced as "Mrs. Christopher Tyler" by the stern young vicar, Mr. Roberts, without ever having really heard any of the service.

. . . . .

The wedding breakfast that followed is no more clear to me now than the service in the church. It was as though all the faces of the guests swam around me, and it was only familiarity with convention that informed me that the gaping mouths and moving tongues and chattering teeth must surely be extending to Kit and me best wishes.

But I could not hear them. I could not see anything clearly except for the laughing faces of *that woman* and Richard, repeatedly standing out in bas-relief against the swirl of the others.

I wanted to smash those two faces, end all laughter.

The only thing that carried me through the ordeal without screaming was the presence of Kit at my side. It did pain me to see him looking so puzzled—why was his bride not looking bright and happy on this grand shared day?—but he was Kit to the bone, always seeing the good.

"I know." He held tight to my hand as he leaned down to whisper in my ear. "You are nervous about the honeymoon. Well," he added with a flash of green eyes and a wiggle of his brows that would have been comical on any other day, "so am I."

"I do love you," I said, placing my hand against his cheek, needing to be reminded that he was still there, that one thing was still real.

"And I do know that," he said, tilting his head just enough to plant a kiss on the center of my palm.

A short time later, it was all I could do not to recoil when *that woman* kissed me on the cheek before Kit handed me up into the carriage that was to take us on our honeymoon.

• Forty-two •

We were to honeymoon in the Swiss lakes region.

It had been Richard's recommendation, he having been so pleased with his own honeymoon there.

"Look how well it ended for your mother and me," he had said with smug satisfaction, indicating Emma.

My mother, I thought bitterly.

I had always been good at doing what needed to be done, whatever was required of me, in the moment. Come home from a pleasant New Year's Day stroll in the park to discover your two closest female relatives bound to chairs and covered in blood, one with her head hanging by a stalk to her body, the other in such an advanced state of shock she can barely form words? Rather than fainting from your *own* shock, and with no one else to rely on for help, you ascertain whether or not the murderer is still on the premises, you do your best to discover what has happened, even if later on you prove to be wrong, you remain cool—even though you do scream—until help arrives.

I had always been good at doing what needed to be done, had learned to do it all myself when no other help was at hand.

And I had followed the prescribed behaviors of this day, my wedding day, by placing one foot determinedly in front of the other. But now the sea of shock I had been swimming in since early that morning washed away and the horror of what I had learned came rushing in, causing my mind to reel with the overwhelming force of it.

The rain battered the roof of the carriage as it swung past the church where we had been married, swung past the cemetery of that church, and I realized for the first time, really realized, that it truly was Aunt Helen buried there, poor Aunt Helen, and the baby she'd been carrying inside her when she was murdered as well.

I wanted to leap from the carriage, scrabble into the earth, hold my aunt in my arms one last time, apologize for all the wrongs the world had done her.

. . . . .

My immediate inclination was to tell Kit what had happened.

But when I opened my mouth to speak, it occurred to me that his day had been spoiled enough already, even if he was not aware of it. I could not bring myself to spoil if further. There would be time enough later. Not to mention, what could we do about it now? Back at the house, the rooms would still be filled with guests—not the most conducive setting for a confrontation. If I went back and made my accusation now, I would probably be carted away before I had the chance to learn any more.

All my life, even though there had been individual moments when I had been *im*patient, I had known how to keep quiet. I had known how to keep my own counsel and simply wait.

Wait for my moment, *my* time.

"You are not yourself," Kit said, a look of concern clouding his eyes as he held my hand in the carriage. I felt his eyes watching me all the while, but it was hard to look at him now, with murder on my mind, lest he see there was something troubling me so severely, there were moments I forgot to draw breath. "In fact, I don't think I've ever seen you at such a loss for words." His laugh was nervous. "You are not already repenting marrying in such haste, are you?"

It pained me to see him so concerned on my behalf, and yet I couldn't tell him what was on my mind, not now.

"I am fine," I said, forcing a reassuring smile. "Or at least I will be soon."

But as the carriage pulled into the railway station and Kit jumped down as best he could with his cane, I spoke one word:

"No."

"No?"

"I do not want to get on that train."

"Not get on . . . ? But this is our train. If we do not get on it now, then we will miss—"

"I don't care about that. Have a driver find an inn for us."

"An inn?"

"Yes, an inn. Are you having difficulty with your hearing today?" Then, to take the sting out of my words, I added, "What does it matter whether we consummate our marriage in Switzerland or right here in London? I do not want to wait."

His smile was wide. "Then I will have the driver find us the finest hotel in London, if that is what you want."

"I don't care if it's the finest hotel, I don't care where it is so long as I am with you."

And I didn't.

The inn, as it turned out, had seen better days. The old floor-boards in the front room warped at alarming angles, a hunting tapestry on the wall hung in tatters, the furniture in the room we were shown to of the poorest quality.

"If you did not insist we stop at the very first place we came to," Kit teased, "I am fairly certain I could have done better for you than this. You know, I did come to this marriage with a fair amount of money."

"It does not matter," I said.

"Would you like some dinner?" he suggested. "I somehow doubt that the food here could be anything we would want to eat, but we could go out, anywhere you like. Do you fancy meat? Fish? Perhaps you would like me to find somewhere we could eat pudding all night? I do not want to rush you in ... anything."

"No," I said firmly. "I do not want food. I do not care if I ever eat again."

Then I pulled the pins from my hair, felt that hair tumble down my back, held that hair out of the way as I turned my back to him, silently inviting him to undo my dress.

I wanted to shut it all away, the knowledge, forget, if only for a little while. I wanted to have *this* ... before I had to go back and do *that*.

With excruciating slowness he began to undo my buttons

and laces. Even though the fabric still separated us, I felt his fingers burn my skin through the dress.

It was maddening.

"You can do this part a little faster, sir," I suggested.

"No."

"No?"

"No. I will only get to do this for the first time once. I want to unveil you slowly."

And that is what he did, one maddening button and lace at a time, at last peeling the garments away until my clothes fell in a great puddle of satin at my feet.

Then he turned me to face him.

His breath caught. "You are beautiful, Lucy."

"I am not, sir," I said.

I did not feel beautiful, did not feel worthy of him, and yet I did not mind being naked before him. I was not being modest in what I said, but rather, I had never thought myself the kind of person others think of as beautiful before.

"But," I added, "I am the only one here without any clothes on." I jutted my chin out at his body. "Your turn, sir."

I did not have to ask him twice.

In a second, his jacket was off, flying across the room. Then his fingers tore at his tie.

"So now you finally remember what speed is." I laughed.

"I will show you speed," he said determinedly, eyes locked on mine as tie followed jacket, shirt followed tie . . . and then everything else.

Now at last we were equal.

The single log the stingy innkeeper had deposited in the

fireplace gave off little light, and it was only after studying Kit for a moment that I saw the scar between his ribs.

"What . . . ?" My eyes asked the question.

"People always see the peg because it is so damned notice- able," Kit said, "but they forget I was stabbed with a spear too." He laughed. "And I do not remind them."

"Does it hurt?" I asked.

"Not now," he said. Kit held his hand out to me. "My wife," he said as I took it.

Before he could kiss or even touch me, I bent my head to that scar between his ribs, traced it with my fingers, placed my lips to it and then my tongue.

Kit lowered his face to mine until there was no space between us, his lips feathering mine. His lips pressing more urgently against my lips, his tongue in my mouth. All of it was sweet tor- ture, causing a rush of naked desire that overwhelmed me with its strength.

Then I felt the weight of him, a weight I did not mind, settle upon me. I had waited for this moment of union, forever it seemed. As for the other, what was waiting for me back home, well, the resolution of *that* had waited for years. It could wait just one more day. Or at least a few more hours.

I pushed tragedy away, reached for joy.

Now, at last, I *did* feel beautiful.

"I love you," he said.

"You make me happy," I said.

And, in that moment, I was happy.

. . . . .

Afterward, I told my secret to the one person in the world that would believe anything I told him, however fantastical, the person I should have been sharing even my most secret secrets with from the very beginning. I put my lips to the entrance of Kit's ear and whispered into the whorls of it my story.

• Forty-three •

I was glad I had waited to tell Kit.

Had I not waited, I was certain the exquisite loveliness of our wedding night would never have been possible.

. . . . .

Born in ice, ended in ice . . .

The rain had frozen to snow had frozen to ice by the time I sneaked back up the steps of my own home—*my home*—in the dead of night. Dawn was still a few hours away as I turned the knob.

I let myself into the dark house, took off my boots so I would not make a sound as I climbed the two stories to their bedroom, opened this second door slowly.

As I pushed the door open, I saw them lying there together in the bed, their bodies intertwined in peaceful slumber.

I wanted to kill them right then and there for the betrayal I believed they had committed on Father.

But I wanted answers even more, so I crept to one side of the bed, slipping my palm over the mouth of the sleeping woman before whispering her awake.

Her eyes over the palm of my hand told me she was shocked at seeing me there, as well she should be.

I pretended to be distressed—not a huge stretch to make, under the circumstances.

"Meet me downstairs," I whispered. "Something has happened."

Then I left, as silently as I had come.

. . . . .

Downstairs in the back parlor, I waited, my back to the fireplace, standing upon the very spot poor Aunt Helen's chair had been that New Year's Day when I found them here together.

Waiting for her to find me there, I had had time to light all the lamps so that the room blazed as though on fire.

It was hard to believe, looking around me now, the furniture and walls and decorations having been redone all in whites and golds, that once this room had seen red drenching the walls, the carpets.

I wondered if any more blood would be shed there tonight, and whose.

She entered, sashing her dressing gown at the waist as she strode toward me.

"Lucy, what is the matter?" Her face was all concern. "You are supposed to be on your honeymoon. Has something gone wrong? Have you and Kit had a fight?"

I had to stop her coming toward me, had to stop her before

she attempted to lay a comforting hand on my arm, which I could not have abided, so I did it with words.

"Hello, Mother," I said.

It was the last time I would ever call her that to her face.

· · · · ·

She laughed nervously. At the harshness in my tone? The look upon my face? It was impossible to say. "You are overwrought, Lucy. Whatever this fight you have had with Kit—"

"Do not *lie* to me about anything," I said. "Never lie to me again."

Father had once said that Aunt Helen would make an excellent solicitor, were it not for her gender, but I saw that he had pinpointed the wrong twin as being the most fit for a life of using words to her own best advantage. Still, I did not see how words could save her this time, and even she had to see now that there was no line of defense against the knowledge in my eyes.

I knew something was wrong, had been wrong all along, and she knew it.

Mother had always had a certain light about her, an energy that was different from anyone else's, but now I saw that light extinguished, turning to ash like the last spark in the fireplace grate.

All the way home from the inn, in the carriage, as the ice clattered the roof and the horses slid on the slick streets, one thing had bothered me. True, nearly everything bothered me now, but for some reason, this one item stood supreme.

"Did Father know?" I asked.

"What are you talking about?"

"Before he died—did he know about you and Richard?"

She laughed blithely. "How could he possibly know? I only met Richard long after Frederick's death." Suddenly she looked wounded. "I cannot believe you would accuse me of such a thing, Lucy. How could you possibly think that *I*—"

"I already told you: *do not lie to me*." I did not give her a chance to respond. "I *saw* you one day, years ago, in the park with Richard."

"I don't know what you're talking about." She raised her dressing gown a bit as though she was about to stride from the room. "I don't have to listen—"

"You will listen!" I stopped her with the steel of my voice. "Your . . . *relationship* must have been going on for a very long time. Now I ask you again: *did Father know about it*?"

The wounded look fled as instantly as it had come. Replacing it was a harsh coldness. "Your father was a weak man." She laughed bitterly. "You ask me about Richard? Well, what of your father and Helen?"

My father and . . .

Then I remembered a day when I had come across a blond woman sitting familiarly on Father's desk and how I'd first assumed her to be Mother, only later realizing it was Aunt Helen; I remembered a time when Mother had gone away to visit Aunt Martha and how I had heard peculiar sounds coming from Aunt Helen's bedroom, sounds I now recognized as man-woman sounds.

My father and . . .

"He *slept* with her!" She spat out the words, a hard gleam in her eye.

Before I could even fully digest what she had told me, she went on.

"And he made a *baby* with her!"

Wait? What? The child Aunt Helen had been carrying when she was murdered was *Father's*?

"Thank God," she said triumphantly, "*that* ended with her death!"

There was something about that triumph in her tone that chilled me to the very core. I had *thought* that my outrage, my need to confront her, had stemmed from my feelings about her betrayal of Father. And yet, really, given the size of my anger— hadn't something else been simmering under the surface all along? As soon as I realized that she and Richard had known each other far longer than I'd previously thought, hadn't I suspected, even if I would not voice that suspicion in my own mind, that something yet darker was afoot?

But no. That couldn't be. Really, I told myself now, it was merely a case of a wife betraying a husband who had already betrayed her. Surely that was all it was.

So my father, whom I had mostly thought to be so strong all the years of my life, had been a weak man, a flawed human being. Well, what of that? We were all flawed, my perfect mother as well. Perhaps, I thought now, she was not the monster I had been making her out to be. Perhaps her behavior was no worse than his had been? But no. It was worse. The way she had treated him after Aunt Helen's death, the contempt, not to mention that while there had been human weakness in his behavior, there appeared to be a real vindictiveness in hers.

"Those years after Aunt Helen was murdered," I said, "the years you encouraged him to eat more, drink more—were you trying to kill him too?"

She laughed at the notion, causing me to immediately recognize how ridiculous had been my fancy. Perhaps she had encouraged him, but he had chosen to eat the food, drink all that alcohol.

"I cannot say I would have minded if he died sooner rather than later," she said, "and I would have gladly hastened it along if I could have." She was so cold. "But I was content to wait."

While we'd been talking, Mother had been slowly circling, like a cat, so I had to keep turning slightly to keep her in direct view until her back was to the fireplace and my back was to the door.

"I was content to wait too," another voice spoke now, a masculine one with a sardonic twist to it.

I felt the knife at my throat without ever having heard the footsteps behind me.

The feel of that voice, that knife at my throat—suddenly I saw something fully in a way I had never seen before. There was more here than just the betrayal of a wife against her husband, or even a husband against his wife. There was murder here as well.

"There never was a red-haired monster, a giant, was there?" I asked, unflinching, eyes steadfast on Mother. "It was Richard."

I felt the knife at my throat press down, just the tiniest bit of added pressure.

"Is this the same knife you used to kill my aunt?"

Richard did not even bother to dignify my question with an answer, instead addressing his words directly to Mother.

"Do you want me to kill her now, my dear?" he asked in a calm, almost cheerful voice, as though he were asking her if she would like a drink of water. "Just say the word."

To Mother's credit, and to my surprise now that I knew what a monster she could be, she looked horrified at the notion of my slaughter. For all I knew, it was an act.

"Won't that be hard to explain?" I asked. "After all, how many women can have their throats slit in the same parlor before the police become suspicious that something is not quite right in this house?"

Richard's laugh told me he was unconcerned.

"I will bury your body in your father's garden," he said. "And if there is blood on the carpet? I will roll it up and throw it away. The servants in this household have always been deplorably lazy. They sleep through everything, and they will not mind having one less carpet to clean."

"No," Mother said. "We can send her away, as if none of this happened. What proof does she have? No one will ever believe her."

There was a pleading quality to her voice, as though she would change this one thing, prevent it from happening if she could.

Of course, there was something else in her voice, in her words. In her . . . *maternal* desire not to see my throat lashed right in front of her, her words were an admission that what I had merely guessed at was the truth: Richard had murdered Aunt Helen, and she had somehow been complicit in that act.

"No," Richard said. "As long as this one lives, she will always be a threat."

Step. Tap. Clack.

It was a sound I imagined in my mind, a sound of footsteps in a tunnel, a sound no one else could hear.

Slam!

"What is that?" Mother jumped at the sound, which could have been a trapdoor snapping shut . . . or open.

"It must be the storm howling the windows in Father's study," I said hastily. Despite the knife at my throat, I cocked an ear, put my hand behind it. "Or perhaps it is his ghost coming back to haunt you?"

A strange thing happened as I watched Mother's face, saw her blanch at my words: I realized that I enjoyed the prospect of scaring her, and that she was in turn indeed scared at the prospect of being haunted.

Step. Tap. Clack.

This time the sound was not in my mind. It was real.

"What *is* that noise?" Mother's voice was strained.

"Perhaps this time it is Aunt Martha haunting you?" My taunting voice rose in volume in an attempt to mask other approaching sounds. "After the way you kicked her out of the house, not once but twice, I am sure she would want to do *that*!"

"Richard?" Mother was puzzled.

"Look over there!" I shouted, pointing behind Mother, drawing their attention away from the door.

"What?" she turned. "What is it?"

"Don't you see Aunt Helen?" And now my voice turned bitter. "*Your own sister*? Now, there's a woman who really does have good cause to haunt you!"

Step, tap, clack.

"Richard!"

Mother wheeled, pointed to the doorway, where stood Kit. In his hand was a pistol, relic from his war.

For a woman who, unlike Mother, had never surprised anyone, I had held one surprise in my sleeve, keeping it from them until now: I had brought Kit with me; Kit, who had stolen into his own house, retrieved his pistol, come to me through the tunnel.

Back at the inn, when I had told Kit the things I knew and what I wanted to do about it, his immediate response was to say that he would come with me. But I had refused, impressing upon him my need to confront her first alone. He had at last conceded that I was a force, a force he trusted, and that for us to be the equals we both wanted to be, he would need to trust me to do this in my own way.

"I can kill you now," Kit said to Richard, "or you can answer all of Lucy's questions and I will kill you later."

"I will kill her first," Richard warned, tightening the knife at my throat once more until it bit into my skin.

"And then I will kill Aliese." Kit swung his arm so that now the pistol was aimed straight at Mother's heart, that black thing that yet beat within her, giving her life. "You would be surprised at how good a shot a peg-footed man can be."

Richard's feelings for Mother must have been stronger than his desire to see me dead, for the pressure at my throat disappeared and an instant later the knife made a dull, impotent thud against the carpet as he released it from his hand.

"Now go and stand by her." Kit waved the pistol at Richard, who obeyed as I hurried to Kit.

Kit dropped his cane, pulled me to his side, kissed my forehead, keeping his eyes trained on them all the while.

"Are you all right?" he asked.

"I have been better," I said, "but I have most assuredly been worse too."

He nodded.

"Now talk," he commanded the others. "Tell Lucy everything she wants to know."

"What happened that day?" I asked Mother.

"You do not have to answer," Richard instructed Mother.

"Oh yes, she does," Kit said, pointing the pistol first at one of them and then the other, "unless she is prepared for you both to die right now."

"It was exactly as I told that Chief Inspector Daniels," she said defiantly. "A man came here on New Year's Day, asking for the loan of the servants to help put out the Carsons' fire. When the servants left, he told your aunt that he wanted to see me, that if she cooperated, I would not lose my life."

"*My aunt,*" I echoed her words. "Your *sister,*" I added bitterly.

She did not flinch at the reminder of her bond.

"Go on," Kit said.

"Helen," she said, careful now in her choice of how she referred to the relative we shared in common, though there was an undeniable contempt there as she continued, "was calm. She did everything in her power to spare me."

"And you repaid her by permitting her slaughter!" I said. I turned to Richard. "And you helped her."

"I would have done anything she asked," he said, as though he did not care what anyone thought of him, unless it was *her*.

"How long have you two known each other?" I demanded.

"For a very long time," Mother said.

"How long?" I demanded again. "Before you learned of Father and Aunt Helen's relationship, or after?"

"What does it matter now?" she countered. It was clear she would not give me satisfaction in this. "It has been a very long time."

"And how did you first meet?" I asked. It had been troubling me ever since my awakening to the truth about them, the question of how two so seemingly mismatched people could ever meet, grow intimate.

"It is a funny story," she said. "We met in the park one day. Richard approached me—he thought I was Helen! He had known her in her previous life." She paused, looked at him. "But once he got to know me better, he decided he liked me more."

A funny story?

I wondered how Richard had known Aunt Helen. Had he been her friend? A lover? And what would he and my mother have possibly had in common to draw them together? Well, I could see what Richard saw in Mother. Beauty. Wealth. But what could she have seen in him? Then it occurred to me: it must have been that he was the opposite of Father, more a part of an almost animal world, where Father had always been so cerebral. Then, too, there was no doubt the appeal of having something that had been Aunt Helen's, and perhaps even possessing it in a way that Aunt Helen never could, but . . .

A funny story?

"Do you see me laughing?" I asked. "Aunt Helen is *dead*."

"Do not blame her," Richard said. "It was my idea that it was time for her sister to die, after what she'd been through."

"But why did Helen have to die?" I said, as if my desperate

asking of the question could make the event not have happened at all. "Why then?"

Mother spoke the words one at a time, so there could be no mistaking them: *"Because . . . she . . . was . . . pregnant!"*

Earlier she'd said that Aunt Helen's baby had been Father's baby. Those years Mother had tried to have a second child, only to fail, then discovering that her sister had not only slept with her husband but that her sister was also carrying that husband's child—still, that was no reason, at least not for a normal person.

"Did Father know the child was his?" I asked.

"You mean Helen's child?" She did not wait for my nod. "Well, of course, when he believed that *she* was the one who had been murdered, he thought it was his. But then later, when he started to believe *I* was Helen . . ."

What?

And yet, that made a queer sort of sense too.

"You must have noticed how guilty he started acting," she said. "With Helen out of the way, I felt free to indulge my contempt for him. And then, too, I was more . . . *energetic* in some of the things we did together, as I imagined she might be with him, so although he never said . . ."

"He believed that you were Helen and that his wife lay in the graveyard with his child," I finished for her simply. "He believed that the wrong sister had been murdered, and that he was the only one who knew it."

"For an intelligent man," she said, "your father did have his stupidities."

I wanted to slap that smirk off her face.

But did she really think any of what she'd said was sufficient cause for what she'd done? She really was crazy. Why had I never seen that before?

Does not a child recognize her own mother?

Clearly, I never had, had never known her.

"That day of the murder," I wondered, "why wasn't your ring on your finger?"

"That was *his* fault," she said, glaring accusation at Richard for the first time. "He ever hated to see me wearing your father's ring, made me take it off every time we met, even that day."

They were a pair, and they were awful.

"Tell me something, Lucy," she said, sounding miffed. "You seem very outraged at our betrayal of your father, but I don't see you as being equally outraged about his and Helen's betrayal of me."

"The answer should be obvious," I said, spitting out my next words. "*They* never murdered anybody!"

And then Mother said something, let something slip, that were Kit not there to witness it with me, had he not told me later that my hearing had been accurate, I never would have believed it.

"That first day Helen came here, knocked on our door," she said, "I had always known she would, and yet I had hoped and prayed that day never came."

Mother had known of Aunt Helen's existence all along? She had known she had a poor twin and had done nothing to help that twin until forced to? And Aunt Helen, poor Aunt Helen, had put her own self forward on that murderous day when Richard came to call in the hopes of saving Mother?

"Do you want me to kill them now?" Kit asked me. "I will do it, for you."

I was sure he had never killed anybody in cold blood before; in war, yes, but never in cold blood.

But this—he would do this for me.

It was so tempting, even though she had given birth to me, it was still so tempting . . .

It was a changed and ever-changing world, where the surface was revealed to be far different from what lay underneath, from what was in fact the real world, the underworld.

How to conduct oneself in it . . .

I thought about Kit's offer for longer than I care to admit.

"No," I said at last. "It is not that they are not worth killing. It is that they are not worth dying for. They are unarmed. They present no threat. It is not worth running the risk of you hanging for it."

Then I started to scream.

. . . . .

Everyone came.

The servants, bleary-eyed, they all appeared one by one in the back parlor, like ghosts summoned to a macabre ball.

What we must have looked like to them: Mother and Richard huddled together in dressing gowns, the knife on the carpet, Kit with his pistol now pointed at Richard's head.

The only one in the household who did not come was Emma.

Poor Emma, my sister—what a world she would wake to tomorrow. How I pitied her. But that did not stop me from doing what I needed to do.

With steadfast assuredness, I raised the finger of accusation, pointed straight at Aliese.

"That woman is not my mother!"

It made sense to none of the others, save Kit, but it made perfect sense to me, for in that moment she had ceased to be.

· Forty-four ·

I have taken up my father's profession.

Or, that is to say, I have taken up his habit: writing, for itself, without any thought of financial gain. One could say that I am a teller of stories, of sorts.

Kit has had a table carried down from the house, so I can sit here in front of the lake as I write my story. Telling one's story—is that not what we humans want, to be heard?

It is summer as I write this.

We finally made it to the Swiss lakes. It is where we live now.

It is different here in this country, with its vast open landscape, the clear greens and blues and whites everywhere after the closed grayness of misty London.

I like the house here in Switzerland. It has only one floor at ground level and one staircase, leading down to a never-used basement, as opposed to the three staircases in my old house. I find this desirable, prefer it this way. Flatness is good. It hides nothing.

I like the lake here in Switzerland too. It makes me think of

Mary Shelley and her monster, a book I have read repeatedly since we have been here. The crescent-shaped body of freshwater, the majestic mountains with their snowy top hats and the narrows on the far shore—it is all quite inspirational, to borrow a word from divinity, divinity being one of those things I do not have much use for any longer.

Mary Shelley—I often wonder what it would be like to be her, to have a book for the ages spring whole from a waking dream. Is that what creation was like for Father?

I will never know. I can only know what it is like for me.

Creating a monster, particularly a sympathetic monster like Frankenstein's, it is quite an ambitious undertaking. "What terrified me will terrify others," Mary Shelley wrote of her waking dream. How remarkable, to have the assurance that what one feels about a thing, others will have too.

Again, was it like that for Father?

Again, I do not know.

Am I happy now? Have Kit and I had a happily ever after?

Such a thing is impossible to say, certainly not before a life story is at its end.

I will say that for the longest time, I was tormented by the notion: *How could I have judged so badly? How could I have not known whom I was supposed to love?* The fact that Aliese and her sister wore the same face seems little exoneration, and I have been further tormented with wondering: *How much of me is Aliese? How much her sister?*

"Happy"? What is that after such a tale?

My aunt was murdered, Father died under pathetic circumstances, Aliese—whom I had once loved *as* my mother—was responsible for all. What is "happy" after all that? It would take another lifetime to cipher it all out.

Some things we will never know the answer to. Kit says this is all right. He says that life without mystery would be like a static story and that it should not bother me that one big mystery remains:

The tunnel that stretched between Kit's and my houses back in London—where did it come from? Was it, as Kit once claimed to believe, a way to connect lovers between one house and the other? Or was there something more sinister there?

Kit says that if this were a novel, we would have found a secret diary in one of our houses to go along with the secret tunnel, and that the secret diary would detail the history of the tunnel's origin. But Kit also says that would be too neat, too tidy. The tunnel was built a long time ago and whoever built it for whatever purpose must now be dead. And while the dead do speak sometimes—I now believe it was Aunt Helen crying out to me from the grave the day of her funeral, begging me not to forget her—they rarely do, and I doubt this will prove one of those instances.

I watch Emma, who was my sister, thought now by those around us to be my first child, as she plays down near the water, her nanny close by her side to ensure that she does not venture too close to the edge, as she is inclined to do if we do not all keep watch. She looks so much like her mother and aunt. Emma is the daughter and niece of twins, the daughter of two murderers. What are her chances for the future? Only time will tell. But we will continue to raise her as our daughter and, when the time comes, we will have answers to her questions.

When news of what happened came out, Mary Williams took it upon herself to visit us at the house in London, which we have since sold, suggesting we place Emma in an orphanage.

I told Mary Williams to go hang.

Kit says it is all right to live in a world of uncertainty. He says that at least it is not boring.

Kit says a lot of things these days. I never mind.

Sometimes, I even say things back.

I talk about being the witness, the observer, and how it's impossible for the observer ever to know everything about the other people in the story—their complete histories, their motivations—and how some things will, by necessity, remain a mystery.

Kit says this is the same argument he gives me. *Do I not realize this?* he points out. Then he says that I expect too much from myself, that I always have, that I am not God—however much I might try to be!—and that I cannot be expected to know everything.

In the beginning, Emma used to ask for her mother and father, missing them. "Mama?" "Papa?" She looked for them everywhere. This was heartbreaking to see, and it hurt me too. For while I knew what her parents had done, I also knew what it was like to lose my own parents, my sun and my moon, even though as it turned out, the sun was never quite the celestial body I believed it to be. Knowing she would never see them again was hard. But after a time, she looked for and asked for them less and less, like a river slowly, drop by drop, overcome by drought. Now she never asks at all. It is amazing how quickly small children forget the past, as though none of it ever happened. I wonder if my own child could forget me so quickly.

Aliese and Richard finished out their days on this Earth at the end of twin ropes. I had to stay for the trial, but I did not stay in London to read about them swinging. Justice decreed that they should, but their end gave me no pleasure. What good could be achieved by yet more death? Some would say justice, some would say revenge, but I had already had enough of death to last me a lifetime.

Kit says he believes Richard loved Aliese greatly, and she him, but that sometimes when two people love, the end result is a dark and twisted thing, and not as it should be. He wonders what their lives would have been if Aunt Helen had never come to knock on Aliese's door. Perhaps they would have gone on doing whatever it was they did together, but without disturbing the fabric of the rest of the world.

I try *not* to think about what Aunt Helen thought about during her last moments on Earth. When I do allow myself to think on it, I prefer to believe that, terrified as she must have been, right up to the end she believed that Richard had come to wreak some sort of revenge on her and that she was nobly defending her sister. I prefer to believe that he slipped in back of her chair, slitting her throat swiftly from behind so that she never saw it coming. I prefer to believe that she never knew it was her own sister's hand commanding the knife.

I no longer wish to dwell on death and twisted things, and so I look up from my writing, look over at the child playing on the lawn with Emma, a much smaller child.

My own daughter, Helen.

Helen is dark, like me, with black hair and flashing eyes, but she is also a resilient thing, reminding me of her namesake great-aunt in happier times. Helen's birth—the pain and the glory—I remember every second.

We raise our girls, as we think of them, as sisters. Hopefully, and with a little luck and care, neither will grow up to hate the other.

Step, tap, clack.

Even though the grass behind me muffles the sharp edges from the sounds, it is always what I hear in my mind's ear when he approaches: my savior. He is simply that.

I turn to look over my shoulder—in a minute, I will lay down my pen—and think, *write* that there is only one thing I know for certain, and it has everything to do with "happy." Indeed, it is the last thing I will say on the subject:

There is not a story, in the entire history of the world, that cannot be improved upon by the inclusion of a character named Kit.

Acknowledgments

A longer-than-usual book spawns a longer-than-usual cast of characters to thank. I offer them now. Thanks to:

- Pamela Harty, for being my agent and friend, and to everyone else at The Knight Agency
- Melanie Cecka, for stunningly spot-on edits, and to everyone else at Bloomsbury
- Mark Bastable, Eliza Graham, A. S. King, Caroline Leavitt, Elizabeth Letts, and Jordan Rosenfeld, for reading, sharing insights, and encouraging
- The Friday Night Writing Group: Lauren Catherine, Andrea Schicke Hirsch, Greg Logsted, and Rob Mayette, for weekly support during the writing of TTD
- Lucille Baratz, for being so sparklingly Mom
- Greg Logsted, for being my husband and writing partner
- Jackie Logsted, for being my favorite girl in the world
- Readers everywhere.